Final Audit

A Novel by

Jim Worth

 A Division of jw publishing

 Mystrigue Press
a division of jw publishing

Copyright © 2004 James Worth

All rights reserved. No part of this book may be reproduced in any form or by any electronic or mechanical means, including information storage and retrieval systems, without permission in writing from the publisher, except by a reviewer who may quote brief passages in a review.

First Edition

The characters and events in this book are fictitious. The events described are imaginary. Any similarity to real persons, living or dead, is coincidental and not intended by the author.

Library of Congress Cataloging-in-Publication Data

Worth, James.
    Final Audit : a novel / by Jim Worth. — 1st ed.
    p.cm.
    LCCN 2005926864
    ISBN 0-9768921-0-3

    1.Detectives--Texas--Houston--Fiction. 2. Murder--Investigation--Texas--Houston--Fiction. 3. Houston (Tex)--Fiction. 4. Mystery fiction. I. Title.

PS3623.0773F56 2005   813'.6
                         QB105-600106

Printed in the United States of America

To my mom, Mary, whose guidance and support have motivated me throughout my life.

∼

A Special Thanks

There are some very special people that I would like to acknowledge. These extraordinary people, through their trust, belief, and vision have made "Final Audit" possible.

I am eternally grateful to the following individuals for the opportunity to pursue this exciting adventure:

Eddie and Donna Salti
Dawn Smith
J. David and Gail Hirstein
Claire Hardman
Mary and Jack Wories

Final Audit

by Jim Worth

PROLOGUE

"*Damn*! I *love* this place." Stephen Carston stared at the distant horizon where the water meets the cloudless blue sky, knowing he might never be able to enjoy this again.

He stood waist-deep in the crystal clear water near the rocks at Ulua Beach, preparing for a new adventure. The sun was warm, a tropical kind of warm. *Just another 80 degree day here in paradise.* The smell of sweet Plumeria was intoxicating, and days like this made him wish every day were a vacation day.

At one point, early retirement was almost a reality. *So close. If only things hadn't...* he stopped in mid-thought. He promised himself he would not think about what could have been—nothing could change that now.

Carston slipped the strap over his head, adjusted the mask to his face, and leaned forward, sliding effortlessly into the serenity of the therapeutic liquid. The soothing water enveloped his body, comforting him, and at that exact moment, took him back to the safety of the womb.

With his fins he began a rhythmic up-and-down motion, one that would carry him out to the point, a rugged, random structure of rocks and bright coral, providing a frolicsome environment for fish, sea creatures, and man. His mind cleared as he watched rainbow-colored Moorish Idols and Ornate Butterfly Fish dart in and out of the holes and crevices of nature's tranquil playground.

Today, his wife and daughter did not feel like snorkeling, and though he knew he shouldn't go out alone, this opportunity to explore further than he ever had before was overwhelming.

He kicked past the last snorkeler, about an eighth of a mile from shore, and set his sights on a section of the point with deep jagged rifts and spectacular spots undisturbed by amateurs.

He reveled in the peace and calm of this part of the point, and swam mindlessly, in and out of the craggy spaces, letting go of all the frustrations and tensions that had strangled him for the past three months. There were new treasures to be found around every turn.

A flash of light caught Carston's eye. He was out nearly a quarter of a mile, but his sense of adventure drove him to the edge. He swam around the outer-most formation of the point, to where he had seen the shiny object. Having been out for some time, he decided that after this new discovery, he would return to relax and have lunch with his family.

The high pitch of an object moving swiftly through the water startled Carston. He turned quickly. Something pierced his skin and lodged deep in his shoulder. The pain was sharp, causing him to expel the last of his precious air through his snorkel.

As he fought the loss of consciousness, he noticed a shadowy figure approaching him—reaching, grabbing. Carston tried to fight back, ripping at his attacker, panicking as he lost focus. The dark intruder seemed swift and powerful, and the substance that was in the sharp object that had violated his body began to incapacitate him. Rays of sunlight from above faded. The water, rocks, and colors around him turned black, leaving only the sensation of being grabbed and dragged through the water—deeper—deeper—and further out to sea…

1

The sultry Texas air gripped his body, tightening, almost choking him, weighing down the jet-black sweatshirt he'd worn to blend into the dark night. Anxious, he stood behind the bushes next to the massive garage, waiting for Benjamin Day to return home. A droplet of sweat dripped off his brow into his eyes, stinging. Tonight, Day would pay for what he did.

The smell of new-mown grass filled his nostrils, reminding him of growing up in Hill Country. Turning to assess the grounds of this lavish estate he wondered why someone with *all this* would take advantage of so many people?

Houston was devastated by the news of the bankruptcy and scandal that had swept through the major energy players that made up the downtown skyline. Day's company was the biggest involved, but the depth of the wound the energy sector inflicted on this thriving business community would not be determined until the knife of corruption and greed had been fully extracted.

Accountants, the Securities and Exchange Commission, and the major stock exchanges were all rummaging through tons of rubble—memos, balance sheets, trades, affiliated companies, contracts, bank accounts, invoices, analysts' statements, and other information—extant from the collapse of this energy giant.

The government investigation was moving way too slowly and rumor had it that Benjamin Day and others might get off without being charged. "Someone had to do something about it," he quietly uttered—words no one could hear—feeling good about what he would do—confident of his resolve.

The man heard the mechanism for the gate jump into action and was abruptly shaken from his preoccupation. He peered through the bushes as the gate opened and a flashy, bright red Mercedes moved toward him up the long ribbon of concrete and brick.

He never did like red; in fact, he *hated* red cars. It was a brand new SL55 AMG. Its Bi-Xenon high-intensity headlamps cast a long beam of light up the driveway. What an ostentatious display of gluttony, he thought. He moved back into the shadows.

The opener whined as it raised the door nearest his position. The Mercedes proceeded into the dimly lit garage, illuminated only by a single 25-watt bulb from the door opener and the ethereal glow of the headlights. Day turned off the car and headlights, but the Magma Red Mercedes was still brightly visible in the cold nefarious darkness of the structure. The man moved stealthily into the garage and slid into the shadows, behind a stack of boxes.

Silently, he watched while his target fumbled with papers and a briefcase in the passenger seat. He waited, focused, ready to move with catlike precision when the driver's side door opened, but Day continued to shuffle through the papers.

The smell of new leather filled the intruder's nostrils doing little to quell his welling desire for revenge. The garage light flashed out, startling him.

Finally Day turned and stepped out of the car, but leaned back in to get the briefcase and folder.

Frustrated with waiting, the intruder moved to a strategic location at the rear of the car, on the driver's side, just beyond the rear bumper, his gun aimed at Day. He had practiced this many times, and it worked just as he had anticipated.

Day turned and saw the silhouetted figure facing him, gun pointed directly at his heart. Startled, he dropped the briefcase from his right hand. It fell to the floor, bounced a couple of times, and settled on the cement beside him. Day raised both hands. In his left hand, he still clutched the bright blue file folder stuffed with sheets of paper.

The intruder glared at Day. The corners of his mouth felt tight. His heart raced, pushing against his chest. He was filled with contempt for this egotistical individual who showed no remorse for the pain and suffering he had caused.

"Wha...What do you want?" Day said, his voice cracking. "How did you get in here? Please. Please... don't shoot, I have money. Just tell me what you want. Please. You don't want to do this."

The man with the gun didn't move or speak. He was an imposing figure in the dark, standing a good four inches taller than his intended victim.

Day continued, the timbre in his voice evidence of his fear. "I don't understand. *Why are you doing this*? Do I know you?"

The stranger stood steadfast, resolute.

"Did someone send you? *Am I on the list*?"

He stood there wishing Day would shut up. He didn't blink, didn't move—just stared. He didn't understand what Day meant about a list; it had *nothing* to do with his task.

Day apparently mistook the trespasser's reticence as a sign of weakness. His attitude toward the shadowy figure changed.

Reaching into his pocket, he said, "Is it the car you want?" He took keys out and shook them in the intruder's direction, taunting him. "Go on take it. It's worth a lot of money. And it was just washed today."

The gunman glared at Day.

"Come on, let's get this done. I have more important things to do," Day said, sounding annoyed. "Just take the car if that's what you want."

Day's patronizing voice incensed him. He despised Day's cavalier attitude.

"*Shut up*! *Just shut up*!" He unleashed a loud bone-chilling explosion, forgetting for a moment about the neighbors.

Day's countenance changed immediately. "I'm sorry. I'm sorry. Just tell me what you want," he pleaded, panic creeping back into his voice.

"I said *shut up*!" The gunman growled, nausea rising up in his gut. He thought about asking Day to explain his heartless actions, but quickly discarded that idea for fear the answer might compromise his decision to exact justice.

"Please don't kill me," Day begged.

"What *part* of shut up don't you understand? I'm not going to tell you again. *You're pathetic*," the intruder shouted, his voice tremulous.

The gun never waivered from the direction of Day's chest. It had steadied in his hand as the once pompous executive pleaded for his life, a life no longer useful. Day had been given his chance and threw it away, taking advantage of his position at the expense of so many.

The gunman noticed the small puddle forming on the floor on the inside of Day's left leg. *Shit, he pissed his pants*! *He's not such a big shot after all. What would Day's investors think if they saw him now? What about his employees? How did he ever become the chairman of the board?*

His thoughts were broken by the abhorrent sound of Day's pleading, whimpering voice.

"I've got money in my safe. I'll give you as much as you want, but don't kill me."

Day's pleas for pardon had no effect. "I thought I told you to shut up!" he shouted. "*It's not your money*! *They trusted you with their money, with their lives, and you didn't give a shit*!" Anger overpowered him. "You don't get it, do you? You greedy bastard!"

A bullet exploded from the end of the barrel and thundered into Day's chest, then a second, and a third!

2

*T*he fusillade was deafening. The killer's frightened inclination was to duck. His knees buckled causing him to falter and lose his balance as the sound of the shots resonated off of every wall, the cement floor, and high ceiling. The two vehicles in the stark structure did little to diffuse the echoing onslaught. He dropped the gun and stumbled, but managed to catch himself.

Day grabbed his chest and slumped to the ground. The front of his $1,000 Versace shirt, a deep scarlet, matched the color of his new wheels. The file folder fell from his hand, and the papers scattered over the garage floor.

Day lay on the floor bleeding, "Who?" he gasped. "Why?"

The killer turned his attention away from Day and began frantically searching for his weapon. Looking first left, then to the right, he tried to focus in the hazy blackness. Clearing his eyes, he noticed the dark object underneath the rear of the car.

A sigh of relief swept over him as he bent down to retrieve the most damaging evidence he could leave at the scene. The hard metal felt warm in his hand. Lifting himself, he straightened his sweatshirt and surveyed the situation.

He hadn't planned to pull the trigger so soon. He had only wanted to move the gun in a threatening manner, but he accidently squeezed the trigger, firing the first round into the center of Day's chest. The other two shots were knee-jerk reaction. Three shots in the chest, just as he had planned.

He wanted to tell Day more—to make him understand what he had done. Though he hadn't gotten to tell Day all he wanted, the shots had the desired effect. Day breathed his last breath.

"It should be obvious to you," the killer whispered. "You left *me* with nothing, now I've left *you* with nothing. I was just balancing the balance sheet."

Day had left thousands of trusting people with nothing. Irony had always intrigued the gunman, and this oozed of irony.

The interior light from the Mercedes and a trickle from some outside landscaping lights provided just enough visibility for him to see Day lying motionless on the floor.

The once spotless garage floor was now permanently discolored by the pools of blood and urine mixing, creating edges of burnt orange, below the lifeless body. No amount of scrubbing would ever erase what had happened here tonight. Even in the ebony silence, he could see the red stains.

Quiet had returned to the dark garage. The endless resonance of gunfire had subsided. The only sound in the structure was his own breathing. He moved closer to the body, listening—he heard nothing.

A cold chill came over him, causing him to shudder. How long had it been since he pulled the trigger? Five minutes? No, it couldn't be that long. Maybe only two or three. He wasn't sure what time Day had come home.

In the excitement of the gate opening and the car moving within ten feet of him, he forgot to look at his watch. He knew he had to hurry and get out of there. He stuffed the gun back in his pocket and turned to run. *Had anyone heard anything? Called the police?*

Surely the shots had alerted someone in the neighborhood. They were loud in the garage, but it happened so quickly. The realization of what he had done sank in as he stepped onto the driveway and slid between the bushes—the same bushes that provided such excellent cover while he waited for Day to come home.

How long had he waited? Panic welled up and his breathing quickened. He glanced at his watch, but his vision fogged and he stumbled a little.

Sprinklers came on somewhere on the property to his left. *The time must be later than my two practice runs.* The sprinklers had not come on during his previous scouting trips.

He continued across the manicured lawn. It seemed much bigger and much darker than he remembered. He was positive the yard was brighter on his other two visits. Tonight he couldn't see a thing. *Were some lights out that may have been on before? No, it wasn't that. There had been a moon.*

Tonight there was barely a sliver of silver. It was the beginning of the first moon and the yard was absent of light. It was dark—too dark to see the tree he bumped as he entered the thick foliage, his last obstacle before the wall. He was still somewhat disoriented and not sure he was going in the direction of his parked car.

Not wanting to leave any clues, he hadn't marked the spot where he had scaled the wall. It should be easy to retrace his steps, but he hadn't planned on being panicked or disoriented. He worried about what he might find as he climbed over the wall. *Would someone be waiting for him? Would he be jumping over right into the hands of the law?*

His hands began to sweat as he thought about making it to his car. How much time? If only he could see his watch. It was pitch-black in the thick brush between the lawn and the wall. If only he had worn his Timex Indiglo.

The same mantra kept running through his head—the time—the wall—the car. He took a few deep breaths, trying to push down the panic as he ran. This would not be a good time to hyperventilate. He turned his thoughts to what he had achieved. *Justice for thousands.* He squeezed between a couple of trees, and crashed through several shrubs toward the wall, and his freedom.

The stone wall was about eight feet high, but its rough surface provided good traction for his running shoes. It hadn't seemed so high when he climbed it to get in, but he knew the car was on the other side. Just enough incentive to get over the wall. He struggled for a grip, found a good foothold, and finally pulled himself to the top.

He paused at the top and sat straddling the wall. His car sat, dispassionate, immediately below him. Nothing had changed on the street. It was the same as when he pulled up: quiet, undisturbed. The earlier fusillade should have alerted everyone in the neighborhood, but obviously it hadn't.

His dark green Toyota sedan was still protected from the streetlights by the beautiful oaks that lined Lost Creek Road. With the exception of a light dew, the scene was exactly the same.

His breathing slowed as he sat on the stone cap. He smiled in complete disbelief that his getaway would be this graceful, this unencumbered.

Jumping down from the wall, he hurried around to the driver's side of the car. The tall oaks, aided by the moonless sky, provided excellent cover. A dark-colored car was the perfect vehicle to use tonight.

He reached into his pocket searching for the keys and his hand brushed against the gun—a stark reminder of what had transpired. His keys were resting just below it. As he pulled them out, he noticed he was bleeding.

There was a cut on his hand. A minor cut. He wiped it on his sweatshirt, now noticing it was damp from sweat. The blood soaked into the wet, ebony material, almost disappearing. Light from the nearest streetlight filtered through the towering, primordial tree, allowing him to see how sweaty and dirty his hands were.

He thought about opening the door with the key instead of the remote, so as not to set off the chirp of the alarm. At this point, he didn't want to disturb anyone.

The key slipped into place. As he gripped it, he came to a sudden realization—*why did I even lock the car in this neighborhood?* *Surely there was no threat of it being stolen.* Not a single car was on the street. As he stood looking down Lost Creek Road, he wondered if anyone ever parked on the street in this neighborhood. His car was probably more conspicuous sitting at the curb than he ever imagined. *It's too late to worry about that.*

His focus returned to the lock. It turned. He opened the door, slid into the driver's seat, put the key in the ignition, and listened as the engine came to life. Two items on the passenger seat caught his eye: the most recent newspaper clipping about Ben Day, and the bill for his son's tuition—subtle reminders of why he was there tonight.

He looked at the clock in the car—11:58. He sighed, took a deep breath, and relaxed. It hadn't been more than ten minutes since Day got home. He pulled the car away from the curb and headed down the street, thinking about the plan, and, despite a couple of miscalculations, how well it had worked.

As he neared the end of the street and approached the corner, he looked in the mirror. Not a soul in sight. Nothing but darkness. Turning the corner, Lost Creek Road disappeared from the rear view mirror, along with his reason for being there.

4

The shooting in one of Houston's richest, most prestigious communities was a little different than the usual early morning investigation.

It was just under two hours since the shots rang out on this usually quiet street. The residents were not accustomed to being awakened at 1:00 in the morning. In light of the event that occurred shortly before midnight, this inconvenience would pale in comparison to the notoriety and activity the neighborhood would receive over the next few days.

The tranquil community, a haven protected from the outside world by the unwavering branches of the 60 old oaks, was suddenly abuzz with activity. Nothing so exciting ever happened in Lost Canyon Estates, aside from the lavish and extravagant parties.

A worn, ugly brown 2000 Crown Victoria moved slowly through the crowd of onlookers and media that had already gathered on the street and sidewalks.

"Can you believe this?" Dave Duncan, the lead detective stated, looking over at his partner in the passenger seat. "You'd think these people would be asleep at this time of the morning." He knew he sounded cranky, but he no longer enjoyed being called out so early in the morning. "This is definitely a different crowd than we get at other crime scencs."

"I was thinking that myself." Stephanie Fox pointed toward a middle-aged couple standing on the curb. "Look at the robes those two are wearing and the sleeping mask she has on her head. Are those real diamonds?"

"I'm sure they are," Dave answered. "No one in this neighborhood would be caught dead with Zircon." Dave chuckled halfheartedly.

"They would actually be comical if that mask wasn't so damn expensive."

Dave nodded. "It looks like a damn sleep-wear fashion show out here. Where the hell do these people get their money? Put that couple down in your notebook, Stephanie," he added. "They look like suspects to me."

"How do you know that?" Stephanie asked, automatically grabbing her notebook.

"Experience, Stephanie. Look at them. They're obviously dressed to kill." He laughed.

"It's too early in the morning for your humor, Dave." Stephanie crammed her notebook back into her purse.

Dave was not a real witty guy, especially this early in the morning. His moment of frivolity was at the expense of the two wearing expensive Christian Dior robes, one sporting golden silk tassels. The other wore a pair of $200 Gucci slippers, no doubt lined with virgin lamb's wool.

The immense estate was completely wrapped in bright yellow police tape—starting at the front gates, around the big oaks down the street, more than 30 feet of the sidewalk and wall about a hundred feet from the gate, and most of the curb on the side of the street adjacent to Day's estate. It covered much more area than the usual crime scenes. A lab tech and a couple of officers were examining the wall in the most heavily taped section of the street, while another examined the gutter adjacent to it. Inside the estate, the garage, the driveway in front of the garage, and the side yard were protected.

Dave stopped next to one of the officers standing at the gate and rolled down the window on Stephanie's side.

The officer was a longtime friend of Dave's. "Mornin', Dave. I see you drew this one, huh?"

"Yeah, Ken, we got the call about an hour ago." Dave yawned, unable to muster much enthusiasm. "I hate these early morning calls. When did you get here?"

"About an hour ago. We were second on the scene."

"Ken, this is my new partner, Detective Fox. Stephanie, this is Officer Meyers." Stephanie and Ken nodded to each other.

"Why can't these guys work from 9 to 5?" Dave asked, not really expecting an answer. "Who's got the forensic team tonight?"

"They woke Jerry for this one." He pointed up the drive. "He's up there with three techs. It's a pretty big case."

"You can be sure of that, if Jerry's got that much help."

A hardened, old school cop, Dave had been through a lot in his years on the force. Although a good cop and a good detective, he had grown weary—tired of the crap he had to put up with on the street, and his lonely life. The years on the beat, and as a detective, had made him cantankerous, sarcastic, and to the point.

After 26 years he hated working, in the early morning, in part because he had a well-known affinity for the bottle, caused, he claimed, by his two ex-wives.

Forty-eight years were beginning to show on Dave, in his deep set brown eyes, receding hairline, and the wrinkles on his brow. Just under six feet tall, his once muscular frame showed signs of too much food and too little exercise. Not unhandsome, he had a rugged, masculine look, but it made him appear a little older than his years. A scar on his left cheek served as evidence of growing up in a tough neighborhood on the south side of Chicago.

The more compassionate, politically correct Houston Police Force was hard for Dave to get use to. Only four years from retirement, he didn't like the recent changes.

Maybe this case would be different. It wasn't the usual stabbing or shooting that happens in the barrio, or after some of the ball games downtown, and not at all like the assaults, muggings, or robberies they get called out for in the bar district. This was definitely uptown.

Dave parked at the curb in front of the property, setting what was remaining of his doughnut and coffee in a styrofoam cup on the dash of the car. Stephanie set her Starbuck's latte on the dash next to Dave's. The new detectives were the latte, bagel, and scone generation, definitely not cut from the same cloth as those who became cops 26 years ago.

They crossed the sidewalk, walked past wrought iron gates and started up the long driveway. Activity at the scene stopped for a moment, as heads turned to watch the duo.

Dave shuffled up the driveway. In her enthusiasm, Stephanie hurried past him and he noticed her firm ass against her tight slacks. Her sinewy thighs pressed against the satiny material, testimony to her years of working out.

"Hey, where you going in such a hurry?" Dave yelled, restraining himself from making a suggestive comment about the slacks.

"Just up here to the garage area," Stephanie called back.

"What's the big hurry? We've got all night," Dave said, though he really didn't want to be here all night. "Wait till Jerry clears us," he yelled at Stephanie, now about 25 feet ahead of him.

Dave had once wondered how she made it through the academy. Not that he would outwardly accuse her of using her obvious assets to get through, but it was a distinct possibility. Her good looks and fantastic body could get her a long way as far as he was concerned.

But Stephanie was more than that. In spite of her good looks—blonde hair, sparkling eyes, nice smile, and other apparent attributes—she was shaping up to be a good detective. She was both athletic and intelligent, a quick learner, and very perceptive.

Stephanie turned and yelled back at him, "I'll wait for you up here, slowpoke."

She was a second-generation cop, had worked hard, studied hard and finished third in her class at the academy. Unlike some of the others in the police department, she had completed two years of criminology at Plano Valley College before entering the academy. It was the deciding factor in her recent promotion to detective. She had worked much harder than many of her peers, and it showed in her testing.

"What took you so long?" Stephanie teased Dave, as he neared the top of the 240 foot driveway.

Dave laughed a little, between gasps for breath. "You had a

head start," he said, not wanting to admit that he was a little out-of-shape.

"Jerry cleared us, so we can take a look. They've gotten everything up here," she said. "This is my first big case, you know?"

"I'm aware of that," Dave said. "That kind of awareness is why they put me in charge."

Stephanie had been assigned to Dave just four months ago, after the retirement of his partner, Danny Brentwood, who had put in 27 years before leaving due to a work-related disability. Dave and Danny made quite a team. After eleven years together Dave knew that Danny was there to cover his back and Danny felt the same about Dave. They knew what the other was thinking and began completing each other's sentences. It was obvious that he missed his longtime partner.

Though Dave expressed reservations about working with a woman, especially one trained to show compassion and trust, something hard for Dave to accept, he was getting use to Stephanie. She showed signs of being a damn good investigator, but this was their first big case together and her first real test.

As they approached the front of the garage, Dave saw the body laying face down on the garage floor, legs askew, one arm hidden under the body, next to a red Mercedes. Papers littered the floor, apparently dropped by the victim, either when he was shot, or when someone surprised him. When Dave drew nearer the body, he could smell a slight uric odor, mordant, diffused by time and the open garage—but still distinctive.

Blood pooled under the body, and a briefcase, not far from the body, lay on the floor among the scattered papers. Little else at the scene appeared disturbed.

"This could be a tough one," the police photographer said in unison with the flash, snapping another picture of the lifeless body. "Not a lot of clues."

"Does that smell like urine to you?" Dave asked him.

"He must have been scared. He peed his pants." The photographer pointed to the lighter puddle near the victim's feet.

As Dave looked around the area for anything specific that he wanted photographed, Stephanie stepped up to the body. "No sign of a struggle," Dave acknowledged in Stephanie's direction.

"Do you know who this is?" Stephanie asked, looking up at Dave, an incredulous look on her face.

"No," Dave shrugged. "Should I? Just some wealthy bastard as far as I'm concerned."

"It's Benjamin Day," she replied. "Don't you ever read anything in the papers except the comics and singles ads?"

"Yeah...I look at the sports section once in awhile. Who's he play for, the Titans?" Dave teased. "So what's the big deal with this one?"

Stephanie rolled her eyes. "He's been on the news for quite awhile—you know the chairman of EnergyDyn!"

Dave just stared and let her continue.

"You know, the energy company here in Houston that went bankrupt? He's being investigated by the Securities and Exchange Commission for stock fraud."

"No," Dave paused, "*WAS* being investigated. I believe the SEC investigation is now officially closed."

Admittedly, Dave was not as knowledgeable of current events as he probably should be, but he knew who Benjamin Day was and what he had done. Anyone in Houston who picked up a newspaper knew of Benjamin Day and his part in the EnergyDyn scandal. Dave really didn't care much. To him this was still just some greedy rich guy who got whacked. But Dave was cognizant that Day's stature in the community had certain ramifications in the solving of this case.

Stephanie stared at him. Dave noticed her look and knew that he would have to watch his comments the rest of the morning or catch Stephanie's cold shoulder in the car on the way back to the station. Stephanie was now getting a little more comfortable with Dave and, at times, made no secret of her disdain for what she considered a lack of professionalism.

But a lack of professionalism wasn't the problem. It was nervousness. Though things were getting better, Dave had not yet fully accepted Stephanie as a partner, which led to some of his nervous sarcasm. He didn't want to admit it, but he was a little intimidated by her womanly charms—maybe even a little attracted.

He turned, and in a more professional manner, asked, "What are the papers scattered all over?"

Stephanie glanced at Dave. "They appear to be copies of a deposition, from an attorney, a Mr. Friedman. But I'm not sure there's a connection."

"What makes you think that?" Dave asked.

Stephanie pursed her lips. "If he were killed because of the papers the killer would have grabbed them when he left, wouldn't he?"

"You're assuming the killer was male, but you're probably right," Dave said. "He would have taken them."

Dave turned and looked out at the numbered yellow card near the edge of the driveway. He took a few steps toward it and noticed the faint footprint, now visible in the light from his angle.

"So, Jerry, you get a good footprint?" Dave asked, pointing to the marked area.

"We did," Jerry confirmed, stepping next to Dave. "We have a photograph of it. We won't be able to get a cast of it, but we've got some prints behind the bushes and down by the wall where he climbed over that we're processing right now. We can get casts of the ones he left by the wall. They're good impressions."

"You sure it was a he?"

"Looks like a man's shoe, Dave, or a woman with awfully big feet."

Dave laughed. "Guess I can rule out the jealous wife, crazy ex, or jilted lover theory."

"You can," Jerry said, smiling, "and the hooker in stilettos."

"We've got prints behind the bushes? So, you think he was hiding, waiting for Day?"

"It sure looks that way. We think he came from behind the bushes, followed him into the garage and shot him." Jerry pointed toward the car. "Probably from about there—from the rear of the car. I'll know more when we check the powder burns. This one looks like it will be easy to reconstruct."

"That's great. How's everything else look from a forensic perspective?"

"We're going to get the footprints and a few other clues, but the perp didn't leave us much, Dave."

Dave grimaced. "This is a high profile case, Jerry. We need everything you can squeeze out of this crime scene."

"I'll try. You know me. We'll get everything that's here." Jerry turned and went back to the body.

Stephanie kneeled over the body, asking Jerry questions and writing furiously in her notebook. Dave walked back to join them.

"What have we got here?" he asked.

"Three shots, all to the chest," Jerry said. He turned to his lab tech and asked a couple of questions, then turned back to Dave and pulled the body up so he could see the victim's chest. "You can see for yourself."

Dave squatted to examine the damage. "Looks like a .38 to me. What do you think?"

Jerry nodded. "We didn't find any stray slugs or any spent casings, so I can't be positive until we get the body back to the lab and pull the slugs out of his chest. My guess would be a .38, at fairly close range, based on what appears to be stippling."

Jerry laid the body down and motioned for the paramedics.

Dave stood up and looked out of the garage. "So the shooter only took three shots, and all from close range? You think Day knew his assailant?" Dave moved out to the driveway, scanning the side yard in the direction the killer may have run to the wall.

"That's a distinct possibility." Jerry said, raising his voice in Dave's direction. "But we can't tell that from what we have. All we know the assailant was waiting in the bushes for him to come home."

Dave turned his attention to Stephanie who was still inside with the lab tech watching the paramedics go about their task of bagging and removing the body. She was like a sponge, absorbing everything she could, wanting to learn more. Dave reflected on what it had been like when he investigated his first case. She asked the lab technician a question and joined Dave at the garage entrance.

"So what do you think, Stephanie?"

"Not sure." She paused. "We can rule out robbery, or a burglary, unless Day surprised the perpetrator. He still has his watch—very expensive—and his wallet. There's about $1,200 in it, lots of credit cards, and the assailant left Day's briefcase."

Stephanie paused, Dave could practically see the wheels turning in her head, searching for the motive.

"Doesn't appear to be a hate crime either, and crimes of passion usually happen in the bedroom," Stephanie said, still mulling over all the possibilities.

"Unless it was robbery, he surprised him, and after accidently shooting him, the perp got scared and ran off," Dave added, "but that's too simple."

"Maybe, Dave. We're open to all possibilities. I think we ought to consider it."

"We'll have to sort it all out at the precinct."

"Okay, but first I want to watch the lab tech dust the car for prints. I've done it before, but I want to see how a pro does it." Stephanie returned to the garage.

Dave looked across the grass and out to the thick shrubbery and activity in the area where the perp went over the wall. He turned back toward the building.

"Jerry, can I get the lights turned off when your tech finishes with the prints? I want just the lights that were on when you arrived."

"Sure, Dave. He's just about done. Let him get these last couple of prints."

Stephanie watched the lab tech dust the Mercedes. He powdered the door, roof, and windows on the driver's side. The tech pulled out some tape and lifted several prints from the door and roof. He turned to Jerry and let him know he'd finished. Stephanie walked back out to rejoin Dave on the driveway.

"Everyone hold your positions, we're turning the lights off for a minute," Jerry shouted, his voice carrying across the estate. Dark greens turned black; light greens turned gray.

Dave turned again quietly searching the darkness, wanting to see what the killer saw while he was on the property. He was puzzled. The detectives would be hard pressed to find a suspect with so little to go on. Cases with this little evidence sometimes never got solved.

What was the possible motive for this murder? Was this a

botched robbery, or burglary, or was this planned for some other reason? Did the perp know the victim? It almost looked like a hit, which was another possibility, one Stephanie hadn't mentioned. The mayor and police commissioner were going to demand some answers.

"All right, Jer. You can turn them back on. Thanks."

"So what did the tech get?" Dave asked. "Anything we can use?"

"They've got something," Stephanie offered, a slightly elevated level of excitement in her voice. "A few prints off the door, window and roof, and what looks like a palm print on the rear fender. The car was washed today. There was a credit card receipt on the floor on the passenger's side, so any fingerprints would be recent. The killer might have been clumsy and left us one."

"Do you really think we could get that lucky? We only have two possible clues so far, including ballistics from the slugs they'll take out of the body. So maybe we'll have three clues."

Stephanie frowned. "You don't think he was nice enough to leave a print for us, do you?"

"Maybe, but don't count on it," Dave said. "This looks planned, so our suspect was probably wearing gloves."

Dave watched the excited gleam in her eye dim. It was a gleam Dave hadn't seen in years. "You never know. We could use a break on this one," he continued, trying to add a positive note, careful not to deflate her enthusiasm. "Prints would be a solid clue."

Stephanie had that youthful exuberance of a new detective. An enthusiasm not yet worn by the years of busting her ass, years of fighting crime and criminals only to see the liberal bastards on the bench let the perpetrators go—released back into society because of mishandled or lost evidence, or a lack of compelling evidence, or some other bullshit technicality.

Dave had forgotten how exciting it was to watch the clues come together, leading to the scum that committed the crime. Twenty-six years had done that to him. It had been a long time since Dave had donned his superhero cape. Almost longer than he could remember.

"This will be a high profile case," he reminded Stephanie.

"I'm sure it will. And I'm sure they are going to want a quick resolution," she added.

"You're right about that." Dave sighed. "Let's wrap this up here and head back to the station to go over what we have."

Dave paused, then turned, remembering one more question.

"Jerry, who called this in? Who discovered the body?"

"Alarm company," Jerry yelled. "Called it in about 12:30."

"Okay, thanks," Dave replied. "We'll check it out. When will you get back to the lab?"

"'Bout an hour. I'll come up to the squad and let you know what else we found."

Dave turned to Stephanie. "We need to come back tomorrow and see if the daylight offers us any additional insights or clues."

"You mean later this morning, don't you?" Stephanie said, reminding him that it was already tomorrow. "God knows we could use some help on this one."

Dave was not a religious man by any stretch of the imagination, but was smart enough to realize a little divine intervention couldn't hurt.

Stephanie walked down the long driveway to the car with Dave trailing behind her.

"How did you know it was a .38?" Stephanie asked, slowing and turning toward him. "I'm impressed."

"Something I picked up during the Army. My MOS was in small caliber ordnance. I had three years of training in various weapons, compliments of my favorite uncle."

"How long were you in the Army?"

"Well…I enlisted for four years. Thought I was going to be a lifer, but things didn't quite work out the way I planned, so I got out after only four."

"What didn't work out?" Stephanie asked, genuinely curious.

"I had dreams of being in Special Forces, even dropped out of college after only one semester hoping to become a paratrooper or Green Beret."

It wasn't that he was a bad student, or not smart enough for college. He just didn't adapt to demands of class schedules and deadlines. Looking back, Dave realized that he just didn't apply himself.

"You wanted to be a Green Beret?" Stephanie asked, as they passed through the gates toward the car.

"That was my plan. I did okay on the physical stuff, but had problems on the academics. I didn't realize you would have to know so much math, and things about electronics, communications, astronomy, and other things. Wish I had studied more in high school."

"My uncle was in Special Forces. I think he was a Ranger or something, and then he became a Dallas cop after getting out of the Army."

"He was in the Army before becoming a cop? How long was he in?"

"I think he was going to be a lifer, also, but he decided to get out after ten years."

"Why'd he want out after serving ten years?"

"He said things changed, and he got tired of it. The opportunity came up in the Dallas PD and he decided the timing was right."

"So he was okay with his decision to get out and join the force?"

"Yeah, he really liked it. He was a good cop—tough, but fair—and he ended up getting promoted pretty fast. He definitely influenced my decision to become a cop. I always admired him, and was always proud of him." She smiled.

They stood on the curb next to the car, Dave enjoying their discussion—one deeper than any they had had since becoming partners.

"So your uncle was your reason for becoming a cop? I wondered what made you join the force. I guess I could have asked, but didn't want to pry." Dave looked at Stephanie a little differently now.

"He was. He always looked so proud, so confident. He used to say how good it made him feel to know he was protecting his community. What made you want to be a cop, Dave?"

"I learned a lot about weapons and decided that becoming a cop would allow me to put my training to good use. And it did."

"Well, it seems to have worked out pretty well."

"Yeah, it has. Kinda lost sight of that over the years. At one time, seems like years now, I felt the way your uncle did." Dave felt a little vulnerable and wasn't sure he liked it. "We should get back and go over what we have."

Stephanie got into the car and grabbed her latte from the dashboard. Dave paused and looked over the property one more time, in awe of the affluence behind the gates of the estates in this neighborhood. Truly a case of conspicuous consumption, he thought, sliding into the worn cloth driver's seat provided by a grateful public. No cushy leather seats for Houston's finest.

He grabbed his styrofoam cup from the dash and pulled away from the curb, heading back to the station to sort out what little evidence they had.

5

*T*he station house was deserted as they entered. Thursday mornings were like that because Wednesdays were generally quiet nights in their precinct.

The 5th Precinct was the best assignment in the Houston Police Department. Only two years old, it was housed in three stories of reflective mirrored splendor, dazzling in its radiant newness, but void of ambiance or character. No beat up doors or rickety stair railings. Absent were the marred wood floors, the old wooden chairs and the hazy, faintly luminous panes of glass. In diametrical opposition to their old digs there was chrome and vinyl, marble tile, and crystal-clear panes of transparent partitions. They now had all the modern technologies they needed to catch unsuspecting criminals.

Though the politicians claimed that crime had gone down in the city for the last few years, those on the force saw no real evidence of that. For many years, the 5th Precinct had the lowest crime rate in the city, aided by the fact that there were several neighborhoods like Lost Canyon Estates in its boundaries. The type of crimes in each precinct varied, and so did the numbers, but homicides in Houston had declined in all precincts over the last half decade. Dave had not investigated a homicide in their precinct in more than six years. The demise of Benjamin Day screwed up the 5th's formidable record.

Tonight's shooting in Lost Canyon was most assuredly a shock to the residents. In fact, there had never been a shooting in Lost Canyon Estates or in either of the two nearby, equally opulent areas: Lost Hills Estates and Canyon Meadows. The cold and brutal murder of one of their wealthy residents would be cause for concern in all three neighborhoods.

It was Dave and Stephanie's job to allay the fears of these influential citizens, most of whom knew the mayor personally. Dave understood that the socialites in this upscale community would place personal calls to the mayor and chief, requesting a swift resolution, demanding more than Dave and Stephanie could offer right now.

"Where should we start?" Stephanie broke into Dave's thoughts. "We don't have a lot of clues here."

Dave tugged at his chin. "Danny and I solved cases in the past with less evidence, so let's focus on what we do have and see where it leads us." He wanted to keep the mood positive, knowing the pressure they would receive as the golden rays of dawn broke through the cold reflective panes that surrounded them.

Stephanie picked up her notebook and scanned the cryptic scribbles on page after page. They were the only people in the squad at 3:00 a.m. The other detectives were home, warm in their beds, steeped in their own innocuous dreams, totally unaware of the event in Lost Canyon Estates.

Dave had stopped by The Beat, his favorite cop bar, on his way home last night and had drinks with some of the guys from the 4th Precinct. They talked about the day's events while he nursed his Manhattens; he headed home around 9:30. He was on call, but hadn't expected to be awakened at 12:30 in the morning. That rarely happened in this precinct. He had just a little edge, but another cup of coffee would help clear his mind for the work ahead of them. Dave poured himself a cup and turned to Stephanie.

Stephanie took copious notes, according to the captain, who seemed to appreciate her enthusiasm. She was deciphering what she had written, her eyes fixed on the page in front of her. Dave, on the other hand, had committed what little they had tonight to memory. He'd put his notebook away years ago. Hell, he didn't even have a clue where it was.

"So what have we got?" Dave asked.

Stephanie looked up, her gaze fixed. "We've got the footprint that you saw, and probably several others that Jerry will get pictures and casts of."

Dave was perfectly aware that the footprints may well be their only "real" clue.

"Speaking of footprints, what were you and Jerry talking about out on the driveway?" she asked.

Dave shot Stephanie a surprised glance, not sure whether she had overheard their conversation. "He was telling me how impressed he was with your work and your questions."

"C'mon Dave," she said, seeing through his attempted smile. "You were talking about more than that, I'm sure. You were talking a long time and that look gives you away."

He grimaced. "What look?"

"That look," she said. "That little half-smile. So come clean."

"You *sure* you want to hear it?"

"Of course. I want the truth. I'm a big girl."

"Okay. Jerry was asking me how I got so lucky and how you got assigned to the 5th?"

"He did? And what did you tell him?"

"I told him I didn't know for sure, but that you were becoming a good investigator."

"How do *you* think I got assigned to this precinct?" she asked, an inquisitive stare on her face.

Dave's face felt flushed. "Who knows, but there were some who questioned it when you got the assignment."

"*Were you one of them*, Dave? Did *you* question it?"

"You've put me in a tough position here. You have to understand." He paused. "I didn't know you then, and there were two other women investigators who were in line for this assignment."

"So, *you were one of them.*"

"I'd heard a lot about you and I *did* wonder, like everybody else, why you and not either of the other two got this assignment," Dave confessed. "But, like I said, I didn't—"

She interrupted. "It's okay, Dave. I knew a lot of rumors were flying around the department—not that I actually ever heard any of them. I'm sure none of them were accurate though, so it didn't really bother me."

"Well, are you going to tell me the real story so we can put the rumors to rest and get on with what we're doing here?"

She nodded. "It's true, the other two were ahead of me for this assignment, and they were offered it."

There were now three women investigators in the Houston Police Department. Despite the low number of female detectives, Houston had done a good job integrating women into the department. There were many women officers, but only three had passed the rigorous detectives exam so far.

The HPD had been honored for its investigative work over the last ten years, and it attributed that to the level of its testing. Qualifying for detective was difficult for both men and women, and women who passed the exam turned out to be sharp, intuitive, and excellent investigators. Stephanie was the most recent to exceed the department's high standards.

"I'm sure a lot of people thought I got this assignment because of my looks," she continued.

Dave nodded, "Yep, quite a few."

"Well, that wasn't the reason." She paused. "I was just in the right place at the right time. Belinda had just been promoted and didn't want to leave her long time partner, and Carolyn's mother had a stroke and she wanted to stay close to her, in case something happened. So that's the story about how I got the cushy assignment, and how you got stuck with me," she grinned.

"I'm glad we cleared that up," he joked. "I may have thought the other before you got here, Stephanie, but I'm glad now that you got this assignment."

"Me, too."

Dave looked back at the desk, "Okay, what else?"

"That's all. I told you everything. Didn't know anyone in the department, didn't bribe anybody, and didn't lay anyone—"

"No." He laughed. "I meant what else have we got for clues?"

Stephanie dropped her eyes to the paper. "Oh. We have three shots in the chest. Small caliber...probably a hand-gun at close range, maybe less than ten feet. If you and Jerry were accurate in your assessment, the slugs will be from a .38 caliber."

"You write all that down in that little notebook?" Dave said, derisive, but in a playful way.

"Thought we could use this information before we got the reports from forensics," she said, looking up from her notebook. "I got everything that I could from Jerry and the lab techs."

Dave was impressed at Stephanie's resourcefulness. "Good work, Stephanie." Dave smiled.

"Well," she said, "do you still think it could have been someone that he knew?"

"I'm not really sure I think that now."

"We know the perp wasn't in the car with Day," Stephanie said.

"True. The shot pattern was tight. He was definitely facing him on the driver's side," Dave said, thinking out loud. "The murderer climbed the wall to get in, and the footprints outside indicate he was waiting. If Day knew him why was the perp hiding in the bushes? I think he surprised Day."

"And," Stephanie added, "the papers were scattered all over the floor. If Day had known him, he probably would have set his case and the folder down."

"You're right." Dave took a sip of coffee. "The assailant snuck into the garage and confronted Day when he got out of the car."

"The scattered papers? Day dropped them when the shooter surprised him?"

"I don't think so. There were papers around him, but not under him, and some on top of the briefcase, but none under it—indications that he dropped them after he was shot."

"They were mostly in front of him, so he dropped the folder as he was falling," Stephanie said. "The papers may have nothing to do with the murder."

"They still might be the reason," Dave said. "We'll know more about that when we talk to Jerry later, and get to see the content. The body was discovered at 12:30?"

"That's what Jerry said." She flipped through her spiral notebook, picked up the phone. "I'll call the security company to confirm that and get the details."

While Stephanie was on the phone, Dave pulled over one of the chalkboards and began listing the clues. Footprint—small caliber handgun—3 shots—close range were written on the top line. Scattered papers—hiding in bushes—climbed the wall—surprise were written on a line below.

"Interesting," Dave stated. He studied the items he'd written.

He turned to Stephanie.

Stephanie nodded. "Yes, I'm here. You're sure about that? Okay, and there was no response? And that was after the earlier check?" Stephanie busily wrote in her notebook. "And the officer was sure the door was closed? All right...Thanks."

Finishing her conversation she turned to Dave, a big smile on her face.

"The body was discovered at approximately 12:30 a.m.."

Dave wrote, "12:30—body discovered," on the board.

"The alarm was deactivated in the garage at 11:49 p.m. and was never reactivated," she said, glancing up. "The garage is on a separate alarm system and since it was not reactivated, and the house never entered, they sent a patrol by to inspect the property. The patrol's earlier check of the property was at 11:10 p.m."

Stephanie paused and turned to the next page in her notebook. "The patrolman could see the garage open from the gate and had the desk call the residence. There was no answer, so the patrolman had permission to enter the property. That's when he discovered the body."

"What time did Jerry put the time of death?"

"He thought between 11:30 and 12:30," Stephanie read from her notebook. "He said it was recent, about an hour or so. He based that on the body temp and ambient temperature when he arrived."

"So we can probably narrow it down to between 11:49 and 12:30," Dave said, as he wrote it on the chalkboard and circled it "—11:49–12:30—time of death."

Officers would canvass the neighborhood in the morning to see if anyone noticed anything out of the ordinary between 11:00 p.m. and 12:30 a.m.

They compiled a lot of information, from what earlier seemed like nothing. There would be more when forensics finished.

"Anything else that we can add to the list right now?" Dave inquired.

"Jerry has the fingerprints from the car that might give us the only clue we need," she said. "It only takes one good fingerprint— if the perp's print ison file somewhere—for us to wrap up this case."

Dave wasn't holding his breath. Even if the perpetrator did leave a clear print, it could lead to nothing. No match, no clue. But it would tie the perpetrator to the scene if they could catch him.

"We need to find out who Day was with yesterday. He must have had an appointment book. Did you see one in the car?" Dave asked.

"No...none in the car, but there may be a book in his case. More likely a PDA."

"Whether it's a PDA or an old fashioned appointment book, we need to get a look at that as soon as we can."

"But what about the papers?" Stephanie asked. "I think we should call this Melvin Friedman, Day's attorney, to see if there is any connection."

Before Dave could answer Stephanie, Jerry burst into the squad.

"We found some things I thought you might be interested in," Jerry shouted across the long, empty room. He was excited, which was uncharacteristic of Jerry. "You asked me to squeeze everything out of the scene. Well...we squeezed."

"You keeping us guessing, Jerry?" Dave laughed.

"No, not at all," he replied. "We have more shoe prints than we thought. Lots of them inside and outside the wall where he climbed over. We also have a partial shoe print, well not really a shoe, but a toe print, from the inside wall."

"So he climbed the wall?" Dave asked, confirming what they thought earlier.

"We are a 100 percent sure of that, Dave. Toe print on the wall matches the one on the driveway and those behind the bushes."

"C'mon, c'mon, what else?" Stephanie clamored.

"We found some blood on top of the wall, on the edge of the cap, where he climbed over. And—we also have a tire track in the street directly outside the wall." Jerry smiled, took a deep breath, and continued. "One of my techs got a great cast of the tread and will begin searching the FBI database for a match."

"The tire track is definitely good," Stephanie said. "And you're sure the footprints all match?"

"They appear to match," Jerry stated. "We'll know more when we get them to the lab for comparison. The FBI's database for footwear is now nearly as extensive as the datum we have for tires."

"So we're dealing with one guy?" Dave interrupted. "We're going back and forth here. What about the tire?"

"Yeah, were dealing with one suspect. The tread mark? It's a good piece of evidence. The cast will be solid, and we have a tire smudge mark on the curb. Looks like the tire hit the curb while he was parking."

"Sure it's from the same car?" Dave asked.

"Not a doubt, Dave. We'll analyze the rubber, and, of course, we'll match it to the manufacturer and model of the tire we get from the tire track. But we have more yet." Jerry paused. "We found some threads we pulled from a tree trunk, and there are some broken branches in the bushes. Important clues if we catch him."

"You mean *when* we catch him, don't you, Jerry? You got Day's briefcase?" Dave asked.

"Yep," Jerry said. "It was never opened or moved. Just supposition, but I'll bet the suspect didn't want anything from the case. We'll dust it for prints to see who handled it, and then we'll open it."

"We need to see if there's an appointment book in it," Dave stated.

"I'm sure there is, or a PDA."

Dave caught Stephanie's I-told-you-so glance out of the corner of his eye.

Jerry continued. "We didn't find either, and guys like this live by their planners. I'll send it up from the lab as soon as they get through with it. You looking for something in particular?"

"Not really," Dave said. "Just want to see who he had appointments with yesterday, and today. You know, just cover all the bases."

Stephanie interrupted. "I'm getting his phone records. I called the phone company, and they're faxing them over to us. We can find out who he talked to the last few days." She turned. "Oh, yeah, we need to find his cell phone, too. Jerry?"

Jerry was already headed out the door. "He didn't have one on him, and there wasn't one in the car. It may be in the briefcase," he said. "If it's there, I'll send it up with the PDA when we're done with it."

"Thanks, Jer," Dave yelled as the door closed behind him.

Dave went over to the chalkboard again and began adding to the list—"tire tracks, blood, fibers, appointments." The list was getting bigger.

"We've got more than we thought," Dave said, stepping back. "Impressive."

Stephanie looked at Dave, a tired look. "I think we should go see the attorney in the morning and see what we can turn up."

"It is morning, remember? But that sounds like a good idea. It's almost 4:00 a.m. Let's get a few hours sleep and meet back here at about 8:00 or 8:30." He glanced at Stephanie, who hadn't answered. "Did you hear me?"

"Uh-huh, then we'll go see Mr. Friedman?" Stephanie asked.

"Yeah, we'll go see this Friedman first thing."

6

"*W*hat evil could create a despair so strong that a man would consider taking his life the *only* way out?"

Eyes watering, the man read those cold, solemn words on the weathered yellow page. Bold black letters, still numbing, reported the sad story behind the largest corporate collapse ever.

The well known professor of business ethics apparently took his own life after the bankruptcy of energy giant, EnergyDyn, wiped out his retirement. The venerable 76-year-old mentor was found in his home early Thursday morning, a single shot to the head. A worthless EnergyDyn stock certificate, bloodstained, was found beneath his left cheek on his antique rolltop desk.

With biting criticism, the newspaper article went on to describe the victim's financial losses. The man stared at the page blankly, as he had nearly one year earlier, again reading the part that implied the old man's greed was somehow the cause of his death. But it was more complex than that, much deeper, more painful.

The story originally ran on page seven of the Metro Section. On that same day, the rescue of a dog from a burning building garnered ten column inches on the front page of the same section. A man's life and death, by virtue of its placement in the newspaper, seemed less important than that of a dog's.

He set the article down, glanced over at the morning paper, and began reading the headline on the front page. "Lights Out for EnergyDyn Chairman," it screamed, across the entire width.

"Day was found lying in a pool of blood as deep as EnergyDyn's red ink," it read below the headline. The incident, covered extensively in the Business Section, gave the reader a detailed account of the murder of the chairman, replete with photos of him, his estate, and various pictures and icons of the company he killed, now symbolic of corporate scandal, corruption, and malfeasance.

A sidebar gave the chronology of EnergyDyn's meteoric rise and astonishing free-fall, and graphed the plummeting stock price. Another gave the list of indictments and the culpability of each of the indicted executives, including Benjamin Day.

It was incredible how many people had relied on EnergyDyn, trusted Day and other executives, with their jobs, pensions, and business. Not only did thousands of employees lose their jobs and pensions, but hundreds of vendors were also victims of their immoral behavior.

Absent, in the news, was mention of the lives Day and his partners in crime had destroyed with their underhanded dealings, fraud, and deceit. Absent were the stories of the individuals, like the gentleman in the article, not only an investor, but a longtime friend, so distraught that they chose to take their lives.

It is difficult to calculate the breadth of the damage, or exactly how many may have chosen the same fate as his friend. As the man continued to read, he tried to make sense of it all, tried to understand the rationale. He could find none.

How could things have gone so awry? Could all this destruction have been prevented, or at least discovered before the stock lost most of its value, and lives were destroyed? What could be done to ensure that corruption of this magnitude never occurred again? And could shattered lives ever be the same after such devastating financial losses?

What price should a man pay for inflicting so much pain and suffering on so many? Those involved continued to profess their innocence, claiming that they had done nothing criminal, that they had broken no law. But, what of morality? What they did, what Day had done, was as criminal as if he had pulled the trigger himself.

His friend was gone. There was nothing he could do to change that. No godly way he could turn back time, or bring him back.

But there was one thing he could do, though it might require great personal sacrifice. There was no question, no second thoughts, no other choice. He had to make that sacrifice.

7

*D*ave stepped aside for Stephanie to walk through the huge double oaken doors, inlaid with beautiful etched and beveled glass. He could tell Melvin Friedman had clients willing to pay big bucks. The etched antique brass sign next to the door said Friedman and Cohen, Attorneys at Law. Cohen had passed away almost four years before, but apparently Friedman was reluctant to take his mentor's name off the firm.

Inside the reception area Dave's beliefs were validated. Plush, expensive furniture and even more expensive art, obviously designer arranged and lighted, filled the spacious room. Soft music, at the perfect volume, reached every beautifully appointed corner. The carpet was spotless and obviously vacuumed every night, a reminder for Dave that he needed to get a housekeeper. Dave was not a slob, but housekeeping was definitely not a priority in his life. Vacuuming once a month was as much as Dave could muster.

"Can I help you?" The well-groomed, professional woman behind the ornate oak reception desk flashed a meaningless smile.

"We'd like to see Mr. Friedman," Stephanie said.

"Do you have an appointment?"

Dave was sure she knew they didn't. He pulled out his badge and flashed it at her.

"We need to ask Mr. Friedman a few questions about one of his clients," Dave said looking straight at the receptionist. "I'm Detective Duncan, and this is Detective Fox."

Without a word or change of expression, The receptionist picked up the phone, dialed two quick numbers and said in a soft, calm voice, "Mr. Friedman, there are two detectives here to see you. Yes, sir." She hung up the phone, looked up at the detectives, with an impassive expression, and said, "Please have a seat. Mr. Friedman will be with you in a minute."

"Thank you," Stephanie said, politely, and headed over to the plush couch, sinking immediately into the soft cushion.

Dave settled beside her. "I wonder how much this baby costs?"

"Probably a few month's salary," Stephanie said, as she leaned back.

It all added up to big bucks in Dave's mind. He just knew that he couldn't afford it, even after more than 26 years on the job.

He was wondering what business Day had with Friedman, just as the attorney appeared through the big oak double doors to the right of the reception area.

"Hello, I'm Melvin Friedman," he said in a jovial, almost laughing manner. He stuck out his short little arm with a stubby hand to shake the detectives' hands. Friedman acted as if he were expecting them. Dave thought that was odd. That wasn't possible, unless Stephanie called without Dave's knowledge. The receptionist didn't seem to expect them.

Friedman was a pleasant enough guy. A stout, 60-ish Jewish gentleman about 5'8" tall, balding hair, eyes that sort of twinkled. This good-natured, fatherly figure in no way resembled a lawyer, Dave thought.

"What's 1,500 attorneys chained together at the bottom of Galveston Bay?" Mr. Friedman started.

Neither of them responded to his outwardly peculiar question.

"Never mind," he said, even before they had time to answer. "I know you've heard it before." He laughed, a deep carefree laugh. It was not one you would normally expect out of someone who had just lost a big client.

Dave reached for his card, drawing Friedman's attention from Stephanie. Friedman quickly raised both hands.

"I give up," he shouted "Don't shoot." Friedman laughed.

He reached down and took the card from Dave.

"Just kidding," he said. "Thought you were going for your piece." He laughed again and smiled at Stephanie. "I'll bet you're packing as well."

Dave laughed, though he knew this was a serious matter, but Friedman's quick wit and insouciant delivery were infectious.

Stephanie shot back, "I am, Mr. Friedman. I also have handcuffs if you're not good," Stephanie said, playfully winking at Friedman.

He laughed at Stephanie's quick return. "I should be so lucky."

"Hello, Detective Duncan," he said, after glancing at the card. "And who is your lovely and witty partner?"

"Detective Fox," Stephanie offered, handing Melvin her card.

"Well the name fits," he said, again smiling at her.

"We're here, Mr. Friedman, to ask you some questions about Benjamin Day," Dave interrupted.

Friedman looked over at Detective Duncan, "It's Melvin. You may be surprised, but I knew that."

"And how could you possibly know that?" Stephanie asked.

"It's all over the newspapers and television this morning. It's big news. He was my client, so it was just a matter of when."

Tired from working the case all night, Dave hadn't seen the news or listened to the radio on the way back to the station before heading to Friedman's office. The radio had been broken in Dave's issued vehicle for a long time.

"What can I help you with?" Melvin asked.

"What were you doing for Mr. Day?" Stephanie inquired.

Melvin paused. "Let's go down to my office where we can talk and I can give you all the information I'm allowed to by law," he said, gesturing to the big oak doors he exited moments before.

The receptionist got up and held open the door for them, her stoic expression never changing as they walked past her, through the door, and down the hallway leading to Friedman's office. "Lenore, hold all my calls, please, while I help the detectives."

The long, sunlit hallway, lined with statues and vases with huge, colorful floral arrangements, extended past the conference room on the right. Dave noted that the panes of etched and beveled glass were identical to those in the front doors, and the room had the same expensive furniture as the reception area.

Friedman's office was just past the conference room. It was even more magnificent than the other areas. He had an incredible view of the city from his corner of the world. It wasn't really a corner, because the glass wrapped around in a half circle, offering an unobstructed panoramic view of the city. Quite a sight and costly, Dave thought to himself, wondering what the rent would be for this place.

"Please sit down." Friedman motioned to the chairs next to another plush couch from which visitors could experience the breathtaking view.

"Can I get you anything? Coffee, tea, soda?"

"We're fine, thanks," Dave spoke for both of them.

"I would like a latte if you can make one," Stephanie said half-joking, and giving Dave a hard look.

"A latte? I can see already that you're high maintenance," Friedman laughed.

As they sat down on the couch, Dave noticed today's paper on the coffee table. On the front page of the *Houston Chronicle* was a big picture of Day, lifeless, face down on the cold, unforgiving garage floor, and another smaller one of Dave and Stephanie exiting the property earlier that morning. No wonder Friedman was not surprised when the two detectives called on him.

Friedman reached over to pick up the newspaper from the table.

"That's not a good picture of the two of you. You look much better in person."

"It was early in the morning," Stephanie joked. "I'm much better after a couple hours of sleep."

"I'll bet you are," Friedman said.

Stephanie casually ignored his comment.

"So, Mr. Friedman," Dave interrupted, "back to the original question. What were you doing for Mr. Day?"

"I think that's something I can tell you without breaching attorney/client privilege. I was representing him in both the fraud and bankruptcy cases," Friedman offered. "Benjamin asked me if I would represent him with any problems that might arise from the EnergyDyn bankruptcy."

"I read the deposition that we found at the scene and wondered if it had any connection to last night's murder?" Stephanie stated.

"You read the deposition?" Friedman asked. "I'm impressed."

Dave's eyes widened. "When did you have time to read the deposition?"

Stephanie shrugged. "I got it from the lab tech before I left and couldn't sleep...so I read it." Turning back to Friedman, "do you see any connection to the deposition?"

"Connection?" Friedman repeated, stroking his chin as if searching for the correct answer. "No, I'm not sure there would be any connection. At least not directly. That was Ben's deposition relating to his knowledge, if any, of the round trip trades." He paused, then shook his head. "So no, I don't really see a connection to what happened last night. Any idea who did it?"

"We don't have a lot to go on so far," Dave said. "We're looking for anything that might lead us to Day's killer. We were hoping you could shed some light on our investigation. Do you know any of his friends or a family member who might have wanted him dead?"

"I don't think any of his friends were angry enough to do this," Friedman said. "He was a very likable guy. He didn't have any enemies."

"*He had at least one*," Dave said, cold and unattached. "Someone didn't like him."

"Did you give any thought to one of EnergyDyn's investors or employees?" Friedman asked, as if he had suddenly made a connection. "It could have been an angry employee...or even a disgruntled investor. He received lots of threats after the bankruptcy."

"But you said that he had no knowledge, nor involvement in the collapse of the company. At least that's what I got from the deposition," Stephanie said, staring at Friedman.

"Right," he exclaimed. "I can't believe that you took the time to read the deposition," shaking his head, and continuing. "Not all employees or investors are willing to wait until this is all sorted out to see what Ben's involvement was. Many of them had just lost their life savings and wanted someone to blame. And many wouldn't believe him even if it were the truth. To most of them, he's guilty merely by association."

Friedman paused, a little tear forming in the corner of his eye. He cleared his throat a little and continued, voice cracking slightly. "In everyone's mind, because he was the chairman of the corporation, he was responsible for whatever happened," Friedman said.

Dave got the impression that Friedman and Day were also friends.

Friedman was extremely cooperative. Dave began thinking about the new angle Friedman had offered them, and how it might help them find a suspect.

"How would we go about getting the investor list?" Dave asked. "And what about the employee list? Is there a quick way we can obtain them?"

"You can get the investor list from the SEC," Friedman suggested.

"And the employees?" Dave repeated.

"I'm sure you could get a list of all the employees from human resources at EnergyDyn. They've been extremely helpful and accommodating since the shredding incident. I'm sure they'll provide you with a list of all who had stock options in the company, and those who were heavily vested in their 401Ks."

Stephanie scribbled notes as Friedman talked. "One more question. About how many investors would you say there were in EnergyDyn?"

"Several million I would guess. There are more than 18,000 ex-employees. Many of them pretty pissed off I would imagine," he added, looking directly at Stephanie. "That's why I think you might find your killer on one of those lists," he said, nodding. "Anything else I can help you with?"

"No, I think that's it," Dave said, standing and shaking Friedman's hand. "Thank you, Mr. Friedman. You've been a great help."

"Anything else I can do, just let me know," Friedman said, returning Dave's handshake. "Could you keep me informed as to what you come up with?"

"Sure, Mr. Friedman, I think we can do that."

"I would really like to know who did this." He paused to shake Stephanie's hand. "You know, I truly believe that he was innocent."

Friedman had not given them a connection to the deposition, but another approach to finding a possible suspect.

"Let's head over to Day's and see what new clues the daylight has to offer," Dave suggested, as they left Friedman's office.

Stephanie nodded. "And we've got a few things Jerry gave us this morning to check out."

As they headed toward the crime scene, Stephanie got out her cell phone and began to dial.

"I'll try to get in touch with the SEC and see if we can get that investor list," she told Dave. "Then I'll get EnergyDyn's number and check with Human Resources."

She was just finishing the calls as they pulled into the driveway at Day's estate.

8

*T*he officer at the scene opened the gate to let the detectives enter the estate. Dave could not believe how big it was and how different it looked during the day. Even the driveway seemed longer than it did last night.

Dave drove up the 240 foot drive toward the expansive circular half moon turnaround in front of the three double garage doors. In the light of day he noticed the patterns of brick up the driveway—intricate curved patterns in basketstone pavers in rich ocher, dark umber, and rosette—every ten feet. The uniquely colored inlays, full width sweeping arcs, matched the circular shape of the turnaround. Dave pulled to the left side of the drive and parked just below the turnaround, facing the garage.

"Well, where shall we start?" Stephanie asked, anxious to get to work.

"Let's start in the garage," Dave said, motioning with a thumb in the direction of the open door, "and see if we can piece together what actually happened."

"That sounds good to me."

They headed toward the west end of the garage and ducked under the yellow police tape that identified the crime scene. The Mercedes, bright red in the daylight, was sitting in the same position as it was earlier, but was covered with dust on the driver's side, remnants of the search for prints. Dave saw small rectangular marks where the lab tech had used the transparent lifting tape to recover the almost imperceptible evidence that could lead them to their suspect.

A noxious odor confronted them as they entered the structure. The combined smell of urine, blood, and death had intensified with the morning heat. Dave looked around the garage, noticing it had three double spaces but was deeper on their end.

"I'll bet Day could fit seven cars in here," Dave said, as he stepped around the chalkmark and looked into the front seat.

Stephanie nodded. "I don't even have a garage at my apartments. It's $20 extra a month."

"You should be able to pay for one now that you've got your promotion."

"I have a carport, but maybe I could move in here for a few months?" Stephanie teased.

"Well, Day won't be needing it."

The body had been removed, replaced by the chalk line drawn on the floor, a fading outline of where the body had fallen, and the position in which it had been found. The car door was still open, and the pool of blood, now sticky and deep crimson in color, defiled the otherwise immaculate floor.

Day was facing his murderer at the time of the shooting. Preliminary forensics indicated his hands were up when he was shot. The briefcase found next to the body had damage to the corners and blood spatter indicating he dropped it before he was shot. He fell forward and was laying face down when he was discovered.

Dave took a position between the body and the car door facing the open garage door. Stephanie took position near the rear of the car, and stood facing Dave, at the location where they thought the shooter would be standing. The lab determined the distance, based on blood spatter and the moderate stippling from the gunpowder, to be approximately eight to ten feet away.

From her location, Stephanie turned to locate the footprint on the driveway. "I think you're right, Dave," she said, noticing how easy it would have been for the murderer to enter the garage after Day had pulled the car in.

The footprint on the driveway was directly in front of the bushes where the killer lay in wait. From that vantage point, the killer could follow the car into the garage completely undetected. Stephanie turned to look again at the chalkmark, at her position, at the footprint, and back at Dave.

"Dave, look here. It's the palm print they pulled last night from the fender. Looks like the shooter leaned on the car. It's from the right hand. He wasn't wearing a glove."

"No kidding? Maybe we got lucky after all," he said. "So our shooter was left-handed? That should narrow down our search. There are fewer left-handed shooters than right-handed."

Stephanie walked out of the garage toward the footprint. It was just eight to ten steps from where the shooter would take aim and kill Day.

Dave walked over to the position where Stephanie had been standing, measuring off approximately eight to nine feet, three average steps, as he did. He turned and looked at the car door and the chalk outline on the floor. "Perfect," he muttered, referring to the distance, angle, and cover.

"Look here, Dave," Stephanie shouted. She was examining the faint impressions in the dirt area behind the bushes. The dirt was lightly wet in the flower bed, from the early morning sprinklers, which helped emphasize the impression. They were definitely made by someone standing there, waiting, the night before. The area behind the prints had been scratched by the gardeners, who came on Tuesday, and it was still fresh and undisturbed.

Stephanie motioned with her hand. "The perpetrator would have an excellent view of the driveway and easy access to the garage from here." She pointed to the impressions in the dirt. "Jerry said the prints were from a size ten or ten and a half shoe."

"We know he came over the wall," Dave said. "He ran across the lawn and hid here, followed Day into the garage, and escaped using the same route."

"How did he avoid the security cameras?"

"There are only two cameras he had to worry about." Dave pointed to one at the other end of the garage directed down the driveway. "It looks like Day was too cheap to spend any money on security."

"You would think he would have cameras everywhere."

"You would think so," Dave agreed. "The killer knew where to climb the wall, and the direction he chose allowed him to avoid both cameras. He's been here before."

"Jerry got the tapes this morning, so we can review them to see if they caught our suspect," Stephanie reminded him. "If he knew the property though, we probably won't get anything."

"Yeah. I definitely think he knew this property and planned his entrance and escape."

"We know which direction he came from," Stephanie said. "If we're done here, let's go check the wall. And we need to inspect the spot where the lab found blood on the cap, Dave. We haven't seen that yet."

"Okay…then we need to look at that tire track outside. There's quite a bit we couldn't see—."

Stephanie interrupted him. "We know he came straight from where he climbed the wall to this spot behind the bushes," Stephanie said, pointing across the yard, "from that direction."

"—last night," Dave finished. "We're pretty sure that's the direction," Dave smiled, a teasing grin unseen by Stephanie.

"Well, let's go see the wall," she said, already moving in the direction she had pointed—across the hundred and fifty feet of emerald green, manicured lawn, and toward the shrubbery.

"Sure that's the way?" Dave yelled, still teasing.

She just laughed. "More than 90 percent sure."

Dave followed her at a slower pace, past the trees, and through the bushes.

"Here it is!" Dave heard Stephanie's excited voice muffled by the foliage. "Right where I pointed."

Dave pushed through the bushes, being careful not to disturb them in case there were more clues, and ducked under the yellow tape. He squatted next to Stephanie, where she was examining the wall.

"There are footprints here in the dirt inside the wall. And here's the partial toe print."

The partial print was visible in one of the smoother areas of the slumpstone. It matched the prints in the dirt.

"What about the blood the lab found?" Dave asked.

"Right here on the edge of the cap," Stephanie declared, standing up and pointing to an area at the top of the wall. "His car must have been on the other side."

Dave turned to look through the shrubs in the direction of the house, only partially visible from their location. "It's a direct route in and out of the property, and out of view of the security cams."

"It does look planned, doesn't it?" Stephanie asked. "We've got the footprints and blood. Anything else we need to see here?"

"We've seen what we need," Dave said, "but I passed the tree where they found the fibers. Let's take a look at that while we're here."

"Okay. Then let's check out the tire tracks," Stephanie said, already moving through the bushes.

"Probably should." Dave said, no doubt unheard by Stephanie, as she was already at the tree tagged last night with yellow tape. There wasn't much to see since the tech removed all the threads.

Finished with that, they slid through the bushes back toward the garage and headed to the gate. The tire track was the final piece of evidence they needed to review at the scene.

In his mind, Dave reconstructed the events of the crime. The perpetrator climbed the wall, avoided the cameras, followed Day into the garage, and shot him. It appeared he escaped by reversing his route, climbed the wall to his car, and, since they found no other blood on the scene, must have left a little blood on the return trip.

It was now obvious to Dave that this had been a planned murder, and not just a botched robbery or burglary. A planned sequence of events. The route was selected to avoid the few surveillance cameras. It was a direct route to the garage, and the hiding spot selected offered the shooter excellent cover and an unobstructed view of the driveway. There was also the element of surprise from the spot where he took position. It had all the elements of a well-conceived and well-executed plan, Dave thought to himself. The objective is to find out who was capable of planning a murder like this. It almost looked like a hit.

Dave felt he should wait to discuss his thoughts with Stephanie until later, after they had viewed more of the evidence. And, of course, because she was about fifteen steps ahead of him again, he really didn't have the opportunity to discuss it with her now.

It was a long walk up the tree-lined street from the gate to where the tire track was discovered. Though it was a warm October day, the big oaks provided lots of shade to both sidewalk and street.

Stephanie was just ahead of Dave, having slowed a bit to let him catch up, as they approached the taped area at the curb. The tire track was now clearly visible in the daylight. Stephanie leaned down and was already examining the area when Dave arrived. It was a good piece of evidence, deep enough for the lab to get a clear impression, make a mold, and determine the exact brand and model.

"This is where the car was."

"Looks like the same location on the wall," Dave observed. "He got out of his car and went right over the wall here."

"You sure?" Stephanie asked.

"Yep."

"How can you tell it's the *exact spot*?" she pressed. "There aren't any visible marks or prints on the outside of the wall that would indicate where he climbed.

"The white birch. The one inside the wall, right next to where he climbed over on the other side," he explained.

"Oh!" Stephanie exclaimed. "I didn't notice that."

"You will," he encouraged her. Dave knew that these things would come with experience. "I planted a few river birches for my ex years ago, so I noticed it when we were inside."

Dave stepped back into the street to look at the smudge on the curb behind the tire track Stephanie was examining in the gutter—a big black smudge about 24 inches long. He looked up and down the pristine street, with pristine curbs and pristine gutters. This neighborhood had the old fashioned high curbs, unlike the new neighborhoods with slightly raised, gently sloped concrete edgings that rise gently to the grassy parkway. It didn't appear anyone ever parked at the curb in this neighborhood.

"There's the black scuff mark that Jerry told us about this morning."

She looked down at the curb from her position. "Yep," she said. Stephanie was already picking up Dave's "yep," after working with him for only four short months. "You think it was from last night?"

"Look at the rest of the curb. Nothing. And the mark appears to be fresh."

She joined Dave and looked up and down the street. "Not a mark anywhere!"

"It's just behind the tire track," Dave stated. "Looks like our killer bumped the curb while parking last night."

Stephanie pointed down Lost Creek Road. "So, he probably left down the street in the direction he was facing."

"I can't argue with that," Dave agreed.

"Wonder if any of the neighbors noticed a car parked here last night? No one we interviewed heard anything, but maybe someone saw something."

Dave nodded. "A car parked in this neighborhood? It would definitely cause suspicion."

"Especially late on a Wednesday night or early Thursday morning," Stephanie added.

"Jerry was positive the smudge came from the same car, and now I can see why. He's always been very thorough, and is usually right about his preliminary findings," Dave explained to Stephanie. "I'm sure it will be in one of the reports when we get back to the station."

Dave started back to the sidewalk and in the direction of the gate. "Let's head back to the station. We've got what we need here."

"We made a lot of progress this morning." Stephanie said.

"We did," Dave agreed. "Let's see what else the lab boys got for us."

9

Dave mulled over the clues while he drove back to the station. Stephanie made contact with someone at EnergyDyn.

Dave had a cell phone, too, but he had held out as long as he could before buying one, and used it as infrequently as necessary. He was the last of a dying breed, champion of those who still saw their privacy as a personal freedom. What was wrong with the old way of doing business, he wondered, hearing bits and pieces of Stephanie's conversation.

Detectives used to go out, gather evidence, return to the squad room, make the necessary calls, and go out and investigate what they found. But now…now they have instant access to anyone… almost anywhere.

What Dave objected to, although he wouldn't admit it, was the inability to hide. Not literally, of course, but figuratively. The department could, with few exceptions, reach them whenever it chose to. Code 7 had not been the same since.

"Dave," Stephanie said, after ending the call, "we need to swing by EnergyDyn before we go back to the station."

"Now?"

"Yep. Now, if we can."

"But it's not really on our way," he said.

"I know, but it's not that far out of the way. A lady in human resources is getting the lists for us—a Mrs. Hanson."

"That quick?" Dave asked. "How's she going to do that?"

"It's called computer technology," Stephanie teased. "Actually, she's getting a couple of lists for us."

"You don't have to be sarcastic," Dave pouted, pretending his feelings were hurt.

"Not being sarcastic. I just know how you feel about computers. How did you ever get things done in the past? You know…in the dark ages." She laughed.

He chuckled. "We managed somehow. I'll admit, computers have their usefulness. I just don't have much use for them."

"Anyway, she's getting those lists together for us right now—employees with stock options and those who have their 401Ks heavily vested in company stock. It saves me a lot of time on the computer pulling up all this information and sorting through it."

"Okay, guess we'll get it then," Dave agreed, "specially if it'll keep me off the computer."

Dave turned the car up the ramp to loop 610, heading toward the I-45, and downtown to EnergyDyn.

EnergyDyn was in big trouble. Trouble with the Securities and Exchange Commission, with investors, and with creditors. It's executives had even bigger problems.

The largest energy trading company in the U.S. was accused of several counts of malfeasance, from 2-way trading, to setting up bogus trading companies, as well as artificially inflating profits to keep the stock price up. All this, while top executives were selling off their shares at record high prices—making millions.

Dave knew two way trading referred to the art of selling the same supply of gas or electricity to one company and showing it as profit, and that company selling it back, also showing a profit. Good business? Maybe, but neither company showed any expense to buy the energy back, therefore, it looked like both companies made a profit from selling energy to each other, improving both bottom lines. That led to inflated profits, better quarterly earnings, and higher stock prices. Dave figured it was obviously more complicated than that, but he heard the program ran into the billions for EnergyDyn and hundreds of millions of dollars for other companies.

A major portion of the trades involved EnergyDyn and was the cause of its downfall. Truckloads of accountants were brought in to identify the extent of these practices, and they were still knee-deep in the minutiae.

Dave did not remember many details from the reports, but the *Houston Chronicle*, *Wall Street Journal*, *Barron's*, and *Business Week* gave descriptive details of the business dealings and practices of EnergyDyn and other energy companies caught in the scandal.

Several government agencies spent months sifting through the mounds of paperwork from EnergyDyn, as well as other corporations, trying to sort out the complicated mess. Adding to the dilemma was the paper-shredding incident, involving EnergyDyn's accounting firm, which the government finally stopped. They're still not sure how much valuable evidence was lost in the thousands of documents destroyed by EnergyDyn's accountants.

The number of companies involved continues to grow, duplicity never before seen in American business. No one is even sure how many executives at EnergyDyn are involved, but, the list might escalate to more than a hundred individuals.

The company's executives told employees that everything was going great and encouraged them to continue investing in the company. EnergyDyn was a darling on Wall Street. Stock prices continued to rise with the increased profit and increased investment. Only a chosen group of individuals knew the profits were false and overinflated.

The most malignant malfeasance occurred when executives, while espousing the success of the company, were engaged in selling *their* positions, banking millions, while unsuspecting employees were kept in the dark. Day was one of those making millions at the expense of the employees, creditors, and investors. The bankruptcy filing left all of them holding worthless paper.

As they neared the exit on the interstate, Dave turned to Stephanie. "Anything in the deposition that might be helpful?"

"Well, Benjamin Day claimed that as chairman, he knew nothing about the 2-way trading, nor had any knowledge of the shell companies. Of course, he didn't have much to say about the nearly 200 million in company stock he sold during the year prior to the collapse when questioned by the government lawyers either."

"Two hundred million?"

"That's a lot of money, isn't it?"

"More than I could ever imagine," Dave said, as he exited to downtown on Smith Street and headed to the EnergyDyn complex. EnergyDyn was only a few blocks from the Houston Police Department headquarters, a place Dave visited only when his presence was requested.

EnergyDyn was once the heart of downtown. The mirrored phallic symbol of cool blue glass—sky and clouds playing on all sides of the majestic oval building—now stood mute at the intersection of Smith and Bell. It's twin tower—inanimate—for sale to recoup some of EnergyDyn's massive losses.

Dave hadn't given the buildings much thought prior to his involvement in this case, but today, as he approached the imposing structures, he felt differently.

"Would you look at those?" he whispered. "They're even more ostentatious than Day's estate."

Stephanie sat silent, staring at the buildings as Dave pulled into the nearly empty parking lot at EnergyDyn.

The once rotating EnergyDyn sign, with the chasing lights proudly lighting up the iconic E, was now dormant. No lights illuminated the sign; black and motionless, placid and stained from its lifeless presence. It mirrored the conditions at EnergyDyn, a corporation once thriving—now defunct. A few numbers and letters were missing from its marble base, further evidence of deterioration.

The parking lot was a mere skeleton of the EnergyDyn of less than a year ago. At its peak, EnergyDyn employed more than 18,000 people in its corporate offices downtown; more than 8,000 in other locations. The corporate complex was once the busiest place in Houston, cars coming and going, creating a unique life of its own.

Dave would be surprised to find 300 people here today. He guessed those who were left were working on the bankruptcy. They parked in front, near the entrance in one of the many vacant handicapped spots.

"You're in a handicapped parking spot," Stephanie said.

"There's still plenty spots available," he said, as they climbed out of the car. There were more than eight open spots on his side alone.

As they walked across the street and up the walkway toward the steps and main entrance, he added, "I never understood why handicapped parking spaces were always the best spots in the parking lot."

Stephanie looked at Dave. "You're not serious, are you?"

"Serious as a heart attack," he replied expressionless. "It's not like a lot of handicapped people are going to park here today." Dave knew she'd think he was uncaring, but he couldn't help toying with her.

"You're right," Stephanie agreed, giving him a sideways glance. She was about to say something else but was interrupted by Dave motioning her to one of the revolving doors at the entrance.

They were greeted by the cold, cavernous lobby, replete with walls of marble and glass, once the warm, vibrant evidence of success. Pools and fountains had long since dried up, evaporating like the company, adding to the lifeless environment.

A long, curved reception desk, with one matronly woman sitting behind it, faced them. She looked cold, bored, almost disconnected—maybe even withered, Dave thought. Flowers in the planters on either side of the desk, once a sign of growth and prosperity, were also withered and dead.

"May I help you?" came her trembling, chilly voice, resonating off the walls of the open space, echoing throughout the building, and down the hallways probably dissipating somewhere near the Energy Trading Department. She looked like she was brought back out of retirement to fill this position.

"We're here to see Mrs. Hanson." Stephanie's words echoed down the halls closely following the still audible words of the receptionist.

"I think she's in Human Resources," the receptionist replied.

"Yes, she is," Stephanie confirmed.

The words bounced off the marble walls in all directions.

"Who may I say is here?" she asked.

"Detective Fox."

"What is this in regard to?" she asked Stephanie.

"It's a police matter," Stephanie said. "I spoke with her earlier. She knows we're coming."

The receptionist raised her eyebrows. "I'll let her know you're here."

She pulled out the huge phone book, evidence of the once massive size of EnergyDyn, and slowly thumbed through the book, her arthritic fingers having difficulty separating the pages.

For the first time, her expression changed. She turned up a little smile when she reached her intended goal. Picking up the phone she punched in the number.

"Three—three—five—one—seven," repeating each number out loud.

"Mrs. Hanson—Human Resources?" she spoke as if she wasn't sure.

"Yes, a Detective Fox is here to see you. Yes, I will do that. Yes, all the way to section three, Room 3517, of course. You're welcome."

She hung up the phone and glanced up at Stephanie.

Her attempt at giving directions was difficult at best, and following them would prove to be equally difficult. They started down the hallway and up the escalator that would take them to the second floor and the skyway connecting all the buildings, with hopes of finding Mrs. Hanson's office.

After what seemed like the better part of a half hour and figuring they had taken six to ten wrong turns, they stumbled into Mrs. Hanson's office. The sign next to the door said Human Resources, so they were sure they had finally found the right place.

Mrs. Hanson greeted them sounding as warm and helpful as Stephanie said she had been on the phone. She put her hand out to shake Stephanie's.

"Hello, Detective Fox."

"Hello, Mrs. Hanson, this is my partner, Detective Duncan."

"Hello, Detective Duncan. How are you?"

"I'm fine Mrs. Hanson, thank you."

"I've got the list you requested, Detective Fox. It's a shame about Mr. Day, isn't it?"

"It is," Stephanie agreed. "Detective Duncan and I are going to find the person responsible for this."

"I hope so. He was a very nice man," Mrs. Hanson offered.

"Do you know of anyone here who may have threatened Mr. Day?" Stephanie inquired, looking directly at Mrs. Hanson. "Anyone that said they wanted to, or would, kill him?"

Mrs. Hanson lowered her eyes. "There were a lot of angry people," she said. "A lot of things were said after everyone found out about the bankruptcy. I'm sure there were, but I don't remember anyone in particular saying anything like that. He was always nice to me. I don't think he could have done what they say he did!"

"You knew him personally?" Stephanie asked her.

"Well, not personally," Mrs. Hanson said, a little embarrassed. "He knew my name and always said hello when I saw him."

"He sounds like a very nice man," Stephanie smiled.

"I thought he was. The lists will help you find his murderer?"

"Maybe," Stephanie said. "We won't know until we go through them, but we're very hopeful."

Mrs. Hanson handed Stephanie a folder and an accordion file. "Here are the lists of employees with stock options, the amount of options and the estimated value, and those vested in the 401K plan, that you requested."

The first file contained more than twenty-five pages of names in fairly small type. The other file, the one of employees who had stock in their retirement plans, was easily 350 or more pages.

"That's a big file," Stephanie grimaced.

"Most of the employees were in the 401K program," Mrs. Hanson answered. "We all thought the company was such a safe investment."

"Did you lose any money?" Stephanie asked.

"Not too much. Not like some of the others." Her eyes seemed to well up a little. "I've only been here for two years. But some, I know, lost everything."

"So, the estimated value is the total of their contributions without what EnergyDyn was contributing?"

"Yes, the employees' contribution. The company matched their contributions. It's a shame what happened to Mr. Day, but even more tragic what happened to the company, and our employees."

Jim Worth 63

"So it affected almost everyone?" Stephanie asked.

"Yes...it hurt so many people...the loss of jobs and life savings. I'm one of the lucky ones. I got to keep my job." She paused for a moment and sighed deeply. "This company was so alive. It seemed like there was no end to the growth. Every week there were more Mercedes, Porsches, and BMW's in the parking lot. Everyone got greedy. It was difficult not to. No one wanted to be left out."

Mrs. Hanson gave her account of what had gone wrong at EnergyDyn. Dave remained quietly in the background during this conversation. He took the lists from Stephanie.

"Detective Fox," Dave interrupted, "we should be going. We still have a lot to do. Mrs. Hanson—thank you, this will be very helpful."

"Yes, thank you for this," Stephanie said. "You have saved me a lot work. Can I call you if we need anything else?"

"Of course, you can, anything to help catch Mr. Day's killer."

After each of them shook Mrs. Hanson's hand, they started the long trek back to the car. Dave had the lists under his arm, and the weight alone was an indicator of the amount of work ahead.

When he pushed through the revolving door and they walked toward the car, he said, "See? Not a single handicapped vehicle."

"You're right," she conceded. "Not a single handicapped vehicle."

As they stood there staring at the empty spaces, Stephanie said, "Day knew Mrs. Hanson's name."

"Yeah," Dave answered curiously. "So what?"

"I find that strange. Mr. Friedman claimed that Mr. Day didn't know Mr. Farrell, and it stated that in the deposition, but Mrs. Hanson told us he knew *her*."

"I'm not following you. What you're getting at."

Stephanie scrunched her brow. "I remember on television, Friedman claimed that Day did not know Mr. Farrell, after Farrell had been arrested. Farrell was the assistant to the chief financial officer, who helped Stephen Carston set up the shell companies."

"What are you getting at?" Dave asked. "What's that got to do with Day's murder?"

"It means he was probably lying."

"How so?"

"He didn't know one of his senior management team, but he knew Mrs. Hanson, from Human Resources?" She went on, "This certainly puts a different twist on this case for me. Maybe he *was* guilty."

Dave just shook his head and opened the car door. "I'm still not totally sure what you're getting at. You can explain it to me later."

They got into the car and headed back to the station.

"Maybe one of these lists will help us solve this puzzle," Stephanie mumbled.

"Maybe so." He sure as heck hoped so.

10

"Captain's looking for you two," the desk sergeant's voice boomed through the entrance of the station.

It was almost noon, and they had not been back to the squad since early this morning. Of course, they had called in three times to let the desk know what they were doing. Still they had not talked to the captain since their call last night. This morning they were gone before he arrived, but Dave knew the captain was curious about what had been accomplished on the case and where they were in their investigation.

Stephanie whispered, "I wonder how many calls Captain's gotten this morning from concerned citizens?"

Dave frowned. "I'm sure more than he cared to get."

A high-profile case like this always drew a lot of inquiries, but this one was different. The mayor and chief had known the victim personally.

At the top of the stairs, Dave and Stephanie heard the same sharp greeting from one of the detectives, "Captain's looking for you." No good mornin's, no how you doin's, which indicated the importance of this case. The squad was now alive with activity, unlike earlier at 3:00 a.m.

"John, how did the canvassing go?" Stephanie asked one of the other detectives on the way to her desk.

"Nobody saw a thing. At least no one that we talked to."

"No one?"

"Not a bite!" John said. "They all want it solved, but they were sorry that they couldn't help."

"How about you guys?" Stephanie asked another team.

"Same, nothing here either. They all claimed they were asleep or not home."

"Anybody hear anything?"

Dave heard frustration in her voice.

"One couple thought they might have heard gunshots," John offered. "But they weren't sure exactly when that might have been."

"Why didn't they call it in?"

"Said they were watching television and couldn't be sure they were gunshots."

"Can you believe that, Dave?" Stephanie said.

Dave was immersed in the reports on his desk that the lab had sent up. He was particularly interested in the reconstruction report, curious if he and Stephanie had come up with a scenario matching the lab's.

"What? Sorry, I wasn't paying attention."

"No one saw or heard anything in the neighborhood!" She threw up her hands in disgust. "They want us to solve the crime, but nobody saw a thing!"

"Not surprised," Dave muttered half-heartedly, still looking for that report.

"You're not?"

"Nope. It's a big neighborhood, big estates, lots of foliage, and not a lot of activity on a Wednesday night."

"But they didn't even hear the shots!" Stephanie said.

"These places are big. They have lots of trees to cut down on the noise. And most of them just downright don't want to get involved," Dave continued. "Whatever the reasons, we're not going to get a lot of help from them."

"It would have been nice to get a little help," Stephanie said, frustrated.

"John, what about the two interviewed on television last night? Which of you interviewed them today?"

"I did. They told me the same thing when I talked to them this morning. They didn't see or hear anything."

"Duncan, Fox, I need to see you in my office." Both detectives recognized the sonorous voice of the captain.

Captain Martin's voice was very distinguishable. It pervaded the squad, hanging thick in the room, commanding action on the part of those to whom it was directed. Though he sometimes sounded gruff, or stern, down deep the captain was a pretty good guy.

"On our way, Captain," Stephanie yelled back.

The captain was sitting behind his desk, reading through all the little slips of phone messages. He didn't appear all that unhappy, but then again, he didn't look happy either.

"Do you know what all these are?" he bellowed.

"Inquiries?" Dave remarked. It was more of an answer than a question.

"Yes, inquiries—lots of them—all asking the same thing. You know what that is?"

Before Dave or Stephanie could answer he continued.

"How is the case going? Have you got any suspects yet? Do you know the importance the mayor has placed on this case? All the usual questions." He added, "Are you two aware that the mayor knew Mr. Day personally? Do you know what I had to tell the mayor's office?" he concluded, finally pausing to take a breath.

Dave shook his head.

"I told them that my star investigators were working hard on the case," he said. "That I would inform them as soon as I found something out myself. Do you know what I really meant?" He glared at them as if he were mad. "I meant to say that I haven't seen my detectives, I don't know where the hell they are, so I really don't have a clue—no pun intended. Do you know how embarrassing it would be to say that to the mayor? That wasn't a lie…was it? You were working hard on this case…weren't you? I was too damned busy answering inquires to even call your cell phones." He took another breath. "So, where have my illustrious detectives been? The ones on the front page of the *Houston Chronicle* this morning," he said. He picked up the paper on the corner of his desk and dropped it right back where it sat.

"We've been hard on the case, Captain," Stephanie offered, apprehensively.

"I'm glad to hear that. So what have you got so far?"

"I think we've figured it out—it was Colonel Mustard, in the garage, with a handgun," Dave joked trying to lighten the mood.

"I'm serious about this, Duncan, you can't appreciate the shit I'm in on this one," the captain said. "I have no love for this guy, but my superiors seem to think he's still important, so when they ask me what we've got I feel obliged to get them the answers."

"We have quite a lot, Captain," Stephanie interjected. "We've talked to Mr. Friedman, Day's attorney; gone back over the crime scene; and collected some information from EnergyDyn. We called in three times this morning, to let the desk know where we were."

"I know you did," he said smiling, "just want you to get a feel for how crazy this case is already. What's it been…twelve hours? All right, what do we have?"

"We have probably an individual, who lies in wait in the bushes, follows the car into the garage, confronts the victim and pops him three times," Stephanie stated. "We're not sure of the motive yet, Captain, but we're working on that."

Dave, listening intently, added, "Appears to have been premeditated, Captain. Maybe even a hit."

"*Premeditated*? A hit? You sure?"

Stephanie looked at Dave blankly, surprised by Dave's new revelation, hearing it for the first time.

Dave nodded. "It looks that way—maybe a hit. We know the crime was well planned."

"Suspects?" Captain Martin inquired.

"Not yet," Stephanie said. "But we're just now putting together all the clues."

"We have a lot from the lab that we have to go through this afternoon, Cap," Dave added.

"Then get to work," Captain Martin said. "Keep me informed. I have a lot of people on my back on this one."

"Will do, Captain," they said simultaneously.

The two returned to their desks and began to go through everything they had. Phone records had been faxed from the phone company; cell phone and appointment book had been sent up from the lab as well as photos, blood report, ballistics, and other forensic reports. Most everything they had found in the early morning was available for them to investigate.

Dave read the report that reconstructed the crime and looked over the diagrams the lab had created.

"It's just as we thought," Dave said, half to himself and half to Stephanie. "Diagrams pretty much confirm what happened."

"By the way," Stephanie interrupted, "when did 'we' come up with the 'premeditated' murder theory? And what about this 'hit' idea? When were you going to tell me that you had a theory, Columbo?"

"Didn't have the opportunity. You were on the cell phone when I put the pieces together," Dave told her, covering up the fact that he had planned to wait for the appropriate time. "Really, I *wasn't* trying to withhold anything from you."

About that time a courier entered the squad looking for Detective Fox. He had a package from the SEC that contained the EnergyDyn investor list. Stephanie signed for the package and set it down on her desk with the other lists. It was about ten times the size of the lists Stephanie received from EnergyDyn.

"That was quick, wasn't it?" Dave asked.

"It was. The lady I talked to at the SEC told me that normally, with a request of this nature, the SEC would take about two weeks to comply," Stephanie said. "She explained that things were different now. With all the corporate malfeasance and pressure the SEC is under, with so many violations, and its inability to police these cases, they have been far more cooperative with policing agencies."

But the other clues were still Dave and Stephanie's first priority. Stephanie picked up the fingerprint report. It showed that the lab techs pulled four different sets of prints from the car. There was a note attached to the report.

"We got four hits on the fingerprints," Stephanie informed Dave.

"That's good," Dave said. "Any we can use?"

"Two of them have matches," Stephanie answered. "One is

Day's, on the door and on the roof. The other, found on the front fender and driver's door, belongs to a small-time criminal," she said. "The lab is searching for a place of employment or a last known address right now."

The tire report caught Dave's attention. He was reading through it when he heard Stephanie's voice.

"Dave, here's the report on the shoe prints. They are all from the same pair of shoes. It's an Adidas running shoe."

"How many of them are out there? Adidas is a fairly popular shoe, isn't it?"

"It is. The model is an adiStar Cushion M, one of the three most popular running shoes in the U.S. But, Jerry found a couple unique wear patterns."

"How unique? Is it something we may be able to trace back to the killer?"

"Nothing specific written in the comments."

Dave raised the report he was holding. "Here's the report on the tire track. Guess what brand?"

"Probably Goodyears," Stephanie said.

"Did you see the report?"

"Nope, just a good guess. My dad always bought Goodyear tires."

"They're Goodyear Eagle Radials—fourteen inch. There's a note here at the bottom in the comments section."

"What does it say?"

Dave laughed. "It's the most popular brand of domestic tire. About 250,000 sold each year in Houston alone."

"That's good to know," Stephanie said, sarcastically. "Couldn't be a brand with only a hundred sets sold, could it?"

"They were fairly new. Tread pattern was real clean, and it has a few distinguishing cuts in the pattern, which should make it easier to match."

"Back to the shoes for a minute, Dave. The lab confirmed that it was a man's size ten or ten and a half. So we know for positive we're looking for a man."

Dave snorted. "Oh, that certainly narrows it down."

They continued searching through reports, hoping for anything that would help them pare the number of suspects. At this point, everyone except Day, Dave, and Stephanie were suspects.

"Where's the ballistics report, Stephanie? You see it?"

She shuffled some papers, then smiled. "You were right, it was a .38 caliber," she said, as she handed him the report.

Dave glanced over it. "Based on the rifling, the slugs came from a Smith and Wesson Model 10."

"You and Jerry were right, but that's the most popular handgun on the market. It's going to be difficult to trace."

The evidence wasn't offering them a lot. None of the clues would lead them to the murderer, but they would serve as solid evidence if they caught someone.

The two fibers recovered from a tree trunk at the scene were from a black fleece sweatshirt.

"The killer must have brushed against the tree in the dark during his escape," Stephanie said.

"That means the sweatshirt will probably have a tear in it and traces of the tree bark in the fabric," Dave said, taking the report from Stephanie.

"There's nothing special about the fabric or dye though," Stephanie added. "Just like everything else we've got."

"Just our luck, everything here, except the possible fingerprint, is pretty generic." Dave sighed. "Shoes, tires, sweatshirt, and gun."

"The only possible clue to positively identify the killer could be the fingerprint." Stephanie stared at the print report. "Several of the matches were Day's."

"Where were his prints again?"

"Some on the door, door handle, window and roof. Two sets had no match, but the other belonged to a Charles Banks. Maybe the fingerprint will be a good lead—" Stephanie paused when the phone rang.

"We've got nothing else to help us find the killer," Dave grumbled, as Stephanie answered the phone. She smiled and hung up.

"The lab came up with a last known address and place of employment on Banks. Maybe we should check him out next," she suggested.

It was better than anything they had so far. The car wash where Banks worked was only about 25 minutes from the station. Dave grabbed his jacket and headed to the motor pool.

Stephanie slid into the car with Dave. "I got Banks's rap sheet," she said. "He's got a record, but it's all small-time stuff."

"Like what?"

"Like simple assault, burglary, joy-riding. He served ninety days for the assault charge twelve years ago. Nothing close to murder."

"Maybe he's trying to move up in the world?"

"I don't think so, Dave. The assault was minor—no gun, no knife, and there's nothing on his sheet for the past ten years."

"Doesn't mean that he's gone straight."

"Maybe not, but our concern is his connection to Day."

"Right," Dave agreed. "Did he own any stock in EnergyDyn?"

"I doubt it. You think a guy working in a car wash owns stock in EnergyDyn?"

"Well, if he didn't own any stock then his only connection with Day is the car wash. We'll know shortly if he was capable of planning anything like this," Dave added, as they pulled up in front of the car wash.

Inside Stephanie held up her badge for the cashier. "We're looking for a Charles Banks. He still work here?"

"He's not here today. He called in sick."

"Sick? Does he call in sick often?"

"Hardly ever. He never misses work, just said he didn't feel very well this morning and wasn't coming in."

"Is he still at 11564 Walker Avenue?"

"I think so. Let me ask the manager."

The manager confirmed that Banks was still at that address as far as he knew. They thanked him and headed to Banks's last known address, which was only about two miles away.

"So, Banks was sick today? Wonder what he was doing last night that could cause today's illness."

"It does sound pretty suspicious, doesn't it?" Dave said. "Let's go ahead and call for back-up, Stephanie."

Stephanie finished the call just as they pulled up in front of the small house Banks lived in. An older, dark burgundy Pontiac Grand Am sat in the driveway on a pair of Goodyear radials.

Banks's beaten-down house was in a rough part of town. It would not be prudent to do anything hasty here. They talked strategies till back-up arrived.

Dave and Stephanie stepped up on the porch while their back-ups, John and his partner, took up positions near the rear of the house. Dave knocked on the door.

"Charles Banks? Houston Police Department." They heard nothing inside. "Mr. Banks," Dave yelled again. "Could you please open the door? We have some questions we need to ask you."

"Yeah, yeah, I'm coming," a voice yelled from inside the house.

Banks opened the door, not looking in top shape, squinting from the bright sun, to see Dave standing in front of him on the porch.

"You mind stepping out here on the porch with us, Mr. Banks?"

The lanky black man stepped out—wearing a tattered shirt and pajama bottoms. "Sure, but ya mind tellin' me what this is all about? Ain't nobody called me mister fo' ah long time. It don't sound good hearin' dat."

"Where were you last night, Chuck?"

"It's Charles, officer, and I was down at da Playpen last night," he said.

The Playpen was a topless establishment on the edge of the bar district. It was one of Houston's seedier bars and had been closed several times for a number of violations—including prostitution.

"How long were you there last night?"

"I don't know. At least till one a'clock or so," he said.

"What time did you get there?"

"Round seven I think. Me and two buddies."

Banks clearly appeared to be feeling the effects of being at the bar for six hours or more.

"And you and your buddies didn't leave the entire—what was it—maybe six hours?"

"Nope, we stayed there. I was workin' some angles with one

of the *fine ladies* at the club. She can vouch for me. Hell, she got mosta my money."

The Playpen was at least 45 minutes from Day's estate. It would have been difficult for Banks to get to Day's and back to the bar without anyone noticing he was gone.

"What's the dancer's name?" Dave asked.

"It's Ebony Nights. She's da finest lady there."

"I'm sure she is." Dave smirked. "She probably looked better by the end of the evening, didn't she?"

"What's dis all about?" Banks asked.

"You happen to know a Benjamin Day? Red 2002 Mercedes SL55 AMG?"

"Him, yeah I do, the cheap bastard. *Very picky* and a terrible tipper. I didn't take nothin' outta his car. He say I did?"

"No, he didn't say you took anything. Did he accuse you of something before?"

"Coupla weeks ago he accused me of takin' his CD case."

"Did you?"

"*Hell no*! He listens ta dat classical shit. I don't listen ta dat crap. It done slipped under his seat. He never apologized to me after he found it neither. Maybe you can get him to apologize?"

"He won't be apologizing to you or anybody. He was murdered last night."

"*No shit*! You don't think I did it—*do ya*? He was cheap, but I wasn't gonna kill him just because he stiffed me and wouldn' apologize."

"We found your fingerprints on the car," Stephanie spoke up. "And you have quite a lengthy record."

"Well, sure ya did," he said, twisting to look at Stephanie. "I did his car yesterday round foe a'clock. Did a *fine* job on it, too, and he gave me a lousy four bits tip," Banks complained. "I been clean for over ten years. It was da drugs made me do all dat crazy shit."

Banks showed no remorse over Benjamin Day's death, but was genuinely surprised when he was told Day had been murdered the night before. If he was at the bar like he said, he couldn't have done it. Charles Banks was guilty of leaving some fingerprints on Day's newly washed car. Surely good reason for a measly fifty-cent tip.

"You're not gonna make me go downtown to da station are you? I ain't feelin' too good."

"No, not right now," Stephanie said, "but you know the routine. Don't leave—.

"Town. Yeah I know."

They returned to the station with no more than they had before, and began to go through the remaining reports.

Both the phone and cell phone records drew blanks. None of the calls Day made or received appeared to have any connection to the crime—calls to Friedman, friends and family, the bank and some local businesses. Nothing that would lead them to believe anyone was even remotely involved. There were a few messages on his phone at home, but the tape revealed nothing that would lead to finding his killer.

His cell phone brought the same results. Dialing the last few numbers produced little. Day's life seemed to be pretty dull since the bankruptcy. Friends and acquaintances were distancing themselves from him for fear of being investigated by virtue of their association with him.

One possibility still existed. Friedman's suggestion of an angry employee or a disgruntled investor might lead them to a killer. They needed to figure out how to break down the information they had and how to effectively investigate the leads.

They already knew that it was a man, with a size ten or ten and a half shoe. The crime re-creation placed the killer at about eight to ten feet away, indicated by the blood spatter evidence, stippling on the shirt, and the shredding around the wounds.

Based on the ballistic evidence, it was believed that the killer was between 6' and 6'2". The lab determined that by taking the angle of entry of the bullets, running a string out to the eight-and ten-foot lengths, and figuring the height of the shoulder and angle of the arm required to shoot the victim from those distances.

Stephanie thought the killer might be living in, or within driving distance of, the Houston area. John's check of all the rental companies in the area failed to produce a rental car using the exact brand of Goodyear tire found at the scene, reducing the probability of someone flying in to murder Day, and renting a car. The possibility of someone from out of town driving to Houston still existed, but they would start with the investors who were in Houston and work their way out.

The lab boys also found about 30 or more threatening letters in a desk drawer when they searched Day's home. All anonymous, with some having Houston postmarks. They also found e-mails from individuals who were upset with the collapse of EnergyDyn. Some from employees, some from investors.

The paper and envelopes were being analyzed by the lab, searching for new evidence, which might even include fingerprints. First they'd check the letters, then the computer files, to identify the individuals from their e-mail addresses. This evidence gave more credence to the investor or employee theory.

Stephanie began going through the investor list from the Securities and Exchange Commission.

"So how's it coming along?" Dave asked, after she had been working on it for a while.

"Better than I thought," she answered. "They sent a disk which allows me to break it down on the computer by zip code and size of investment."

"Smart thinking, which way first?"

"First by zip code, then into sixteen areas and then I'll assign one section of the list to each of our sixteen teams."

"Sounds complicated to me. Glad you're doing it."

"It's really not complicated, but it's a little tedious to break it down by areas. I have to ask the software to give me all hits in specific map grids."

"Where'd you learn all this?"

"Had a couple of classes in Computer Aided Investigative Techniques at Plano Valley College," she said, glancing up at Dave.

"Well, I have to admit, I am impressed."

"Thanks. I should have the lists in about an hour. We'll have the patrols distribute them to each of the teams at the other precincts so they can get started today."

After a couple of hours of sorting, Stephanie identified more than 7,800 individual investors, male, living in the Houston area.

She finished packaging the lists for all the teams, took the one that she and Dave would check, gave the rest to the patrols, and headed for the lab.

Dave was further impressed when she took the list to the lab and asked them to cross-check the names on the list with firearm registrations, searching for an investor who also had a gun permit for a .38 caliber handgun. In the meantime, they would begin their interviews searching for suspects.

The four additional lists that stayed in the 5th Precinct were split up and given out to each of the four investigative teams. This was going to be a big job.

Each area contained between 110 and 125 names. It was just after 3:00 p.m. when Dave and Stephanie prepared to hit the streets.

The only way to finish this task was to get out and "pound the pavement."

11

*D*ave believed one of the hardest parts of a detective's job was field interviews. Computers and the Internet had revolutionized some parts of police work, sped up information gathering, and enhanced investigations, but one area that would never change was face-to-face interviews. Legwork was always a necessary part of any investigation and would always be.

Dave did not relish having to go from house to house, business to business, but searching for suspects made interviewing the only conceivable method they could use.

Dave and Stephanie had taken the Northwest section of Houston. Their list included Lost Canyon, Lost Hills, and Canyon Meadows.

After earlier discussion among the detectives, they started with the biggest investors, figuring those who had lost the most had a greater motive for revenge.

The first dozen Dave and Stephanie interviewed turned up nothing. They encountered a lot of angry investors, but no real suspects.

The afternoon faded into dusk, and with it, hopes of finding a suspect today. By the time evening slipped into night, Dave and Stephanie had conducted 25 interviews and were feeling the effects of the long day with little sleep.

"You ready to call it a night? It's not going anywhere till morning. We can pick it up then," Dave said.

"Sounds good to me," Stephanie said. "I'm getting tired. Let's head back to the station. I want to do a little computer work and review a few of the reports before going home."

"You got it. We can find out how the others did."

When they arrived, one of the teams was already back at the station. John informed them that another of the teams had already gone home and that they had met with similar results.

"We had two on the list that might be worth checking out again," John, the detective who backed them up at Banks's, told Stephanie. "But, that was about it."

"How many did you interview?"

"I don't know, maybe a couple dozen. This is tough work, interviewing all these people."

Dave nodded. "Face-to-face interviews are slow."

It was an arduous task, one the detectives did not particularly enjoy. The other team came in, reported the same experience, and were done for the night. They agreed to pick up where they left off the next morning.

"It's a good thing our case load is light right now," John said.

Stephanie shook her head. "I don't think it would matter. This case is high on the chief's priorities, and I think he wants to throw all of our resources at this one." She paused, glancing around. "Where's Kevin? Is he back?"

"He and Greg are in I-3."

"*What's he doing in there?*" Stephanie asked.

"They brought in a suspect, and they're interviewing him."

"Great, John. Why didn't you tell me?" she said, annoyed. "Dave, Kevin's got a suspect in three."

They were already interviewing the suspect, so Stephanie and Dave stepped into the viewing room to observe the interrogation. Kevin was asking him a question as Dave reached up to turn on the speaker.

"—me again, so we can get this straight. Where were you on Wednesday night?" Kevin asked, frustration in his voice.

"I told you, I was in Beaumont on business."

"Yeah, you said business. But what kind of business? You told us you weren't working."

"I went there for an interview. A job interview. I haven't worked since EnergyDyn filed bankruptcy," he added.

"With what company?"

"I didn't actually have the interview."

"What do you mean you didn't have an interview? Didn't you just tell us that was your reason for being in Beaumont?"

"The guy that was supposed to interview me wasn't there."

"Let me get this straight. You tell us you were in Beaumont for an interview, but it never happened. You expect us to believe that? What else are you lying about?"

"I'm not lying. The guy wasn't there...honest."

"Well, when did you return from Beaumont?" Kevin questioned. "It's not that far away. You could have been back easily Wednesday evening, killed Day, and made up this story."

"I didn't. I mean I didn't come back Wednesday night. I stayed in Beaumont."

"What motel'd you stay in?"

"I didn't stay in a motel. I slept in my car at a rest area there."

"You what? Come on...who do you think you're talking to?" Kevin shouted.

"I did. I was so upset about driving all the way to Beaumont and the guy wasn't there, that I went to a bar."

"Did anyone see you at the bar?"

"I'm sure the bartender remembers me. I sat at the end of the bar."

"What bar?"

"I don't remember the name. It was near the interstate."

"Was it in Beaumont...outside of Beaumont?"

"I don't remember. I just pulled into a bar."

Kevin slammed the chair against the table. The sound of metal on metal resonated through the tiny room.

"Wow, this just keeps getting better!" Kevin turned to his partner. "Can you believe this guy?"

"I'm trying," he answered. "But it's getting more difficult."

"It's the truth. I had nothing to do with Day's death," the suspect pleaded. "Sure, I said I could have killed him. But I didn't do it. Am I going to need a lawyer?"

"*Do you?*" Kevin asked. "How are you going to pay for one? You don't have a job, no money. Do you want a public defender? We can get you one right now if you think you're guilty."

"I agreed to come in and answer a few questions about my investment in EnergyDyn. You *didn't* tell me I was *a suspect* in Benjamin Day's murder."

"You weren't, but you're doing a damned good job painting yourself into one."

"I didn't have anything to do with it," he argued. "I wasn't even here."

"How about some gas receipts? Did you gas up while you were on the road?"

"No, didn't have to. I filled up the day before here in town."

"Got a receipt for that one?"

"I paid cash."

"Very convenient," Kevin said. "Greg, let's go outside for a minute." Turning to the man being interviewed, he said, "Don't go anywhere, we'll be right back."

Kevin and Greg came out of the interview room as Dave and Stephanie stepped out of the viewing room.

"How's he look for this one?" Stephanie asked.

Kevin shrugged. "Hard to say. How much did you two see?"

"From the 'where were you Wednesday night?' What did you bring him in for?"

"He was cooperative, but he said he was glad Day was dead and that he got what he deserved. He's real angry and wouldn't let up so we asked him to come in and help us by answering a few questions about his investment in EnergyDyn."

"We were talking about that while watching your interview," Stephanie nodded. "He's definitely the best candidate we've got so far. What else have we got on him?"

"He's about 6'2" and he has a car with Goodyear Eagle Radials. He told us he owned a handgun, a .38 caliber," Greg said. "Keeps it in his car for protection. Told us he used to carry large sums of cash in his previous job."

"They're cross-checking for any gun registrations right now," Kevin added.

"How about his alibi?" Dave asked.

"You heard him, Dave," Greg said. "He said he paid cash for gas, so we have no gas receipts, restaurant charges, or sales receipts. We haven't had time to check any of this out yet."

"He claims he was asleep in a rest area, 70 miles from here, at midnight," Kevin said. "So I guess we're going to have to find the bar and interview the bartender."

"He did say earlier that he had no idea where Lost Canyon Estates was," Greg added.

"Do you believe him?"

"Not sure. He could be lying about everything."

"How much did he lose in his investment?" Stephanie inquired, wondering how badly he would want to seek revenge.

"It said he had $50,000 invested in EnergyDyn."

"That's a hefty chunk!" Stephanie exclaimed. "But is it enough to be a motive for murder?"

"Not as much as some, but it was a lot of dough for him," Kevin answered. "You guys want a shot at him?"

"No, you go ahead. You're doing a great job," Dave said.

"We've only got a few more questions. Unless we get something from the lab, we'll have to let this guy go," Kevin said. "Still, he looks awful good for this one."

"Did you check out his hands or arms?" Dave asked. "Probably the right one. The perp cut either his hand or his forearm, probably climbing the wall."

Kevin and Greg returned to the interview room and asked to see the suspect's hands and arms. He complied without hesitation. There were no cuts on either hand or arm. They excused themselves and exited the interview room.

"No cuts or scrapes," Kevin said.

"Cut him loose," Dave told Kevin. "He's not the one." He turned to Stephanie. "You disappointed?"

"A little," she said. "I really thought he might be the killer."

"Would have saved us a lot of work," Dave told her.

"Sure would."

"I'm going home. You should, too." Dave headed toward the doors, noticing Stephanie lagged behind at her desk.

* * * *

Kevin released the suspect. Stephanie lingered at her desk, tired and discouraged. She sat down, leaned forward, and shuffled through the evidence hoping to find something they might have missed. It was only 7:30. Though she thought about going home, it was too early to go to bed, and she knew she couldn't sleep anyway. Too much to think about.

For more than an hour, Stephanie looked through the evidence and read the reports, turning up nothing new. Nothing that would lead her to any suspects.

They would get additional reports from the lab in the morning, and she would go through the new stuff then. She tossed the report in her hand onto the pile on her desk, got up, and walked over to the chalkboard.

"Footprint," she read aloud. She read the rest of the things Dave had written on the board, saying them slowly. "Small caliber handgun—close range—surprise." She paused, turned away from the board, then mentally added: hiding in bushes—snuck into the garage—surprise—planned escape. "Planned escape," she repeated quietly. It suddenly became evident to her that Dave was right; this was premeditated murder.

If it was planned, it surely could have been an investor or angry employee. They could be on the right track.

Energized by the thought that the investor list might produce a suspect, she decided to go home, get a good night's sleep, and start fresh in the morning. She turned to leave the squad room, paused at the door, looking one more time at the pile on her desk, and started down the stairs—a little more bounce in her step.

The morning looked much brighter to Stephanie, in part because of last night's revelation. Though she didn't get as much sleep as she had hoped, she was clearly motivated to continue with their interviews. She had awakened a couple of times during the night thinking about the case and an active mind made it difficult to get back to sleep.

Stephanie was the first to arrive at the squad in the morning on Friday. She had her latte and bagel and was raring to go. It was early—7:15 to be exact. Dave probably wouldn't get in till around

8:00. Anxious to start, she called him at home. He answered on the first ring.

"Hello."

"Dave," Stephanie said, almost before he finished his hello. "You were right!"

"About what?" he asked.

"About it being planned."

"Yeah, what makes you suddenly so agreeable?"

"I looked over the evidence last night and it all added up. It was too well executed to be random," she acknowledged.

"That was my gut feeling," Dave said.

"I think it could be an investor or employee. We could be on the right track."

She wanted to get moving on the investigation.

"You sound pretty enthusiastic. You already on your way to the station?"

"Already here," she informed Dave. "What's your ETA?"

"Leaving right now," Dave said. "Just have to put my shirt on. Be there in about twenty."

"Okay, see you when you get here."

Stephanie hung up and turned to the investor list. She went over the people they managed to interview yesterday, making sure that they hadn't missed anything important.

Her notes from yesterday helped her eliminate most of them again. Some were obviously too short. Others had feet that were likely too small. One even wore a seven and a half. Stephanie chuckled to herself, wondering if what they say about the relationship to foot size was true. *Or is that the size of the hands*? She couldn't remember, and laughed again.

Most had the wrong tires. The rest had good alibis or at least ones that seemed credible when they reported where they had been or what they had been doing on Wednesday night. When combined with other elements, they were ruled out as suspects.

Stephanie put an asterisk by a couple indicating they might be worthy of a second look if it became necessary. She put a checkmark by everyone who was angry about the bankruptcy—which was more than two-thirds of the list.

It was a slow process, and they had more than 120 to interview. Stephanie wanted to do at least 60 today. It was Friday and she didn't want to spend all weekend interviewing possible suspects. Not that she really had anything else to do.

She looked at the rest of the list, trying to organize it by the size of investment and geographical location, hoping to make the process as efficient as possible.

By that time, two other teams had already come in and were out in the field starting their interviews. Greg was there, waiting for Kevin so they could get started.

"Morning, Dave," Stephanie greeted him cheerfully. "Ready to go?" she asked, as Dave headed for the coffee.

"Can I get some coffee first?" he raised his empty coffee mug.

"Sure. Sorry. I'm anxious to get going."

Dave poured himself a cup of coffee. "I can see that."

"I went through the list," she informed Dave.

"You did?"

"Yep," she answered, "and I have our first nineteen interviews organized."

"You do?" Dave asked. "I'm impressed. You continue to surprise me."

"I got in early this morning," she continued, as if reading Dave's thoughts.

With cup in hand, Dave motioned to Stephanie, "Let's get going then."

They drove to their first interview, Stephanie talking nonstop. She couldn't help her renewed enthusiasm. The first contact proved to be the same as the others. He wore a size nine shoe and was home in bed with his family on Wednesday night. The next one wasn't much better, nor were the next fifteen on her list. A couple were red flags, and Stephanie put an asterisk by their names.

They met with the same unbridled anger from most everyone they interviewed—evidence of the deep pain the bankruptcy had inflicted. One even suggested lining up all the top executives from EnergyDyn and shooting them—he got two asterisks. If he hadn't been 5'9" and looked like he hadn't ever owned a pair of running shoes, she might have taken him in for questioning right then.

Nearing noon, Stephanie's enthusiasm faded. She was hot and tired, and they didn't have anything more than when they started.

"You getting hungry?" Dave asked.

"And tired," Stephanie confessed. The bagel Stephanie ate that morning had worn off about ten o'clock.

"How about if we stop at Bernie's?"

"Sure, we haven't been to Bernie's in awhile, and I could use a rest," Stephanie said. "Let's do these two quick interviews first."

The last two interviews of the morning proved much the same as the others. No suspects. They would go over what information they did collect, during lunch, and set up their next interviews.

* * * *

Finally they pulled into Bernie's.

"I just need a tuna salad," Stephanie said, as she stepped up to the window, "and an iced tea."

"You want that sweetened, hun?"

"Just plain, if I can get it."

"For you, hun, I think we can do that. And what about you, Dave?"

"I'm going to have my usual, Myrna, and don't skimp on the meat this time," he chuckled.

"You give me any trouble today, I'm gonna send you down to the Krab Shack," Myrna lashed back, flashing a toothless grin. "Go have a seat, and I'll get that right out to ya."

Bernie's was just a greasy, neighborhood drive-in sandwich shop. It had been part of this area of Houston for as long as Dave could remember. The wooden picnic tables had been varnished so many times over the years, that customers probably sat three inches higher now than when the tables were first purchased. Names, initials, hearts with arrows, and various other symbols were chiseled deep in the wood grain beneath glassily transparent layers of varnish—those with dates—annalistic of this tattered and beaten neighborhood. Dave had been coming to this restaurant for more than 20 years. He told Stephanie his initials were carved somewhere in one of the tables; he seemed boyishly proud of that.

Bernie's had the best Reuben in town—hell—the best Reuben

in the Southwest. Bernie took great pride in the Reuben he served and had spent years perfecting it. People from all over Texas, and as far away as New Orleans and Little Rock, came here just to get his Reuben sandwich, an epicurean work of art that had been written up in food magazines at least a dozen times.

He started with shaved lean corned beef, tender and mouth watering from hours of slowly simmering in Bernie's special broth of mustard and spices, time-tested to give the beef its ultimate flavor. He heaped it on a perfectly baked and perfectly sliced dark rye, with a savory crust—crispy—but not too hard. Bernie then layered thinly sliced Swiss on the hot corned beef, creating a delicate fusion of meat and cheese. Next came piles of tangy, steaming sauerkraut, moist, but not too wet, on the melting cheese. He topped it with a special 1,000 Island sauce of his own formulation. The finished concoction would please and delight even the most discriminating gourmand. A culinary masterpiece. It was one of the reasons Dave had put on a few pounds over the last few years.

They went over the list and talked about the interviews while they ate. Stephanie picked at her tuna, while Dave devoured his gastronomic delight. He glanced up at Stephanie who was watching him stuff his face.

"Do you know how many calories are in that? Not to mention the cholesterol and carbs," she admonished. "*That*…is a cardiac nightmare."

For the first time, Dave felt a little self-conscious and left some of the sandwich on the plate.

They worked together to set up their next interviews.

"It doesn't look like we'll get the 60 interviews I wanted to do," Stephanie said, looking up from the list. "But we can get 45 or 50 today."

Dave didn't think 60 was possible, but hadn't said anything to Stephanie.

"We should be able to do that," Dave agreed. "Let's get out there then."

They had just gotten in the car when Stephanie's cell rang.

"You got a hit, John?" Stephanie asked.

She turned to Dave. "He says they have a possible suspect, but a couple of minor things don't quite fit."

"Well, what matches?"

"He says the lab confirmed that the suspect has a registered .38. And that he was as loud and angry as last night's suspect. And he's the right size and looks like a runner," she explained.

"All right, let me know either way," Stephanie said, closing her cell phone and turning back to Dave. "Looks like John has another possible, but we better continue until we hear for sure."

The first twelve interviews after lunch produced more of the same. Plenty of anger, but no real suspects.

John called to let them know that their possible suspect was not the one.

They were only able to do about six interviews an hour at their current pace. Some were quick—eliminated within two or three minutes. Others took a little longer. It was the time between interviews that was slowing them down.

A check with the other teams turned up two more possibilities, but not strong ones, and they were quickly dismissed for one reason or another. They would have to keep going. Stephanie checked the twelfth off and they headed to the thirteenth name on their list.

Dave pulled up in front of a nice, middle-class home, and was first out of the car. He walked around it, stepped up onto the curb, and caught a glimpse of Stephanie writing 2:48 down in the log.

They were halfway up the walkway when Dave noticed the car in the driveway, a dark green Toyota Camry. What caught Dave's eye was the scuff mark on the right front tire.

"Stephanie, the tires are Goodyear radials, right?"

"Goodyear Eagle Radials," she said. "Fourteen inch."

They walked over to the car and noticed the numbers on the sidewall confirmed that it was a fourteen-inch tire—185/70/14.

"Who is this?" Dave asked.

"A Phillip Hobart," Stephanie said, glancing at the list. "He lost quite a bit in the bankruptcy. Shall we call back-up, Dave?"

"Not yet."

He motioned her to a safer location on the sidewalk behind the car and away from the house.

"We should be able to handle this one ourselves," Dave said.

"Dave, I think we should have back-up. If he is the one, let's not forget, he shot Benjamin Day, and that makes him potentially dangerous. Let's just do this one by the book—okay?"

"All right, go ahead and call."

She made the call while Dave moved their car from in front of the house. He returned as Stephanie closed her cell.

"This could be our guy!" Stephanie said to Dave as he approached, excitement in her eyes.

Dave had the same feeling—something he hadn't felt in a long time. *This could be him.*

12

*D*ave and Stephanie watched the house from their position, behind the car, at the edge of the property.

"What do you think we should do?" Stephanie asked. Dave thought he heard apprehension in her voice.

"I think we should try the old 'car possibly in an accident ploy.' What do you think?"

"Isn't that a bit overused? Don't you think he'll be on to it?"

"Maybe not. I think he'll go for it as long as we put on a good act," Dave assured her. "Got anything better?"

"Well, no…but…"

"Okay, let's go for it then, but we need to stay on our toes."

The objective would be to knock on the door and tell Phillip Hobart that an accident had occurred in the area and they were checking out all the cars that matched the partial plate a witness gave at the scene.

Their concern between the two of them that this ploy may not work was real. It had been used on television numerous times and might be transparent to Hobart. They would have to be ready for anything in case it didn't work.

"Adam 5, 1 Adam 5." Dave and Stephanie listened as the police band informed them that there were no warrants on a Phillip Hobart. They also learned that he had a registered .38. Dave was glad the FBI's database had recently been updated and now included registrations as far back as 1976.

"So he has no record," Stephanie said. "But he does own a .38 caliber."

This heightened the anxiety immediately. It increased the possibility that they might be dealing with someone dangerous.

"We have to be cautious and prepared for anything," Dave told Stephanie.

They talked about changing their plan, but finally agreed it might still work.

"I got your back, Dave," Stephanie promised. "We just have to stay alert."

Hobart's house was in an upper middle class neighborhood, well maintained, with the yard neat and trimmed. The eaves looked like they were about due for a coat of paint, but other than that the house was in good shape.

Dave glanced up and down the street. This looked just like his neighborhood, he thought. He wondered, for a moment, if they might not have the wrong guy.

Two back-up units and one detective team pulled up. It was Kevin and his partner Greg. They met with Dave and Stephanie, were informed of the plan, and were assigned the areas they would be covering.

When each officer was in place, Dave proceeded toward the porch with Stephanie close behind. He was still not sure what they might encounter when he knocked on the door, but he gave it a hard rap with two knuckles. Stephanie took position off the porch, just off Dave's right shoulder, with an unobstructed view of the front door.

There was no way to predict whether Phillip Hobart would answer the door calmly or with a gun. They had to be careful, had to follow procedures, and had to expect the unexpected. Dave knocked on the door again. The dead-bolt turned, the knob rattled, and the door opened. Dave could see a man standing inside, through the screen door, but he couldn't see him well enough to determine if he had a weapon.

"Can I help you?" the man asked.

"Phillip Hobart?" Dave asked, calm and unwavering.

"Yes," he answered with some hesitation.

"Is that your car in the driveway?"

"Yes," he said again with even more hesitation.

"I'm Detective Duncan, from the Houston Police Department. Were you by any chance involved in an auto accident a couple of days ago?"

"No, why?" he inquired, a little more relaxed.

"We're investigating an accident, a hit and run. A witness got a partial plate, and we're checking out all the possible matches. It's probably nothing," Dave said, still cautious, waiting to see if Hobart would take the bait.

"Oh...no, I wasn't in any accident recently."

"Would you mind if we took a look at your car?" Dave searched for any reaction, any unexpected movement from Phillip.

"No problem," Phillip said. He opened the screen door and came out on the porch to accompany the officers to the car.

Dave motioned to Stephanie, a slight sweep of his hand toward Hobart's feet. He had noticed that Phillip appeared to be wearing a pair of Adidas running shoes that matched the description in the lab report. They looked to be the right size.

Dave walked over to the car with Phillip, informing him that it would be damage to the right front.

Stephanie excused herself to make a call on her cell phone. Dave knew she wouldn't take her eyes off them near the car. There was no indication that Phillip had a gun, or had any suspicions he was being investigated.

"Doesn't look like there's any damage here," Dave said, looking over at Hobart. "Looks like you hit a curb, though." He bent down to look at the smudge.

"Yeah, a couple of days ago."

"I usually do that right after getting the car washed," Dave said in an easy, nonthreatening tone. He didn't want to do anything that would alert Hobart. "It always seems to happen when I pay a little extra for the Armor All." He laughed.

Dave's laugh put Hobart at ease. "I know what you mean. Happens to me, too."

"How do you like these Goodyear radials?" Dave continued.

"They're good tires. I've had them on a few other cars."

"They new?" Dave asked.

"Few months," Hobart answered.

"What kind of mileage you get out of 'em?"

"I think I got over 40 thousand out of the last pair, but they were on another car."

"That's damned good mileage."

Dave continued the light banter with Hobart while Stephanie was on the phone getting some additional information. Dave was trying to distract Hobart so he couldn't hear her conversation.

"Yes. Yes, we can. I'll do that. Maybe we can use the phone here," Stephanie said.

When Stephanie finished, Dave turned to Hobart, "Sorry to have bothered you. It obviously wasn't your car."

Stephanie walked over. "Mind if we use your phone, Mr. Hobart? It'll only take a minute to call the station. My cell phone is going dead," she said, shaking her phone, as if shaking it would give the battery a little more life.

"Sure, come on in."

He opened the screen inviting them into his house. He seemed too relaxed to be their killer, Dave thought. Maybe this Hobart wasn't their suspect after all—but there were matches to four of the items of evidence. Dave followed Stephanie and their casual suspect through the front door and into the living room.

"Nice place," Stephanie said, looking around.

"Thanks," Hobart said, cheerfully, "I try to keep it up. The phone is there in the kitchen." He motioned to the door at the end of the living room.

Stephanie walked toward the kitchen. As she passed the desk, she noticed the newspaper article with the big picture of Day from the cover of Thursday's *Houston Chronicle*. It was on top of a small stack of clippings and other papers. The picture of Dave and Stephanie had been trimmed from the piece he kept. She went on to the kitchen and dialed the number.

"Hello, this is Detective Fox," she said loud enough to be heard in the living room. "Put me through to Captain Martin."

She paused and looked out at Hobart and Dave.

"Yeah, we're done here," she said. "Sure about that? Okay,

we'll drop this and pick up the investigation there."

Stephanie returned to the room, gave Dave a little wink, and faced Hobart.

"Phillip Hobart," she said in her best cop voice, "you're under arrest for the murder of Benjamin Day. You have the right to remain silent…"

She put the handcuffs on Phillip and finished giving him his rights.

"Do you understand your rights as I've explained them to you?"

"Yes," he said, without emotion.

Stephanie led her handcuffed suspect out the front door, to the yard, and turned him over to Kevin.

"Take him downtown and book him," Stephanie said with a big smile. She looked at Kevin, "I always enjoy saying that."

Kevin led Hobart toward the car in handcuffs. Stephanie turned to rejoin Dave on the porch.

"Nice work, Stephanie," Dave said, proud of his new partner.

"You, too," she said. "We worked well together, didn't we?"

"We sure did, partner," Dave said, giving her a warm, approving smile. "Yep, we did good."

They had made their first big bust together and Dave enjoyed the feeling. Stephanie was so excited it was hard to contain her. Dave could see her exhilaration from the bust, an exuberance much like he felt when he made his first big arrest, too many years ago.

"Lab boys are on their way," Greg informed Stephanie. "Captain Martin's getting the search warrant and having John bring it right over."

"Thanks, Greg. Thanks for your help."

"What made you decide to make the arrest?" Dave asked.

"Aside from the tires, there were lots of matches. Size ten to ten and a half Adidas running shoe, the black sweatshirt on the couch, and clippings of the murder on the desk."

Dave nodded approval.

"I didn't know about the clippings," Dave said. "They're on the desk?"

"Yep. But, the one that really did it was when Kevin told me on the phone that he had confirmed Hobart had a registered Smith & Wesson .38 caliber Model 10. I had that in the back of my mind the whole time you were talking to him."

Dave went quickly over the list. "Tires, curb smudge, shoes, sweatshirt, clippings, gun. Pretty compelling list of evidence."

"When I cuffed, him I noticed a cut on his right palm," she stated. "I'd be surprised if he wasn't our guy."

"Well," Dave said, "let's see what else might be here."

The detectives started searching the house, careful not to disturb anything before the lab techs arrived. Stephanie looked closer at the sweatshirt on the back of the couch. It was definitely black, and she could see a slight tear on the shoulder, visible the way it was laying. There were lots of clippings on the desk.

Dave noticed Hobart's awards in the big display case in his living room. Several big trophies, plaques, and pictures filled the shelves.

"Stephanie, I recognize this guy," Dave said, staring at Hobart's picture in his burnt orange Texas Longhorn uniform.

"You do? From where?"

"I didn't connect the name till now."

"How do you know him?"

"He was one of the best safeties in the University of Texas's history. He was good enough to go pro."

"How do you know that? I thought you were from Chicago?"

"I am, but my uncle lived in Dallas, and he took me to a Texas/OU game at the Cotton Bowl. That was before I became a Houston cop. Hobart was brilliant that day."

"Why didn't he make it to the pros?" Stephanie asked.

"Don't know. I came down to the academy and never heard of him again. He was the star of the OU game. Man, could he tackle." Dave couldn't believe Hobart was the same guy. He pointed to the large plaque in the middle. "See this, Stephanie? It's for Southwest Conference Player of the Year in his sophomore year." He paused, then pointed to a picture on the top shelf. "And this—this is a picture of Hobart with Daryl Royal when he received the award, and Daryl was named College Coach of the Year."

"Sounds like he was a good player," Stephanie smiled. "But

that was before my time."

"Yep, he was good. I wonder what happened to him?"

"This is a long way from pro ball. My dad is still waiting for SMU to come back," she said, laughing.

Dave, a little more serious, "Yes, it is—a long way," looking at Hobart's All-American Defensive Player plaque from his junior year.

John showed up with the search warrant and brought it into Dave.

"Well, maybe we'll find out what happened," Stephanie said to Dave, as Jerry burst in the front door.

"That was some nice detective work," he said to both of them.

Dave had to grin. Jerry always enjoyed identifying and gathering evidence at the scene. He often told Dave he thought of himself as somewhat of an artist. Gathering evidence, he painted a picture for them to use in court. Kind of like Picasso, finding the abstract pieces and weaving them into a work of art, a tapestry so to speak. Not only did Jerry enjoy his work, he was fun to work with.

"So you think this is the guy?" Jerry said to Stephanie, as she and Dave were gloving up. He had already heard how excited she was about making her first big bust.

"Sure do," Stephanie assured him.

"What do we have?" Jerry asked.

Dave had been relatively quiet to this point watching Stephanie interact with Jerry. She was on an adrenaline high.

"Jerry," Dave said, "we've got the tires, Goodyear Eagle Radials, with a scuff mark on the right front tire."

"We'll measure it," Jerry said. "I sent one of the lab techs out to measure the smudge on the curb yesterday. My tech's out taking the tire impressions right now. What else?"

Stephanie showed Jerry the sweatshirt and the newspaper clippings in a pile on the desk. Jerry had the photographer get pictures of both the desk and the sweatshirt. He picked up the sweatshirt to examine it and noticed the tear on the right shoulder.

"Bet the threads came from this tear!" he exclaimed.

Jerry put the tattered sweatshirt in a large evidence bag, sealed it, and catalogued it. Then he went over to the pile of newspaper clippings, looked through them and prepared them for collection. Dave waited nearby.

"Jerry, I'd like to take a look at those when you're finished," Dave said.

"Give me a few minutes. Let me bag 'em, then you can look at them if you'd like."

Jerry proceeded to bag each item in a polypropylene bag and compiled a list of items. Dave went over to see what Stephanie had found.

"They're all yours," Jerry said, rising from the desk chair. "Just keep them in the same order for me."

Dave sat down, tightened his latex gloves, and examined the first clipping.

There were five articles about EnergyDyn's bankruptcy, four related to Benjamin Day, and twelve downloaded pieces of the EnergyDyn demise from various Internet sources.

Near the bottom of the pile were time-lines, hand drawn diagrams of Day's estate and of Lost Creek Road, and a map showing the escape routes. It looked like he had been working on this plan for awhile. Just over five weeks by Dave's calculations.

Hobart had included dates and detailed information about Day's schedule in some of his notes. He could have been planning this longer, but his first recorded entry was just over five weeks earlier.

So much incriminating evidence. Dave rejoiced that Hobart had created and preserved it. This evidence tied him to the crime with almost absolute certainty.

As he moved through the articles and assorted papers, something near the bottom of the pile caught Dave's eye. The subject matter changed. There were a few items that had no connection to EnergyDyn.

"We have the gun," Jerry announced, as he came back into the living room.

"Where did you find it?" Stephanie asked.

"You won't believe this. It was in his night stand." A puzzled look crossed his face. "He didn't even try to hide it!"

"It's like everything else. Why didn't he get rid of it?" Dave asked, shaking his head. "Surely he had time."

"It's been fired recently," Jerry said, raising the muzzle to his nose to smell. "He didn't bother to clean it."

"You think this is the gun, Jerry?"

"Three spent casings still in the cylinder. He didn't replace them either."

Dave turned back to the clippings. He counted six bags containing stories from Florida newspapers.

"Stephanie, take a look at these," Dave called out to her.

"What are they?" she asked, moving toward the desk.

Dave said nothing, just handed them to her. She read each one carefully, shuffled through them again, and reread a little bit from each one.

"Why would he have clippings from Florida newspapers from over five months ago?" she asked. "These are about GlobalNet."

Stephanie handed them back to Dave. "I don't know," he said. He shuffled through them once more. He slowly began to read one of the headlines and then the subhead:

"Exec Falls To Death"
"Indicted GlobalNet Exec Falls 3 Stories From Scaffolding"

13

Dave stood inside interview room three. An officer opened the door and Phillip Hobart entered the room. Dave wasn't sure he liked the new term "interview." It didn't have the same punch as "interrogation." But this was the newer, kinder, politically correct Houston Police Department. Different name, same drab rooms, mirrored walls with one two-way—same kind of suspects and the same questions.

The officer removed the handcuffs and left the room.

"Have a seat," Stephanie said, "anything we can get you?"

Hobart had a blank look on his face. "No, thank you," he uttered, sitting at the table.

Dave paced back and forth at the end of the room, stroking his chin as if he were figuring out where to start. His stride was deliberate—determined.

"We will be taping this interview, Mr. Hobart," Dave informed him, finally speaking. "Do you have any objections?"

Hobart shook his head. "No."

It was now about 6:30 in the evening on Friday. Not exactly what Dave wanted to be doing on a Friday night. He could tell Stephanie was raring to go, almost supercharged. He wanted to interview Hobart and get this to the district attorney tonight. Things had moved much more quickly than Dave expected. He couldn't have imagined they would be questioning a solid suspect less than two days after the murder.

Call it luck, or karma, or whatever, but they got their suspect, and in almost record time. With all the evidence, this suspect was positively dead meat.

Hobart had said nothing since his arrest. He had been cooperative, but had not talked. He hadn't asked for an attorney either, which surprised Dave.

"Your rights were read to you at the time of your arrest, weren't they?" Dave asked.

"Yes."

"You understood those rights?"

"Yes."

"Would you like an attorney present?"

"No," he said quietly. "I've got nothing to hide."

"Are you waiving those rights, Mr. Hobart?" Dave asked him, something he would not have considered asking a few years ago.

"Yes."

"Where were you two nights ago, on Wednesday night, Mr. Hobart?" Dave began.

"I was at home."

"Doing what?"

Hobart mumbled. "Watching TV, I think."

"Sorry, I didn't hear that. Could you speak up?"

"I said, watching television."

"Anyone see you at home—*watching TV?*" Dave probed.

Dave asked the questions at a fast pace at this point—a pace he had used before. It had worked on other suspects, and he was trying it now, attempting to disorient Hobart.

"Nope, no one." Hobart said, without a change in tone.

"What'd you watch?"

Hobart thought a moment. "I don't know," he paused, "Uh… maybe *Friends*, or… maybe it was *Frasier*."

"Which one was it?"

"I don't remember," he paused again, searching for the right answer. "Whichever is on Wednesday nights."

"C'mon…you don't expect us to believe that, do you? What do you take us for?" Dave pushed.

"I was watching television."

"Call anyone that evening? E-mail anyone?"

"Nope, not that I can remember," he said, shaking his head.

Dave raised his voice a little. "So *no one* can vouch for you on Wednesday night?"

"Not really."

"Sure you weren't at Lost Creek Estates?"

"Where is that? I really don't know where that is."

"Never been to Lost Creek Road?"

"Nope," Hobart repeated.

Despite the rapid fire questions, Hobart kept his cool. Dave continued his questioning hardly taking a breath.

"We have strong evidence placing you at Lost Creek Road on Wednesday night," Dave continued. "You want to change your story?"

Quietly, unflinching, Hobart responded, "I told you, I don't know where that is."

"Very strong evidence! Shoes, sweatshirt, curb smudge, the diagrams of Benjamin Day's house." Dave was painting a picture for Hobart. "And I'm sure the blood from your cut will match the blood we found at the scene. And if the tire tracks and ballistics match, we've got you."

"You're wasting your time," Hobart grinned. "It really doesn't matter what you have."

"What about the diagrams we found on your desk in your house, Mr. Hobart?"

"What diagrams?" he said, shaking his head as if he knew nothing about what Dave was talking about.

"The ones we found with the newspaper clippings. The ones of Day's property."

Stephanie sat back, silent, and watched while Dave interviewed Hobart. She would occasionally move the evidence folders around the table so Hobart could see them. The evidence was strong and pointed right at Hobart. Everything they found at Hobart's place matched what they found at the crime scene. The lab would surely confirm that.

"Why don't you just make it easy on all of us? Confess and we can all go home."

Dave walked around the table a couple of times, stroking his chin again. He stopped and whispered something to Stephanie. She nodded, got up, and left the room.

* * * *

As she left, Captain Martin came out of the viewing room next door to talk to Stephanie.

"Not very talkative, is he?" Captain Martin asked Stephanie.

"Not yet," she said to the captain. "But all the evidence matches. We know he did it, so we'll just have to show him. He'll come clean when we show him the lab results."

"I hope so," the captain said. "Would sure like to wrap this up and get it to the DA tonight."

"Dave is going to try another approach, while I run down to the lab and see if they're finished with the ballistics, blood work, and the tire tracks. They could be the final pieces needed to get his confession," she added.

"What's he got planned?"

"He's going to talk football, which might loosen him up."

The captain looked puzzled. "*Football*?"

"Yeah, football. I know it sounds crazy, but Hobart was an All-American at Texas," she explained. "Dave knew who he was and thinks it might work."

"Hope so. Getting this guy would take a big weight off of my shoulders. By-the-way," the captain added, "an ADA is on the way over to observe and support us."

"How long?"

"Probably five or ten minutes."

"Well, I should be back with the evidence by then, and I'm sure it will all point to Hobart. If so, then we've got him…even if he doesn't say a word."

"Go get 'em!" Captain Martin said. "Let's wrap this up."

* * * *

Dave was still strolling slowly around the room, stroking his chin, when the captain returned to the viewing room to see how the interview was progressing.

"I saw your trophy case in your living room," Dave said to Hobart. "Pretty impressive."

Hobart stared at the table. "You think so?"

"Yep, I do. I saw you play in the Texas/OU game in your junior year. You were headed for the pros."

"That was a long time ago, and world's away. I try to forget about it."

"So what happened to you, man? You had it made. How did you end up like this?"

"Like what? You mean a regular guy instead of a pro football player?"

"Yep, something like that," Dave said, sarcastically. "Why didn't you go pro?"

"Career ending knee injury, the game after you saw me play."

"Sorry...I didn't know," Dave genuinely felt sympathetic. "But why did you kill Benjamin Day?"

"Didn't say I did," Hobart said, withdrawing slightly as he answered the question.

"You know, when Detective Fox returns with the lab reports on the gun, blood, and tire tracks, it's over. Why don't you just tell me now what happened? You did this—you know it and I know it, so why put us all through this?"

"It doesn't matter."

"What do you mean it doesn't matter? You killed Benjamin Day."

"Day was scum. But, even that doesn't matter."

"Let's talk about your little library." Dave opened the file containing all the clippings. "What are all of these? Were you planning on writing Day's biography? Or maybe *his eulogy*?"

"Something like that."

"Your silence isn't going to help you. In fact, it's beginning to piss me off."

Hobart didn't say anything. He just stared blankly at Dave who stood in front of him, glaring, trying to intimidate him.

"I don't understand—" Dave began, but a knock on the interview room door interrupted him.

The door opened and Captain Martin stuck his head in. "Dave...a minute?"

"Sure, Cap." He glanced at Hobart. "Think about what I said."

Dave was greeted in the hallway by Captain Martin and the ADA.

"Good work, Duncan," the ADA spoke first. "Looks like you wrapped this one up in record time."

"We're not done yet, but a lot of the credit goes to my partner, Detective Fox."

"Yeah, we heard she did a good job," he said. "Word of the apprehension spread through the office fast."

"I'll bet it did."

"Where's your partner?"

"She's down at the lab. Should be right back."

"Where's his attorney? On the way?"

"Nope, he refused counsel. He waived his rights."

"Is that right?" A look of surprise crossed the ADA's face.

"What do you think, Dave?" the captain asked. "Think he's going to give us anything tonight?"

"He's tight-lipped, but that will change when Steph comes back with the lab results."

"Well, let's give him a breather and let him sit there and think about things for a minute. Take another stab at him when Stephanie returns with the confirmation."

"Okay, the football idea didn't seem to work," Dave admitted.

The captain and ADA returned to the viewing room and Dave leaned against the wall outside the door to gather his thoughts. Stephanie would be back momentarily with the lab reports that would clearly point to their suspect—Phillip Hobart.

Maybe being confronted with conclusive evidence, Hobart would tire of the interview and confess.

I sure hope so.

14

Despite Hobart's unwillingness to be forthright about the murders, and Dave's questions becoming more aggressive, he maintained remarkable civility. He just wasn't going to tell Dave anything.

Dave thought about The Beat, and how nice it would have been to be having a drink there right now. He had long ago given up being married to the job, and the enjoyment of working well into the night, interrogating suspects till they broke, had lost its luster. Dave knew the guys would be gathered at The Beat to hear the story of his and Stephanie's big bust.

Tired of waiting in the hallway, Dave returned to the room, closed the door, leaned against it, and stared at Hobart. The suspect sat stoic in the center of the stark room.

Stephanie returned and handed the reports to Dave. They spent some time discussing them in a whisper. After the discussion, Dave walked over, leaned on the table directly in front of Hobart, and looked straight into his eyes. "We know you did it. Detective Fox has some evidence you'll want to hear."

"You know what these reports say?" she asked, looking at Hobart who was now looking down at the table. She didn't wait for his answer. "This one says it was your gun that put the three holes in Day. The other two show that your car was parked on Lost Creek Road, and that you made a blood deposit on the wall at Day's house."

She paused, turned, and walked back toward the viewing glass. She could see Hobart's reflection in the glass. He made no movement to look up at her.

"So how did the bullets from your gun end up in Day's chest if you were never there?" she asked sharply.

Dave glared at him. "You were angry. We understand that. You lost a lot of money." He paused. "Hell, if I had lost that much money, I might have considered it myself."

"Why don't you just tell us what happened? We have your diagrams, notes, and all the evidence to convict," Stephanie said.

"Here's what I think happened, Phil," Dave broke in. "You were upset. You lost everything because of EnergyDyn and GlobalNet. You became angry...no, I'll bet you were *livid*. And you had every right to be. Am I right so far?" Dave looked at him for any possible sign—any change. "Just nod if any of this sounds good." Dave looked at Stephanie. "You know what else I think, Phil?"

"It's Phillip."

"You know what I think, Phil?" he repeated. "I think you saw the newspaper article where Day said he had no knowledge of the problems, and that *pissed you off.*"

Dave reached down and grabbed the first newspaper clipping from the folder on the table. "This upset you, *didn't it*? How could he *not* know?"

"You were an investor in EnergyDyn," Stephanie added.

"A lot of investors are pissed off. You just took it a little further than the others, Phil. You're not the only one who got screwed," Dave pounded. "I think you started following him right after that," he said, pointing at the date on the first article.

Stephanie handed Dave a small leather book.

"You kept pretty good notes in your journal," Dave said, thumbing through Hobart's book. "This is going to be a big help in presenting our case. You've laid it all out for us."

Hobart sat mute, but the expression on his face changed slightly.

"Great checklist, too." Dave smiled. "You even wrote to double check the bullets and remember to load the gun. Pretty damned thorough if you ask me."

"Don't forget the map, Dave," Stephanie reminded him.

Dave nodded in her direction. "Oh no, I wouldn't forget the map. You were even gracious enough to show us where you planned to climb the wall, Phil."

Dave paused, then picked up the diagram of the house and yard. "You knew where the cameras were, didn't you?" Dave grinned. "Look at this path across the side yard. *Brilliant*! I couldn't have planned this any better."

Dave caught a slight smile on Hobart's face as he glanced up from the drawing. Dave thought it was a smile of pride.

"Were you nervous, Phillip? You must have been nervous, because you don't look like a stone cold killer. And despite all your preparation, you made some mistakes."

Hobart's eyes glazed over, and Dave noticed him withdraw a little.

* * * *

Phillip felt his heart rate increase, his skin warm. He thought about how nervous he was that night, when he was turning onto Day's street.

It all rushed back. He remembered how his heart began to beat faster as he passed 1432 and neared 1442—how his pulse quickened. None of it was part of the plan. Nor were the sweaty palms. He thought about the difficulty he had catching his breath. Breathe, he thought, in a near panic. Breathe dammit!

He tried to take a couple of deep breaths, hoping to slow down his heart. He remembered reaching down to unzip his heavy sweatshirt—already damp from the humidity—trying to give himself more room to breathe.

His thoughts were momentarily broken by something Stephanie said. Phillip wasn't sure if it was directed at Dave or at him, but he heard something about a tire smudge. Though distracted by her voice, he easily returned to his thoughts of that night.

Thoughts of pulling the car to the curb, about a hundred feet before Day's gate. His chest was tight as he looked over at the wall. Suddenly, one of the tires hit the curb, which brought the car to an abrupt stop, and allowed him to finally take a breath.

Sweating, Phillip turned off the engine and sat in the car for a moment, trying to regain his composure. The sweat on his hands had dried by the time he reached into the glove compartment for the gun. His Smith and Wesson .38 revolver. Phillip hadn't fired it in several years, and hoped that it would fire correctly one last time. He knew it couldn't be put off one more week. Others may have had that luxury, but delaying a week or two was not an option for Phillip.

"Phillip…Phillip," Stephanie's voice broke into his thoughts.

Phillip clenched his hands. He looked up blankly in the direction of the voice.

* * * *

"We know you must hurt…losing your life savings because of the bankruptcy," she said.

Hobart took a deep breath. "You want to know what happened?" he said angrily, breaking out of his calm. He looked straight at the camera. "You really want to know why?"

"Before you continue Mr. Hobart, are you waiving your right to an attorney?" Stephanie interrupted.

Dave gave Stephanie a stern look. Hobart had already waived his rights, and Dave didn't want Stephanie to remind him.

Hobart shot a hard look at Stephanie. "Of course. I told you that already. Why would I need an attorney?"

"I just wanted—"

"Do you remember the professor who was in the newspaper about a year ago?"

Dave shook his head. "Not really. Should I?"

"Yes, you should! They said he killed himself."

"Is that why you killed Day?" Dave repeated.

"Didn't say I did. But I find his death very interesting," Hobart continued. "He was a greedy bastard!"

"The professor?" Dave asked.

"You mean Day?" Stephanie asked, at the same time.

"No…not the professor…yes…Day. He didn't care who he wiped out, or who it hurt. None of them did. Lousy bastards. Didn't they make enough as company executives? They stole millions and screwed their investors."

The two detectives stood and listened as Hobart explained the reasons for killing Day. Once he started talking, it was like a dam broke. He continued with his explanation.

"And Benjamin Day was one of the worst. I lost almost everything because of him. A big portion of my retirement was in EnergyDyn stock."

He paused, a little tear forming in the corner of his right eye. He looked first at Stephanie, then at Dave. "There's nothing left to leave my kids," he continued. "How am I going to pay for my kids' school? He wiped me out, 25 years of hard work, down the drain. And he walked away with almost $200 million."

Stephanie broke in with a question. "So you did this because you lost money when EnergyDyn crashed?" she asked.

Hobart didn't seem to hear her.

"I lost my retirement, my job, my dignity. I had nothing left. He had to die for what he did. Now he has nothing." He paused. "There are others who need to die for what they did," he said, this time with hatred in his voice. "Others who deserve the same fate."

Dave threw the clippings from Florida on the table in front of Hobart, one at a time, where he could see them. This caused him to pause. He glanced at each of the five articles.

"You mean like Brett Galivan, from GlobalNet?" Dave said forcefully, moving each one of the clippings, forcing Hobart to look at them.

"Yeah, like Brett Galivan. He was just as bad."

"Did you kill him, too?" Dave shouted.

Hobart's earlier calm, easy-going personality had turned. He now had hatred in his voice, the bitterness of a man who had lost everything.

Taking a slow, deep breath, Hobart said, "Wish I had. But you won't be able to pin that one on me." He looked straight into Dave's eyes, almost defiant. "Besides, that one was an accident, wasn't it?" Hobart smiled at Dave.

"Then why all the newspaper clippings? What's so fascinating about this accident in Florida?" Dave asked.

"Because…" Hobart paused again as if searching for the right answer. "Interesting case," is all he said, both answering and not answering Dave's question.

Jim Worth

Hobart's return to noncompliance bothered Dave. Though he seemed to admit to Day's murder, he never said that he actually did it.

"Unfortunate accident, wouldn't you say?" Hobart added with another smile, almost a smirk, on his face.

"We'll just have to find out, won't we?" Dave opened the door. "Officer, get him out of here."

Stephanie reached up and turned off the camera. The door closed, and Hobart was on his way back to his cell.

They stood in the room alone—quiet. They had gotten a lot out of Hobart, but not the confession they wanted.

Stephanie looked over at Dave. "What's the matter, Dave? You don't look too happy. We just got a confession."

"Not really, Stephanie. There are a couple of things that still bother me."

"Bother you? Like what? He just told us that he killed Day."

"Did he? Maybe he implied it, but he didn't admit it," Dave said. "It's what he didn't tell us that bothers me. Why did he bring up the professor?"

"That's true," Stephanie agreed. "He didn't tell us why he had those articles from Florida, either. What's with that?"

"I'm curious about that, but even more about why he didn't get rid of the evidence," Dave frowned. "He didn't get rid of *any* of it."

"What about Florida? I think we should look into that case," Stephanie said.

Dave hated to think about the entire weekend being spent on work, but he agreed with Stephanie. "You're right. Arrange it."

15

Stephanie looked out the airplane window at the long beaches of Ft. Lauderdale and Hollywood, as the attendants prepared the plane for final approach. She had never been to Florida.

It was after 5:00 p.m. on Sunday. They were only four days into the investigation and the new information they discovered at Hobart's had led them to the east coast of Florida.

The Brett Galivan articles discovered at Hobart's house were cause for concern. Could Hobart have been involved in two murders? Though the death of Brett Galivan in Florida was determined to be an accident, Stephanie had a piece of the puzzle that the Florida authorities did not have. Why was their suspect so interested in Galivan's death?

Brett Galivan was the chief financial officer of GlobalNet, the recently failed telecommunications company that followed in the footsteps of EnergyDyn. It was now the largest bankruptcy filing in history, eclipsing EnergyDyn in size, just months after the energy giant held that infamous distinction.

When GlobalNet filed bankruptcy, it left investors with almost worthless paper, while executives of the failing company sold hundreds of millions of dollars worth of stock before the filing—mirroring the circumstances in the EnergyDyn scandal.

Stephanie had learned that Galivan had sold more than $95 million worth of fraudulently inflated stock. Other officers from GlobalNet had sold even more before it was discovered that the company showed more than $7 billion in overstated income. The ramifications of that discovery: free-falling stock prices.

While executives had sold their stocks at high prices over the past year or more, the sudden announcement of the accounting problems and the bankruptcy filing left thousands of investors holding stock that was selling for pennies on the dollar. Most were unable to sell their stocks at all.

Shortly after the bottom fell out, the CFO of GlobalNet fell 24' to his death when scaffolding on the third floor of his new digs failed, causing the accident.

"That's a long way to fall," Dave quipped, when Stephanie read that part of the report to him.

"Not nearly as far as GlobalNet's stock," Stephanie countered.

From what Stephanie had gathered so far, no one could explain why Galivan was on the scaffolding, and it still had not been established when the investigation concluded almost five months ago. The Boca Raton Police Department determined it to be accidental death—backed up by the medical examiner's findings.

As the plane made its final approach, Stephanie reviewed the newspaper clippings from Hobart's and some articles she had retrieved from the Internet. There was more than enough information and photos available of Galivan's new Boca Raton residence to get a good picture of the magnitude of the estate.

"You want to look at what I found on Galivan's new place?"

Dave yawned. "Not really, but I'm sure you're going to tell me about it."

"I'll just give you the highlights," she told him. "It's really not a home; it's more like a mansion on the water in Boca Raton. The main part of the house is three stories. It's about 8,500 square feet of absolute self-indulgence, this article says, and it would be worth $15 million if it were completed."

Dave's face was expressionless, but his voice dripped with sarcasm. "*Is that all*? So, he's building in the low-rent district."

"No, smart ass. That's not all. He brought in custom-made chandeliers, purchased from Tiffany's for the entry and dining room, and matching Tiffany sconces to add style and function to the walls in the entry, billiard room, and home theater."

"I don't know about you, Stephanie, but I've always wanted Tiffany sconces in my home theater and billiard room," Dave said laughing.

"You jest," she said, "but he also has a factory-equipped boat house and a fully furnished pool house. It also says the mansion has an unrivaled waterfront view."

Obviously a shining jewel, as another of the articles stated. But it now stood vacant and unfinished—spectral—manifest of what was wrong with unbridled competition and the unchecked desire to accumulate wealth.

Stephanie compared it to an opulent white elephant, a gaudy reminder of greed and selfishness, evidence of how messed up the capitalistic system can become when the proper checks and balances are not enforced.

"The mansion was about 65 to 70 percent completed when Galivan fell to his death," she said.

Stephanie hurried to put her things away as the plane touched down on the runway. She was anxious to get started on this part of the case.

Walking toward baggage claim, the two Houston detectives discussed their strategy for investigating the incident and their role in working with the Boca Raton Police Department.

They picked up their rental car, a Chrysler Sebring convertible. Stephanie was informed by the attendant that it was the only thing they could get on such short notice. "Fine with me." Stephanie smiled as she threw Dave the keys. They headed toward Boca Raton, about 25 or 30 miles north of Ft. Lauderdale.

"How about putting the top down?" she asked Dave, more as a command.

"We have to be stopped to put it down."

"Well, pull over then. It'll only take a minute, won't it?"

"I guess." Dave sounded annoyed.

"This is nice, isn't it?"

"It's okay," he grumbled.

Stephanie playfully poked him in the side. "C'mon, admit it, Dave, this is great. It's a perfect evening for a convertible."

"Uh-huh," he managed.

It was nearly sunset, and the weather was perfect, as they drove up Highway 95 to their hotel. The reservations were set up by Detective Doug Morris, the Boca Raton investigating detective on the case.

"Morris told me that he put us up at a hotel right on the water with a great view of the ocean." Dave playfully nudged Stephanie. "I think he said the Radisson Resort."

"Resort, huh? I like that. That should make this trip easier for you, Dave."

"I don't mind coming here. I'm just not sure why we're here."

Stephanie laughed. "I saw an opportunity to see Florida for free. Seriously, I think Hobart was involved, and I wanted to find out for myself."

"Morris filled me in on the phone. He said it looked like an accident to them, pure and simple."

"But why would Hobart have all those newspaper articles if he weren't involved?" Stephanie wasn't happy with the unanswered, nagging details in this case.

"I can't tell you, but Morris said there wasn't a lot of evidence, and none that indicated there was another person involved."

"We'll just have to see for ourselves," she said. "Besides, the assistant district attorney wanted us to connect Hobart to this one. Didn't Detective Morris say he was sending the file over to the hotel?"

"Yep, said it would be at the front desk when we arrived."

On the drive, they decided to review everything that night and be up to speed when they met with Detective Morris in the morning. He had offered to pick them up, but they had the rental car and were only about 20 minutes from the crime scene. Detective Morris wanted them to meet him there at 8:00 a.m..

A package was waiting for them when they arrived at the hotel. It was not a big package, indicating to Stephanie, a short investigation. It also indicated there was little evidence to go over.

After settling into her room, they met in Dave's room to go through the file.

"Great rooms, huh? We'll have to thank Detective Morris," Stephanie said, as she stepped onto Dave's balcony and stared out at the ocean.

"Not bad," Dave conceded.

"We have a great view of the ocean and of the boats in Lake Boca Raton."

"Lake Boca Raton?"

"Yep, I pulled out the map and found that this is a lake on the Intracoastal Waterway and that the inlet below us connects the Intracoastal to the ocean."

Dave gave Stephanie a puzzled look. "I didn't know that. I haven't even looked out there yet."

"You should," Stephanie said, taking a deep breath. "Come out here and smell the ocean."

He moved out onto the balcony and took a deep breath.

Stephanie savored the air. "This is the first time I've seen the Atlantic Ocean. Isn't this fantastic?"

"Very nice," he said, "but we do have work to do."

"Okay, Okay, I guess if we have to."

They tore into the file, dividing up the reports.

The evidence showed that bolts had given way on one end of the scaffolding, on the third floor near the main section of the house, causing Galivan to lose his balance and fall to his apparent death. There was no indication of tampering or foul play. The report revealed that one of the nuts had worked loose and the bolt pulled out of the framing.

"This report says that Detective Morris and an insurance investigator interviewed two of the contractors on the job," Stephanie read from a report, breaking the silence. "It says they interviewed them twice."

"Twice? Why?"

"Doesn't say, but it looks like they eliminated both of them as suspects."

Dave glanced at Stephanie. "Which contractors?"

"It looks like the general contractor, a Rich Williams, and the tile guy." Stephanie said. "We should interview both of them again."

A report to Dave's right contained Williams's name. He reached over to pick it up. "Williams was the last one to leave the site on Friday night, and the one who called the police on Saturday morning. Maybe we *should* talk to him again."

"Not a single witness," Stephanie said, shaking one of the reports. "Just like our case, no one saw a thing."

"What was the time of death?"

Stephanie pushed the coroner's report over to Dave. "Between 6:00 and 7:00 p.m. on Friday. A work crew discovered the body the next morning when they arrived at the site. Galivan had been there all night."

There wasn't a lot more in the file. The report on the bolts showed no manipulation, no file or saw marks and did not indicate any apparent tampering. Detective Morris would fill them in on the details in the morning.

They had been through nearly everything they could go through that night and it was almost 9:00, so they agreed to retire and pick up things in the morning.

Dave yawned and stretched. "How about meeting downstairs for breakfast at 6:30?"

"Fine with me, unless that's too early for you," Stephanie teased.

"You just worry about making it down on time. Late one buys breakfast."

"Nice try. You know you're going to buy. Good night, Dave," she said, smiling as she closed the door, eager to start fresh in the morning.

"Night," Dave said, "See you in the morning."

"Uh, huh. Don't be late," she mumbled as the door closed behind her.

* * * *

After Stephanie left, Dave noticed Galivan's appointment book sitting on the table. They had set it aside and had not yet looked at it. Dave had read in the report that the book was found at the scene in Galivan's car. His car had been there, unlocked, all night. Maybe an appointment would establish why Galivan was there Friday night.

But Dave found no appointment in the book for Friday evening. Galivan's only appointment on Friday was late morning with his attorney. There were several items in the book for Wednesday and Thursday, but nothing that would lead Dave to believe Galivan was meeting someone at the construction site on Friday night.

The only thing written was scribbled to the side on the right-hand edge of the page. It appeared to be a name with a "6" next to it, but it wasn't written in the book in the area for 6:00 p.m. "Johnston-6" was all that was scribbled on the edge of Friday's page.

The report indicated that the interview with Galivan's attorney turned up nothing unusual. It was one of many meetings he and his attorney had over the previous few months. His attorney's name was in the 10:00 a.m. section for the following Monday and several other dates during the next few weeks. Galivan obviously didn't make the Monday appointment.

Dave put down the book, turned on the television, and got ready for bed. He was tired, and tomorrow would be a long day for him and Stephanie.

* * * *

The alarm went off at 5:30 a.m. in Detective Fox's room. She hadn't gotten as much sleep as she would have liked. Like so many people, she never slept well the first night in a strange bed in a strange hotel. And there were a lot of things that kept Stephanie's mind active all night. Maybe a quick hot shower would help wake her up.

By the time she headed down to breakfast, she was refreshed and ready to go. She had always been good at throwing herself together quickly. Stephanie knew she was very lucky, never wearing much makeup, because she really didn't have to. She felt comfortable with her natural look. And she didn't have to do much with her hair. Although she wore it a little longer now than she used to, she could pull it back in a ponytail and be confident it still looked good.

Dave was already sitting with a cup of coffee when she came out onto the patio. Stephanie walked to the table and pulled out the chair that gave her a view of the boats. She noticed Dave had the file with him, no doubt so they could reexamine things at breakfast.

"How'd you sleep?" she asked.

"Not bad—considering," Dave answered. "Had a little trouble

getting to sleep."

"Me too," Stephanie confided.

"Thinking about the case?"

"Yep," she said, in a way she thought would impress Dave.

"Any revelations?"

She shook her head. "Not really. The same things kept running through my mind. You?"

"Nothing that we didn't see last night."

Stephanie ordered a latte and a bagel when the waitress came over. Dave ordered two eggs over easy, crisp bacon, hash browns and wheat toast. "A lot of cholesterol," she joked, looking at Dave.

He managed a little laugh. "Cholesterol you're paying for. Or did you conveniently forget?"

"Enjoy it, because it won't happen again," she challenged.

They talked about the case during breakfast.

"Why was Galivan on the scaffolding on a Friday night?"

"I don't know," Stephanie confessed. "Thought about that several times last night."

"I went through Galivan's appointment book after you went to your room. There was nothing unusual except one strange entry."

He passed the appointment book over to Stephanie pointing to the scribble on the edge of the page.

"Johnston-6. What does that mean?"

Dave shrugged. "Not sure, but it's the only entry on Friday."

"Were any phone records in the file?" she asked, not remembering everything that was in the file last night. "Maybe Galivan called this Johnston before Friday evening."

"Not that I saw," Dave replied. "But I didn't go through it page by page."

They hadn't found anything yet that would connect Phillip Hobart with the case, except the clippings. She had hoped she could make a connection through Phillip's phone records, but she might find the answer in Galivan's records.

Maybe she'd find the connection when they investigated the scene.

16

Dave drove along the private road bordered on either side by exotic tropical flora of a type not visible from the interstate—tiny flowers of magnificent mango, huge trumpets of hot pink and deep corals. Beds of yellow and white clusters, so brilliant they could only be enjoyed in indirect glances, lined the ocean side of the lane.

"Who can afford to live here?" Stephanie exclaimed, eyes wide in disbelief and appreciative awe.

Each place they passed was more grandiose than the last, porches of slate and imported tiles, columns and fountains defining each stately entryway.

"Look at these on the bay side, Dave. These look like the houses you see on the cover of *Architectural Digest*."

The mansions on the bay were strategically positioned to take full advantage of the view, each set close to the water with pristine white docks offering the rich a rare and privileged door to the world.

"Wonder if there is any legal way to make the kind of money it takes to afford one these places?" Dave asked. He guided their car over a bumpy transition from asphalt to gravel. As the car bounced through a thick section of tall tropical foliage, including varieties of palms the two detectives had never seen, the $15 million estate came into view.

Even in its partially dressed state, Galivan's new mansion was visually impressive and worthy of its lofty place on the water.

Though they already had details about the mansion, Dave would never have guessed its full magnitude if he hadn't seen it. The actual number of rooms were difficult to determine, but blueprints at the planning commission's office showed that there were twelve bedrooms, eight bathrooms and four half baths, and four leisure rooms, including the billiards room, card room, and theater.

The theater was set up to show the big games on a new Diamond Plasma 96" HDTV, mounted on a wall behind the retractable movie screen. There were two dining areas, a huge office overlooking the water, and two wine cellars: one connected to the bar and one adjacent to the culinary kitchen. The kitchen had two regular ovens, a convection oven, a huge Sub-Zero refrigerator, and granite countertops.

This lavish estate was situated at the end of the road on 2.5 acres, with water on three sides. It had access to the Intracoastal through a private inlet from the virgin white boat dock. The boat house was almost twice the size of Dave's house.

An Infinity pool and two spas sat on the edge of the property overlooking the bay, surrounded by more than 5,000 square feet of patio and deck. Two large balconies overlooked the pool. A spiral water slide sat majestically on one corner of the pool, while the waterfall spa sat lanquid on the other corner.

Dave was surprised to see the scaffolding was still in place. Morris had said things were mostly undisturbed since Galivan's death, but this seemed extreme.

Construction had stopped immediately after the incident. The yellow tape, though broken in some places, still surrounded several areas on the property, indicating the areas of investigation. Galivan had used his new home as collateral for his $10 million bail, but bail was no longer necessary. Galivan would never enjoy the superfluous amenities of his estate.

Dave turned into the property and parked in the graded, but unpaved area in front of the main part of the house. Stephanie got out of the car and stared at the unfinished 12' by 12' scalloped base of the fountain that Dave guessed was to be the centerpiece of the entrance. Set at a 45 dgree angle—like a diamond in the rough—the framed, partially tiled base provided a hint of the size and magnificence of the entry.

Some of the statues, and planters had already been set in place near the structure. Most of the electrical fixtures were laid out for special lighting. It would be centered in a 60 foot oval of deep emerald green, surrounded by exotic palms and sprays of colorful annuals—a beautiful jewel inset in the tiled 300 foot circular driveway.

As they walked up the steps toward the huge double doors, a car pulled into the property and parked next to their rental. Dave guessed it was Detective Morris.

They waited on the porch as he got out of the car and headed toward them.

"Hello, I'm Detective Morris," he said. "But Doug is fine." He reached out to shake Dave's hand as he stepped up on the porch.

"Dave Duncan," he replied, shaking Detective Morris's hand, "and this is my partner, Detective Fox."

Dave could tell Detective Morris was immediately attracted to Stephanie. He began to stutter a little, and she spoke up.

"Stephanie," she said.

"Nice to meet you," Morris finally got out.

Dave figured Doug, as he preferred to be called, to be about 32 years old. He was ruggedly handsome, and a little taller than Dave. He was on the slim side, but muscular.

"So, you got into the hotel okay?" Doug asked. "What do you think of it?"

Stephanie smiled. "Yes, we did, thanks. It's great. Haven't had a chance to enjoy it yet," she said.

"You may not get much chance. Let me show you around," he said, looking right at Stephanie and almost ignoring Dave. "Anything in particular you were interested in seeing first?"

"The scaffolding is most important," Stephanie said.

"We were wondering why Galivan would be out on the scaffolding in the first place, especially on Friday night," Dave said.

"We wondered that ourselves," Doug answered. "There was no sign of a struggle, and no evidence of anyone else here."

Stephanie glanced up at the third floor balcony. "How would he get up there? He wouldn't climb, would he?"

"He went upstairs to the bedroom and through the slider onto the balcony." Doug paused. "You saw the pictures. He wasn't dressed to climb and there is no evidence that he had. We found a few shoe prints on the balcony that were clearly his."

"You confirmed he was inside that night?" Dave asked.

"We're pretty sure he stepped from the balcony, onto the scaffolding, and fell when it collapsed," Doug explained. He pointed to the balcony on the corner of the main building. "That room has access from a hallway off the main stairway."

"Let's take a look," Dave said.

Detective Morris waved his arm toward the massive doors. Stepping into the entry, Dave nearly lost his breath. It was three stories high, a rotunda, easily 20 feet across. The ceiling, mostly glass, allowed the light to fill the entry and brighten the stairwell. Rays of light in various sizes danced off the marble floor creating interesting patterns and angles of light on the walls and steps.

"How much did you say a place like this cost?" Dave asked, turning in a complete circle to take in the magnitude of the entry.

"A lot more than you and I have, Dave." Doug answered. "Fifteen million is a conservative estimate."

"I can see why!" Stephanie exclaimed, mesmerized by the light patterns on the floor and designer-colored walls.

They continued through the entry to the base of the sweeping circular staircase which curved gently to the second floor landing. From the landing, another equally beautiful circular stairway would take them to the third floor.

They climbed the stairs and continued down a long hallway to the room where Galivan had climbed onto the scaffolding.

The sliding glass door gave immediate access to the balcony and scaffolding.

"No railings on any of the balconies?" Dave asked.

"Apparently they were going to be installed in three weeks," Doug explained, "as soon as they finished the masonry. Unfortunately, it was three weeks too late for Galivan."

Detective Morris opened the slider and stepped out onto the

balcony. This was one of the smaller balconies and one of only two on the front side of the house. Dave paused to look at the area in the room near the slider. The large open windows provided plenty of light to see footprints on the floor.

The room had been sealed since the accident and the prints were still faintly visible in the undisturbed dust. Stephanie followed Dave and inspected the same areas. He looked through the door and onto the balcony.

"It's well preserved in here. There's no sign of a struggle here or on the balcony," Dave said. But he was more interested, at the moment, in the shoe prints. He was looking for an imprint of an Adidas running shoe. One that might match Phillip Hobart's.

"Did you find any prints from a running shoe?" Stephanie asked.

Doug shrugged. "Not that we noticed. All the prints we found were from boots and from Galivan's shoes."

"Any of them distinct or different?"

"Not really. Rich Williams's boot pattern is unique. He's the general contractor, and we found his prints all over the site," Doug offered. "I asked Mr. Williams if he could meet us here at 9:00 this morning."

"Good," Dave said. "Saw you interviewed him twice, but we'd still like to interview both him and Hector Nuñez, the masonary contractor."

Dave had trepidations about stepping out onto the section of scaffolding adjacent to the section that had fallen.

"Is this okay?" Dave asked, apprehension in his voice.

"Don't worry, it's safe," Doug assured him. "Our guys tested it."

Dave bent down to inspect the location of the failed bolts, carefully examining both sides of the frame. The holes had been damaged and elongated from the impact of the bolts being ripped out.

Dave glanced up and saw Detective Morris admiring Stephanie from the open door as she looked around the balcony. "Tell me about the bolts," he asked. Morris stepped out on the balcony next to Stephanie and looked down at the section Dave was inspecting.

"They were loose," Doug started. "The nut on the outside bolt had worked loose and fallen off. It likely fell out when Galivan stepped onto the scaffold."

"What about this other side?" Dave asked.

"The lab determined that the other nut was already loose and gave way—apparently unable to handle the pressure and stress created by the falling weight."

"No sign of being cut, or purposely loosened by someone?" Dave inquired.

"None at all," Doug assured him. "They found that several other nuts were loose throughout the scaffolding."

"Does that happen frequently?"

"Yes, that happens on jobs of this size when the scaffolding is up this long," Doug explained. "It is usually not a problem because they inspect it every week or two."

"What did Williams say about the scaffolding?"

"He told us that it had been checked and tightened less than two weeks prior to the accident."

"How about Hector Nuñez?" Dave asked, looking up at Doug.

"He told us the same thing. Said he wouldn't let his guys out there if it wasn't safe."

"And we know for sure it was checked?"

Doug glanced at his file. "Williams produced the docs signed and dated by the leasing company. He said he has used them for a long time and has never had a problem. Just a freak accident."

"Freak indeed," Dave said, glancing at both sides of the framing. The frame had been twisted, but was intact. No cut marks from a saw or cutters on either side and no obvious evidence of tampering. Someone sawing the bolts while still in the frame would have left markings on the frame. Shavings would have also been present. But neither was evident.

"He fell down there?" Dave asked, not really expecting an answer as he looked at the bent section of the framing.

"That's what we figured. He hit his head right there below you on the cross framing," Doug explained. "medical examiner said he died from the first blow to the head and not from the fall itself."

"The pictures did show a lot of damage to the head," Dave agreed.

The blood stain, though faded, was still visible on the cross framing below them. Additional blood stains further below showed that he hit his head on the edge of the lower board as well. The Boca Raton Police Department had done a great job preserving the crime scene.

"The medical examiner's report said he died sometime around 6:00 p.m. or later," Stephanie said, more as a question.

Doug turned quickly to answer Stephanie's question. "Yes, between 6:00 and 7:00 on Friday night is the established time of death."

Stephanie shuffled through the file. "Is it at all possible someone could have been here with him, forced him out on the scaffolding somehow?" Stephanie asked. "Maybe rigged it to fall?"

"That's possible," Doug answered. "But there was no visible evidence that anyone else was here."

"And just to confirm, he was found by some of the workers in the morning?" Dave asked.

"Yeah, by the work crew that got here first."

"Was Williams with them?"

"No, he got here a little later."

Stephanie glanced up. "But the report said he called it in—"

"Who is that?" Dave interrupted when he saw the pickup pulling into the driveway.

"That's Rich Williams, the general," Doug answered.

"He's a little early," Dave said, glancing at his watch.

"We'll be down in a minute, Mr. Williams," Doug shouted.

"I'm almost done here, Stephanie. Why don't you go down and start the interview?"

"Sure," Stephanie smiled.

Dave was glad of her enthusiasm. She wouldn't miss any clues with her eager curiosity.

"I'll introduce you," Doug interjected, obviously looking for an opportunity to go with Stephanie. He turned to ask, "Do you need me here, Dave?"

"Nope," Dave answered, "I'll only be a few minutes."

* * * *

Stephanie led the way down the stairs to where Williams was

waiting. He was examining the railing at the end of the porch when they came through the front door.

Detective Morris made the inrroductions.

Stephanie and Williams shook hands, and Stephanie started apologetically. "I know you've answered quite a few questions already, so I hope you won't mind answering just a few more."

"Sure, I don't mind. Anything to help."

"Did you discover the body, Mr. Williams?"

"No, actually one of the electrical crews…the first crew here in the morning did," he answered.

"Saturday morning?"

"Yeah, Saturday about a quarter to eight. I was on my way here."

"You usually work on Saturday?" Stephanie asked.

"On this place? Absolutely! There's someone here every day."

"And you contacted the police?"

"I did," he nodded. "The crew supervisor called me when they found him, and I called the police immediately."

"What time did you leave on Friday?"

Williams looked down at the ground. "Around 5:00 p.m., with the dry wall crew. We were the last ones to leave that night."

"Was Mr. Galivan here?"

"No, he hadn't been here in probably three days."

"And you didn't come back that night?"

"No, I went home to get ready to go out that night with some friends."

"And they can vouch for you?"

"Of course, they can. We met at one of our favorite clubs in Delray Beach."

"What time was that?"

"I got there a little after seven," he answered.

"Anyone ride there with you, or pick you up?" Stephanie inquired.

"No, actually I met everyone there. I drove myself."

Stephanie sensed she had taken that as far as she could so she changed directions. "Did you notice anyone suspicious hanging around?"

Williams smiled. "There was always someone suspicious hanging around here. This is a construction site. We had a lot of people coming and going then."

"Anyone you didn't recognize?"

"Lots I didn't recognize." Williams laughed. "There were subs and crews in and out constantly, and Galivan was the worst. He had friends and acquaintances dropping by all the time."

"Difficult to keep track of everyone?"

He laughed again. "More than you can imagine. We had a deadline to meet. If they could shoot a nailgun or hold a trowel, we put them to work."

Stephanie looked at Doug as if searching for the next question. "What about security? Did you sign people in and out?"

"Did at first, but we didn't really enforce security. There were too many people to keep track of," Williams said, waving his arm in a sweeping motion. "This place is pretty isolated anyway, and we never had a problem."

"Was there anybody who really stood out?"

"No more than any others. Now, if *you* had come to the site, I think I would have remembered," Williams said.

Stephanie felt her cheeks redden as she pulled out the picture she had of Hobart and showed it to him. "Ever see this man around here?"

She had hoped the picture would jog his memory. If he had seen Hobart here it would be the proof she needed.

Williams looked at the photo carefully. Finally, he shook his head. "No, he doesn't look familiar."

* * * *

Dave stepped through the entry, he turned for a moment to look at the massive doors, and shook his head in disbelief. Everywhere they had been on this case amazed him. He walked over to the others standing on the end of the porch.

"Dave," Stephanie said, "this is Rich Williams. Rich, this is Detective Duncan."

Dave extended his hand to Williams. "How you doing? Thanks for coming."

"No problem. Glad to help."

"Anything you need to ask?" Stephanie inquired, looking over at Dave.

"Did you go over everything we discussed?"

She read from her notebook. "Pretty sure I did. Timing on Friday, whereabouts, alibis, Hobart."

"I guess we've got what we need," Dave said.

Another truck drove in at that moment.

"Do you know him?" Dave asked Williams.

"Yeah, it's Hector Nuñez, the masonry contractor on the job."

"Well," Dave said, "thanks for coming. Can we contact you if we think of anything else?"

"Sure, of course," he said.

Williams descended the steps and headed toward his truck.

"Oh…I almost forgot. Does Johnston six mean anything to you?" Dave yelled to Williams as he neared his truck.

"What…Johnston what?"

Dave repeated. "Johnston dash 6."

"No, that doesn't mean anything to me. Should it?"

"No…just asking. Don't worry about it."

Williams turned and greeted Hector as he passed.

"You want to take this one?" Stephanie asked. "I'm going to check in with the squad and see if they've got anything new for us." She pulled out her cell phone, handed Dave the photo of Hobart, and walked toward the cars.

Dave and Detective Morris headed over to question Nuñez. Detective Morris introduced them, and Dave began the usual questioning. He could see Stephanie writing in her notebook the whole time he was conducting the interview.

She jotted down a lot of information and sounded excited. Nuñez didn't recognize Phillip Hobart from the picture either, but Dave was more interested in what Stephanie was writing, than what Nuñez was saying.

Dave thanked him for coming and asked if they could contact him if they needed anything else. When he headed back to his truck, Stephanie came over to give Dave the news.

"You won't believe it," she shouted.

"What are you worked up about?" Dave smiled. He was beginning to enjoy her enthusiasm. It added a little life to his mundane work.

"Phillip Hobart was an investor in GlobalNet!"

"Okay, but so were a lot of other people," Dave reminded her.

"Yes, but he was in Florida at the time of Galivan's accident. He has a friend in Naples. How far is Naples from here?" she asked Doug.

"About an hour to hour and a ha—"

She only heard part of Doug's answer. "They checked his phone records, and he made eight calls to his friend, Brian Porter, during the weeks before the accident."

Dave knew this new evidence was the connection she was hoping for to prove that Phillip Hobart not only killed Benjamin Day, but also killed or participated in the death of Brett Galivan.

Their investigation would now take them from the east coast of Florida, to the west coast of Florida.

He couldn't help but be happy for her.

17

*T*his weather was made for the silver convertible as it sped along Highway 75, aptly called Alligator Alley. The road stretches across the lower portion of the Florida peninsula, and they were heading west to Naples with the top down.

Dave looked over at Stephanie, her blonde hair blowing in the wind. "So what do we know about Naples? Did Doug give you any info?"

"He told me it was a quiet, upscale beach community south of St. Petersburg," she said pulling out her notebook. "Said he really liked the Gulf Coast, and thought about applying for either the Fort Meyers or Naple's departments."

"Sounds great, but we're not going to have any time to enjoy it. I meant what do we know about Naples PD?"

"Oh, Doug said it was a good department and would be extremely helpful."

"I hope so," Dave said. "This is sure a boring drive, isn't it?"

Alligator Alley took them through the Miccosukee Indian Reservation and the Big Cypress National Preserve.

"You don't find this interesting? Doug gave me this brochure of the area." She opened it up and spread it out on her lap. "Did you know that Florida is in the middle of a ten-year drought so we may see more gators than we would normally."

"Gators?" Dave groused. "I didn't come to Florida to see gators."

She glanced over at Dave. "Don't be so melodramatic."

"I'm not being melodramatic…I was just saying—"

Stephanie read from the brochure, "If you keep your eyes open, you might see some of Florida's other natural wildlife—egrets, herons, cormorants, and belted kingfishers," she teased, as she opened her cell phone.

Dave knew she had called the Naples Police Department and asked for their assistance. The Naples PD already had Brian Porter's address for her and was standing by, awaiting their arrival.

She closed her phone ending her call to Houston and turned to Dave. "It looks like he was in Florida for five or six days at the same time as Galivan's death."

"Hobart or Porter?"

"Hobart. Kevin said they just confirmed the information."

"You don't think it was a coincidence, I take it?"

"Awfully coincidental that the guy we arrested for Day's murder happened to be in Florida at the same time another executive falls to his death," Stephanie said, staring out the window at the endless swamp. "Don't you think?"

Dave didn't answer, but looked over at Stephanie as she watched a flock of snowy egrets begin a westerly takeoff from their marshy roost. Sixty or more magnificent white birds stirred, then accelerated across the long watery runway, with graceful ease, in a natural unison he'd never seen. Dave saw Stephanie's steely gaze fixed on the event, as the flock rose together to a height of no more than twelve feet, wings in perfect syncopation.

"How do they do that?" she wondered aloud, shaking her head.

"Do what?" Dave asked.

"Look at their wings. How do they keep the same effortless rhythm?"

Dave glanced out the window at the sea of white, slightly ahead of the car, "It is unbelievable, isn't it?" He paused for a moment, as enthralled as Stephanie.

It is more *unbelievable* than either of them knew, considering this majestic, pure white inhabitant of coastal wetlands was nearly wiped out in the early twentieth century, during the great plume-hunting era. Women's hats were adorned with the fine plumes of this graceful, 24" bird—sporting a full meter wingspan—until protective legislation passed in 1910 helped re-establish the Snowy's population.

"Now, back to Hobart," Dave said, looking back at the road.

"Sorry, I got lost there for a moment," Stephanie apologized. "Anyway, Hobart filled up at a gas station in Pensacola on Wednesday, and again in Hollywood on Friday."

"The Hollywood we just went through? The day Galivan died?" Dave asked, a little surprised.

"Yes, and yes. That very day. He was only 30 or 40 minutes away on Friday."

"What about his friend in Naples?" Dave asked.

Stephanie read further from her scribblings. "Brian Porter... evidently our suspect made eight calls to Porter in the three weeks prior to his trip."

"So you're thinking Porter was an accomplice?"

"Well, it definitely puts a new slant on the case, doesn't it?"

Dave peered straight ahead. "It could," he mumbled. "You might have something."

The snowy egrets turned north and caught their gaze for a moment. Stephanie paused to again watch them soar, effortlessly, only feet above the woody brush of the Glades, to an unknown destination. "If only our lives were that uncomplicated," she mused. Turning back to Dave she said, "There's more." Her voice rose slightly. "Hobart was an investor in GlobalNet, but they couldn't find Porter on the list, and he wasn't on EnergyDyn's list, but that doesn't mean he didn't help Hobart."

"Remember, Hobart lost his job," Dave reminded her. "Porter's company could have encountered the same problems as Hobart's."

"That's possible," Stephanie agreed.

"Do you know what Porter does?"

Raising her head as if searching the sky for the answer, she said, "I don't know. We'll have to ask him when we see him."

They were only about 20 minutes from Naples and the Naples Police Department. Naples PD was going to have two cars escort them to Porter's house and assist with the interview.

Stephanie was now thinking they might be making an arrest in Naples. Though Hobart had proven innocuous, there was no assurance Porter would be. She sat in silence, staring out the window, listening to the drone of the engine and the wind swirling in the convertible.

"Hobart lost a lot of money in GlobalNet's collapse," Stephanie said, breaking the silence of the last few minutes.

Dave didn't say anything. He was focused on the road, not wanting to miss the turn-off. The car got quiet again, and Dave could see Stephanie was deep in thought about something. "What are you thinking about?"

"I'm just wrestling with the connection between Hobart and Porter—between EnergyDyn and GlobalNet."

At this point Dave knew they really had nothing on Brian Porter—nothing regarding his possible involvement, and did not have time to find out much more. The Naples PD was trying to get some additional information for Stephanie before they arrived, but he knew they would have to get what they needed from the interview.

"Dave," Stephanie said, "I don't quite get it."

"Don't get what, Steph?"

Dave had started calling her Steph because it was easier. He was beginning to feel more comfortable with her.

"I can't quite get a grasp on the connection," she said. "Why would Hobart kill Galivan, five and a half months ago, when he lost way more money in EnergyDyn? Why wouldn't he kill Benjamin Day first?" She paused, a blank look on her face, then added. "Especially since Day was in Houston, and EnergyDyn filed bankruptcy first."

"That's why we're here investigating, Steph. It's our job to put the pieces together. Sometimes they don't all fit until the end." He frowned. "Sometimes they never fit."

"I know," she said, "but things don't add up."

"Like what?" Dave had some ideas of his own, but wanted to see how Stephanie's skills of deduction were working. "What doesn't add up?"

"Well," she paused, "The MOs are completely different."

"Not necessarily," Dave said. "Maybe Hobart was going to shoot Galivan, and just got lucky. Hobart could have gotten him out on the scaffold and Galivan fell before he pulled the trigger."

"So you think Hobart did it?" Stephanie asked, the level of excitement rising in her voice.

She had been working hard to find the connection that would bring Dave on board with the conspiracy theory. He could tell she thought he was beginning to come around.

"*I didn't say that*," Dave said. "Porter may shed some light on it for us. I'm just saying, if Hobart did kill Galivan, the MOs could appear different."

"Well, the new evidence puts Hobart in Florida. That makes him more suspect," she justified, the gleam returning to her blue eyes.

"That's why we're following this thread of evidence, to see if we can connect the dots," Dave reminded her. "But we've got nothing solid yet."

That explanation seemed to satisfy Stephanie for the moment. She pulled out her notes, turning page after page. She had a curious nature and Dave found that refreshing.

As Dave eased off the highway at Collier Boulevard, he watched Stephanie put her notebook away. He didn't know what to expect but quietly hoped for Stephanie's sake that Porter was involved.

18

*S*tephanie's questions were put on hold as Dave pulled up in front of the Naples Police Department, a cozy, historical building in the downtown area. Nothing like their new facility in Houston, the quaint building had character and old world charm. It had a welcome ambiance that wasn't present in their cold concrete and glass structure.

The desk sergeant told Stephanie they were prepared to assist. Stephanie informed the sergeant that they anticipated the contact to be an ordinary interview, but confessed that they were not exactly sure what they might find.

The Naples Police Department had been thorough. Brian Porter had checked out in their inquiries. He appeared to be a normal citizen—had never been in trouble as far as they could tell.

"But Phillip Hobart checked out clean, also," Stephanie reminded the officers.

The Naples officers were also interested in the case in Houston, and what connection a citizen of the sleepy little beach town of Naples could have to do with their case.

Two teams were at the station and ready to accompany Stephanie and Dave to Porter's.

"So we're in agreement?" Stephanie asked the desk sergeant. "I think it's the best way." Her eyes were clear and her voice confident. "I'll conduct the interview and your officer will back me up on the porch."

The desk sergeant looked at Dave and then at Stephanie. "Okay," he agreed, after seeing the determination in her eyes. "We're doing this as a courtesy, you know?"

"I know," she said, "but it would take too long to go over the questions we need to ask him. Did you make the call?"

Another officer came into the room. "He's home. We made the call pretending to be a wrong number.' It seemed to work."

"Good," Stephanie said, as she turned, an energetic spring in her step. "Let's get to work."

The three cars drove down Terrace Avenue and pulled up in front of the house next door to Porter's. He, like Hobart, lived in a comfortable middle-class neighborhood. It was fairly close to the police station and a few blocks from the airport.

It was now 4:00 p.m. A car was in the driveway and they were sure that Porter was home. As they exited the car, Dave reminded her that caution was the better part of valor. "I don't want anything to happen to you. You're my partner," he added, giving Stephanie a little wink.

"I'll be careful," she assured Dave, returning the gesture.

The element of surprise was important in this interview. They didn't want to give Porter time to get rid of possible evidence.

Stephanie took a deep breath, and moved onto Porter's porch, the Naple's officer behind her. "You ready?" she said, turning to the officer.

"Whenever you are."

She went over the questions she would ask and quickly reviewed the order. She took a big nervous breath, reached for the doorbell, and heard it ring inside the house as she depressed the little plastic button.

She took another nervous breath. Stephanie could feel her stomach churn. They hadn't eaten since breakfast, so it was difficult to tell whether the cause was hunger, nervousness, or fear. She rang the bell again.

She heard a voice inside yell, "Coming." The door opened and an older, portly gentleman stood facing Stephanie.

"Brian Porter?" Stephanie asked, hand poised near her gun as a precaution.

"Yes," he said. He glanced at the officer with Stephanie.

"I'm Detective Fox, from the Houston Police Department. and this is Officer Tilton from the Naples PD. I wondered if I could ask you a few questions?" she continued.

"About what?" Porter asked.

"Would you mind stepping out on the porch, Mr. Porter?" she requested.

"I guess so," he said, opening the screen door and stepping outside. "What did you want to know?" Porter frowned. "What would a Houston detective want with me?"

Stephanie glanced inside before turning slightly to confront Porter. The officer remained in position where he could easily see Porter and the door.

"Information about your relationship with Phillip Hobart. And more specifically your contact with him five and a half months ago." Her mouth suddenly felt dry.

He paused and looked at Stephanie. Finally, he said, "Sure—I guess—what do you want to know?"

Stephanie observed Porter's behavior and body position, watching for any changes as he answered questions. She could still see the concern on his face but was unsure how to read it.

"Phil's a good friend," he confirmed. "Is he in some kind of trouble? I haven't heard from him in weeks."

"A little," Stephanie informed him.

"What did he do?" Porter inquired.

"Shouldn't tell you that because it's an ongoing investigation." Stephanie thought about that. Maybe if she told him he'd loosen up with her. "He's been arrested for murder."

"*Murder*? You've got to be kidding. You have the wrong guy. Who did he supposedly kill?"

"He's being held for murder…the murder of Benjamin Day."

"I saw that on the news. *Real shame, isn't it?*" His voice dripped with sarcasm. "And you think Phillip was involved in that?"

"We do. We also have information that Mr. Hobart was here in Naples approximately five and a half months ago. Was he here?"

"Yeah, he was here," Brian said. "What's the Houston thing got to do with his vacation in Florida?"

"How do you know Mr. Hobart?" Stephanie asked Porter, not answering his question.

"We worked together in Houston at a drilling equipment company. I was his boss for several years," Porter informed her. "What's that got to do with me and Florida?"

"Do you still work for the same company?"

"No, I retired almost five years ago."

"Did he stay with you while he was here?" Stephanie asked.

"No, I was up in Philadelphia when he was here."

"What were you doing in Philadelphia?" Stephanie asked, rapidly firing questions at him.

"My dad was ill, and I went up for a couple of weeks to help my mom out," he told her.

"Do you have proof of that?" she asked him, realizing as she said it that she probably shouldn't have asked it in quite that way.

"*Yes, I do*," he said sharply. "I have my round-trip tickets from the trip. What's this about? I thought you were here about Phil?" His voice began to change, and his answers became increasingly sharper.

"I'm sorry," she said. "That must have seemed dispassionate."

Stephanie noticed his frustration with both her and the questions. His body language tightened.

"We just want to establish Mr. Hobart's whereabouts during the five-day period that he was in Florida," she said.

"He stayed here while he was in Florida," Porter barked.

"He stayed here while you were gone?" she asked, a little gentler. "Any idea what he did while he was here?"

"How do I know? I was in Philadelphia."

"I mean, do you know why he was here?" more confidence in her voice.

"Just a short vacation," Porter said. "He said he just needed to get away. So," Porter paused for a moment, "I offered my place if he came to Florida."

"He didn't tell you anything else?"

"I didn't ask. He did say that he was thinking about going to California for a few days to get away. San Francisco, I think."

"San Francisco? What was he going to do in San Francisco?"

"I don't know. Said he just needed some time. That's when I offered him my place, told him to come east instead."

Stephanie looked out at the street. "So you offered? He didn't bring it up?"

"No, I'm sure I was the one who offered. We talked about it for a couple of weeks before he decided to come. I told him he would have the place to himself," he added.

Stephanie was thinking they were losing Phillip Hobart's connection to this murder. Maybe he wasn't involved at all. But he was here, and they had the gas receipts from Hollywood. So he was on the East Coast on Friday. She tried to think of anything else she needed to ask Porter. She suddenly thought about the investment.

"Do you own any shares of GlobalNet?" she asked.

"Thank God, no!" Porter answered. "Phil did, and he was pretty upset about what happened."

"Upset about GlobalNet or EnergyDyn?"

"Both of them. Between GlobalNet and EnergyDyn he lost nearly 85 percent of his retirement, and really had no savings to speak of."

"So he was angry?" Stephanie was now in a comfortable rhythm. "How angry was he?"

"He wasn't angry enough to kill someone, if that's what you're implying," Porter said. "I hope I didn't get him in any trouble by saying that. Phil is a great guy. I worked with him for quite a few years, and rarely ever saw him get angry."

Despite Porter's effort to dispel Hobart's level of anger, his last few statements renewed Stephanie's belief of a possible connection. But they had to prove that he was involved with this incident, one that had already been determined to be an accident.

"A few more questions, Mr. Porter. Did Hobart use your phone while he was here?"

"I don't think so. He had his own cell phone."

"Would you mind providing your bill for that month? Did he leave anything here—notes, clothes?"

"I can get you the bill, and no, I don't think he left anything."

"Do you have any tools he might have used?" Stephanie asked.

"I have tools, but they're locked up. Phil would have no way of getting them," he explained. "Besides, I have the only key."

"Okay, Mr. Porter, I think you've answered everything. Could you get that phone bill for me?"

"Sure, no problem," he said, turning to open the screen door. "Would you like to come in for a moment?"

She shot Dave a glance before answering. "Okay." She followed Porter inside, Officer Tilton right behind her.

Stephanie took the opportunity to look around Porter's living room, while he retrieved his phone bill from a file cabinet. Looking at his desk in the small room off the living area, she hoped to find newspaper clippings similar to those they found at Hobart's. Porter's desk was neat, no sign of clippings, maps, or diagrams of either incident.

Porter turned, bill in hand. "This is the bill for May. You never told me what Day's murder has to do with Phillip's stay here."

"Are you familiar with the death of Brett Galivan, over in Boca Raton?" Stephanie asked, watching for a reaction from Porter.

"Vaguely," he answered. "That happened while I was gone."

He seemed genuinely unsure, Stephanie thought. "Your friend, Phil, may have been involved in his murder."

Porter stared blankly for a few seconds and then spoke, "Murder? I thought that was an accident."

"That's what we're trying to determine," she explained.

"You're not serious, are you?" A look of deep concern crossed Porter's face. "There is no way Phillip was involved in that. If you knew him, you would know that, too."

"For his sake, I hope you're right."

Stephanie thanked Porter and asked him if they could contact him again if they had any additional questions.

When she left the house, she headed straight to Dave. "Hobart stayed here, but Porter was gone the whole time."

"So you don't think he was involved?" Dave asked.

"No, if Porter is telling the truth, he couldn't have been," Stephanie explained. "But Hobart could have pulled it off by himself from here. Porter said he was angry. Maybe he was angry enough to kill someone."

"Let's go ahead and check out the gas station in Hollywood where he filled up the car," Dave said. "It's on our way back."

She nodded. "Someone there might recognize him." She did not really believe that would happen after five months.

It was nearly 5:00 p.m. and, even though it was still daylight saving's time, it would be getting dark by the time they got to Hollywood. In October, in Florida, the sun set around 6:30 p.m. Dave followed the Naples officers back to the station so Stephanie could get a copy of Porter's phone records.

She thanked them for their assistance, climbed into the car, and they headed back east.

Another dead end, and little chance that Hollywood will offer any hope.

19

Stopping in Hollywood on their way back to Boca Raton was the next thing on their agenda. Dave was skeptical that it would produce any worthwhile results, but Stephanie wanted to show an attendant Hobart's photo on a slim chance someone would remember seeing him. Obviously, there was no assurance the person on duty that day was even still working there.

"You know, Porter said several times that Hobart was a great guy."

Dave turned to Stephanie. "We've heard that from virtually everyone associated with him," he said.

"I know," she said. "His neighbors said he was a great neighbor, and his co-workers said they enjoyed working for him."

"Don't forget he was a coach, volunteer, team sponsor—all noble virtues," Dave reminded her.

"Then why did he do it? Would he just crack after losing his retirement?"

Dave glanced at Stephanie, a sympathetic look on his usually tough face. "He did lose an awful lot."

"I guess he did, but enough to commit two murders?"

On the way back, they talked about the possible connections. How could they link Hobart to this murder? They knew that he was on the East Coast on Friday, placing him closer to Boca Raton, but that didn't put him at the scene.

"I'm still puzzled," Stephanie said. "Why didn't he just shoot

Brett Galivan, like he did Day? Why have him go up on the third floor?"

"Maybe he didn't need to. Galivan might have been already up there," Dave said. "Shooting him could have been his plan, but, it's possible that Galivan fell from the scaffolding before he had time to pull the trigger."

"That would be convenient."

"Stranger things have happened," Dave told her.

"I guess," she said. "He would still be guilty of murder, even though he didn't pull the trigger."

"More like attempt to commit murder—but no less guilty. We just have to put him at the scene," Dave added, knowing how difficult that was proving to be.

Dave thought the trip back seemed longer than the trip to Naples. He was sure it was just that he was tired, and the sun was going down. But it should have seemed shorter, because they talked all the way back. They still hadn't eaten since breakfast, and there was nowhere to stop until they got closer to the coast. Perhaps they could get a bite in Hollywood somewhere.

Stephanie pulled out her cell. "I'm going to call Doug…fill him in on what we found out."

"Oh…it's Doug now?" He chuckled, having fun teasing Stephanie a little.

"Easier than saying Detective Morris," she snapped back. "You're starting to call me Steph."

Dave just laughed. "I didn't think you even noticed."

Stephanie gave Dave a "gimme a break" glance, and dialed Doug's number at the police department.

"You're still at the station?" Dave heard her say.

Dave was curious about what Doug may have found. "Put it on speakerphone so I can hear."

"Hey, Stephanie. Yeah, I'm still here. Any luck?"

"He did stay there," Stephanie said, "but his friend, Brian Porter wasn't there. He was in Philadelphia, at his parents. We'll have to check out his alibi, but we haven't ruled out Hobart."

"Where are you now?" he asked.

"We're almost back to Hollywood. We're going to check out

the gas station where Hobart filled up."

"Stephanie, before you do that, we received some additional information from your department about half an hour ago. They tried to reach you, but you must have been in a dead zone driving through Alligator Alley. This will definitely interest you."

"They found something new?" she asked, opening her notebook. "Shoot."

Dave could hear some of what Doug was saying, but not all. "What's he got?"

Stephanie glanced at Dave. "I'll fill you in on anything you miss," she mouthed.

Doug was still talking. "They said they found credit card charges for Hobart from South Beach on Friday. It looks like he had a couple of beers down there at one of the bars."

"He did?" she asked. "When?"

"In the afternoon."

"Where's that, Doug? I know it's south of us, but where is South Beach exactly?"

"About an hour south of here. Maybe thirty minutes from where you are right now." There was a brief pause, then he said, "The credit card receipt said 2:34 p.m. if that helps."

"That would still give him time, wouldn't it?" she asked.

"Yeah, but here's the kicker—he had dinner down there, too."

"What time?" she questioned.

"Around 7:00 p.m."

Dave felt out of the loop. He was able to hear only bits and pieces of Doug's information from the speaker selection on Steph's cell phone before she turned it off. He could tell from Stephanie's end of the conversation that Morris had passed on some important information.

"You're saying he couldn't have been up there? What was he doing in South Beach?" Stephanie asked, frustration in her voice.

"Kinda looks that way," Doug said. "Unless someone was using his credit card, he was having dinner in there at the time of the accident."

She looked at Dave. He saw the frustration in her furled brow and felt badly for her. Every time she thought she was about to connect Hobart to the murder another bit of evidence seemed to exonerate him.

"There is one other thing, Stephanie," Doug said. "Rich Williams was an investor in GlobalNet."

"Doug, *we'll need a picture of Williams.*"

20

*T*he case had taken an interesting, and sudden turn, a completely new twist. Dave looked over and Stephanie was writing furiously. Dave could see the sun in the rear view mirror approaching the western horizon. Minutes ago it was about to set on their first day of investigation in Florida, but now, twilight handed them new information taking them south, down the eastern coast.

"So, Hobart was in South Beach at the time of Galivan's fatal fall?" Dave asked.

"Seems that way," Stephanie said, looking over at Dave. "He was there in the afternoon. He had a couple of drinks at a place called The News Cafe, around 2:45."

Dave grinned. "That would still give him plenty of time to get back to Boca Raton."

"That might be possible if he hadn't had dinner at a restaurant a block away called Scandals, in the Boulevard Hotel, placing him about an hour or more away at the time of death," she continued.

Dave sighed. "Doesn't look like he could have done it, does it?"

"How long would it take him to make the round trip?" Stephanie asked.

Dave could hear the strain, the disappointment, in Stephanie's voice. "I don't know," he said. "He could probably do it in about two hours or a little more, depending on traffic."

Dave looked over at her. She was so sure, with the evidence

they had—placing him in Florida at the time of the accident, his investments and losses in GlobalNet, and the phone calls to Brian Porter—that he was involved in Brett Galivan's death.

"We'll have to gauge the time on our way back," Dave offered. "It may be less than an hour each way—it may be more."

"Does this mean you're in?" Stephanie's eyes lit up.

Dave shot Stephanie a puzzled look. "In?"

"Yep, in," she repeated. "You think he still could have done it?"

"I just meant we need to check the time. That may confirm whether he did or didn't have the time," Dave explained.

"Well, he would have an hour to get back. That should be sufficient time."

"Not really, don't forget that he had dinner sometime between six and seven o'clock." Dave reminded her. "He would have to be back at Scandals no later than...say 6:30."

"I wasn't thinking about that," she groaned. "Thirty minutes wouldn't give him enough time."

Dave didn't think Hobart had done it, but they needed to be thorough and check out all the leads. Stephanie slumped in her slump in the seat. He knew it was tough on her. She had been on an emotional roller coaster for the last four days.

"We've now got Rich Williams as a suspect," Dave offered. "How much did Doug say he lost?"

"A lot," she said. "His investment went from $100,000 to a measly $7,500. That sure looks like a motive for murder to me."

"Motive, opportunity, access," Dave added.

"His boot prints were all over the crime scene. We should have another talk with Mr. Williams." Stephanie grinned, excited about the possibilities of finding a new suspect.

Dave shot a glance at Stephanie. "Out of our jurisdiction, but so is everything else we've done here so far."

"But we uncovered this new evidence. We should at least be allowed to find out if he was working with Hobart!"

"Good point. We could probably get away with that." Dave smiled, thinking how Stephanie could easily make that case with Doug. Though he originally wanted to be done with the whole

Florida thing, events were changing so rapidly, he was beginning to become intrigued.

It was now almost 6:00 p.m.. There were only wisps of pink, orange, and gold behind them and nothing but waning darkness in front of them as they approached Highway 95 and turned south, heading toward Miami.

The gas station in Hollywood was at the third or fourth exit on Highway 95, at Hollywood Boulevard.

Dave got off at the Hollywood exit and found the station. They weren't expecting much, but had to check it out anyway. Stephanie walked over to the booth and flashed her badge. He watched her and listened from the car.

"And what can I do for you, *officer*," came the sarcastic comment from behind the protective glass.

"Do you recall seeing this guy here about five months ago?" Stephanie showed the picture to the attendant sitting safely behind two-inch-thick glass, with only a six-inch by three-inch hole to communicate through.

She hardly looked up. "Nope."

Stephanie pushed the picture hard against the glass, immediately gaining the attention of the attendant. "*Take a good look*," Stephanie shouted through the glass.

"All right, all right," she said, focusing on the picture. "I've worked here for over a year, but I never seen him."

"You've *never* seen him?"

"*No*," she snapped back with distinct finality.

"*Thanks* for your help," Stephanie snapped back.

"Glad to be of help, *officer*."

Stephanie stormed around to the passenger side of the car and swung open the door.

"Not much help?" He had never seen Stephanie so angry.

"That bitch was a *lot* of help," she growled.

Stephanie slid into the car and half slammed the door. Dave decided to keep quiet as he exited the station and headed back to the 95 on-ramp.

After settling down a bit, Stephanie turned to Dave. "Ever been to Miami Beach?" she asked.

He nodded. "Years ago. With my first wife. It's probably much different now."

"How long ago?" she probed.

"When you were a little girl."

Those words rang in Dave's ears, a sudden and stark reminder of the age difference between him and his partner. More of a huge gap than an age difference. He hadn't really thought about it before that moment, at least never that blatantly.

Whatever attraction he had for Stephanie, his chances had just been minimized with a single statement. Getting involved with a partner was not good. It would interfere with their working relationship. But he had never been confronted with this issue before—never having had a woman partner.

Look at me. Even the notion of something happening was fatuous. This sexy young lady, 20 years his junior, probably had a line of suitors. And no matter how he felt about her, he would always be at the end of that long line.

"Dave!" Stephanie's sharp voice woke him from his thoughts. "Are you here?"

"Yeah. Yeah, I'm here."

"You were in some other place," she said.

"I guess I was," he said, declining from explaining any further. "Sorry, guess the drive was getting to me."

Dave had just admitted that he had an attraction for his beautiful partner. He knew she would be far more interested in someone like Detective Morris than someone like him. *Detective Morris*?

"Detective Morris—Stephanie, did you let him know we were going to South Beach?"

"That's who I was talking to…remember? I told him we were going to both locations and got the addresses from him. I'll call him when we get done."

"Are we still planning on meeting with him tonight?"

"If we get done in time," she informed Dave. "If not, we'll see him in the morning."

"Good."

"He's going to set up another meeting with Rich Williams for us. We need to ask him some questions about his investment and his feelings toward Brett Galivan. And we need to find out if he was lying to me about knowing Hobart," she said.

"Okay," Dave blurted out, surprising himself with the overly exuberant outburst. "Let's see what we can find in South Beach."

21

Stephanie felt the case, her quest to connect Hobart to Galivan's death, slipping away. But, she wasn't ready to give it up yet. She had convinced Dave of her need to investigate the new evidence in South Beach.

Dave turned left up the on-ramp and headed south down Highway 95 to Miami. Stephanie checked the maps they had grabbed at the rental agency, searching for the two locations Hobart visited in South Beach on that eventful Friday. Stephanie wanted to question the servers and bartenders at both locations.

"Looks as if the two places are close to each other," she said, pointing to Ocean Drive and the 800 block. The News Cafe was on the corner of Ocean Drive and Eighth Street, and Scandals was one block south, somewhere in the middle of the 700 block. "I wonder if Hobart was alone at the News Cafe?"

"I guess Hobart could have met someone."

"How about Rich Williams? Our new suspect, for starters."

Dave glanced at her. "You interviewed him. Do you really think Williams knew Hobart?"

Stephanie paused before answering, "He might have met with Hobart to finalize plans for that night. They could have been working together. Isn't that possible?" she asked. "Hobart could have gotten Williams to do it, couldn't he?"

Dave shrugged. "Sure, it's possible. He could have slipped away from the site that day," Dave added. "We didn't have any reason to ask him that. You think he was lying about recognizing Hobart?"

"Not that I saw, but they both lost a lot of money in GlobalNet. Sounds like a good connection to me."

"Yep, it does. They did lose a lot of money. And I *did* say that the money could be a motive for murder."

Stephanie gave him an approving smile. She felt he was finally beginning to see what she saw.

"But why conspire way down here in South Beach?" he asked.

"So you believe it was a conspiracy?"

"I didn't say that. Maybe I shouldn't have used the word conspire," he smiled. "Just wondering out loud, I suppose. Why would they meet so far from Boca Raton? Surely there were other places closer to meet."

"Maybe Williams wanted to be sure he wouldn't be seen with Hobart. He would still have time to get back and do the job, and no one in either place would suspect them."

Stephanie had a new confidence in her voice. She was sure something was there in South Beach. Their first stop would be the News Cafe.

She gave Dave directions. "We'll be going east on Highway 195. It'll take us over the causeway toward Miami Beach."

"You're the navigator," Dave smiled.

"Yes, I am. I'm in charge, aren't I?" She laughed.

"Only because I don't have a clue where I'm going, so don't get too comfortable barking orders," he joked.

"I wouldn't think of doing that. We'll be turning south on Collins, and then we'll cross over to Ocean on 14th Street. Think you can remember all that?" Stephanie sallied, enjoying the light banter with her partner.

They cruised down Ocean Drive, a two-lane asphalt strip, divided by a single yellow stripe, pressed tightly between the buildings and the ocean. By the time they started down Ocean, evening had edged into night—twilight. The radiant lights of the South Beach clubs and restaurants brightened up the street, in anticipation of the nightly revelry for which this hot spot had become renowned.

"Wow, Dave! Look at this place. It's...fascinating."

As they approached the heart of South Beach, Stephanie took in its neon and retro glory. The Art Deco buildings, circa 1930s, stood defiant—resplendent. Their freshly painted facades of lime, turquoise, raspberry, and banana, with splashes of lavender and purple, breathed life back into the skyline of this vibrant stretch of beach. The magnificent buildings, making up this four-block piece of real estate, had weathered time, attitudes, and decay only to be reborn and sizzle at night, just as it had in the 20s, and 30s.

"This is spectacular. Every building is different, but every building is the same."

Stephanie could feel Dave's excitement. "And everything is so colorful."

"I'm talking about these buildings—the architecture," Dave clarified. "I was never much of a fan of Art Deco, but when you see it like this, it takes on a whole new meaning." Dave was more animated than Stephanie had seen him since they became partners.

Stephanie looked down the street. The jutting sky blue tower, with deep blue neon letters, announced the Colony Hotel. Stylized floral motifs set in decorative panels, frets, and chevrons coalesced with the iridescent glow of neon to create an electrifying backdrop for the energy of the refurbished hot spot.

"I thought you said you've been here?" Stephanie frowned.

"I said Miami, but I never saw South Beach. I heard about it, but when I was here, it was run down and not the place to go—more of a slum," he explained to Stephanie. "It certainly is the place to go now."

"You mean it hasn't always been like this? This place is wild."

"I heard it was like this years ago."

South Beach was abuzz with activity. The street was crowded with people. The clubs and restaurants were on the right as they approached the main part of South Beach—the beach and Atlantic Ocean on their left.

It was exciting to Stephanie. Every nerve in her body seemed to be firing. *Very hot*! This was 180 degrees from her conservative upbringing. Not that she didn't get a little wild from time to time during her college days. She had let her hair down, but this was different—wild—frenetic. She imagined what it would be like on a weekend, in the summer. *Untamed—primal.*

People were everywhere, a mixture of beautiful people and curious tourists; interesting; colorful; dynamic people. The streets were so alive.

"I wonder what it would be like to spend a week here during the summer."

"You think you could survive a week down here?" Dave laughed.

"I would sure love to try. It might kill me, but I'd love to try."

Salsa music, from one of the clubs, poured into the street and into the rented convertible instantly elevating Stephanie's heartbeat, as they approached their first destination—8th Street.

"The News Cafe should be just ahead," Stephanie said, spotting the forest green awnings, less than a half block in front. "Right up there, Dave, on the corner!" Her body began to move as they passed the source of the stimulating beat. The street already began to weave its esoteric magic.

"I see it, Steph."

"There's a parking spot right near it," Stephanie announced.

Dave pulled up to the spot and parked. It was the only spot available. They were just a short distance from the News Cafe. Parking was a commodity here, even on a Monday night.

Stephanie opened her door and stepped out onto the sidewalk. She smelled the excitement in the air. The salty fragrance of the beach and spicy aroma of the foods filled her nostrils. She inhaled deeply—the smell of Cuban steak and black beans lingered, reminding her that they hadn't eaten since breakfast.

The top of the convertible settled on the frame of the windshield. Dave reached up, latched both latches, and got out on the street side.

Stephanie caught Dave staring at the car. "You're beginning to enjoy the convertible, aren't you?"

"I was just thinking about how lucky we were to find this spot so close."

"I see that smile. You're loosening up. You're glad we came," she teased and watched Dave's face redden.

A gentleman in a crisp, heavily starched white shirt, sharply creased, sporting military type epaulets, approached Dave and informed him that this was valet parking.

"Would you like for us to park your car in the lot, which is $15…or we can—"

Dave instinctively reached for his badge, interrupting. "Police business," he proclaimed—firm, and authoritative.

"Yes, sir." He glanced at Dave's badge and immediately snapped his heels together military style. "How long will you be?"

"Thirty minutes to an hour…that okay?"

"No problem, sir. Take your time. It will be safe here," he assured Dave, bowing slightly.

Stephanie was already on the sidewalk in front of the café when Dave joined her.

The News Cafe in big white letters, old English style, was emblazoned on the front scalloped flap of the canvas awnings that stretched lazily over the full length of the patio. It protected some of the round, marble-topped tables and humble steel-framed, wooden-slat chairs out front, from the elements; but its most important function was to let patrons know they had arrived.

This 24 hour cafe was open, airy, and crowded—an ideal locale to people watch. Stephanie could understand why Hobart would have a beer here in the afternoon.

Stephanie walked between the tables, up the four steps, and into the restaurant. The inside was not as big or as noisy. The rich dark woods and overstuffed booths blocked out some of the din from the street. It was more subdued inside, lacking the fervency of the patio.

Stephanie headed to the bar to ask the bartender for the waitress listed as server on the credit card receipt Kevin found in Phillip's files.

A young man stood behind the long, well-kept bar, eyeing Stephanie as she approached down the narrow aisle between the booths against the windows, and the bar.

"What can I get for you?" he asked, in his best macho voice.

Stephanie couldn't pass up the opportunity to burst his bubble and flashed her badge. "Is there a server named K. Echberg here?"

He grinned, seemingly unfazed. "You don't look much like a cop. Sure that thing is real?"

"Oh, it's real—K. Echberg?"

"Yeah, that's Katie, but she's not working tonight," the bartender said, still staring. "She in trouble?"

"No, just wanted to ask her a few questions. How can we get hold of her?"

"You'll have to talk with one of the managers," he replied.

The bartender fixed his eyes on Stephanie's body. She waited for him to call the manager, starting to feel a little uncomfortable. It was like the badge excited him.

"Do you think you could get him?" she asked, flustered.

"Uh…yeah, sorry."

When the bartender returned, Stephanie pulled out the picture of Hobart. "Do you remember seeing this guy in here?"

He was more business like now. "No, can't say that I have. When would that be?"

"About five months ago."

"No, but he may have been at the other bar."

"There's another bar here?"

"Yeah, just on the other side. Out the front door and left through the other doors."

This multi-level Café, newsstand, and gift shop had two bars. Stephanie didn't think it was big enough. She and Dave would have to ask the other bartender if he recognized their suspect.

From somewhere behind the bar, the manager appeared. Stephanie explained what she wanted with Katie, and he agreed to try and get in touch with her.

"She only lives a few blocks from the restaurant," he told them. "If she's home, I'll ask her if she can come down."

He turned, heading back to the office. Dave was leaning against the end barstool. Stephanie looked around and noticed the inside was beginning to get busier.

"Is it always this busy?" she asked the bartender.

"Usually a lot busier, but this is a Monday. You should see it on a weekend in the summer."

"Looks like a great place to work," she said, merely to make conversation.

"Great scenery," he said, again staring. "Lots of scantily dressed chicks," he added, in a cocky manner Stephanie didn't particularly appreciate.

"Tell the manager we're over in the other bar."

"Sure thing. Come back when you're done over—"

"Dave, let's go ask the other bartender a few questions," Stephanie said, cutting him short.

"We're open 24 hours at this bar," he yelled after Stephanie. "I'll buy you a—"

"That guy gave me the creeps," she said, looking over at Dave.

The other bartender was not what Stephanie expected. She was an attractive young woman, maybe 25, pleasant and helpful. She did not recognize Hobart from the photo either, but informed them that the bartenders don't really see many of the customers unless they're sitting at the bar.

The manager found Stephanie in the main bar and informed her that Katie would be here in about ten to fifteen minutes if they could wait.

"We'll wait," Stephanie nodded.

"Would you like a drink while you wait?"

"No, thank you," they both said in unison. "Not right now," Stephanie added.

"If you'll excuse me then, I've got to take care of a few things," he told them. "You can see how busy we are. Are you sure I can't get you anything?"

"We're fine. Thank you, anyway."

Stephanie walked back over to the bar. "What do you know about Scandals?" she asked the bartender.

"I know they're our competition," she said, laughing. "Really, it's a great place," she continued. "A little high priced. Why do you ask?"

Stephanie explained that the guy they were investigating had evidently eaten dinner later that evening at Scandals. She explained that they had to interview one of the servers and bartenders there as well.

"It's just half way down the block, but you can't get there from here," she joked.

Stephanie gave her a funny look, not quite understanding.

"I'm just kidding. You can walk there," she said.

Stephanie smiled.

"Excuse me for a second, I need to get these customers. If you need anything else, just let me know," she smiled, a warm smile, "Katie ought to be here any minute."

She and Dave sat at a vacant table on the small balcony overlooking the patio. It was unlikely that Katie Echberg would remember Hobart, but you never knew. Dave and Stephanie didn't talk much as they waited. It had been another long day.

As they sat—tired—silent, watching the throngs of people moving between the tables on the patio and the tables out on the edge of the sidewalk, Stephanie caught a whiff of something from the kitchen. "Dave, are you hungry…because I'm starving."

"I was just thinking that myself. You know we haven't eaten since breakfast."

"So what do you feel like? Fish, Cuban, pasta, steak?"

"Anything at this juncture. How about if we eat after the interview at Scandals?"

Stephanie's stomach growled. "I'm good with that," she grinned.

A minute or so later Katie walked into the restaurant. They asked her a few questions about the Friday that Hobart would have been there. She explained that it would have been at the end of lunch. On a Friday they were always busy and she told them she probably waited on 40 or 50 people every Friday in May.

"If he didn't order anything unusual, it would be hard for me to remember," she said. "I always remember the odd drink orders."

Stephanie showed her the picture.

"I'm sorry," she apologized, "but I don't remember him." She explained that it was difficult for her to remember who she waited on yesterday, let alone months ago.

It was not really a surprise to Stephanie. There was nothing really distinctive about Hobart—not too bad looking, but not noticeably gorgeous either. He had no visible scars, tattoos, or other features that would make him stand out. Stephanie knew it was a long shot and thanked Katie for coming down on her day off to help them out.

They thanked the manager and headed down to Scandals to interview the server there. Approaching Scandals, Stephanie still hoped for some tiny bit of evidence that would connect Hobart.

* * * *

Dave's stomach grumbled the closer he got to Scandals. He wasn't used to going all day without eating.

"This place looks incredible, too. How about if we eat here after our interview? My treat," Stephanie offered.

"Your treat?" Dave turned, allowing a big grin to spread over his face. She had never offered to buy before. "This has got to be upscale, which is another way of saying expensive. You sure you want to spend that kind of money?"

"I know," she said, "but the experience will be worth it."

Dave shook his head. "I couldn't let you do that, but this place does look like it would be worth the experience," he admitted.

Slowing to look at the posted menu, they were greeted by an exuberant barker. He stood on the sidewalk just outside the stylish restaurant—his job, to interest passers-by in dining at Scandals. His sales approach was at first, slightly aggressive, but light-hearted and genuine. Almost ignoring Dave, he worked to convince Stephanie that her decision to dine there would be a wise one and greatly appreciated.

"You'll love Scandals," he smiled, his voice inviting, not as forceful as the barkers one encountered at a carnival. "Is there anything I can answer for you?"

Dave spoke up first. "I'm Detective Duncan, and this is Detective Fox."

"Listen…I swear I'm going to take care of those parking violations next week," the barker said, laughing.

A barker with a sense of humor, Dave thought.

"We've heard that before," Stephanie said, smiling. "Should I just slap the cuffs on him here, or do we take him out back and beat it out of him?"

Dave couldn't believe what he was hearing, but decided to play along. "I think the beating," he said, stroking his chin. "I haven't beaten anyone this month."

They all laughed, enjoying the moment and the quick, good-natured jousting.

"John...John Karl," he said, extending his hand to Stephanie.

"Do you have a last name?" she snickered.

Dave laughed again, admiring his partner's quick wit, and enjoying the levity. Stephanie and John joined in. Their laughter bounced off the white canopies, which protect the restaurant's alfresco patrons all the way to the curb.

"That's Karl, with a K."

"Well, Karl with a K, how long have you been a barker?" Stephanie asked bluntly.

"Oh...that hurt," he grimaced, placing his hand over his heart as if she had stabbed him. "We prefer host," he smiled, bowing his head slightly in a gesture of service.

Stephanie smiled.

John had done his job, and done it well. There was no other choice for Dave now. He knew that Stephanie would want to eat here. John's personality and irresistable humor helped in making the decision. It didn't hurt having the exotic specials of the evening conspicuously displayed on a table near the entrance—masterful displays of culinary delights—tempting—erotic.

Dave looked over at Stephanie and nodded his approval. Stephanie informed John that they would be dining there, but had some business to take care of first.

"I will hold the best table on the sidewalk for you," he promised, bowing again.

Like Katie at the News Cafe, the server at Scandals didn't recognize Hobart and didn't remember serving him. Dave let Stephanie ask the questions, which lasted only a few minutes. The outcome was the same with the bartender. Dave was concerned about Stephanie; worried that she might be getting depressed..

As promised, John sat them at one of the premiere tables on the sidewalk, one with a complete view of the passing spectacle. The off-white linen table cloths, potted palms, and candles created an ambiance worthy of South Beach.

A glass of Chardonnay for Stephanie and Cabernet for himself arrived at the table, compliments of John. Stephanie raised her glass to the host, a symbolic gesture of thanks, then turned to Dave. "Cheers."

"Cheers," Dave responded, holding his glass up to Stephanie and then in the direction of their host.

"Whew," Stephanie exhaled, and every muscle in her body relaxed.

She took a sip of her Chardonnay, a California vintage. "This is very nice…a hint of oak…with a long finish," she stated, an air of expertise. "A buttery finish," she extolled, smiling at Dave. *"Very nice."*

Dave raised his eyebrows, an admiring look. "And where did you learn that?"

"My parents were into wine and I picked up a little knowledge over the years," she explained.

They talked through the entire dinner. Dave relaxed, and was having fun. He laughed and joked, enjoying this opportunity to bond with his partner, hoping to present a side he had never shown Stephanie.

"You look relaxed," Dave said.

"I am…*very*," she answered.

Dave basked in her radiance. The flickering light from the table candle softened her features, the glow brightened her already sparkling smile.

This was the most open they had been. They were talking about their lives, their days in high school. Dave saw a Stephanie that was animated, playful.

"No…*really*?" Dave teased.

"I was…*seriously*," she stated.

"And a cheerleader, too, I'll bet?"

"I was," she laughed. "Do I detect just a little sarcasm in that statement?"

"I guess there was," he confessed. "It has nothing to do with you, or the fact that you were a cheerleader. I didn't want to upset you," Dave continued, hoping not to change the mood.

"It's okay; I'm not upset. That was a long time ago," she smiled.

"It was something I did as a teenager and am still glad I did it."

"I just had a different opinion of cheerleaders when I was in high school, "Dave explained. "Guess I still harbor some of that resentment."

"Well, what's your opinion now?" she asked, still smiling. "You know, I also played soccer and softball. And played an instrument."

"Ah," Dave said. "I have a well rounded partner. And an attractive one, too." He raised his glass to toast.

Stephanie raised hers. "Why, thank you, kind sir. Here's to diversity."

Dave looked into her crystal blue eyes, the flame dancing playfully, inviting.

"Do you know how beautiful you look right now?" he blurted out.

A blank, silent moment followed.

Dave was just about to say something else. "You—"

Suddenly, there was an explosion of sound. A rich aria filled the canopies and echoed down the sidewalks, surely mixing somewhere down the street with the oldies and samba music emanating from other clubs.

Thank God. Dave hoped his momentary flirtation had gotten lost in the music.

Under the influence of the wine, the night, and South Beach, Stephanie sat mesmerized by the sultry sax of the musician who walked down the front stairs to entertain Scandal's patrons. Dave had seen the poster inside. His name was Vadim, and Dave could see that he was equally entranced by Stephanie. He sat down at their table and played a song of his own composition—especially for her.

The dinner was exquisite. Stephanie had the decadent special of lobster and prawns, piled atop a tower of garlic mashed potatoes, while Dave enjoyed the succulent seafood pasta with prawns, scallops, and lobster complemented with an exquisite mild bisque sauce. He decided it was a well-deserved perk, made even more enjoyable by the company.

True to her word, Stephanie sprung for the bill.

Relaxed and thoroughly satiated, they bid John farewell and thanked him for a most memorable experience, one that stoked Stephanie's desire to return.

Except for dinner, the trip to South Beach had been a strikeout. Walking back to the car, Dave noticed the intensity of the street was rising, becoming more electrifying—the smells and sounds more intoxicating.

"Dave?"

"Yeah, Steph."

"Nothing. I was just—"

She didn't finish her thought, but Dave was sure she was going to ask if they could stay just a little longer. It was getting late and he knew they should head back to Boca Raton. He was glad she didn't ask.

Stephanie had lots of time to think on the hour or so ride back. She told Dave she was disappointed they couldn't place Hobart at either location, and couldn't place Rich Williams with him.

Dave knew that Williams was now a suspect, given his connection as an investor in GlobalNet and his access to Galivan.

Stephanie fell silent. Vadim was playing softly from the car CD player, a sexy version of "Unbreak My Heart," which was the sixth selection on the CD she purchased at the restaurant. Dave knew she no longer had the energy to think. He watched her slump down in the passenger seat as exhaustion gripped her body. The last four days Stephanie had been running on adrenaline, pumped into her system with every new angle, every new lead, and *every* new suspect.

Tomorrow, however, Dave smiled, was another day. The day would start with Stephanie interviewing Rich Williams, the newest suspect in the death of Brett Galivan. Maybe he could help Steph link Hobart to this case after all.

22

The phone rang at 7:20 a.m. in Stephanie's room. She thought it was her wake up call. It was Detective Morris.

"Are you awake?" she heard him say, even though her groggy hello should have tipped him off. She was supposed to meet Dave and Doug downstairs for breakfast at 8:30. She wouldn't need her 7:30 wake up call now.

Stephanie had talked to Doug on the phone last night, but they didn't meet as previously planned, since she didn't get back to the hotel until around 10:00 p.m.

"We're on with Williams at 10:00 a.m.," Doug informed her.

Still a little groggy, Stephanie mumbled, "Thanks for setting up the later appointment. I'm sure Dave will thank you, too."

"No problem," Doug said, way too cheerily for Stephanie.

The two glasses of Chardonnay had an effect on her this morning. It's too bad he couldn't have made it 11:00 o'clock.

"Where are we meeting him?"

"Out at Galivan's," Doug answered. "It's about the halfway point. See you at breakfast."

Last night Stephanie agreed to meet Doug in the morning, fifteen minutes before Dave, but she didn't expect him to call at 7:20. She jumped out of bed and into the shower, hoping that it would wake her. Sleep had come much easier than the night before, probably because it had been a longer day. The wine may have contributed also.

Doug was already waiting at the table when Stephanie came down. He had even ordered her a latte. He was a cappuccino kinda guy and didn't hesitate to mention that to Stephanie during their conversation. It was easy to see that he was interested and trying to impress her.

"We showed Hobart's picture to several people, but no one remembered seeing him," she told Doug, allowing him to hear the disappointment in her voice.

"It's tough after five months," Doug consoled her. "Especially down there. It would have been pretty crowded."

"Dave and I discussed that on the way home. We thought it was unrealistic to think that someone would remember him after that much time."

"At least you got to investigate it."

Stephanie looked at Doug with faux sad eyes and a protruding lip. "I know, but I so wanted to connect him to Galivan's murder."

"Accident," Doug corrected her. "Now you should focus on Williams."

Stephanie had asked Doug to get Rich Williams's phone records and credit card statements from April, May, and June. The Houston PD was faxing over his investment information.

"Were you able to get his information?" she asked.

"Right here," he said. "I thought we could go through it this morning."

"I searched Hobart's phone records last night and found nothing related to Rich Williams," Stephanie said. "Nothing to his home, business, or cell phone."

"We may find the same thing with these phone records. I didn't see any calls to Houston, or the southern Texas area," Doug said. "Did Hobart have a cell?"

"He did, and incoming calls are listed on his wireless bill. Did Williams make any calls to Naples?"

Dave came wandering into the restaurant then, and Stephanie waved him over to their table. He had showered, but she thought he looked a little unsteady, too.

"I'm surprised to see you two sitting inside on such a beautiful Florida morning," Dave said, as he approached the table.

Stephanie was engrossed in the paperwork.

"You aren't talking about the case without me are you?" he asked, smiling.

Before Stephanie could answer, Doug spoke up. "Stephanie has been filling me in on Naples and South Beach. It doesn't sound promising."

"Uh-huh," Dave mumbled. "Can I get a cup of coffee?" he said to the waitress as she passed by the table.

"Why sure, suga'," she said, in a pleasing southern drawl.

"Have to have some coffee before I can discuss business," he said, turning back to Doug. "No, it doesn't sound promising, but neither did our case when we found Phillip Hobart. When is our meeting with Williams?"

"I asked him to meet us at Galivan's place at 10:00 this morning."

The waitress returned with Dave's coffee, a smile as warm as her southern drawl. "Here you go, suga'."

"I think she likes you," Stephanie teased, as the waitress sauntered away.

Dave pretended to ignore her.

Stephanie went through the phone records while Dave and Doug talked. She was trying to cross-reference numbers and dates. She was also quickly looking for any calls Rich Williams might have made to Brian Porter in Naples, or vice versa.

"Find anything yet Stephanie?" Dave asked.

"Nothing yet," she said. "I don't find any calls between Williams and Porter."

"Anything from Naples?" Dave inquired.

"Or South Beach or Hollywood?" Doug added. "Maybe the pay phone at the gas station?"

Stephanie had been through most of the records and hadn't found a single call connecting the three to anything remotely resembling a conspiracy.

"Nothing to or from Naples. From this, it appears they didn't know each other," she answered.

"Or they were very shrewd," Doug offered.

"I'm not sure we can connect Williams with Hobart," she said, still confident Hobart had something to do with Galivan's accident. "If they communicated, it must have been by e-mail, or carrier pigeon," she joked, managing a slight laugh.

Suddenly Stephanie looked at both of them, and said, "What about e-mail?"

"I don't—"

"Dave, we need to have the lab check Hobart's computer and hard drive for e-mails," she continued.

"It's your—"

"I'll call them before we meet with Williams."

Before Dave could speak again, Stephanie was dialing her cell phone.

The lab told her that they had already run through Hobart's computer. They checked his hard drive and floppies, going back eight months, and found nothing that might be a part of a scheme or plan to murder any other executive. Hobart hadn't put anything in his computer regarding the Benjamin Day murder either.

"He might have communicated by instant messenger," the lab tech told her. "In that case, there would be no record of the conversations."

"No record of the IMs?" she asked. "You can't get those off the hard drive?"

"When they're gone, they're gone," he said. "Never stored on the hard drive."

"Can we check for screen names on all three computers on the buddy or friends lists?" she asked.

"We can, but we'll have to subpoena the other computers," he explained. "We have to get cooperation from three different jurisdictions.

"So I'm guessing that's difficult?"

She hung up, a look of disappointment on her face. "Let's eat breakfast." She motioned for the server.

They hadn't ordered yet, and it was getting close to 9:00. As the waitress approached, Stephanie noticed her warm smile directed at Dave.

Stephanie ordered her usual bagel, with cream cheese, but this morning, as well as a bowl of fruit.

Dave and Doug had big, manly breakfasts—bacon and eggs—three eggs instead of just two, four strips of bacon, advertised as their Lumberjack Breakfast for only $3.99—with hash browns, toast, and juice. So high in artery-clogging cholesterol and fat. It made Stephanie shudder. She saw right through their boyish, competitive attempts to impress her.

"Is it hash browns, or hashed browns?" she asked the guys.

They stared at each other and shrugged their shoulders. They didn't really know. So much for intellectual repartee. Stephanie switched subjects.

"There was nothing on Hobart's computer," she told them, after they ordered.

Another dead end. They talked more about what Stephanie needed to ask Williams. Who put up the scaffolding and who had access to it were at the top of their list. They needed to get a list from Williams of all his subs. Stephanie wanted to know if any of the sub-contractors were investors in GlobalNet, anyone who might have helped Williams get rid of Galivan.

Revisiting the story about his friends, the ones he went out with that Friday night, was important. Stephanie would request phone numbers for each of them. They were his only alibi.

Knowing that he lost more than $92,000 on his GlobalNet investment gave them something new. It was definitely a motive for murder, Stephanie thought. To her, a thousand dollars was a lot of money and $92,000 was beyond her comprehension. It had to be tough to lose.

"We need to ask him again if he *knows* Phillip Hobart," Stephanie stated.

"You did that," Doug reminded her. "I heard you ask him."

"I asked him if he *saw* Hobart hanging around the job site," she said. "His answer was no. If he wasn't hanging around the site, then he wouldn't have been lying. This time we'll also ask him if he knows Brian Porter."

23

They finished breakfast. Dave reviewed Stephanie's list. It was complete. They would arrive at Galivan's a little early, but that would give Dave time to take another look at the crime scene.

Dave was impressed with Stephanie's continuing enthusiasm and her skills as an investigator. Her hard work was evident as he watched her plow through page after page of information before breakfast.

He was beginning to trust her judgment and her instincts. "While you're conducting the interview of Williams, I want to have another look around. You got everything?" Dave asked.

Stephanie's smile answered his question. "I do. You don't want to have a go at him this time?"

"Nah. I have complete confidence in you. You know what you need to ask him, right?"

"I sure do. We're going to find out what we need to know today."

"That's the right attitude," Dave said, as they approached Galivan's.

Doug came to a stop in front of the house. Dave pulled up next to him. Nothing had changed. Dave told Doug he was going to take another shot at the scaffolding and headed toward the stairs. "I don't want to overlook anything." He turned to Stephanie, "Good luck with Williams. Call me if you need anything."

* * * *

Stephanie and Doug walked up to the porch and waited for Williams. They talked about what Brian Porter had said in Naples. She told Doug about Porter's statement—telling her that Hobart was angry.

"Times on Hobart's credit card receipts from South Beach showed 2:34 p.m. and 7:08 p.m. Would Hobart have time to get up to Boca Raton, commit the murder, and get back?" she asked.

"Not on a Friday night," he said, without hesitation. "Not if the time of death is correct."

Stephanie brought up another possibility. "How sure is the coroner on the time of death? Could it have possibly been 5:30 or 5:45?"

"It could be, but he's pretty positive about the six to seven o'clock range."

Doug assured her that the Broward County Coroner was good at his job and extremely good at determining time of death.

"I'm not second guessing him, but could it have been a little earlier?"

"Anything is possible. What are you thinking?"

Stephanie kept figuring all the times: time of death, time of happy hour, time it took to eat dinner, drive time, and it all kept coming out the same. She took a deep breath. "Hobart couldn't have been in both places. But if the murder—"

"You mean if the time of death—"

"I mean, it was fourteen hours or more. He laid there all night. Couldn't the coroner have been off by a half hour?"

"Maybe. That's always a possibility, because it's not an exact science. And a half hour would make a big difference."

"Yes, it would. I'm not giving up on Hobart yet."

"But I thought you were looking at Williams now?" Doug asked. "He had a firm alibi."

"*If* Williams was being truthful about when they left that evening," she questioned. "It wouldn't be the first time some employee left the job early and lied about quitting time. I just want to go over all the possibilities before Williams gets here."

"If this will ease your mind, we interviewed the crew and separately they all told us it was a little after 5:00. Two even confirmed that Williams was ahead of them in his truck and headed up A1A for at least three miles."

"I was just thinking—"

A truck turned into the driveway, interrupting Stephanie in mid-sentence, and pulled up next to the other two cars. It was ten minutes till 10:00.

"He's early," Stephanie said, looking at her watch. "He was early yesterday morning also." Stephanie wondered if he was always so punctual. That would be important in regard to his Friday rendezvous with his friends.

Doug met Williams by the truck and explained that they needed to clear up a few final details. He didn't indicate that Williams was now a possible suspect in the case.

Williams walked up to the porch. "Good morning," he said, cheerfully.

"Good morning," Stephanie replied. "Thanks for coming back out." Stephanie took a deep breath and asked Williams the first question. "Tell me again...who assembled the scaffolding for the job?"

"The guys that brought it out from the leasing company," Williams told her. "They always put it up."

"I know we've gone over this before," Stephanie apologized, "but if you'll just bear with me. Who had access to it?"

"Most everyone working here."

"So anyone could have sabotaged the scaffolding?" she asked.

"Yes, I guess so," he answered, a look of confusion. "Sabotaged?"

"Even you?"

"Yes—but, I thought it was an accident?"

"We're not so sure of that anymore," she answered. "That's why we're here again."

"So what's that got to do with me?" he said, looking over at Doug for some answers. "I wasn't even here."

Stephanie watched for a reaction. Noticing Williams's confused glance at Doug, she decided to change directions. "You said you went home to get ready to go out with friends?"

"Yes, I told you that," he said, a little defiant now. "Wait a minute…you don't think I had anything to do with this do you?"

"Not sure," she said, "so we need to check out everyone again."

Williams looked at both Stephanie and then Doug. "So you're saying this wasn't an accident?"

"We've just come across some new evidence that we need to check out," Doug said, speaking for the first time.

"We'll need the name of the friends you went out with that night," Stephanie told him.

"That was a long time ago."

"You should be able to remember that night," she said, looking straight into his eyes. "The night before a murder? I think I would remember that."

"I'll try to remember who was there that night," Williams said, "but it's not going to change anything.'

Dave walked out on the porch.

"Maybe not, Stephanie said, then asked. "Did you have an investment in Galivan's company? In GlobalNet?"

"Yes, I did," he answered. "So did a lot of other people."

"Why didn't you tell Detective Morris that?" she questioned.

Williams shrugged. "He never asked."

"You didn't think it was important?" Stephanie asked, suspicion in her voice.

"I thought it was an accident!" Williams emphasized.

Stephanie probed deeper. "You lost a lot of money in that investment…didn't you?"

"I wouldn't say a lot."

"You don't think $92,000 is a lot of money?"

He squirmed a little.

She continued, hoping to uncover something important. "Is it a lot of money?" she asked again, pushing a little harder.

"Well, yes, it is a lot," he admitted, "but not enough to kill for!"

"Why did you buy GlobalNet stock?"

"The same reason I buy any stock—because it was doing good," he said. "And I thought if Galivan had this much money, it had to be a good investment."

His statement didn't surprise Stephanie, but she wanted to know more. "You bought it…because?"

"I talked to Galivan about it before finally buying some shares a year ago. He told me it was a great investment. I wish I had known that he was selling his."

"Didn't it make you angry when the company filed bankruptcy?" she challenged.

His body tensed. "Well, yes, but I wouldn't kill him over it!"

"Not even when you found out he was a crook?"

"No, that would be stupid," he said.

That statement stopped Stephanie for a moment. She thought she had him on the ropes.

Williams continued. "Why would I kill him?"

"Because you lost a *lot of money*," Stephanie raised her voice. "*You lost $92,000!*"

"Sure, I lost about $92,000, but I'm making well over a million on this job. So I lost a little money," he said, throwing his hands out to make a point. "It was less than 10 percent of what I'm making on this job when the stock crashed. Actually more like 7 or 8 percent."

"Yeah…but that's still a *lot* of money," Stephanie said, trying to make her point.

"It is, but I had over $300,000 more to make on this job. That was what I would have gotten on the final draw upon completion," he explained. "When he died, my $300,000 died with him."

Stephanie had not considered that when figuring his motive for murder. Though his losses at GlobalNet were big, he lost much more as a result of Galivan's death.

"So you see, it would have been stupid to kill him for a few thousand dollars before the job was completed. The only thing I'm guilty of is being greedy."

That's a valid point, Stephanie thought. She was a little embarrassed. "I see your point," she mustered. "Do you know Brian Porter?"

"Brian Porter? Should I?" he shrugged. "He might have worked on this job, but I don't know him."

"I guess that's all we need for now." She smiled. "Thanks for your help. You're free to go. But don't leave town."

"Thanks," Williams said, heading for his truck.

"I always wanted to say that," she joked, turning toward Dave and Doug. "That was interesting. Didn't see that coming."

"Don't beat yourself up," Dave told her. "Ninety two thousand seemed like a good motive to me, too."

* * * *

Williams backed his truck up and started down the road. Doug had asked the insurance investigator to meet them there at 11 a.m.

"What's the point? It's a nonevent now," Stephanie said.

Dave sensed that Stephanie was at the bottom of her investigative roller-coaster again. "I'll take this one, Stephanie." He didn't like seeing her this way, but every detective had been in this position before, and he knew this wouldn't be her last.

With a blank stare she said, "I'm going for a walk; let me know when you're done."

"Anything new upstairs?" Doug asked, after Stephanie had walked toward the boathouse.

"Nothing that I could see. It's basically the same."

"Doesn't look like Stephanie's going to find what she was looking for, does it?"

"Unfortunately, it doesn't look good for her at this point. You think your investigator friend will have anything for us?"

Doug looked over to where Stephanie was standing. "He'll be here soon, so I guess we'll find out."

Shane Larson, the investigator for Fleetwood Life and Casualty, also arrived early.

"Does everyone in Florida always get to their appointments early?" Dave asked. "It must be the orange juice." he laughed.

Shane joined Dave and Doug on the porch. Doug introduced them.

Shane had his investigation notebook under his arm. He took a few moments to discuss some of the details with Dave and pointed to a couple of important items.

They went over the crime scene again—the boot and shoe prints, blood evidence, the nuts and bolts, and the scaffold framing. Shane told Dave that he felt, as did Detective Morris, that without any evidence of a struggle, the only possible conclusion was just an unfortunate accident.

Doug nodded. "It still looks that way."

"It *is* odd, however, that four executives, *all* of failed corporations, have died in the last nine months," Shane mentioned.

"*Four?*" Dave's eyebrows raised. "What do you mean by four?"

This information surprised Doug as well. "You didn't tell me this. There are four?"

"Yeah," he said. "Our company also investigated the death of James Digást, the president of AmeriCable, three months ago."

"I remember seeing that," Dave said. "But I didn't make the connection with these two murders we're investigating."

"Digást died under suspicious circumstances," Shane said. "But it appears, like this one, to be an accident. Our investigator in Pennsylvania is not ready to close that case quite yet."

"You said there were four," Doug said.

"The first one was nine months ago. That one's not ours. It was Stephen Carston, from EnergyDyn," Shane informed them.

"From EnergyDyn?" Dave asked. "Our EnergyDyn?" He had missed that one in the *Chronicle*.

"I know about that one," Doug stated. "It was the drowning in Hawaii."

"Yes, that's the one," Shane remarked. "Carston was EnergyDyn's CFO."

Dave was curious. "How'd you know about that one, Doug?"

"I'm a swimmer and snorkeler. When I read about it, I realized I had snorkeled in the same location where Carston disappeared."

"Carston's disappearance was not too long after EnergyDyn filed bankruptcy," Shane added.

"That was the first one?" Dave asked.

"Right," Shane said. "Carston's death was listed as an accident, too."

Dave turned to look at Doug. "This info will get Stephanie going again. I'm sure she'll want to look for the connection."

Dave asked Shane if there was anything else he could give them, but that bombshell was enough. Dave took the name and phone number of the investigator working the Digást accident in Philadelphia. "Stephanie'll call," he told Shane, "and get more information from him." They thanked Shane for his help.

"Maybe," Dave said, "Stephanie has a case after all."

"You have to admit, it seems a little more than a coincidence," Doug said.

"Doug, can you do me a favor?" Dave asked.

"Sure, what do you need?"

Dave leaned against a post. "Would you get Williams and Porter's bank records? Go through them and see if you can find anything suspicious. Don't say anything to Stephanie yet…I don't think it's a good time right now," he confided.

"I can do that. And I won't say anything."

"Let me know what you find. We'll look into these two cases, also," Dave stated. "But I'm not going to say anything till we get back to Houston."

* * * *

It was a good motive. Ninety two thousand is a lot of money.

Stephanie was so sure that a loss of that amount was a perfect motive for murder. But Williams didn't seem stupid. A wise man would have waited until after he completed the job to kill Galivan.

This whole trip seemed like a waste of time, she thought. Maybe Dave was right. Galivan's death had no connection to their case, and Hobart had no involvement, despite being in Florida.

Stephanie's thoughts returned to how this entire place had been obtained with bad money. Standing firmly on the $50-a-square-foot terrazo-tiled patio, she thought about the number of people who had lost most of their retirement in order to obtain it. Their money, hard work, years of saving was in every square inch of the building, in every one of the ornate windows and doors, every tile of the artisan-style patio, every technical advance in the boathouse, and every board in the dock. She wondered how Galivan could ever live there knowing that.

She walked to the end of the boat dock, the sound of each step resonating off the water below, and looked out over the ocean.

While Dave and Doug talked to the insurance investigator, she walked around to the back of the property. Her stroll took her by the theater and around to the pool at the edge of the water. She thought about how beautiful it was, how much was here, wondering how much work it would take to earn this kind of money—legitimately.

Staring out at the water and the lush foliage that made this place so beautiful, Stephanie conceded that this part of the investigation was over—Galivan's death was an unfortunate accident.

The investigator was leaving as Stephanie returned to the front of the house. She joined Dave and Doug on the porch. "I think we've done all we can here," she said, disheartened. "We ready to go, Dave?"

"Yep, I think we're ready," he said.

Doug was going back to the hotel with them. They would finish packing and head to the airport.

Dave shook Doug's hand. "Sure appreciate your help, Doug."

"Me, too," Stephanie added, giving her new friend a hug.

Doug asked Stephanie if he could look her up when he came to Houston. "I'll take you out to dinner," he offered.

"That would be nice," she said, smiling as she got into the car.

She waved good-bye to Doug as Dave pulled out of the parking lot, heading toward Ft. Lauderdale. Stephanie was on her way home, tired, empty-handed, with nothing more to investigate.

The flight home would be a little more than two hours. Stephanie decided to get some rest, if she could, and put this disastrous trip behind her.

24

*W*ednesday morning at the station was very different.

Dave found Stephanie sitting at her desk, a blank stare on her face. He knew how difficult it was for her to get focused after all the failures she had been confronted with in Florida. He knew because he had been through similar situations when he was a young detective.

"Hey, Steph."

"Mornin', Dave," she managed.

"You okay?"

She looked over at him by the coffee pot. "At least some things don't change," she smiled. "I'll be all right."

"No they don't." He laughed. "You're still here before me, and I can't start work without a cup of Joe. Did you get any rest?"

"Some. I laid in bed, but my mind wouldn't shut off."

Dave was trying to figure out how to tell her about the other two victims. He knew full well that this information could put her on a new high again.

"I still think there's something we missed—something that would connect Hobart, or prove that Williams or Porter were involved."

"You still think there's something else here?" he said, searching her face.

"I do, and I want so much to prove it. *It's got to be more than coincidence.*"

Dave thought she could handle what he was about to tell her, so he went with it. "What would you say if I told you there were two more victims?"

"Two more what?"

"Executive deaths...two more victims."

"How...where?" She frowned—big wrinkles on her brow. "When and how did you discover this?"

Dave was ready for what she might ask. "Shane told Doug and me yesterday during our talk, while you were walking."

"Why didn't you tell me?" her voice elevated.

"I didn't want to get your hopes up until you got a little rest," he said. "And it was something that could wait until we got back here."

"So fill me in, Dave. What two victims...and when?"

Dave gave her all the details he had about the two cases: Stephen Carston in Hawaii, AmeriCable's Gordon Digást in Pennsylvania, and Fleetwood Life and Casualty's involvement. He gave her the name and telephone number of the insurance investigator in Philly and asked if she would check out the two incidents. He knew the answer.

"Absolutely. This could be the link we were looking for."

She was on that coaster again, and Dave wanted her to have a softer landing if these didn't play out with her conspiracy theory. "Don't get your hopes up too high," he cautioned. "These were both listed as accidents, too."

"Don't you think this is a bit more than coincidence, Dave? I sure as hell do."

"I'm just saying...more like warning you, that these could turn out to be just what they are—accidents."

"I understand, and I'll approach them that way."

Dave nodded. "Good. Let me know what you find."

* * * *

Stephanie was pumped and ready to go again. But was she setting herself up for another fall?

She was anxious to pick up the investigation again and thought she would start with victim number three. *Victim #3.* Despite the warning, she wondered if Hobart had any connection with this victim, or the one in Hawaii.

The new information Shane supplied offered Stephanie new hope that there was a conspiracy and Hobart had complicity. Dave had mentioned that the investigator still had suspicions in Pennsylvania. *Suspicions*—Stephanie's interest piqued at the word. Calling Shane's friend at Fleetwood this morning would be her first priority. She was determined to get all the details.

Since Stephanie had no contact in Hawaii, she thought the Digást investigation would be more prudent. She started a case file for Hawaii and would get the information from the Maui Police Department later.

She and Dave were scheduled to meet with the assistant district attorney, Eric Manly, later in the morning. That gave her an hour and a half for Pennsylvania; plenty of time to get on the Internet and do some digging. Stephanie was good at using the Internet to do her preliminary research.

First, she pulled up the incident report to get the dates and other information about the case from all possible sources.

She ran a search for the local newspapers, logged into their archives, and found out the Digást death was an auto accident, outside his boyhood town in the Pennsylvania mountains. The president of AmeriCable, son of the founder, drove off the road and into the Allegheny River, just eight miles from town.

The investigation had been the jurisdiction of the Pennsylvania State Troopers. Stephanie pulled up the report on the Web site and printed it out. Reading through it she decided to place a call to the Trooper's office in Williamsport.

The report said that Gordon Digást had apparently missed a curve on Highway 6 and crashed through the rail and down a steep embankment into the Allegheny River, the same river that formed the northern boundary of his extensive estate. The report also showed that he had been drinking that night, and the call would confirm that. Drought conditions had left the river at its lowest level in many years, possibly contributing to the death.

"And that was Thursday night on the eighteenth?" she asked Lieutenant Cameron, from the Pennsylvania State Troopers.

"Thursday, sometime between 11:00 p.m. and 2:00 a.m.," he confirmed. "We've narrowed it down to between 11:00 p.m. and midnight," he added.

"How did you determine that?" she questioned.

"Our investigation discovered the approximate time he left Pittsburgh, then we calculated the amount of time it would take for him to reach the location of the accident."

Stephanie could sense his pride, even through the miles of cable that separated them. "That's good investigating. I'll have to remember that," she added.

"Thanks, our guys do good work."

"What about the clock?" she asked. "If the Porsche was so badly damaged, did the clock stop on impact?"

"Damnedest thing, as badly as that car was damaged, and despite the fire, the digital clock was still running," he said. "Everything is digital nowadays. Porsches are so well built, even an analog clock might have continued running."

"It's that German engineering," Stephanie said.

"We didn't find him till the next morning. A stopped clock would have made our job easy."

"No witnesses?"

"Not one," he told her. "We couldn't find a single person that claimed they saw his car that night."

Like the accident in Florida, there were no witnesses. The winding mountainous road was desolate that evening. Not a soul on that section of the road—that late—on that night.

Digást was returning to Coudersport from a day of meetings in Pittsburgh.

"He made this trip frequently?"

"At least once a week," the lieutenant confirmed.

The cozy little town of Coudersport was nestled against the Allegheny River in the heart of North Central Pennsylvania, away from the hustle and bustle of big cities, protected from corporate scandals and malfeasance—the unlikely home of AmeriCable.

Coudersport is a Victorian canvas of rural America, a nostalgic stroll back in time. Its warm, friendly citizens, and buildings with old charm facades would inspire, and encourage Norman Rockwell to buy dozens upon dozens of brushes, and tubes of rich earthy oils: umber, sepia, gold, brown, and brick red.

The Victorian lamps that line Main Street between First and Third Streets cast their soft, protective light on middle American sidewalks—middle American values. Warm greetings and time-tested recipes, passed down from generation to generation, are discussed and exchanged daily in Courthouse Square.

Incongruous, indeed, that one of the largest cable operators in the country would have corporate offices just three blocks from a late 1800s gazebo, sitting tranquil, in the center of a serene expanse of rich emerald green. This grassy rectangle, a place where upstanding citizens gather for annual social events in this peaceful mountain community, is host to the Victorian Christmas Festival, Coudersport Expo, and Judy Bolton Day, honoring author Margaret Sutton.

The venerable white-washed lattice bandstand was the perfect place for the townspeople to stop, talk about the day's events, catch up on the latest news, and, of course—gossip a little.

But on July 19th their usually upbeat and cheerful chatter turned to conversations of surprise, death, and loss—to the family and to the whole town.

Gordon Digást, one of five individuals accused of illegally taking money from AmeriCable for personal use, was being tried for his part in pilfering the once family business—now a public corporation—and using it as a personal piggy bank. But he was still one of the residents of this tight-knit community and would be missed by many.

In the ensuing days, *The Daily Grind*, Coudersport's local newspaper, would tell the sad story of the loss of Gordon Digást. Trash and Treasures, and Garters and Gowns closed that day, as did Buchanan Brothers' Pharmacy. A hurriedly scribbled, handwritten sign, in black marking pen, was posted in one of the store windows—a similar one in AmeriCable's corporate offices: "Closed due to death in family." They were all closed on the 24th, except Kay's Hometown Restaurant. Kay graciously provided coffee and doughnuts to all of the attendees.

On that day, the day of the funeral, the new "Welcome to Coudersport" signs, usually beckoning tourists to Chamber sponsored sidewalk sales, and Moonlight Madness, stood drawn and somber.

Almost the entire population of Coudersport—population: 2,854—turned out to pay their respects. The procession ambled through most of this small community. It started west on Third Street, then south on West to Water, and back to Main. The long parade of friends and mourners headed north, past the AmeriCable buildings, between Water and First, and on past the Potter County Courthouse. Courthouse Square sat empty—in mourning. The Maple Sugar Shack was lifeless, like those attending the funeral. There was no sound, no children's laughter, no idle conversation on the square this morning, as the procession somberly made its way to the cemetery.

This was the same grassy square where Gordy Digást, while growing up, engaged in fisticuffs, danced, loitered, kissed, cussed, drank, wrestled, played the slide trombone with the band, dreamed—lived.

There were no witnesses in Florida, now no witnesses in Coudersport, and Stephanie would later discover that there were no witnesses in the drowning of Stephen Carston, the chief financial officer of EnergyDyn, in Hawaii. In *each* of these unfortunate accidents—*not a single witness.*

Stephanie took a moment to think about that. She heard the lieutenant say again: "*No*, there were no witnesses."

"He was out on bail wasn't he?" she asked the lieutenant.

"Yes, he was."

"So, he was under a lot of pressure?" she asked, assuming the answer.

"The whole family was," he informed her.

"Lieutenant Cameron, did it appear to you that he might have been trying to commit suicide?"

"No," he said, without hesitation. "Our investigation showed skid marks from his attempt to brake just before crashing through the barrier." He paused. "A man trying to commit suicide doesn't brake going over the side."

"Could he have had second thoughts?"

"Don't think so," he said. "It was the way he applied the brake, going straight off the embankment as if he had been surprised," the lieutenant said. "He didn't attempt to try to turn the car to avoid going over the railing." The lieutenant tried to explain further. "If he was having second thoughts, he would have tried to turn the vehicle away from the guard rail. He didn't do that."

"I understand," Stephanie said. "I'm just trying to rule some things out. Any suspicions of another person being involved?"

"Not that our investigators could determine," Lieutenant Cameron told her. "Do you think your guy had anything to do with this?"

Stephanie had filled Lieutenant Cameron in at the top of the telephone conversation. She explained the other mysterious coincidences. The lieutenant hadn't heard of the other accidents prior to his conversation with Stephanie, but was interested in the circumstances. "Rather suspicious," were his exact words.

"That's what we're trying to determine," she said. "We couldn't connect him to Florida, at least we haven't *yet*."

"What made you think he was involved in Florida?"

"We found evidence that he was in Florida at the time of the accident. We're looking for similar evidence in your case," she told the lieutenant.

"I see," Cameron said.

Stephanie paused for a moment to gather her thoughts. "I would love to connect him to this one and maybe go back to the Florida accident and connect him to that one." She paused, then finally said. "I believe there's a conspiracy here."

"*A conspiracy*?" he questioned. "You really think so?"

"I think there is, but not everyone here agrees," she confessed.

"Well, let me know if you find anything that you think we should take a second look at," Lieutenant Cameron offered. "I can't promise you anything though."

"I will Lieutenant…and thank you for all your help. Can we count on your assistance if we have to come to Pennsylvania to investigate?"

"Sure can," he answered. "Just let me know when. You'll love Coudersport."

Stephanie hung up the phone and turned to open the new file

on her desk. She had already written, "Victim Number 3"—neatly on the tab. She began to scribble some additional notes on a blank sheet of paper and stuffed it and the other notes she'd just taken in the folder.

There wasn't much in the file, but Digást's phone records would soon be faxed from the Pennsylvania phone company, as well as the AmeriCable investor list from the Securities and Exchange Commission.

Dave had been busy reviewing the lab reports and the interview with Hobart for their meeting with Manly. Discussing what she had just learned would have to wait until after the meeting.

25

*P*hillip Hobart had already been indicted and held over for trial, on Tuesday, while Dave and Stephanie were in Florida. He was in jail, unable to post bail—or, more likely, unwilling. He didn't seem to care.

Dave was rarely confronted with feelings about his suspects, but something about this case bothered him. He thought Manly was rushing this trial, and though he believed they had the right man, he didn't like the pressure put on them to finish the investigation. Hobart's trial—most unprecedented—was scheduled in just two weeks.

During the ride over to the DA's office, he and Stephanie talked about the Pennsylvania accident.

"What did Shane's contact tell you?" he asked. "What was he suspicious about?"

"I didn't have time to call him yet. I was able to talk to a Lieutenant Cameron at the State Trooper's office," she explained. "He was very helpful."

Dave was waiting for further explanation. When it wasn't offered he spoke up. "So what did he think? Was it an accident?"

"He said their initial findings indicated an accident," she said.

"But you're not buying it?"

"Well, I'll be a better judge of that after I talk to the insurance guy."

The assistant DA wanted to know if they could connect Hobart with the Florida case. Like so many other politicians, he was looking for an opportunity to advance his career and that would require being in the spotlight. If they were able to connect Hobart with another murder, or better yet, a conspiracy, it would be a big boost for the prosecuting attorney's career.

Dave had let Stephanie run with this investigation, and she seemed happy to take the lead. He had already decided that she would give Manly the details. He hadn't told her yet, but the less contact he had with Manly, the better.

Stephanie had an abundance of energy and was adamant about connecting Hobart with Florida, and now the other incidents. Her feeling was—if the guy committed murder then he should fry. *Manly would appreciate that.*

Dave was supportive of Stephanie and would help her put this case together, but he still had an undefined reluctance about this case that was unlike him. He was actually sympathetic with Hobart.

The more he learned about the victims, or alleged victims, and the more he discovered about their involvement and circumstances, the more he began to feel that they deserved what they got. Couldn't have happened to a nicer bunch of guys, he thought.

Unlike Stephanie, Dave was closing in on retirement. He would be 50 in just two years and had more than 26 years in the department. Another four and he would retire after 30 long years on the force. If he could get through those four it would make a big difference in his monthly retirement income.

Most of Dave's retirement was his city plan with the police department, but he had some in a 401K retirement plan and in mutual funds. Of course, his retirement from the police department was probably sufficient, but he couldn't be sure of that and, by itself, might not be enough.

His long-time partner, Danny Brentwood, had talked him into a 401K twelve years ago, even before they became partners. Danny convinced him that he needed more—some extra money to supplement his department pension. Though he had paid little attention to his retirement funds, he suddenly had an interest in finding out more.

Dave now wondered if any of his funds had positions in EnergyDyn, GlobalNet, or AmeriCable? He wondered if he had anything left to retire on. Maybe, like Phillip Hobart, he was wiped out and just didn't know it yet. Hell, he thought, his last ten or eleven statements were still in the envelopes, unopened. He vowed to find out—today!

"So..." Stephanie began as they walked into the courthouse, "what about this meeting with our illustrious district attorney?"

"I think he just wants to know if we can connect Hobart, but who knows, with him? *You know*, he's just trying to boost his career and is using this case." Dave added, "I'm going to let you lay it out for him."

"I know he's using this case," Stephanie confessed. "But so am I. I know this one doesn't matter much to you, but I would love to get my first big conviction."

"Oh, it matters to me," he conceded. "You know about me and Manly...right?"

"I've heard things."

"Well, they're probably all true," Dave smiled. "He has been trying to boost his career since he got here."

"I know that...everybody knows that."

Dave looked over at Stephanie as he pushed the up button on the elevator. "Don't mistake my intentions, Stephanie. I would really like to see you get this conviction. You've worked hard and done a great job on this case," he said, pride in his voice.

"Thanks, Dave. That's good to hear."

"If you want, I can do all the talking."

"I'll be okay. We can just go with the flow, and you can answer questions if you want to."

Dave looked at her, not sure what her answer would be to his question. "What are you going to tell him?"

Stephanie thought about it for a moment. "I don't want to lie to him, but I still believe there's a connection. We just haven't found it yet."

"I thought we agreed on the plane last night that it was an accident?" Dave questioned.

They stepped into the elevator and she pushed 3. "We did, but this new information from Pennsylvania…I can tell him truthfully that we haven't made the connection, but that we aren't quite ready to wrap up the investigation. I would still like to research the accidents in Pennsylvania and Hawaii to see what I can find out."

"You sure you still want to do that? We could probably wrap this up right now if we wanted to," he said, folding his arms.

"I still think there's a conspiracy here," she said, as the elevator slowed. "It's a gut feeling I have."

"We haven't found anything solid yet," he emphasized, "but I'll back you, partner, if you want to pursue it. I know a lot about gut feelings."

"I *do* want to pursue it, Dave. Lieutenant Cameron could find something for us. So I wouldn't really be lying to Manly. And we haven't checked out Hawaii."

"That's fine," Dave said. "Let's go in with just that information, and see if Manly wants us to keep digging."

Dave approached the receptionist. "Manly?"

"Conference room," she answered. "Go right in, Detectives."

The captain was already there and looked up as they entered the conference room at about two minutes till nine.

Manly immediately jumped up to greet them. Dave knew Manly's sudden enthusiasm wasn't on his account. His interest in Stephanie was obvious. Dave and Stephanie were currently his star detectives—his chance to climb the political ladder. But Dave could be absent and Manly wouldn't care.

Dave always considered Eric Manly, assistant district attorney, to be rather sleazy, maybe even a little perverted. He wasn't sure what the authorities might find at Manly's place if they ever raided it, but nothing would surprise him. He always hit on Stephanie when he was in her presence. Dave didn't like it, but Stephanie wouldn't let him do anything about it.

Stephanie was taller than Manly. Her five-nine towered over Manly's five-feet six (five-seven if he stood on his toes).

A portly man, Manly always looked tousled. His clothes never seemed to fit right—shirt out, tie crooked, jacket wrinkled. His thousand-dollar suits weren't purchased off the rack, but he had a knack for making them look that way.

Stephanie, on the other hand, dressed impeccably. Her appearance was always neat and clean, clothes always pressed. She purchased quality clothes, and it showed. Dave's appearance was improving, helped by Stephanie's example.

They both took seats at the end of the long table next to the district attorney's assistants and investigators.

Manly looked down the long table. "Got anything for me from Florida?"

"Nothing yet," Stephanie spoke up, "but we're not through with the investigation."

"Well, I need you to find me something to go with this case, Detective Fox. If you do, I'll be obliged to take you to dinner," he added shamelessly.

It didn't take long for the sleazeball to hit on her, in front of everyone. It was almost comical.

"You can keep dinner, but I'll still try to connect Hobart to the incident in Florida, as well as the others," she snapped back sharply.

Anyone else may have been in trouble for talking like that to Manly, but not Stephanie. Manly appeared to even enjoy her feisty remark.

"Others?" Manly sat up straight.

"Yep, two more cases," she said. "We just heard about them. Haven't even had time to tell *you* about them, Captain Martin."

"Well...go out and find the connection," Manly barked before the captain could speak, and ignoring her obvious rejection.

"You know, we'll just do that," Stephanie replied sarcastically.

The detectives excused themselves.

"I'll see you two when I get back to the station," Captain Martin said.

On their way back to the station they laughed about Manly's futile attempt at taking Stephanie out to dinner. Dave was bothered, but mildly amused by Manly's constant attempts and his ability to shrug off rejection.

"Can you believe him?" Stephanie said, laughing.

"You don't have to put up with that, you know," Dave reminded her.

"He's harmless…but thank you for being concerned."

Dave could see that Stephanie was anxious to get back to the station and continue her investigation into the Digást accident.

I hope, for her sake, this doesn't end up like the Florida investigation. But I've got to let her run with it.

26

Stephanie sat down at her desk and immediately picked up the Digást file. Dave went over to get some coffee. Her positive attitude had returned, and she was more determined than ever to find the connections to Hobart that she was sure existed.

She was deep in paperwork as Dave came over to her desk. "The cheap bastard didn't even offer us coffee," Dave stated, half laughing, half serious.

Stephanie giggled. "No latte either."

"And after we drove all the way over there." Glancing down at the new pile on her desk Dave said, "Looks like you accumulated more lists."

"Lieutenant Cameron faxed over the phone records I requested and I had Kevin get me the list of AmeriCable's investors from the SEC."

"You need a hand going over any of this?"

"Not really," she said, "but you could go over the Florida stuff one more time for me to see if we missed something." She paused, then looked at Dave with a frown. "I know you don't really want to, but I would certainly appreciate it if you would."

Dave agreed to do that while she searched the AmeriCable investor list hoping to find Phillip Hobart's name. They had been over the Florida evidence several times already, but sometimes investigative work was redundant.

"I will, but if I find something you'll have to take me to

dinner," Dave said, mocking Manly. He laughed and looked at Stephanie. She laughed also. "First, tell me a little about this guy in Pennsylvania," Dave insisted, "then I'll go through the Florida material again."

Stephanie explained the accident as Lieutenant Cameron had explained it to her.

"He was drinking and ended up in the river. Sounds like an accident to me."

Stephanie went on, ignoring his comment. "AmeriCable filed bankruptcy. Seems the Digást family still thought the company was their personal piggy bank."

"I thought AmeriCable was a corporation—on the New York Stock Exchange?"

"It was a public traded company—but the Digást's didn't act like it."

"Why did AmeriCable file bankruptcy?"

"The state attorney general estimated the family took more than $300 million out of the corporation, forcing the company into bankruptcy," she explained, then added, "They even built a $13 million golf course on property they had already taken from the company."

"*Thirteen million?*"

Dave listened and secretly hoped that Hobart had done it and would get away with it. He wondered how many other people felt the way he did. With each new case and each new story, Dave became more sympathetic to Hobart. "Amazing," he said, "all that money and still greedy for more." Dave went back to his desk shaking his head and half-heartedly reviewed the Florida file.

Stephanie went through page after page searching for Phillip Hobart, Rich Williams, and Brian Porter. After an hour of searching, she hadn't found any of them on AmeriCable's investor list. Nor did she find them in any of the mutual funds or 401K plans.

Dave came over to Stephanie's desk to see how she was doing. "I found nothing new in the Florida files."

"It doesn't appear any of them were investors in AmeriCable either," she pouted. "Still have to go through the phone records for that period."

As Dave walked over for another cup of coffee, Stephanie turned her attention to the new phone records. She began to notice several numbers that were becoming repetitive. Calls to two Houston phone numbers and several to the 214 area code—more specifically, the Dallas area.

She decided to call the numbers and find out what was going on in Hobart's life at that time. She called the first Houston number.

"Doctor's office," the pleasant voice on the other end of the line answered. "Can I help you?"

Stephanie didn't know what to expect, but even this surprised her. She paused, searching for the right words.

"Hello," came the voice again.

"Hello, this is Detective Fox with the Houston Police Department," she said to the receptionist. "Can you tell me what office this is?"

"Yes, this is Doctor Tanner's office," she informed Stephanie. "Is there anything I can help you with?"

"I need to find out if one of our suspects is one of your patients," she said. "A Phillip Hobart?"

"He is," she said. "Shame about what happened to Mr. Hobart, isn't it? Especially after all he's been through."

"Yes, it is," Stephanie said, in a sympathetic tone. "May I ask you a couple of questions?"

"I suppose," she said.

"Can you tell me what kind of treatment Phillip Hobart was receiving at your office?" Stephanie requested.

"He is one of our regular patients," she told Stephanie. "He wasn't feeling well, and we ran some tests, trying to find out what was wrong."

"What was your diagnosis?" Stephanie asked.

"We weren't exactly sure, so we referred him to a specialist in Dallas to run some more tests."

"What kind of specialist?" Stephanie asked.

"I'm not able to tell you that. I can give you the name of the specialist if you would like."

Stephanie paused again. "Yes, please do."

"We referred Mr. Hobart to a Dr. Finnik."

"Is Dr. Finnik's office in Dallas by any chance?"

"Yes, it is," she informed Stephanie. "I can give you the number."

"That won't be necessary. I have the number," she said, her mouth dry.

Stephanie thanked her for the information and hung up the phone. She sat staring blankly, not sure what to do next.

Her eyes returned to the records. An eerie feeling swept over her as she stared at the number. It wasn't a good feeling. *I know this number, but from where?*

27

The young attorney sat motionless, contemplating the events of the morning and his next move.

Which book was it? He remembered seeing the precedence late last night and made a mental note that it might be useful. But he was tired, hadn't marked it, and finding it again in this pile of legal opinions might prove to be difficult. This was his chance to show everyone in Houston that he was a good lawyer, so he would find it if it took him the rest of the day.

Anthony J. Baker, Esq.—that's what the walnut name-plate on Tony's desk stated in bold capital letters. The public defender assigned to defend Phillip Hobart was proud seeing the Esq. after his name. It was a symbol of achievement, especially in the Baker family.

A graduate of the Thurgood Marshall School of Law, Tony had worked hard to get where he was today. At times he struggled to get through even one semester. It was the price you paid for being accepted at one of the most prestigious law schools in the country, he thought, every time he scraped by. He had made it, though, and the public defender's office was just a temporary stop on Tony's journey.

Appointed or not, he was going to do the best job he could for his new client. But Tony was a realist and knew that the evidence was overwhelmingly stacked against them. It was the biggest case he ever had. He was smart enough to realize he was in over his head.

Help can come sometimes when you least expect it and in the most unusual way. Tony Baker was about to find that out. He was both surprised and a little relieved when he received the phone call.

"Hello," Tony said, after answering the phone that rarely rang prior to two weeks ago.

"Hello—Anthony Baker?" the caller asked in a calm, slightly inquisitive voice.

"Yes," Tony answered, apprehensively, "what can I do for you?"

"I'm calling in regard to the Phillip Hobart matter," he said. "You are representing him, aren't you?"

"I am," Tony confirmed. "Who is this?"

"Names are not important; what I'm prepared to offer you is," the caller said, his voice firm—direct.

"And what might that be?" Tony inquired.

"My employer, who has a special interest in this case, would like to pay for Mr. Hobart's legal fees."

"He has no legal fees," Tony informed the caller rather sharply, "and what special interest?"

"We're prepared to pay for the best legal counsel available for Mr. Hobart. I suspect you're feeling a little overwhelmed with this case."

There was a brief pause. "Yes," Tony confided, "just a little. It *is* the biggest case I've ever tried," he added, still not sure he should admit that to the caller, especially one he didn't know.

"We thought so, that's why we would like to make this offer," the anonymous benefactor continued.

Tony was still not sure he should be giving this caller this much information, but his voice was sincere and reassuring. "What is your interest in this case? Why would you want to help Mr. Hobart?" he asked. "The evidence is overwhelming."

"Suffice to say, Mr. Baker, that *some people* believe what Mr. Hobart did is not necessarily a bad thing."

Tony thought about what he had just heard—someone other than himself *actually believes* in Phillip. He also thought about the benefits in Phillip getting the best representation. "Of course, I would have to confer with my client," he informed the stranger on the phone.

He still wasn't sure about this, but after all those hard years in law school, he knew a good offer when he heard one.

"Please do. I will call you tomorrow to get his answer. If it is to the affirmative, we will make all the necessary arrangements."

"I'll ask him. Can I call you back tomorrow?"

"No...I will call you. Expect a call at 11:00 a.m. *sharp*, your time."

"I'll talk to my client this afternoon," Tony said.

"Not a word of this to anyone else, all right?" the mysterious caller's voice was stern.

"Of course," Tony said, not sure exactly what he was agreeing to, but willing to take a chance if it would help his client.

The caller hung up. Tony stood behind his desk, still holding the phone, now feeling a little numb from the conversation that had just transpired. Hanging up the phone, he began to go over in his mind what he had to do.

His first priority, if in fact he had to prioritize, would be to discuss with Phillip this incredible, unexpected offer. He would sort out the details on the way over to the jail. One thing he understood, above all other things, is that the onus would be suddenly lifted from his shoulders. Tony gathered the materials he needed, dropped everything else on his schedule—not that there was much to drop—and headed to the county jail to share the good news with his incarcerated charge.

Tony Baker's heartbeat quickened as he picked up his pace, anxious to get to his car and see his client.

In his haste to give Phillip the good news, Tony flooded the engine. He was only months from getting better transportation, but for now all he could do was wait. The smell of gas infuriated him. "This crappy piece of shit!" he cursed, knowing his impatience was equally to blame.

On his way to the jail, Phillip's appointed counselor thought about the opportunity this revelation would mean for *him*. He would be able to work with some of the most revered criminal attorneys in the country. "What an incredible opportunity," he thought aloud. He stopped himself for a moment and thought about how selfish that sounded. Selfish—maybe—but also a once in a lifetime opportunity for him and Phillip.

Phillip has a chance now—a "real" chance.

28

Stephanie had held off as long as she could. She busied herself with paperwork, but it hadn't quelled the struggle going on in her mind. Several times she picked up the number, but set it back down—unable to dial it.

It was now late afternoon. Dave had asked several times if she was okay. She had managed to deflect his concern thus far, but realized she couldn't do it much longer.

There was something about the number that bothered her—haunted her, but she couldn't identify her fear. There was only one way to find out. Stephanie reached for the receiver and began dialing the Dallas number from the phone records. An uneasy feeling stirred in her stomach as the phone rang once—twice—three times.

"River Shore Oncology Center...Dr. Finnik's office."

There was a long silence, again she heard the voice.

"Hello...can I help you?"

"River Shore Oncology Center?" Stephanie repeated, her voice trailing off to barely a whisper.

"Yes, may I help you?" came the calm voice from the other end of the receiver.

Stephanie shivered. She felt faint. "I'm sorry...could you give me just a moment?" she said.

"Of course," the voice remained soft and patient.

After a short pause the voice came back on line. "Are you

there? Are you okay?"

"Yes...yes, I'm here. This is Detective Fox, with the Houston Police Department. I wonder if I could ask yu a few questions about one of your patients."

Her voice was as pleasant and soothing as the receptionist's voice at Doctor Tanner's office. "Yes, Detective Fox, how can I help you?"

"It's regarding a Phillip Hobart. He would have been a patient of yours three or four months ago."

"Yes, Mr. Hobart is a patient. Let me get the file."

Stephanie waited while the receptionist retrieved Mr. Hobart's file. It seemed like a lifetime to Stephanie, but was really no more than about half a minute. She could hear the shuffling of papers over the phone and then the receptionist's voice.

"Detective Fox, I'm fairly new here and was just informed that I cannot give you specific information," she apologized. "I can tell you that he was referred by Dr. Tanner's office in Houston."

"Yes," Stephanie said, pausing for a moment. "I spoke with Dr. Tanner's office."

"What would you like to know?" she asked.

"I wanted to ask about his diagnosis."

"I'm not sure I can give you that information," she said.

Stephanie explained the situation and emphasized how important it was that she obtain information that might help Mr. Hobart.

"We could get a subpoena," Stephanie threatened, "but I was hoping we wouldn't have to do that."

"Let me talk with Dr. Finnik, and see what information I can release," she said. "Can you hold?"

"Sure, I can do that," Stephanie said. She hoped that she wouldn't have to get a subpoena and go to Dallas to get the information. Although, it would be an opportunity to see her parents, she thought.

The receptionist was gone for approximately four minutes. When she returned, she again apologized to Stephanie. "I'm so sorry, but I'm unable to give you any other information about Mr. Hobart."

"It's all right; I understand. Is Mrs. Dorman there?"

"Yes, she is. May I put you on hold for a minute?"

"Of course."

The "on hold" music almost put Stephanie to sleep. After about a minute she heard the hold button click and the music ended.

"*Detective Fox*?...This wouldn't be Stephanie Fox, would it?" Her voice sweet and friendly.

Stephanie remembered that warm voice. She'd heard it at least a hundred times or more. "Yes, Mrs. Dorman, how are you?"

"It's still Jean to you, Stephanie," she said. "I'm fine. So it's detective now? When did you get promoted?"

"About four months ago."

"Well, congratulations. I expected you would make it, but not *this* soon. How's the family?"

"They're great, Jean. Just talked to Mom last week. Dad still complains about his gout, but they're fine. How about ya'll?"

"We're all doing good. Nothing really new. Jenna's a big ol' senior this year and thinks she's somethin' *real* special."

"Well, ya'ar special when you're a senior," Stephanie said, slipping back into her drawl.

"She's following right in your footsteps. She's been nominated for homecoming queen. She looks so precious in her gown."

"I'll bet she does. Good for her, I hope she wins. She's a cutie," Stephanie added.

"What can I do for you, honey?" Jean asked.

Stephanie's relationship with Jean Dorman went back five years. Jean was a pillar of support for Stephanie and her family.

The number to River Shore Oncology Center was familiar to Stephanie, even though she couldn't place it at first. She hadn't dialed it in almost two years, but had reason to dial it frequently the previous three.

Stephanie's grandmother volunteered at the center for more than five years before she was diagnosed with cancer herself. She had spent her volunteer years providing assistance, support, a shoulder, and always love to the many families who came to the center. Then, suddenly, without warning, she was in need of the same understanding and support she had given so many—selflessly.

Jean was there when the family was first informed of the illness and remained steady—a rock—through the three years that Stephanie's grandmother fought the awful disease. "It's the least I can do," she remembers Jean saying when they found out. "Your grandmother has been such a blessing to this center—an angel of mercy. She has provided so much to so many since she came here."

Those words reverberated, in an instant, through Stephanie's head as she thought about Jean's question.

"I'm working on the Benjamin Day case, Jean, and I need a little information on one of your patients, Phillip Hobart."

"I saw that on the news," she hesitated. "What has Mr. Hobart got to do with it?"

"He's our suspect in the murder."

"*Oh my*," Jean gasped. "I can't believe that. Do you really think he did it?"

"Yeah, I do."

"What do you need, Stephanie?"

"Although I think I know...I need to find out why Hobart was seeing Dr. Finnik."

A moment of silence followed. "I'm really not supposed to tell you any of this, you know—doctor/client privilege and such, but because it's you, darlin'—"

"I know. Obviously he had cancer of some sort. What do you know about him, Jean?"

"First and foremost, honey," she began, "Phillip Hobart was a model patient. I don't believe he could do anything like this."

"We've gotten that impression already. Everyone we interviewed told us he was a great guy."

"He was a lot like your grandmother," Jean said. She paused to gather herself, and then, voice cracking a little, she continued. "Phillip was diagnosed with Pancreatic Cancer," she stated. "When we first saw him, the case was already in the advanced stages. He was diagnosed at T4, which is the most advanced stage."

"What was the date that you first saw him?" Stephanie inquired, wanting to get all the dates straight.

"I've got his file right here. Let me check the dates for you.

Here it is. His first visit was on July 10th, a Wednesday. We ran tests on Monday, the 15th, and additional tests over the next few days. He was released on the morning of the 18th."

"When did he actually find out he had cancer?"

"Let me find the exact date. I believe it was in August."

There was again a slight pause, the shuffling of papers, and then Jean's calm, professional voice. "Yes, it was on Friday, August 2nd. He was pretty much aware that he had cancer before he came to us," she added.

"How did he take it?" Stephanie asked.

"Extremely well," she said. "Like your grandmother, he was one of the few patients who actually touched me. It was their attitude, Stephanie, their unwavering strength."

"What form of cancer did you say he had?"

"Pancreatic Cancer...it's a *bad* one."

"And...and how long did Dr. Finnik feel he had to live?" Stephanie finally asked, not really sure how to ask a question of that nature.

"Around six months," she told Stephanie.

"What about treatment?"

"There really is very little we can do in the way of treatment for someone as advanced as Mr. Hobart was."

She paused for a moment and added, "The only thing available is chemotherapy, and he refused that. Something else that might help...we found out later that he had lost his job and the insurance was going to run out."

"That's what we're figuring out," Stephanie said.

"I hope this helps him," she said quietly, shedding her usual decorum.

"It will," Stephanie promised her. "You tell Jenna I said good luck."

"I sure will, honey," Jean said, her voice as sweet as ever. "It was so good to talk to you. Give the folks my best."

Stephanie thanked her for the help and hung up. She ran the dates through her head again—July 10th—July 15th—July 18th. Hobart was in Dallas for four days, from the 15th through the 18th. That would mean he was in Dallas when the Coudersport accident occurred. He couldn't have done it. *He couldn't have killed Digást.*

29

*P*hillip Hobart shuffled into the interview room in leg chains and his bright orange jail attire. He greeted his attorney with his usual smile. Tony responded with a level of exuberance unfamiliar to Phillip. The usually stoic and somber Tony was uncharacteristically excited.

Phillip smiled. "Tony, what's got you so worked up?"

"Good news!" Tony exclaimed.

"You look like you're going to wet your pants."

The guard finished removing Phillip's leg irons, and he walked over to sit down in one of the two chairs at the lone table in the center of the cold cement room. The room depressed Phillip. He was tired, his eyes devoid of color. His health seemed to be declining more each day, but he was determined not to let his attorney see it.

The gray walls and biting cold floor, with the stainless steel chairs on either side of the same gray and stainless steel table were stark reminders of the desolation and emptiness Phillip felt. The guard closed the door, and he turned his attention to Tony.

"Tony, sit."

"I'm too excited to sit. We have a guardian angel," he blurted out. "Someone has offered to pay for the best counsel available for you." His voice climbed a few octaves higher than normal.

Before Phillip had time to ask questions, Tony told him about the phone call. He pointed out all of the benefits of having one of the top attorneys in the country representing him. Phillip listened intently while his counselor droned on.

He stared at Tony—expressionless.

"Phillip, did you hear what I said?"

"I have good counsel," Phillip replied in a calm voice, looking directly at Tony.

"But we're talking about getting you the *best* attorneys in the country," Tony declared.

"Tony, you're doing everything you can for me, aren't you?"

"Yes, I'm trying," Tony said, "but I have limited resources."

"Tony, it's fine. Trust me, we don't need other counsel. Everything will work out fine." Sensing Tony's lack of confidence, he said again, "trust me," and shot Tony a reassuring smile.

"I don't understand," Tony said.

"If I told you why, would it be just between you and me, you know—like attorney/client privilege?" Phillip asked.

"Absolutely," Tony stated. "Except under some very limited circumstances."

"I'm going to take a chance here," Phillip confided. "I don't need another attorney." He paused and took a deep breath. "Because I'm going to die in three months."

Tony's mouth dropped. He didn't say a word—just stood there shocked, mute. He turned away from Phillip.

"Tony, maybe you should sit down," Phillip said, noticing that the young lawyer was wavering and had turned pale.

Tony sat down and finally uttered, "*Dying?*"

"Unfortunately, yes."

After a very long pause, Tony asked, "Dying—*from what?*"

"Cancer," Phillip stated calmly. "One of the worst ones—pancreatic cancer. I have less than three months to live if the doctors are correct."

"How could you keep something like this a secret?" he said feebly. "You didn't appear to be ill, except for the recent cough and slight fever."

"I can assure you, it's cancer."

"Now I see why I was assigned this case—and why you refused outside counsel," Tony said, cold and distant.

"It's going to work out, Tony," he assured him. "I've accepted my fate."

"Who knew this?" Tony finally asked. "Am I the only one who doesn't know? Was I given your case because—"

"No one knows. You're the first," Phillip promised. "And no, that wasn't why you were assigned to represent me."

"God dammit. What do we do *now*?"

"Exactly what we've been doing," Phillip said, his voice calm and reassuring. "You're defending me the best you can. Nothing is different."

"Everything is different!" Tony exclaimed. "How can I proceed with your defense now, knowing what I know?"

Phillip looked at Tony, a look of confidence. "I've watched you. You're a good attorney, Tony. I know you can do this."

"But why…why didn't you tell me?"

"I should have. I'm really sorry. I didn't think it would make a difference."

"Well, *it does*."

"I need you to help me get through this," Phillip said, looking at Tony with another reassuring look.

"I can try," Tony said, "but I can't promise anything."

"Look at me. Just tell me you'll try…*promise* me you'll try," Phillip said, looking for a sign from Tony that he was okay.

Tony agreed to continue in spite of this new, disheartening information. "What do I tell the mysterious caller tomorrow morning when he calls?"

"Tell him thank you, but I refused the help."

"But I don't think that will satisfy him," he informed Phillip. "There was something about him. Something in his voice."

"Then tell him the truth if it will make you feel better Tony. It really doesn't matter at this point. Go ahead and explain it to him," Phillip continued. "See if you can find out who he is. I'm curious, too, about who would be willing to help me."

Tony shook his head slowly back and forth. "I'll ask, but I don't think he'll tell me. He wouldn't give me his name earlier, when he first called."

Phillip once again reassured Tony that everything would be

okay, but it didn't appear to make the lawyer feel any better about what he had just discovered.

* * * *

The attorney stared as the guard returned to take the prisoner back to his cell. The guard locked the leg chains, with a cold metal snap, and followed Phillip through the door. Tony watched him noisily shuffle out, the door clanging behind him, knowing now that the chains that imprisoned Phillip, were not the heavy metal chains he had around his ankles. For nearly ten minutes, Tony stood motionless, drained, in the cold, colorless confines of the interview room.

Finally, he took a deep breath, grabbed his briefcase, and turned to head back to the office. His thoughts bounced from Phillip's revelation, to the mysterious caller, and back to Phillip. It was now obvious to Tony why he did it. Right or wrong, Phillip had made the decision to get even with Benjamin Day and did it with no uncertainty. It was over for Phillip, and it was over for Day.

30

The dynamics of their case against Phillip Hobart changed dramatically with just one word—"cancer."

Stephanie got up from her desk, still in shock, and went over to Dave who was pouring himself another cup of coffee. "Dave," she said in a hushed voice.

Dave turned to Stephanie, standing in front of him, pale, with glassy eyes. He could hardly hear her say his name. "Steph, you okay?"

"Dave," she repeated in barely a whisper. "He has cancer!"

"Who?" Dave asked.

"Hobart," she stated, almost inaudible.

"He has *cancer*?" Dave's eyes widened. "How did you find this out?"

"I noticed calls in the new phone list to two particular areas—here in Houston and the 214 area code—Dallas."

"Before the accident in Pennsylvania?"

"Yep...six calls in two weeks to the number in Houston, and nine to Dallas in just over two weeks. So I called them."

"And what did you find out?" Dave asked, on the edge of his seat.

"The specialist in Dallas was an oncologist and his office told me Hobart had advanced pancreatic cancer."

"Cancer," Dave repeated. "*Wow*! And you're sure about this? How'd you get them to tell you?"

"Yep, I'm sure. A friend at the center gave it to me. He *didn't* do it!" She blurted out.

"Didn't do what?" Dave asked.

"Didn't kill Gordy Digást," she said. "He *couldn't* have. He was in Dallas that morning."

"You know that?" he asked. "You said he was there in the morning?"

"Yeah, I did. He was in Dallas on the morning of Digást's accident. He was finishing the tests at the oncologist."

"I think you should check that out when we're done here," Dave told Stephanie. "He could have hopped a plane and went straight to Pittsburgh. Better check his credit card records for that month."

"So you think he still could have done it?" she frowned, surprised by Dave's comments.

"I didn't say that, I just said it was a possibility and that we should check. What did you find out about the cancer?" Dave probed.

Stephanie went into a verbose explanation about the cancer—the stages, possible treatment, and his refusal of treatment. Everything Jean had told her—dates, tests, reactions. "He wasn't angry when he left," she said. "He must have been pretty rundown from the tests. I know my grandmother was."

She told Dave that Hobart was informed he had six months to live on August 2nd. Exactly two weeks after Digást's death. "So you see, I don't think he could have done it!"

"What about the conspiracy theory? Did you find any friends in Pennsylvania?" Dave asked.

"Didn't look for that yet," she said. "But I haven't checked through the entire phone list. I saw the two repetitive phone numbers and that's as far as I got," She looked up at Dave. "I will though. I still think he had something to do with this—just not sure how."

Stephanie thought, at the time they found out about Brian Porter, he might be involved. Then she thought Williams might have helped Hobart. But that didn't work out either. A thorough search through the list was disappointing to her. Porter was from

Pennsylvania, so she thought he was involved, but nothing popped up. She was beginning to believe that maybe the others were just accidents and merely coincidental.

"The MOs were so different," she stated, perplexed by the variations in the deaths. "Maybe Hobart wasn't involved in the other cases."

"Yeah, but think about it," Dave challenged. "If he had cancer, what did he have to lose at the time he shot Day?"

"*You're right*!" she exclaimed. "He knew he didn't have much time to live. It really wouldn't matter."

"He probably thought he would die before being discovered," Dave said.

"In that case, he wouldn't have to conceal it."

"I can't believe I'm going down this road," Dave said smiling. "I'm on Hobart's side."

"Maybe there has been a master plan all along, and we just haven't seen it," Stephanie stated.

Dave nodded. "A possibility. Now that I know he has cancer, I feel even more sorry for the guy."

It was obvious to Stephanie that Dave had mixed emotions. His feeling of sympathy for Hobart had grown stronger as they got further into the investigation. Knowing Hobart had cancer strengthened that feeling. But she could tell he was also becoming more interested in the conspiracy theory. She just had to find something—any bit of evidence that would tie the events together.

Stephanie began seeing signs of the change. Dave was so close to retirement himself. Maybe it was because he saw himself, alone, lonely—even a little depressed, after he retired. What would he have done if someone like Benjamin Day, or Brett Galivan—or any greedy, selfish, overpaid executive—wiped him out, like they did Hobart?

"Thanks for letting me continue with this investigation," Stephanie said, smiling at Dave. "I know sometimes I'm a little gung-ho."

"You're doing a good job, Stephanie. I had always been taught to follow every lead, to look at the improbables and the impossibilities, and didn't want to discourage you from doing that same thing. You've reminded me a couple of times that this is your first big case. I was there once, and have an idea of what you're going through."

She knew that she needed to learn to look at all the evidence—pursue all the angles, but not jump to so many conclusions. It was now obvious that Hobart would have needed some help—if he was involved in these other deaths.

"Thanks for the vote of confidence, Dave. I'm going to find the connection," she grinned. The sparkle returned to her earlier dormant eyes.

So, bolstered by Dave's encouragement, Stephanie continued her search for Phillip Hobart's accomplices, or co-conspirators.

31

*I*t was difficult for Stephanie to sleep Wednesday night, having found out about Hobart's cancer. Despite the lack of sleep, she was at the station early—she had a job to do and she was going to do it. That's what the City of Houston paid her to do—investigate crimes and catch the criminals.

Hobart may have had cancer, but he was still a criminal and Stephanie was determined to prove that he was involved in the other cases. If not the actual killer, he was involved with others in a greater cause—a conspiracy.

The coincidences in Florida, and now in Coudersport, were too much for her to let go. She decided to check for calls to Pennsylvania, Ohio, New York, and New Jersey—anywhere close enough to Coudersport for accomplices to be involved in this case.

Stephanie knew Hobart was in Dallas on July 10th and from the 15th through the 18th. Although she was beginning to hate searching phone records, it had to be done. If he was involved in Pennsylvania in a plan to eliminate Digást, it would show up in June and the first weeks of July. If Hobart worked with someone, there would be calls to Buffalo, Pittsburgh, Philadelphia, or areas around those cities.

The credit card statements showed nothing. No gas receipts, car rentals, or airline tickets that would put Hobart in or around Coudersport on the day of Digást's accident.

In fact, she found a gas receipt from an Exxon station between

Dallas and Houston on that day, indicating he was on his way home that afternoon. So Stephanie found herself searching for a ghost again.

Stephanie had already been through the investor list from AmeriCable. The Securities and Exchange Commission was still cooperative, providing the lists she requested.

Phillip Hobart was not on the list. At least not as an individual investor. He apparently had no financial reason to kill Digást. But Hobart was angry at corporate executives.

Could knowing there was something terribly wrong have caused Hobart to accelerate any plan he might have put together? Stephanie thought, in today's business environment it wouldn't be too difficult to find a number of people willing to help him. There were a lot of angry investors out there. *Where is the connection?*

Neither Rich Williams nor Brian Porter's name showed up on the AmeriCable list. She continued to shuffle through the massive pile of paper looking for mutual funds or retirement plans that matched—she found nothing.

After spending most of the day examining the endless documents, Stephanie was tired, still feeling like they were on Florida time. She'd had a short night of sleep, and her concentration was waning.

She glanced over and saw Dave on the phone. She would have to wait till he finished to talk with him.

Her eyes closed briefly, and the commotion around her dulled. If she was going to solve this case, or find a conspiracy, she would have to fight the fatigue that was beginning to grip her.

32

Tony arrived at his office around 8:00 a.m. in the morning and sat nervously behind his desk. He wasn't sure where the mysterious benefactor telephoned from and did not want to miss the call, in case he had mistaken what was said.

He spent some time putting away books, shuffling papers, and filing, but didn't accomplish much—more focused on what he would say to the anonymous caller. He knew one thing with almost complete certainty; he would receive a phone call at 11:00 a.m. sharp, either his or the guardian angel's time.

Hobart's counselor was deep in thought when the phone rang startling him. He glanced at the clock. It was exactly 11:00 o'clock, and the first ring continued to resonate through his little office, broken only by the second. Tony leaned forward and picked up the phone.

"Hello," he stammered.

"Mr. Baker?" It was the same quiet, composed voice from yesterday.

"Yes, sir, this is he."

"Did you inform Mr. Hobart of our offer?" he asked, his tone serious and direct.

"I did," Tony answered. "He told me to thank you for your generosity, but regretfully, he must decline."

"*Decline?*" the caller questioned, losing his earlier calm. "*Surely* Mr. Hobart understands the offer and the gravity of his situation?"

"Yes—he does—entirely."

"And he doesn't want to accept this opportunity of possible freedom?" The caller paused briefly. "May I inquire as to why?"

"He has cancer," Tony informed him, barely able to say the word, even though he had practiced it since he arrived at his office earlier in the morning.

"Did you say he has *cancer*, Mr. Baker?"

"Yes sir—cancer—he only has three months to live. So, you see he really doesn't see the need to obtain his freedom. He said he really has nothing to live for."

"I am sorry to hear that," came the unwavering voice at the other end of the line. "Give him our best. We sincerely wanted to help him."

"I truly believe you did. Can I at least tell him who his benefactor was?" Tony asked.

"I can't do that—you understand—but please inform him that some out there, besides us, understand his plight and are sympathetic with his position."

"Thank you for your offer. Under other circumstances, I'm sure my client would have gratefully accepted," Tony was saying, before hearing the click at the other end.

Tony again found himself standing, holding the phone, a little dazed. He slowly came back to reality and realized that his opportunity to work with someone like Jerry Spence had just faded.

He scanned his tiny office. Phillip had asked him to continue to represent him, and he was determined to do the best he could. Maybe a little prayer would help also. He turned back to the paperwork on his desk.

Tony would spend the rest of the day assembling his case. The trial was only a few days away, and there was still lots of work to do.

He had made a promise to Phillip, and was going to keep it.

33

"Stephanie...Stephanie," Dave repeated, as he gently shook her shoulder. "You look tired."

"Just resting my eyes."

"Uh-huh. It looked that way."

"No...really, I was. What's up?"

"I was just talking to Detective Morris," Dave said.

"That's good...how is Doug?" Stephanie asked, sounding only moderately interested.

"He's good. He asked about you. I think he was disappointed it was me who called," he added, laughing a little. "He told me they might have something new and interesting that they're checking out right now."

Stephanie sat up and leaned toward him. "Something new? Did he say what?"

"He didn't say exactly what, but thinks they found something they hadn't noticed before."

"So they're still investigating?" she asked. "I didn't think they were doing anything further."

"You sparked their interest, I guess, so they reopened the investigation. That's why they checked out Williams and Porter again, and are taking a second look at the evidence."

"He didn't even give you an idea, not even a hint, of what they found?" she frowned.

"No, he didn't, but he said he would call us as soon as they confirmed their new evidence."

"That's not fair," she said, "to get me all excited and make me wait. What else did you find out?"

"He interviewed all of Williams's alibis, and they checked out. Everyone said the same thing. Their stories put him at the club in Delray Beach a few minutes after 7:00 that night, and he was dressed up. Two of them confirmed that he was there till some time after 10:30."

"Does that match their statements before?" Stephanie asked.

"Doug said they hadn't interviewed them earlier. No need to. Williams wasn't a suspect."

"That's right," she nodded. "And all their stories were the same?"

"Pretty much. They said he had showered, his hair was combed, and he was wearing slacks and a nice shirt. And they all claimed Williams acted normal that night."

"What about Porter?"

"His story checked out, too. His dad was sick, and his mom told Doug he was there for almost two weeks."

Stephanie sighed. "And he was there the whole time Hobart was at his place?"

"The whole time, as far as Doug could confirm. Porter has been there several times since to help his mom and brother out."

"I guess we can cross Porter off my list."

"You turn up anything new?"

"Nothing yet," she said, stretching to work out the kinks. "I've been going over these lists all day. It would have been nice if we had gotten a call for a stabbing, or a shooting, or even a car accident—*something* that would have gotten us out of the squad today. How about you?"

"Not a thing," he said. "I called Naples and Miami Police Departments, and the Florida State Police for parking or moving violations—nothing."

"So we can't even bust Hobart for parking violations," she said laughing.

Dave laughed with her. At least, she still had a little humor.

"Well, I've got nothing from Pennsylvania either," she told

Dave. "No calls to any location near Coudersport, and none of them are on the AmeriCable investor list. We could identify the investors in the area and get someone to check them out?"

"*Who on earth would do that*? No one else is that crazy." Dave laughed.

"Yeah, I'm sure you're right. No one has the same interest in their cases as we do in ours," she winked. "You don't think we could get Lieutenant Cameron to go for that?"

Dave shook his head. "Don't think so. It's getting late. This'll keep, and I don't think we'll get the new findings from Boca until tomorrow."

"I guess it will," she yawned. "I'm pretty tired."

Thursday had taken its toll on Stephanie. It was one of those days where nothing happens and they had to pour over mounds of tedious, boring information.

"I know you're excited about the new info we might get from Doug," Dave said. "You can stay if you want."

Without another word, Stephanie got up, grabbed her jacket, and—not even glancing at the mess on her desk—headed for the door. Dave was right behind her as she headed for the stairs. He reached up and turned off the lights in the squad.

"This was an extremely long day," she said, looking back at Dave.

"Yep," he said. "You better get used to them if you want to be a detective."

"It's not always like this, is it?"

"Only on the bigger cases," he assured her. "The rest of the time it's damned boring."

"That's good to hear," she giggled. "Have a good night Dave."

"You too, Steph. See you in the morning."

Dave would do what he did most every night he finished early, head to The Beat to have a couple of drinks with the guys. He didn't particularly enjoy going back to his house.

About 1,400 square feet, filled with furniture that was about ten years old, it was all he could afford after his second divorce. It was acceptable, and it was his, but it was cold and lonely, and seemed much smaller since the start of this investigation. He definitely preferred the noise, clamor, and conversation of The Beat, over the quiet of his home.

Dave knew most of the people—mostly police officers and staff—that socialized at The Beat. He didn't drink with anyone in particular, but he had a few friends from other precincts who were there as often as he was. They talked about their recent cases—and the Hobart case was the biggest in the city right now.

One of his longtime drinking buddies and close friends was Paul Robertson from the 4th Precinct. Paul and Dave worked together years ago when they were beat cops at the 8th Precinct. He was sure Paul would be there tonight.

Paul was already at The Beat when Dave arrived and excited to hear all the new developments. He ordered Dave's first drink. Paul acted interested in the Hobart case, and Dave spent the next hour explaining the new developments, including Hobart's cancer.

"Only a couple tonight," he told Paul. He needed to be in good shape tomorrow to give Stephanie a hand and, maybe, wrap this case up. They had exhausted all their leads, and under normal circumstances, it would be time to close the file. This wasn't a normal case though, and Dave realized that the new information Doug might have could extend the investigation.

That was something Dave didn't really care to do, but he was beginning to enjoy the roller coaster this case was on and he would do whatever he had to in support of his new partner.

True to his word, Dave headed home after a couple of drinks to get a good night's sleep and help Stephanie close the Hobart case.

* * * *

Stephanie, on the other hand, headed to her car anxious to get home and get a full night's sleep in her own bed. She thought she might hit the pillow early tonight. She was on her way home to her small apartment and her cat, Charlie, a lovable mixture, though noticeably absent of any pedigree.

That didn't matter to Stephanie. What meant more to her was how he was always there when she came home. She loved his big Cheshire grin when he knew he had done something bad. She was going home to spend some quality time with Charlie, and maybe let him curl up on her lap while she watched a movie and ate popcorn.

She knew he had been feeling pretty neglected of late. He would be happy to see her home early tonight.

She was sure that after a solid eight hours of sleep she would find the one thing that could break this case wide open.

34

There was a note on Stephanie's desk when she arrived at the squad. Manly wanted to see them again in the afternoon. She had a bombshell to drop on him today.

They had to meet with Captain Martin first, to fill him in on what they had come up with since their meeting with Manly yesterday morning.

Stephanie was debating whether to go over Rich Williams's and Brian Porter's phone records one more time before their meeting with the captain. Making such little progress, she was now beginning to think it was a waste of time.

It had been another restless night for Stephanie. She was troubled by their inability to make the connection with the other cases, and was thinking about the new evidence they might get from Boca Raton. Were they missing the obvious, some important element that would connect Hobart with the other two deaths? She felt that the answer could conceivably be in Florida and was eager to hear what Doug had to say.

Dave grabbed a cup of coffee, and they headed to Captain Martin's office together.

"Tell me what you've got," the captain started, getting straight to the point.

"Not much more than yesterday," Stephanie said. "Except, I discovered Hobart has cancer."

"*Cancer!*" the captain wheezed, his voice filled with surprise, rising to a level of excitement Stephanie had not seen in him before. "*When* did you find this out?" he asked.

"Just yesterday, Captain, late in the afternoon."

"How does this affect the case?"

"It really doesn't," Stephanie answered, before Dave could say anything.

"I would think it would have a big impact on the case," the captain said frowning.

"Not really," Stephanie said. "We know Hobart killed Day, and we still think he had something to do with the others, so nothing has really changed."

"Did you find anything yet connecting him with the other deaths?"

"Not yet, Cap. We're having a little trouble finding the connection, but we know it's there," she told him. "Dave talked to Detective Morris yesterday in Florida, and he might have something new for us today."

He turned to Dave. "Something new? You think it might be a link?"

Dave shrugged. "Not sure. He wouldn't say what it was, but we'll know more when he calls back."

"You know Manly is pushing us to make a connection," Martin told them. "So if there is a conspiracy, we need to find it—and quickly. Otherwise, I'd wrap this investigation up *right now*."

"We're trying, Captain," Dave said. "We'll know more when we see what they found in Florida."

Stephanie added, "One day it seems like we've exhausted every lead, then the next day there are several new, unresolved, or suspicious elements."

"Does Manly know about the cancer?"

She shook her head. "I doubt it. Not sure that anyone knows."

"Well...find out. See if Hobart's attorney knows," the captain instructed.

"Yes, sir," Stephanie nodded. "We're meeting with both Baker and Manly this afternoon."

"What else do you have, Dave?"

"We've gotten some leads in the other cases, but they've turned out to be dead ends." He paused for a moment. "But things are changing hourly. And we're not sure yet what part the cancer has to do with all of this."

"It still feels like a conspiracy to me," Stephanie interrupted.

Dave agreed. "She's right, Cap. It is beginning to look like more than coincidence."

"So what do you think?" he asked, firmly.

Dave paused again. "We may have to just try Hobart for the Benjamin Day murder and drop the others," he said. "But before we do, I think we should give it some more time."

"Well, we can give it a little more, because Manly wants us to find that connection...but we can't spend a whole lot more time on this, Duncan," Captain Martin bellowed. "If we can't make a connection soon, then there is *no* conspiracy, Manly or no Manly. *Got it, Fox?*" he emphasized, looking over at her.

She nodded. "We understand, Captain."

"Go out and get something done," he said. "Find the connection, or close the file."

The meeting with the captain went well considering the case should have been closed already, and they had little more to tell him, aside from the cancer and the possibility of new evidence in Florida.

"And let me know what happens in your meeting with Manly," he yelled as they closed his door.

Captain Martin knew how much time they had put into the case and Stephanie could see that he was more sympathetic than usual. It helped that they had the suspect in custody and were going to try him for murder, which was solid. The high-profile case had been solved quickly, getting people off his back.

Doug had called while they were in the meeting. He left a message that the new evidence would be of interest to the two of them and to call him back as soon as possible.

"Why don't you call Doug, then head to Baker's on your own, Steph?" Dave suggested. "I've got something I have to do at lunch today."

"You sure you trust me?" she teased. "You got a date for lunch you don't want to tell me about?"

"I'm sure," he smiled. "Nope, just something personal."

She wanted to meet with Baker on Thursday, but he told her he wouldn't be available until Friday morning. "I can handle it."

"Boca Raton Police Department, this is Detective Doug Morris," Stephanie heard the confident voice say at the other end of the line.

"Detective Morris—Detective Fox," Stephanie said.

"Oh, so it's detective now," Doug said, laughing.

"Just teasing you a little."

"So how are things going on the case?" he asked.

"Up and down," she sighed. "I haven't talked to the insurance investigator but did get a state trooper in Pennsylvania, a Lieutenant Cameron. He didn't have much more for us than you did, but he is very interested in the developments in all the cases."

"So are you on your way to Pennsylvania? You're getting to be quite the jetsetter." He laughed.

"No, this one we'll handle from the office for now."

"And how are you? You getting any rest?"

"Some," she said. "Got to spend some quality time with Charlie last night."

"Charlie?" he said. "I didn't think you were seeing anyone." His surprise and embarrassment were evident in his voice.

"I'm not, silly. Charlie is my cat."

"Uh…uh…oh," Doug stuttered.

"Are you jealous, Doug?"

"*No*," he said, defensively. "I'm not jealous. I don't have a jealous bone in my body."

Stephanie laughed. "Uh-huh…come on, Dougie, you can tell me if you're jealous."

"I'm not jealous…really…I'm *not* jealous."

"Jealous of my cat."

Doug snickered. "How long—"

"I've had Charlie for almost ten years," she said, before he finished asking.

"That's quite a while."

"He helps me keep my sanity." Stephanie confided.

"I have a therapist for that," Doug joked.

"Charlie's better than therapy," she said. "Dave said you might have something new for us on the Galivan case. I didn't know you were still investigating."

"Yeah. That's why I called. We're still looking into it because of your visit, and we found something related to the nuts from the scaffolding."

"Well, what is it, Doug? You're driving me nuts waiting. No pun intended." She laughed. "I'm going to need the name of your therapist if you don't tell me soon."

"Okay, Okay—we checked the nuts again, the ones that had loosened and fallen at the site, against some that were loose elsewhere and some that were tight. We removed them from the scaffolding and brought them into the lab. The lab tech found microscopic teeth marks on the ones we bagged up at the scene," Doug explained. "The marks look like they could have been made by a small pair of pliers."

"*On all of them?*" Stephanie asked in a rush of words, barely able to contain her excitement.

"Yep. The lab checked each of them with the electron microscope and found that the small mark on each matched. We couldn't see them with the naked eye. Some were less pronounced than others…but they matched. They appear to have been removed by the same tool. Those marks weren't on the ones we took off of the scaffolding for comparison."

"So that means we were right? It was a homicide and not an accident?" Stephanie said, raising her voice.

"Don't jump to conclusions," Doug said. "We're still evaluating the evidence and what it means—but yes—it does look like the scaffolding was tampered with."

"So you think that someone removed the nuts to make it look like an accident?"

"It looks that way Stephanie," Doug confirmed. "Based on the new evidence, we've reopened the case. We're looking at it as a possible homicide now."

Stephanie was excited by this new revelation, which she felt confirmed Galivan's death was not an accident—that it was definitely murder.

"But who, Doug?" she asked, knowing that he wouldn't have the answer to that question yet. "So many had access to that construction site."

"We don't know," Doug answered. "But we are going to look into it further, and there's one other thing…"

"Something else?"

"Could work out to be something big. Williams was in Hawaii, on the island of Kauai, at the time of Carston's disappearance," he told her.

"*No shit!*" Stephanie blurted out, uncharacteristically."

"No shit," Doug repeated. "We have the Kauai PD working on it right now."

"I'll call Maui," she said. "I was going to talk to them anyway. You sent them a picture?"

"We did. They're going to get back with me as soon as they have something."

"This is great, Doug."

"Don't get your hopes up, Stephanie. That was nine months ago and we can't expect anyone to recognize him after all this time."

Stephanie let out a sigh. "I know," she said. "I'll keep my fingers crossed. What else have you found?"

"That's it, so far. We're checking out Williams's credit card statement, trying to put him in Maui on the day of Carston's accident."

"This is exciting news, Doug!" Stephanie exclaimed.

"I thought you would think so."

"I have to go now, Doug. Have to meet with Hobart's attorney in a few minutes. Did Dave tell you Hobart has cancer?"

"No, he didn't," Doug said. "When did you find this out?"

"I'll tell you later, gotta run. Call me with any new developments…okay?"

"Sure will, Stephanie. It was nice talking with you again," Doug added.

"You, too. Bye, Doug."

Stephanie hung up, barely hearing what Doug was saying as the receiver cradled. She was eager to meet with Tony Baker, hoping he might be able to provide some additional information she could work with.

Before she headed to Baker's office, she left a message for Lieutenant Cameron in Pennsylvania, letting him know what Detective Morris found in Boca Raton and asking if he found anything new in his investigation. Stephanie rushed out the door and headed toward the motor pool.

Things were beginning to heat up, and she was right in the middle of the fire.

35

Baker's office was in the court building, one floor above Manly's. It was much smaller than Manly's. He sat behind an old metal desk in a high-backed chair with one slightly worn arm. There was barely room for the two wooden chairs in front of the desk for visitors.

On the stark, aged beige walls hung three framed items, one in dire need of straightening: a picture of JFK, Baker's Trial Lawyers Association certificate, and an award for something Stephanie had never heard of.

In the corner stood an old four-drawer metal file cabinet, the gray paint chipped and scratched—the second handle from the top, significantly bent, probably from being moved far too many times.

Stephanie couldn't believe how poor the lighting was in Baker's tiny office. One of the fluorescent lights surged on and off creating the effect of a weak strobe light. It was a simple matter of replacing the ballast, but no doubt, Baker's work order was at the bottom of some pile, in some state office.

He greeted her as she came through the door. "Nice to see you, Detective Fox."

Stephanie stood behind one of the hard wooden chairs, as he fiddled with the folders on his desk, trying to tidy up a bit.

"Please have a seat," he said, pointing to the two chairs in front of Stephanie. "What can I do for you?"

Stephanie and Dave had spoken to Baker a couple of times, but had not been to his tiny office. He seemed much calmer today than he had in their two previous meetings. She knew he was relatively new to the public defender's office and could tell that he was overwhelmed with this case, evidenced by his nervous shuffling of the folders on his desk.

Stephanie sat down and got right to the point. "Did you know that your client has cancer?" She studied his face looking for a reaction.

"I do," Baker answered quietly, after staring at Stephanie for a long moment. "How do *you* know that?"

"I found out from his doctors," Stephanie informed him. "Why didn't you tell us you knew, Tony?"

"I just found out!" Baker exclaimed. "Besides," he snapped, "there is a thing called attorney/client privilege, you know."

"*You just found out?*" She let the surprise show in her voice. "When?"

"Phillip told me night before last," he said. "You know, I *don't* have to tell you this, and if you didn't know about the cancer already, we would not be having this conversation."

"Why didn't he tell you before?"

"I don't know, but he might have never told me if it hadn't been for the phone call."

"*What phone call?*" Stephanie asked.

"A call I got—someone offering to pay for Phillip's defense."

"Someone wanted to pay for an attorney? Who?"

"He wouldn't say, but he was very serious," Tony added. "I shouldn't be telling you this. In fact, that's *all* I'm going to say about it."

"Why was he interested in the case? Where was he calling from? Who was he?" she asked.

"I don't know that either, but this part of the conversation has *ended*!"

"Is he calling back?" Stephanie tried again.

Tony ignored her question.

"We need to get your phone records!" Stephanie exclaimed, again reviving her feelings that there might be a conspiracy. "When did you get these calls?"

"That won't happen," he said "You know that. I—"

A colleague of Tony's popped his head into the office at that moment.

"Tony, sorry to interrupt, but could I have just a moment of your time?"

"Sure. Excuse me for a second, Detective Fox," tony said.

The young attorney turned to Stephanie. "This will just take a moment." He smiled, apologetically.

"No problem," she smiled, as Tony got up to go out into the hallway. "Mind if I borrow a piece of paper? I left my notebook back at the squad."

"Sure, go ahead."

Stephanie leaned forward to grab Tony's pad and pen. She scribbled a note for herself. It was a simple note, written in the middle of a big legal pad. She tore it off and shoved it into the folder she brought with her.

Tony returned, and Stephanie again approached him for the phone number, but he was steadfast in his refusal to give her any more information regarding the call. She found out what she came for. Tony Baker knew about the cancer. Now she needed to find out if anyone else knew.

Stephanie thanked Tony and left his office at a hurried pace. She had renewed enthusiasm from the information she received from Doug, and the new information she just received, inadvertently, from the public defender. The search for accomplices was again in full motion.

Thoughts raced through her head as she got closer to the station. Anyone willing to pay for Hobart's legal costs must be involved in the conspiracy, she thought—maybe even the mastermind.

Stephanie reached for the folder in the passenger seat and pulled out her note, held it up, and stared at it almost trance-like. She glanced at the simple statement on the paper and read it slowly, aloud—"Get Phone Records." With the page backlit in front of her, she noticed the ghostly impressions above her scribbled words. One was partially covered by the pencil, but was still discernible.

"*Yes*," she screamed in jubilation.

36

Dave's stomach churned at Manly's obnoxiousness. It took him one minute and forty-two seconds to hit on Stephanie this time. Dave had set his watch to time and record the event.

"So, Detective Fox, are you available this evening?" he said, wearing a weird grin, one that Dave couldn't quite describe. "Do you have time this evening to meet and go over what you have?"

"I don't think so, I have plans," she said.

A sleazy sparkle entered Manly's eye. "What could be more important than meeting with me, going over a few things, and helping your career?" he said. "Maybe over a vintage glass of wine?"

"I'm not fond of vintage glass," she joked.

"Then we'll drink it right out of the bottle. You sure you wouldn't want to join me?"

"I don't think you *really* want to hear the answer."

His faced dropped a little and he mumbled, "Well, perhaps tomorrow night?"

"Perhaps," she said, ready to move on to business.

He perked up, ready to see what they brought him. "Okay, what have we got?"

Dave stopped the watch at 1:42, which might even be a new record for Manly. He would have preferred Stephanie walking out on the pervert; however, it was good to see she was finally tiring of his innuendos. They had to tell the assistant DA about Hobart's cancer. Stephanie handled the verbal fencing with Manly well.

"We have some new developments in the case," Stephanie spoke up.

"That's good. Let's hear them."

Stephanie looked straight at Manly and began with the most important. "Hobart has cancer," she said, stoic, absent of emotion.

"*Cancer?*" he shrieked. "Where'd you hear that?"

Stephanie explained only what she and Dave had discussed.

"You said developments—what else have you got?"

She went on to explain the information she received from Detective Morris, which Dave was also hearing for the first time.

"Cancer?" he repeated, non-chalantly, then quickly shifted. "So you got them to reopen the case in Florida? Nice work."

He didn't seem to be affected by the news of Hobart's cancer, except for his brief surprise. Dave watched Manly's reaction. He seemed more interested in the new discoveries in Boca Raton, than the fact that his prime suspect had cancer and was dying.

"They're just checking out a few things. They may be the pieces we need to make the conspiracy," she added.

"Good. Keep digging. I've got everything set for Hobart's trial, but I would love to break open this conspiracy thing."

Stephanie told Manly that she had another new development, one she had not had time to research yet. Dave had received the high points of this new evidence from Stephanie downstairs. She went on to explain. "We won't know exactly what value it has in this case until I can check out a couple of phone numbers."

Manly seemed even more fervid after absorbing this new information. He turned to Dave. "How do you feel about these new discoveries?"

Dave had remained silent thus far, but was becoming increasingly upset over Manly's reaction, or lack of one. He tried to stay calm. "Definitely interesting developments."

"Do you think we can tie Hobart to a conspiracy?" he asked, visibly excited.

"We won't know until we go through the new evidence," Stephanie said.

"Can't really tell," Dave stated tersely, offering as little to Manly as he could.

"It would be good for the case," Manly stated, directed at both detectives.

Dave glared at him. "How so?"

"A conspiracy is way bigger than just a local homicide," he said. "It's like having a royal flush, instead of a full house."

"So…will you drop the death penalty for Hobart…if there's no conspiracy?" Dave asked.

"*Absolutely not…even if there isn't a conspiracy*," he said, looking right at Dave. "And if there is, think of what it will do for my career to expose the conspiracy."

"*But he has cancer*! He will *never* make it to the chair anyway," Dave yelled. "Surely you *don't* intend to go through with it if he has cancer?"

"But I have my career to think about," Manly repeated. "And he's going to die anyway." His voice cold—callous

"The hell with your career!" Dave said angrily. "What kind of animal are you?" Dave surprised himself. He had never felt this much passion about a case, or a suspect before.

"If I don't think of my career," Manly said, further angering Dave, "who else will? I may never get an opportunity like this again."

"Should we continue to look for a connection?" Stephanie interrupted.

Manly turned his attention to Stephanie. "Yes—*absolutely*—go ahead and pursue the investigation, in Florida, Pennsylvania, and the new one. And keep me informed."

"Okay," Stephanie said. "We'll let you know what we find out."

Stephanie grabbed Dave's arm. He thought about wrenching it away as he felt her grip tighten, but allowed her to guide him out of Manly's office.

Stephanie rolled her eyes. "Can you believe him?"

"I *can't* believe him, Steph. He has no conscience."

"How long did it take him?" she asked.

"How long for what?" Dave asked, his rage still simmering.

"How long before he asked me to meet him?" she smiled. "I saw you time him with your watch."

"Oh...I thought you meant how insensitive he was about Hobart's condition. He still wants to go for the death penalty, can you believe it?" Dave slowed and shot a glance at her. "You saw that?"

"Yeah...I did," she said, laughing.

Dave looked at his watch. "A minute forty-two seconds."

"A minute forty-two?"

"Yep. But what about Hobart?"

"It seemed a lot shorter than that!" she exclaimed. "What about Hobart?"

"I don't believe Manly *still* wants to ask for the death penalty after what we told him."

"Hobart did commit cold-blooded, pre-meditated murder," Stephanie said.

"Yeah, but Steph, you have to admit, there were mitigating circumstances."

"I know," she said, placing a hand on Dave's forearm, "but we can't let the guy go because he has cancer. It's the law that keeps us from anarchy. It's a *very* thin line, I must admit."

He smiled. "You learn that in college?"

"Anyway, I think Manly is just blowing smoke. I don't think he'll really ask for the death penalty," she assured him, as she opened the door to her car.

This was a complete role reversal, Dave thought. He was now the compassionate one and all signs of compassion for Hobart had vanished from Stephanie. It was probably because this was her first big bust, and, though she didn't want to see Hobart get the death penalty, she did want to see him convicted.

She's right, but it doesn't stop my pain for Hobart.

37

Stephanie held up the sheet she'd taken from Baker's pad to the afternoon light. Her pulse quickened as it had earlier, when she made this incredible discovery on her way back to the station.

Tony was more curious about the mysterious caller than he let on.

There were two numbers—impressions—on the page. "4-1-5—5-5-5—4-3-4-2," she read. Then, 4-1-5—9-4-4—0-1-7-1." Two different numbers. She could not believe her good fortune. Dave's phone call asking her to meet him at Manly's forced her to put her excitement on hold—difficult to do when she was only two blocks from the station.

Stephanie's hands began to sweat as she pulled out the white pages and turned to the section in front with the area codes. She had beaten Dave back and was eager to find out where the calls came from. The customer guide had the area codes listed numerically and she found the 415 listing. It was the code for the San Francisco area.

"San Francisco," she mused. "Why not Houston, or Florida?" she said aloud. Picking up the phone, she dialed directory assistance.

Dave walked in and approached her as she hung up the phone. "Sounds like you did a lot while I was at lunch."

"I did," she nodded. "I'll fill you in after I make this call to California. This could be big."

Her heart raced as she picked up the phone to next dial the San Francisco Police Department. She really felt this was the one lead that would tie the conspiracy together.

"San Francisco Police Department, Homicide Division."

Dave turned and went and sat down at his desk.

"Hello, this is Detective Fox from the Houston PD."

Stephanie explained their case to the detective and laid out her theory of a conspiracy.

"You think someone from San Francisco is involved?"

"I have two phone numbers from your area, made by an anonymous caller, offering to pay for our suspect's legal fees."

"How do you think he fits into your puzzle?" the detective asked.

"We feel that he may be responsible for coordinating the conspiracy," Stephanie explained.

"You said you had two different numbers?"

"Yes, two. Both in the 415 area code. Do you think you could track them down for us since they're in your jurisdiction?"

"Sounds like you might have something. Let me have the numbers, and we'll look into it for you."

Stephanie's voice softened, but did not completely conceal her excitement. "Thanks," she said, after giving him both numbers. "You'll call me as soon as you get anything?"

"Will do. I'll handle this myself and get back to you."

She was energized by his enthusiastic assistance and the possibility of finding something bigger than just a murder. She busied herself straightening up her desk and putting things back in the proper files.

As she waited, she thought about Dave and the secrecy of his lunch today. She was beginning to feel closer to him and was concerned that he was not yet comfortable enough with her to share his problems.

Her thoughts were broken by the loud ring. It wasn't the call she was expecting; it was Lieutenant Cameron.

Stephanie explained to Lieutenant Cameron what they found in Florida and asked if his investigators had turned up anything new in their case.

"We're going over things again because of your inquiries," he informed her, "but it's going slowly because it isn't a priority. The lab hasn't found anything out of the ordinary so far, but they're at least looking," he continued. "The information from Florida might speed up their investigation a little."

"You'll call me right away if you find anything, won't you?" she asked the lieutenant.

"You'll be the first on my list," he assured her.

"All right," she said. "Thanks, Lieutenant Cameron. I'll be talking to you soon."

Like a cat in heat, she paced the squad room. She decided to go over and give Dave the 4-1-1 to bring him up to date.

"—and Doug found out that Williams was in Hawaii at the time Carston disappeared," she concluded.

He smiled. "Very interesting developments."

She fully explained the phone numbers and the offer to pay for Hobart's legal fees. Stephanie showed him the paper with the two numbers.

Dave took it from her and set it on his desk. A blank stare washed over him. After a moment he read aloud, "get phone records." He looked up at Stephanie, a perplexed look on his face.

"Hold it up to the window," she instructed.

"You little sneak," he scolded.

"I couldn't believe it when I saw them," she said, shaking her head.

"It looks like Baker wanted to know, too," Dave stated. "He wouldn't give you the numbers, though?"

"Nope, claimed attorney/client privilege."

"This may not have fallen under that, but he was better off playing it safe, and he protected himself," Dave added. "It doesn't matter. You got them, anyway. You got lucky." Dave grinned.

"I've already got the San Francisco PD working on it. They should have something for us later."

Dave seemed proud of her, and this made her feel good. She had done well the first time he had trusted her on her own.

"Did you get everything done?" she asked, concerned.

"What I could," was his short answer.

"Was it something you can share?"

"Not right now, Steph. Maybe I can tell you a little later, but not now."

"Well, I just want you to know you can talk to me."

Dave was caught off-guard. "Thanks for your concern, Steph. We still have a lot to do, so let's get to work."

She wouldn't push Dave any further, but was glad she let him know she was there. And he was right. They did have a lot of work to do. *This case was not over yet.*

38

The afternoon moved slowly.

After the phone call from Doug, the information from Baker, and the meeting with Manly, it was difficult to get back to the task of going through old evidence. Stephanie was anxious to get the information from the San Francisco PD. They should be calling soon, she thought, and was certain they would provide the information that would lead to the perpetrators of the conspiracy. She was already preparing mentally for a trip to San Francisco.

She busied herself with the lists and again drew blanks, though she really wasn't looking all that hard. There were no calls between Williams, Hobart, or Porter during the period surrounding Digást's death; and none to Philadelphia while Porter was visiting his parents. There were calls to Philadelphia before and after Digást's death, but they were all from Porter to his parents.

"Calls to Philadelphia, before and after Digást's crash," Stephanie said aloud. "I wonder what Porter was doing in July?"

The information Porter gave, regarding being at his parents at the time of Galivan's death, checked out. His dad was indeed ill, and Porter had flown up to help his mother take care of him. He was there for two weeks, just as he said. She found Porter's credit card statements and looked for any July charges. There were two charges for airline tickets in July. They *definitely* needed to be checked out.

Before she could dial the number to the airline, a call came in from Lieutenant Cameron. He had some new information he thought might interest her. She put it on speaker-phone and motioned Dave over to hear what he had to say.

"The lab found a tracking device attached to the frame of Digást's smashed-up Porsche."

"When?"

"They found it about an hour ago," the lieutenant confirmed.

"So you think someone was tracking him?"

"Not just *someone*," he said. "These people had state-of-the-art equipment!"

"Who would have that kind of equipment? And why would someone be tracking Digást?"

"We don't have a clue," he told Stephanie. "CIA—FBI—SEC, we really don't know. It was badly burned, and all the identifying marks and serial numbers were filed off. Whoever planted this transmitter, did not want it traced back to them."

"Any way of finding out who wanted to know what he was doing, and where he was going?" she asked.

"I doubt it," he said. "We're talking ultra high-tech stuff here. We'll look into it a little further, but honestly, we can't spend too much time or resources on this right now. If it was one of the big boys, we would be chasing a specter, I'm afraid."

"So you've reopened the case?"

"Not officially, *and won't*, based solely on this bit of evidence. I requested this because of your interest and the other deaths," the lieutenant told her. "If we get something else substantial, we might."

"I realize that," Stephanie said. "If you do find anything more, you will let me know *immediately*?"

"Sure will, Detective Fox."

Stephanie hung up the phone and turned to Dave.

"So they won't open the case unless they find more in this *unofficial* search."

"It is an interesting bit of information," Dave offered. "Why would someone be tracking a white-collar criminal?"

"Another suspicious piece of the puzzle that leads nowhere," she sighed. "I wonder if there is anything we missed in the Digást investigation?" She paused, as if organizing her thoughts. "I should call that investigator from Fleetwood Life and Casualty, and let him know what Cameron found."

"Yeah, he should know."

"Could you call the airline and get Porter's flights and dates of arrival and departure for me? I wrote down the number and credit card information here." She handed Dave the slip of paper.

"I can do that," he smiled. "What are you going to do next?"

"I'm going to check his credit card statements for other charges surrounding Digást's death."

She paused and watched Dave walk back to his desk, slip of paper in hand.

"Dave, would either of them have access to state-of-the-art electronics?"

Shaking his head. "I doubt it, Steph…if they did, it wouldn't be on a credit card."

Stephanie returned to the statements scanning for charges that might make Porter a suspect. After a few minutes, she realized that there was nothing—not a single charge that might connect Porter to Coudersport.

Dave had made the call and returned to inform Stephanie. "They were both round-trip tickets to Philadelphia. Looks like he went to his parents," Dave added.

"I guess that's another dead end. You feel like Hawaii?" Stephanie asked.

She had not been able to look at the circumstances in Hawaii yet. Given the new discoveries, she wanted to search for connections there.

"You think the captain would approve a few days in Hawaii?" she said jokingly, as she handed him the Hawaii file.

Dave laughed, looking over at Stephanie. "Not a chance."

"Maybe I could get Manly to approve it," she said, winking at Dave. "I could promise him pictures of me in my most revealing bikini, on the beach in Maui."

* * * *

Dave laughed at the thought of bribing Manly. But he also thought he wouldn't mind seeing Stephanie in a bikini, especially her *most revealing* one. Maybe Hawaii was a good idea.

"You could ask," Dave said. "We could use a couple of days in paradise."

She nodded. "We sure could."

Dave returned to his desk to get to work, while Stephanie waited anxiously for a case changing call from San Francisco.

Stephen Carston, the chief financial officer of EnergyDyn, mysteriously disappeared during a day of snorkeling, while on vacation in Hawaii. Dave learned that Carston had been accused of being the mastermind of the shell-trading companies at EnergyDyn, which helped falsely bolster profits and helped the EnergyDyn stocks climb in value. He disappeared in January, less than two months after EnergyDyn filed bankruptcy.

The circumstances were more suspicious in this case than in the others. There was no body. It was called an accidental drowning based on witness testimony that he was seen entering the water, but never returned. They assumed that he drowned out near the end of the point and the currents took him out to sea.

Carston was the first of the three accidents. Would there be more to follow? For the first time, Dave thought they might be working under a timeline.

"Dave, if these cases are actually murders and not accidents, you think there could be more?" Stephanie interrupted.

"It's definitely a concern," Dave confided. "If it is a conspiracy we could be seeing more victims."

"Then we'd better find the conspirators and end this thing before it gets out of hand."

Dave went back to the Hawaii incident. He got in touch with a detective at the Maui Police Department, and they discussed the investigation. The detective agreed to fax Dave the police report and other pertinent information that he could review. He looked up at Stephanie after he finished the conversation. "The Maui detective on the case said there were still suspicions centered around the drowning."

"What kind of suspicions?" she asked.

"They've discussed two possibilities," he explained. "Number one, that Carston faked his death, to avoid prosecution. And two, that he was eliminated so that he couldn't testify."

"You mean a professional hit? Did they pursue both possibilities?"

"Both," he said, "but they dismissed them for what seemed to be good reasons."

"Let's hear 'em."

Dave leaned back in his chair. "They said he has not been sighted since his disappearance: not at airports, cruise lines, or any of the marinas on any of the islands."

He went on to explain that no money was moved from any of his bank accounts for months prior to the government freezing his funds, and he has no access to it now. So they determined that the faked death probability was a dead end.

"Of course, he could have had money in a Swiss bank account or in the Caymans," Dave interjected.

"Hmmmm," Stephanie mumbled. "How would they check?"

"Not sure," Dave answered. "Never had that come up. The Treasury Department had surely found any accounts and froze them along with the others."

"Why didn't they pursue the 'hit' theory?"

"They said that there wasn't any evidence to suggest foul play," he said, "so they haven't ruled it out completely, but they have nothing to go on."

"The detective told me they conducted the normal search in a drowning case and had divers from the Maui Fire Department's Search and Rescue Division search the entire point and reef areas where Carston started his dive. They searched for two days, but didn't find a single piece of evidence," he added, "and called off the search, as they would in any missing persons investigation."

Dave knew this made sense, but it still bothered him that there was no body. Despite their explanation of the body being carried off by ocean currents—and that the currents were strong enough there to take a body—he thought it would have washed up somewhere on one of the islands by now.

As Dave was mulling over the possibilities of Hawaii, the phone rang on Stephanie's desk. She hurried to her desk and picked it up on the third ring. It was the call she was waiting for—from San Francisco.

It was around 6:10 p.m. She started speaking quietly at first.

Dave could tell, watching Stephanie's expressions and hearing part of the conversation, that it wasn't what she wanted to hear. Her voice elevated.

"Oh yeah," he heard her say. "From two different pay phones? Well, did you get any fingerprints? You don't think so?"

There was a long pause, and Dave could see that Stephanie was listening intently.

"Yes—yes, you could be right. Okay, sure, I'll call if we get any new developments on our end."

Stephanie hung up the phone, disappointment on her face. It was easy for Dave to see the investigation hadn't turned up what she had expected.

"Well, Steph, what did they find out?"

"The caller called from two different pay phones," she told Dave. "One in —"

The phone rang on Stephanie's desk before she could finish explaining to Dave. She answered it on the first ring.

"Detective Fox. Yeah, Dave's still here, too. Looks like we may be working late tonight. I know," she said. "It's after 7:00 there, isn't it? What are you still doing there? Really?" Her voice trailed off.

Dave watched Stephanie as Doug was giving her details of their investigation. He could see Stephanie's face and saw her shake her head several times. It didn't look too promising. When she hung up, she threw her head back, hands behind her head, and stared at the ceiling.

Dave approached and leaned a hip on her desk. "Well?"

"Not good," she managed. "They can't go any further with the nuts. It looks like another dead end."

"What'd they find?" he asked.

"They can't determine the tool, so they have no way of tracking it down. They suspect it was homemade."

"What else?"

"The Kauai PD told Doug that the hotel recognized Williams and that he was with his family the whole time," she frowned. "They're faxing his hotel bill."

"Well, at least they knew him. What about Maui?"

"He didn't have any charges in Maui, and he didn't rent any boats, or book any tours to Maui. Hell, he didn't even rent a kayak while he was there," she laughed.

Dave looked at her, not sure she could take any more negative information.

She threw her arms up in the air. "Damn, everything is falling apart."

"What about San Francisco?" Dave asked. "You said one—"

"Oh, yeah, this is good, *too*. One number is in Sausalito, wherever that is. And one in Daly City, which is south of Sausalito," she frowned. "They say that they are on opposite ends of San Francisco, about 40 miles apart."

"What else did they say?" Dave asked.

"I asked them about dusting for prints. They said they didn't feel it was necessary."

"Did they say why?" Dave asked, fairly sure what the answer would be.

"They said that anyone careful enough to call from two different pay phones—that far apart—would not leave fingerprints. And they didn't have time to go through the hundreds of prints they might find on the two phones and booths."

"So I guess our conspiracy theory has again hit a dead end."

"I guess so," she said, unable to hide her disappointment. "I really thought this might lead us to bigger fish. This looked really promising." Stephanie stood, picked up a folder and threw it on top of the pile. Papers scattered everywhere. Dave had never seen this kind of temperament from Stephanie in the four months they had worked together.

"Another long day with nothing to show for it," Stephanie said, not looking up. "We now have theory, with no conspiracy."

"There are days like that," Dave said, trying to ease her frustration. "In fact, too many of them."

"I'm ready to wrap it up, Dave. How about you? There's *no* urgency on this case now," she said, finally admitting that they may have reached the end. "Our search for connections and accomplices appears to be over."

"It looks that way," Dave agreed. His gut instinct was right.

He had wanted to close the case right after arresting Hobart, and before South Beach, but he kept that to himself. "What are you doing tonight?"

"No plans tonight," she admitted, almost complaining. "Kinda thought I'd be here working on the case putting together all these pieces." She shrugged.

"But you told Manly you had plans."

She rolled her eyes. "I told him that to get him off my case. Duh."

Dave laughed, realizing his error. "I'm heading over to The Beat. Buy you a drink?"

"I could use one tonight," Stephanie said. "Besides, it's Friday, and we have the whole weekend off."

"So is that a 'yes'?"

"Yes. Why not?" she said. "It's been a while since I've let my hair down."

"Great, I'll introduce you to a couple of the guys," he said, trying to hide any excitement in his voice.

Dave had already been ribbed plenty by the guys at The Beat since being partnered with Stephanie. None of them had ever seen her, but they had heard about her. Dave couldn't begin to count the number of times he'd been asked if he'd slept with his partner yet.

The more he knew Stephanie the less he appreciated the remarks. Sure, it was fun at first. He enjoyed all the attention, but after getting to know Stephanie, he'd gained respect for her. Especially since they started this case.

The ribbing no longer seemed appropriate—maybe even inappropriate. Dave felt things would change after they met her.

"Great," he said again, "You know where it is?"

"Yep," she said. "Been by there a few times, but never stopped in."

"Okay, I'm heading over now. First drink's on me."

39

*A*n ashen haze greeted Stephanie as she swung the door open and walked into the crowded, exiguous police bar. A rancid, stale odor, from years of spilled drinks, smoke, cheap cologne, and sweaty bodies hung in the air.

Everything stopped when she entered. All eyes were on her, as she walked, confidently and gracefully through the scattered tables to the one where Dave was seated.

The Beat was a typical cop bar. Smoke filled, with dark wood, old mirrors, 50¢ pool tables, neon beer signs, and thick wooden tables with heavy wooden chairs. Texas was not a nonsmoking state, and patrons still smoked in bars and restaurants. Stephanie, a non-smoker, couldn't understand why they didn't change the law, and that was one of the reasons she rarely went to bars. She did not appreciate her clothes and hair reeking of smoke when she got home. But, tonight she was here to have a drink with Dave and meet some of the other officers. She decided she could tolerate it for one night.

The bar was owned by a retired cop—a longtime detective—Lieutenant Jack Fletcher. Jack had purchased the bar from another retired cop. He was a 25 year veteran of the Houston Police Department, and a friend of Dave's for nearly 20 years.

Dave was sitting at a table near the back of the bar with three other guys.

Stephanie maneuvered her way to their location.

"This is my partner, Stephanie Fox," Dave said, standing up to introduce her as she neared the table.

"Tom Barnhart," one of the detectives introduced himself, almost falling over his chair as he jumped up to shake Stephanie's hand.

Tom reached out to shake Stephanie's hand. He was the youngest of the three, maybe in his late thirties, she guessed. She also knew Tom was the detective from the 9th Precinct.

"Obviously...Tom Barnhart," Dave said, smiling. "And this is Paul Robertson and this one...this one is Rafael Martinez-De La Rosa," Dave pointed to the other two detectives from the 4th Precinct, "but we call him Rafe. He's the most anglicized Mexican I know," Dave smiled. "Paul and Rafe are partners."

Stephanie extracted her hand from Tom's, looked over at Paul and Rafe, gave them a big smile, and reached out to shake their hands.

"Paul and I worked together at the 8th Precinct years ago," Dave told her. "They assisted us last week with the interviews of the individuals on the investor list."

"Great work—using the list to find this guy," Robertson said to Stephanie.

"Thanks," Stephanie said, a little embarrassed. "It was really Dave's idea."

"Is that so? You expect us to believe he came up with a plan that good?" Paul joked. "He never was that sharp when we worked together. You must bring out the best in him." Paul winked.

"No, *really*...he did," she said, trying hard to convince the disbelievers.

Tom, still standing, grabbed a chair from the next table for Stephanie. "Have a seat," he said, sliding the chair between himself and Dave.

"Thank you, Tom," she smiled. "Such a gentleman."

Tom blushed, turning a few shades of red.

"How many had you interviewed when you got the call that we had a suspect in custody?" she asked, turning back to Paul and Rafe.

"Everyone in Houston, I think." Paul ssaid, looking at Rafe.

"Yeah, it felt like it," Rafe said laughing. "I am definitely getting too old for this shit. Seriously...I think it was 45 or 46," Rafe confirmed.

"And you decided that it was someone in or close to Houston?" Paul asked.

"Wasn't sure, but we had to start somewhere. Then, Kevin called all the rental car companies and found out that none of them had cars with Goodyear Eagle Radials. So I figured it had to be someone local."

"And the class," Dave announced proudly.

"Yes, I took a class in geographical profiling in the Criminology program at Plano," she explained.

"That's what made you think it was someone here in Houston?" Paul asked.

"Not entirely. Most of the evidence we collected indicated it might be someone with a personal grudge," she explained. "And it had the appearance of someone working in his comfort zone—someone who knew the neighborhood and the escape routes."

"Interesting," Tom said, his gaze fixed on Stephanie's eyes.

"We would have used the computer to break it down further, had there been more criteria, such as multiple murders," she added. "It's really useful for profiling serial killers—a tool for identifying their comfort zones and habits." She beamed, seeing that they were all interested in what she was explaining.

"Why didn't you use the computer for this one?" Tom asked.

"I did use the computer, but not in the same way. I was able to break down the list of investors using zip codes and size of investment. There really wasn't a pattern we could set up in the computer to narrow the killer's zone. That's why we asked everyone to follow the same criteria—largest investors to smaller investors, closest to the area, working their way outward."

"Well, it definitely worked," Paul said, nodding at Dave.

"Yes, it did," Stephanie said, pride in her voice.

Stephanie noticed she was the only female in the bar. She was sure this was probably the case many nights here. But this was Friday night. *Do all the female cops have dates tonight?* "I'm the only female in the bar," she stated.

"You know, you're right," Tom confirmed, looking around as if he hadn't noticed before.

"Do women ever come in here?" she asked, teasing the guys.

"Sure—" "Uh-huh—" "Of course," they all said at the same time.

"A lot of women officers come in," Paul told her. "A few will probably be in later. There just aren't any here right now."

She knew that several of the female officers and the female detectives drank at The Beat, but she wanted to see if she could get a rise out of the guys. It was important that she start things off here on her terms, so making them a little uneasy was a good start.

"How's the case going?" Tom asked.

"Well," Stephanie paused. "we've got Hobart for the murder of Benjamin Day, but we can't find any connection to the other deaths, despite all the new pieces of evidence we're receiving. I'm sure Dave told you that already."

"I wonder how Lou Dobbs is going to score this one on his EnergyDyn scoreboard," Rafe broke in. "He's going to have to create a whole new category. Maybe two," he laughed.

No one else laughed. They were not familiar with Rafe's reference to *Lou Dobb's Moneyline*, and the scoreboard created to track the convictions of the executives—predators—who were responsible for EnergyDyn's collapse.

"One could be 'executives murdered, and the other—',"

He stopped in mid-sentence, realizing none of them knew what he was babbling about. "No one here watches *Moneyline*?" he asked, looking at their blank expressions.

"I guess not," he said to himself.

Paul moved the conversation back to the investigation. "Dave told us about Florida, Hobart's cancer, and all that new stuff in San Francisco."

"Yeah, what a coincidence that Hobart was in Florida at the same time as the death of this Galivan guy. And finding out yesterday that the scaffolding had been tampered with," Tom added.

"But that's just what Galivan's death may end up being, despite the new evidence—merely coincidental," Stephanie stated. "And, as far as San Francisco…"

"A little disappointing?" Paul asked.

"It sure is!" Stephanie frowned, taking a moment to organize her feelings. "I really thought Hobart was involved in Digást's death, but there was nothing connecting him to Pennsylvania. Then they find a tracking device—a transponder, in Digást's Porsche, that could have been placed by CIA, FBI, or SEC, or maybe AARP," she laughed. "And it probably has nothing to do with our case."

"We were talking, before you got here, about the odds of four executives from bankrupt corporations having accidents less than nine months apart, and how unlikely it seems that they could be merely coincidences," Tom said.

"Too much of a coincidence," Stephanie said. "One of the lab techs ran the numbers. You know what the odds were? Once in every 7.879 million years."

"Are you kidding?" Tom gasped.

"Based on those odds, our theory was way more likely. I really thought we had found the connection to the conspiracy when we found out about San Francisco."

"Someone from San Francisco *really* offered to pay for one of the best criminal attorneys in the country?" Paul asked.

"According to Tony Baker they did, but the San Francisco PD said it wasn't worth pursuing given what little evidence we had."

"So that's already a dead end?" Paul asked.

"It is for now," Stephanie declared. "They won't do anything more unless we come up with some more evidence."

"Dave told us how surprised you were when you found out about the cancer," Tom stated.

"It was a *big surprise*! No one knew. Baker didn't even know about it until Wednesday night."

"*He didn't even tell his attorney?*" Tom asked.

Dave shook his head. "That's why he never asked for an attorney when we arrested him," he interjected. "He thought he was going to die before it ever got to trial."

"Why didn't Baker drag this out?" Paul asked. "He could have gotten a continuance."

"I don't think Hobart would let him. He wanted to go to trial as soon as possible," Stephanie said. "And Manly fell right into it."

"The trial was the only way to get his message heard," Dave added. "If he died after being caugh, and hadn't gone to trial, no one would know why he did it."

Tom smiled. "And now, the state will have to care for him till he dies."

Paul turned to Stephanie. "So how do you think he's involved in the conspiracy?"

"Not really sure he is anymore," she said. "We have had so many changes in this case that it feels like one big roller coaster ride."

"It sounds like it," Paul said. "What else could happen?"

They mulled over the possibilities, all agreeing it was more, much more than just coincidence.

Detective De La Rosa seemed to know a lot about the deaths. "The disappearance of Carston in Hawaii was the first. He was the chief financial officer of EnergyDyn. He disappeared in January, only about two months after the corporation filed bankruptcy."

Rafe and Stephanie continued to discuss the Hawaii disappearance among themselves while the others talked about other things.

Stephanie was interested in Rafe's insights into the case. He explained that Carston was an amateur diver and an adequate swimmer, but he suddenly disappeared while out snorkeling. She listened intently.

"The newspaper article I read said that the rocky point at Ulua Beach goes out in some areas for over a quarter mile," he said. "It's a popular beach between two big hotels in Wailea, and a great place to snorkel. There were a lot of people there that day."

"Have you read anything about Carston faking his own death to avoid prosecution," Stephanie asked.

"I didn't see anything about that," Rafe told Stephanie. "But I did read that all of Carston's accounts were frozen, so if he faked his death, he wouldn't have any money."

"The Maui Police investigated that possibility for over a week before finally calling it an accidental death," she told him. "They said their investigation showed that *no one* saw him during the week after his disappearance."

Rafe told Stephanie he was into stocks. He had been a day

trader for some time. That's why he knew so much about the cases; because he had owned stocks in both EnergyDyn and GlobalNet, at one time or another, before they filed bankruptcy. He was aware of each of the accidents when they occurred, because they were widely covered in the financial community.

"You still day trading?" Stephanie questioned.

"Not anymore," Rafe said. "Not for awhile now."

"Why did you stop?"

"The stock market is not the place to be right now, for starters," he said. "It was too crazy, too involved. You become obsessed with watching the market—a market, you eventually realize, you have very little control over."

"So is that why you quit?"

"No, it was when I realized, as the market started to slide, that most of the professionals didn't know anymore than I did. And in many cases, they were the reason everything in the market was so screwed up."

"So what did you do?"

"I sold almost everything off and quit—cold turkey. And I'm glad now that I did."

"You didn't get hurt too bad then, I take it?"

"Not too bad—except in my 403B," he said. "But didn't everyone?"

Stephanie had just finished her third drink and was ordering her fourth when the 10 o'clock news flashed on the television behind the bar.

She had been there longer than she'd planned, but found herself having fun shooting the bull with Dave and the guys. Though she was drinking more than she wanted to, it had been a long time since she could remember having this much fun. What the hell, she thought, tomorrow's Saturday and I have absolutely nothing to do. She was just thinking how glad she was that she took Dave up on his offer—when something stopped her in mid-thought.

"Ex-CEO of TriCorp, Eugene Wimkowski," she heard the news anchor say, "died today. The 65 year old executive was found dead in his home in the Hamptons at approximately 9:00 a.m. this morning."

"Turn that up!" Stephanie yelled to Jack behind the bar. "Dave, did you hear that?"

Dave turned to see the television.

The reporter continued, "Wimkowski had apparently slipped and fallen in the shower, hitting his head—the fall—the preliminary cause of death."

Stephanie stood shaking her head. "I don't believe this."

"He had been dead for approximately eight to ten hours, according to the Suffolk County medical examiner, when he was discovered by the maid on Friday morning. The Southampton Police Department is calling it an apparent accidental death, citing no evidence of robbery, breaking and entering, or struggle of any kind."

The news anchor went on to explain that Mr. Wimkowski was free on $10 million bail, after being under indictment for tax evasion by the New York attorney general. He was also under investigation for wire and securities fraud by the Securities and Exchange Commission.

Stephanie glanced at Dave. Her eyes caught his. He had the same blank look on his face that she was positive she had, and probably the same thought. *Coincidence*?

Hobart was still a guest of the Houston Police Department, comfortable in a Houston jail. So who did this one?

This was the fifth executive of a bankrupt corporation that had died in just nine months. Benjamin Day was not an accident. They had their suspect, and it was *definitely* a homicide. The three other deaths were still suspicious, and now there was a fourth.

Stephanie felt numb. "I wonder what the odds just went up to?" she asked the group.

Since Hobart didn't do it, who did? Did he work on a plan with someone before he was arrested? There was no evidence of that in anything they had collected, but they weren't looking for anything involving New York, Long Island, or Southampton.

"We'll need to check this one out in the morning, you know?" Stephanie said to Dave, stating fact rather than asking a question.

"I know," Dave said. "Exactly what I wanted to do on my weekend off."

"I'll call Southampton in the morning."

"Okay," Dave nodded. "I will admit, Steph, it gets curiouser and curiouser."

"Yes, it does," she agreed.

Stephanie finished her drink, gave Dave a hug, and thanked him for inviting her. She said good night to Paul, Rafe, and Tom, thanked them for a great evening; and promised that she would definitely be back. "I'll see you bright and early in the morning," she said to Dave, and headed for the door.

On the way home she continued to think about Wimkowski's death and how strange it was that these accidents kept occurring, if in fact they were accidents. Either it was an incredible set of coincidences or something sinister was going on. She recommitted to looking at the accidents for a possible conspiracy, even though it appeared that they might be chasing the wind.

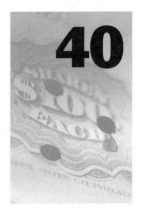

40

"You're sure?"

Dave heard Stephanie's voice as he entered the squad room.

He set his bag down near the door next to Stephanie's. She had called at 1:30 in the morning to let him know that they were going to be flying to New York that morning and to pack a bag for at least two days. He wasn't sure this was such a good idea.

It was now almost 7:45, and Stephanie had been hard at work, for more than an hour, gathering the files she thought they would need in Southampton.

"Would you mind getting his phone records for me anyway?" There was a short pause. "Humor me," she said. "Great—thanks Detective Taylor. We'll see you this evening."

"Good morning, Dave," Stephanie greeted him cheerfully as she hung up the phone.

Their conversations seemed to start this way every morning—Stephanie hard at work at her desk; Dave, over in the coffee area, getting his first cup of coffee.

"How you feeling?" he asked, looking at Stephanie to see if there were any signs of a hangover.

"A little edge this morning. But not as bad as I expected. I had a good time last night, Dave—thank you," she added, a coquettish smile on her face

"Who was that?"

"That was Aaron Taylor, the lead on the Wimkowski case." She was anxious to tell Dave what she had discovered in her conversation with him. "Detective Taylor told me their preliminary investigation indicated an accident. Wimkowski slipped in the shower in his master bath, hit his head, and died."

"If it was an accident, Stephanie, why are we going to New York?" Dave asked, still groggy from last night.

"Because the medical examiner has some suspicions regarding the cause of death," she told Dave. "I'll explain it to you in a minute."

She turned to her notepad and wrote down a few more things that she'd gotten from the conversation. Dave couldn't help but admire her thoroughness.

"There was no evidence of forced entry, robbery, or foul play," she explained. "But the M.E. is still concerned about the amount of damage the skull sustained from the fall."

"If the M.E. still has suspicions, why did he sign the death certificate?"

"Good question. We'll have to ask him," she continued. "I explained our case to Taylor, told him about our suspicions and about the other deaths."

"What did he say about it?"

"He was definitely interested. Like everyone else, he doesn't believe it can be just coincidence," Stephanie smiled. "Told me we would get their full cooperation."

Dave took a sip of his coffee. "Did the detective say what else they had?"

"He's faxing everything over to me in a few minutes. I've asked him to send Wimkowski's phone records so I can cross-check his calls. I want to see if he received calls from any of the three over the last couple of months."

Dave grinned. "You're getting so good at that."

"Maybe…getting tired of it, though, but someone has to look for Long Island calls."

"How does this one look compared to the other cases?" Dave asked. "Any similarities?"

"Just like the others. From what Detective Taylor told me, it looks like an accident, but it has those nagging, underlying suspicions," she said. "The Southampton Police and the lab are still going through the evidence. We'll have to see what they come up with. But the case that bothers me the most is Hawaii."

"Same here," Dave agreed. "My problem *still*—is the body. You would think a body would have washed up on shore by now." Dave stroked his chin, gathering his thoughts. "That's what I keep coming back to. Where is the body? Search and rescue looked for two full days and found nothing."

"No sign of him. No mask, no snorkel or fins, no trunks, and *no* body parts," Stephanie mused aloud.

"Nope. It still has me baffled," Dave said, answering her quiet observations. "I still have some questions about Florida, also."

"*You do?*" Stephanie asked. "I didn't know that. I thought you were ready to close that case, especially after what Doug told us yesterday."

"I was," he said. "It may not be that important, but I still don't understand why Galivan was out there on the scaffolding by himself, at 6:00 on a Friday night. What would have brought him out there? It's been bothering me since we got back."

"Yep," Stephanie agreed.

"And Johnston-6 on the edge of his day planner may be more important than we suspect. It just doesn't add up."

"I didn't get that either," Stephanie said. "I mean, why was he there on a Friday night when he hadn't been to the site in several days? And now that we know the scaffolding was tampered with, I'm even more skeptical."

"I think you're right. If we could just figure out what got him to the site, we might be able to prove it was a homicide—and not merely an accident."

"That's the missing link," Stephanie agreed.

Dave surprised himself—Wimkowski's death spurred his interest and rekindled his suspicions regarding the other cases. Images of each of the incidents ran through his mind, and he had difficulty sleeping after seeing the newscast. He heard Stephanie's voice and turned his attention back to what she was saying.

"Maybe we should call Doug back and let him know about this new case…if he hasn't already heard," she said.

"It might be worth a try," Dave nodded and headed back over to the coffee pot.

* * * *

Stephanie wondered why Dave hadn't brought up his suspicions about Florida earlier. She again questioned Digást running off the road, a road he'd driven hundreds of times. And Carston, an amateur diver and excellent swimmer, disappearing. Now Wimkowski slips in the shower. The new accident created more questions.

Stephanie picked up the phone and dialed Florida. Before she finished dialing, Dave answered a call. It was Doug. Stephanie waited while they exchanged pleasantries.

"You can tell her, Doug. She's right here."

"Hi, Doug, it's Stephanie. You have some news for me, I hope."

"Yes, but I'm afraid it's not what you want to hear," he said. "We've closed the case again. We couldn't find any evidence that supports, or goes along with the tampering of the scaffolding."

"*Nothing*? Are you sure?" Her frustration grew. "Nothing at all?"

"Not a thing, Stephanie. Sorry," Doug apologized. "We're sure the scaffolding was tampered with, but we can't find *any* evidence that will tell us who, or why."

"*So that's it?*"

"I'm sorry, Stephanie. We've been told that we have to close it...*today*," he added. "Dave says you're on your way to Southampton because there was another accident."

"Yeah, we are. Like the others, there are some questionable elements," she said. "We have to go check them out. It'll only be two days, and then the trial is going to start at the end of the week."

"Well, I'd better let you go...I know you've got a plane to catch. I'll talk to you when you get back. Good luck in Southampton."

"Thanks, Doug. I'll talk to you during the week," she finished. "Oh...and if we find anything, you'll reopen the case, right?"

"You are persistent," he laughed. "We'll see."

Stephanie hung up the phone, disappointed, and not sure how much more time they could devote to these cases, especially after what she had just heard from Doug. She wasn't sure how many resources the Houston Police Department would allow before it cut off the investigation.

The request for travel to New York was already in the works. Stephanie was hoping that Southampton would offer the missing pieces to their frustrating puzzle, and the department had already approved it.

Detective Taylor had sent the forensic report which she would quickly review before heading to the airport. Her gut still told her that there was a connection—something that would link all these deaths, but she was running out of time.

41

"**W**hy couldn't we have gone to Maui to investigate that one?" Dave thought aloud. He caught himself uttering—"here today, gone to Maui." He snickered, suddenly remembering the old cliché. This was clearly evidence that he was getting his sense of humor back. Something that had been missing from his life the last few years.

Stephanie was walking back to her desk with the new information Detective Taylor had faxed to them.

"What are you laughing about?" she asked Dave, glancing up from the papers she was reading.

"It was nothing," Dave said, laughing again.

Captain Martin burst through the door and greeted them in his usual gruff, morning voice.

"Anything new?" he snarled.

"Just what I told you on the phone. We just got the reports from Southampton."

"Another one?" the Captain rhetorically. "How many does this make?"

"What are you doing here on a Saturday morning, Captain?" Dave asked.

"This is number five," Stephanie answered.

"Something about a request to send two detectives to New York. I had to come down to sign some requisitions. I'm supposed to be on vacation. Number five? Hmmmmm."

"How's the fishing?" Dave asked.

"Not bad," he said. He turned to Stephanie. "What's all that?"

"The information from Southampton. They were able to send it over to me already. Isn't technology a wonderful thing?"

"You really think there's a connection here?" Captain Martin asked.

"I do, Captain, even though the proof has been a little elusive, the deaths all fit in the framework of my theory," she nodded.

"What about you, Dave?"

"Can't say for sure yet, Cap, but we'll know more after this trip. I think we've found a pattern in the cases."

"A pattern?"

"A weak one, but definitely similarities," Dave explained, "and one worth looking at."

"Well, check it out, but you can't waste a lot more time on this. These trips are costing the department money," he added. "Most of it comes out of *my* budget."

"We'll run through the investigation fairly quickly," Stephanie said. "We think we know what were looking for."

"What time is your flight?"

"Hour and a half," Stephanie told him. "We're going to go over the evidence before we leave."

"Okay, have a good flight. Keep me informed. We'll meet again on Tuesday morning."

"Why not Monday, Cap? We'll be back in the morning."

"I'm going back up to my cabin and baiting a hook for the next three days," he groused. "Get things up to speed and I'll see you first thing Tuesday morning."

Dave and Stephanie returned to their desks to review the case files and prepare for their trip to the airport.

"All right, Steph, let's take a look at the Southampton stuff together."

"Here's the coroner's report. It indicates Wimkowski apparently died from the head injury sustained in the fall." She read the comments section. "There was no blunt object trauma, but the coroner wrote that the damage to the skull was excessive and not consistent with a normal fall in the shower."

"Looks like the maid found him in the morning," Dave read. "She said the bedroom carpet was wet, and the bathroom was flooded when she went up to the bedroom."

"This report with the drawing shows that he was partially blocking the drain," Stephanie said. "They estimated the body was in the water for nine or ten hours."

Dave glanced up from his paper. "Makes time of death about midnight, doesn't it?"

Stephanie nodded. "Between 11:00 a.m. and midnight."

"Add another similarity," Dave suggested. "He laid there all night...just like Galivan."

"Yep. And Digást went off the road at midnight and was found in the morning also."

Dave could see the wheels turning in Stephanie's head. He thought about how her enthusiasm had brought so many things to light. "Hobart killed Day around eleven."

"Like I said...a definite pattern. Now, if we can find the link."

Dave nodded and looked at the clock. "We'd better get packed up and head to the airport. We can finish this on the flight."

"Okay. One last thing. This report indicates there was no other evidence that would dispute the initial findings," Stephanie said. "The coroner listed cause of death as: 'Accidental Death due to head trauma from fall in shower,' but in the comments section he notes his suspicions."

Dave packed up the papers and reports. "We'll go over that on the plane."

Stephanie stuffed the report in a briefcase along with reports from the other cases.

They grabbed their bags and headed out the door. Another adventure, Dave thought. The flight would be a little over two hours into Atlanta, a quick change of planes, and about two hours and fifteen.......... minutes into JFK in New York. It would give them plenty of time to go through all the preliminary paperwork. Dave agreed with Stephanie. There was a pattern developing. *Stephanie might have been right from the beginning.*

42

*D*ave took out his notebook and dusted it off. He had had to search for it early this morning to bring along on this trip. He found a blank page, pulled out a pen, and prepared to take some notes. "Okay,mpton PD."

Stephanie looked over at Dave. "What is this? What are you doing?" She was shocked when she saw the notebook in his hand.

"I'm writing down information about the case," he told her.

She had not seen him write anything down since starting to work with him four months ago. "I thought you committed everything to memory?" Her eyes fixed on his.

He remembered details very well and included them in his reports, but encouraged her to write down everything relative to each investigation for future reference. "I do, but this case seems to get more complicated every day, so I thought I'd better find the old notebook and use it."

They had been silent up to that point, diligently going through the paperwork they brought; Dave through the old information and Stephanie the new.

Stephanie paused, so Dave spoke up. "Hold that thought," he smiled. "Let's try this first. Galivan on the scaffolding on Friday night."

He wrote on the clean page in his notebook:

Galivan / Scaffold / Alone / Friday Night / Johnston-6 / Nuts

                    5/02
Below that he jotted:
            Hobart / Porter / Williams

"Carston's disappearance and probable drowning in Hawaii," Stephanie said, when he was finishing writing down the names.

He wrote:
Carston / Drowned / Alone / Experienced Swimmer / NO Body
                    1/02
And below:
                Williams

He wrote the NO in capital letters emphasizing his biggest concern in the first accident and most mysterious.

Stephanie continued. "Digást driving off the side of the road, off an embankment into the river. On a road he had driven hundreds of times."

Dave wrote:
        Digást / Auto Accident / Alone / Plunge to River
        Tracking Device / Lapse, Sleep, Alcohol, Suicide?
                    7/02
And:
                Porter
"And now we have Wimkowski," Stephanie said.
        Wimkowski / Fall / Alone / Excess Damage to Skull
                    10/02
Then:
                    ?

As he finished writing, they looked at each other. The list was a powerful visual reminder.

"One element stands out in each of the deaths," she said, her eyes focused on the page.

Dave understood. "What's that?"

"ALONE. Every single one of the victims, including Benjamin Day, were alone at the time of their demise…and there were no witnesses."

"Alone," he repeated. "Now that bothers me. Why not an auto accident at a busy intersection in Pittsburgh, or Galivan falling while the crew was around?" he asked. "And if we add 'between 11:00 p.m. and midnight,' it becomes more than coincidence."

"That is interesting," Stephanie confirmed.

Dave nodded. "Carston is the only one who doesn't fit in that narrow time range. These cases might just be related after all." Up to now, he had to admit that he'd been enjoying Steph's enthusiasm and the fact that he was on a second trip with her in only one week. He stared at the words he'd written on the page. Before, they were just random accidents, but now he saw a pattern. He had to focus, focus on the clues and try to keep his mind off thoughts of his partner. "Now, tell me what else we know about the Wimkowski case."

* * * *

Stephanie's attention was directed at the clouds outside her window as her thoughts raced from one case to the other trying to identify another connection. Dave's question brought her attention back inside the plane.

"What, Dave?"

"I was just saying we should go over the things you got from Detective Taylor."

"Oh, yeah, there were a few other things he told me that aren't in the reports."

She shuffled the papers around and found her notebook and opened it.

"Am I going to need to write this down? I've written about all I can for one day," he joked.

Stephanie laughed. "No, I think you can commit this to memory. Taylor said that Wimkowski had gotten home around 11 p.m., had gotten undressed, and was taking a shower sometime between then and midnight, and apparently fell."

"That was determined by time of death?"

"And something about the alarm system," Stephanie said. "Wimkowski had reset it sometime after getting home. The maid got there around eight the next morning and after hearing the shower running for an hour went up to check on him."

"Did she know he was dead?"

"She told Taylor that she could see the blood in the shower

through the open door."

"What kind of trace do they have?"

"Forensics is running the water they collected through a special sterile pump with state-of-the-art filters, designed to pick up every element that might be evidence," she explained. "Detective Taylor said they had just begun the process while we were on the phone."

"We'll have to see what they find."

"The most important thing, still, is the M.E.'s suspicions about the injury."

The plane was starting its descent into JFK International on Long Island. Stephanie could see the Statue of Liberty on Ellis Island. She had never been to New York. *What an incredible sight.* She wondered how on earth the French could have gotten that huge statue over here in the late 1800s.

The statue, a gift from the French government to the United States, was a marvel in granite and took months to transport from France. Ellis Island was expanded to accommodate Ms. Liberty, with tons of earth from construction of the subway system. The pieces were assembled on the base, using big barges and huge cranes, and has stood as a symbol of freedom for more than 100 years.

Her thoughts then turned to 9/11. She wondered where the Twin Towers would have been in the New York skyline. Stephanie shivered, coming to the sudden realization that she would never have the opportunity to see them.

She packed up the reports and lists, as Dave folded his notebook. The tires screeched as they set down on the runway. She was eager to get started on this new chapter in the investigation.

43

"So this is New York?" Stephanie said, as she and Dave walked up the ramp. She could not believe she was in New York to investigate another case, and that just a week ago the two of them had been in Florida.

Nicole Hill stood at the gate to meet them as they came off the plane. She was Detective Aaron Taylor's partner. "Nicole Hill," she greeted them, reaching out to shake Stephanie's hand. "But Nicky is what I go by."

"Hi, Nicky—Stephanie Fox…and this is my partner Dave Duncan."

"Nice to meet you, Detective Duncan," she said.

"Dave is fine," he said.

"Aaron told me you're trying to connect Wimkowski's death with your case in Houston and a couple of others," Nicole said.

Nicky was a perky, attractive woman, about 30 years old, and just a few inches shorter than Stephanie. Her eyes sparkled, and Stephanie couldn't help but notice her enthusiasm and the friendly warmth in her voice.

"Anything new you can tell us, Nicky…since Aaron faxed us the reports this morning?" Stephanie asked.

"They've retrieved some hair and fibers from the water collection."

"Have they identified them yet?"

"They're just now examining them, and we got a number

of fingerprints," Nicky continued. "Some were the victim's, but they're still running the others to find a match."

"Where are we going first?" Dave asked.

"We'll go back to the station first and you can meet Aaron, then I'll take you to the hotel so you can check in."

"Will we be able to see the crime scene tonight?" Stephanie hoped they'd arrived on time.

"It'll be too late, but we've scheduled that for tomorrow—late morning—as well as seeing the body at the medical examiner's in the afternoon."

"I was hoping we could get started this evening." Though obviously disappointed, Stephanie understood. She was eager, but would have to put her enthusiasm on hold.

"Southampton is about an hour from here," Nicky explained. She stepped onto the moving sidewalk in front of Stephanie, facing backwards, and continued giving details.

"Aaron and I will take you to dinner, and I'll show you some of the Hampton's nightlife. That is, if you're up to it."

"I am," Stephanie said, "but I can't speak for Dave." She laughed. "Think you're up to it?"

"Am I up to it? Is the Pope...?" He laughed.

They made it through baggage claim and headed out to Nicky's car parked at the curb in front of the American Airlines terminal. They were on their way to the Hamptons, the playground of the East Coast rich and famous.

"This is my first time to New York," Stephanie said.

"First time?" Nicky asked, surprised.

"I saw the Statue of Liberty as we came into JFK," Stephanie said. "I'm trying to figure out where the Twin Towers would be."

They were heading west, exiting the airport, and Nicky was able to show them where the towers stood prior to 9/11.

"See that hole beyond the top of those red brick buildings?" Nicky pointed, almost directly in front of them.

"No kidding...in that space *right there*?" Stephanie stared in disbelief at the vast emptiness in the New York skyline. "Are we going to have time to see Ground Zero? I would really like to see it while I'm here."

"I don't think so. When do you leave on Monday?" Nicky asked.

"Pretty early."

Nicky turned to Stephanie. "Probably not, then. We're way out near the end of Long Island, and tomorrow's schedule is pretty tight."

The Belt Parkway, Highway 27, would take them all the way to Southampton—almost at the eastern tip of the island. They would exit at North Sea Road taking them right into Main Street and the heart of Southampton. The weather was, surprisingly, still pleasant for this late in October. It had been awhile since they had such summery weather this far into the fall.

Nicky thought about taking them the scenic route, Highway 27A, but they didn't have time. The trip took them a little over an hour. The sun was fading, and though it was an Indian summer in the Hamptons, a chill was in the air. As they got out of the car in front of the Southampton Police Department, Stephanie could feel it. Though it was pleasant during the day, when the fiery orb descended in the west, there was that touch of dampness that befell northeastern beach towns this time of the year.

At the station, Nicky introduced them to her partner, Aaron Taylor." She had been a detective in Southampton for about two years and had been partnered with Aaron when she arrived.

Stephanie guessed Aaron to be around thirty.

Nicky made all the introductions and, after a short discussion of the case, Aaron suggested that Nicky take them to the hotel and get them checked in.

"Nicky informed you about dinner?" he inquired.

"She did," Stephanie confirmed. "Sounds great to me. I'm starved. It's been a long day, but I'm good to go, and Dave took a nap on the plane," Stephanie teased.

"Great," Aaron said smiling. "It's on the Southampton Police Department tonight. Nicky will take you back to the hotel, let you get checked in, cleaned up, and she'll pick you up about 7:00, if that's okay. My wife will be joining us also," Aaron added. "We'll meet you at the restaurant."

"Perfect," Dave said. "I'm pretty hungry myself."

"It's a short distance from the station to the hotel, and not far to the restaurant. There are some excellent restaurants here," Nicky said, as she drove them to the hotel.

"I'm sure there are," Stephanie replied, remembering Scandals, and the fun they'd had in South Beach. "Probably high priced, too!"

"Not too bad," Nicky told her. "What do you feel like tonight? Or should I say…is there anything in particular you don't like?"

"Not really," they both answered. "We pretty much like everything," Stephanie added.

"Good, that makes it easier," she said. "I'll discuss it with Aaron before I pick you up. After dinner, I'm taking both of you out to a great club!"

After checking into the hotel, they agreed to meet in the lobby a little before 7:00 p.m.. Stephanie was elated that they were going to experience a little of Southampton's nightlife.

44

After showering, Stephanie picked up the phone and dialed Dave's room.

Dave was showering when he heard the phone ring. He stepped out, dripping wet, wrapped a towel around himself, and answered the phone beside the bed. "Hello."

"Hey, Dave, what's the dress tonight?"

"I don't know," he replied. "I'm wearing a pair of slacks, a long sleeve shirt, and a leather jacket."

"I have a skirt and a hot top— "

Dave's laugh interrupted her. "Yes, you do," he said.

"Or," she continued, ignoring his obvious sexual innuendo, "I was wondering if it would be better to wear slacks tonight?"

"You'd look *great* in both," he said.

She wondered if she imagined a flirtatious tone. "Thanks," she giggled, "but I was referring to the temperature—you know, the cold weather?"

"Oh," he laughed again. "I didn't mean what you thought." He paused. "What I mean is—"

"It's okay," she laughed, "quit while you're ahead."

"Why don't you give Nicky a call and find out where we're going and what she's wearing."

"Good idea. I knew there was a reason why I brought you along," she teased.

"Brought me? Don't you mean dragged me?" he said. "I could be at The Beat right now enjoying a stimulating conversation with the guys."

"So, what you're saying is thank you?"

Dave just laughed.

"Back to the point. I think I'll give Nicky a call."

"Great, because I'm getting cold standing here all wet with just a towel wrapped around me."

"Go get dressed. I'll see you in the lobby in a little bit."

"I'm gonna jump back in the warm shower," Dave shivered. "I'll catch ya downstairs, Steph."

Stephanie was in the lobby when Dave came down. She opted for the leather pants, moderately tight, and a colorful top, also on the tight side, and a nice jacket, short and open in the front, showing what she had decided was a tasteful amount of cleavage.

"You look *very sharp*," Stephanie said, looking Dave up and down.

He bowed. "Why thank you, Stephanie. You're looking *very* hot yourself," he added, shifting his eyes playfully as he looked her up and down the way she had him.

Stephanie realized these two trips had lightened the relationship between them. Dave had opened up a little, and Stephanie had become more aware of his softer side.

Nicky was parked in front, waiting. As Stephanie stepped out the front door, she felt the October chill and was glad she chose pants and a jacket.

Nicky greeted them as they got into the car. "You two ready?"

"We are!" Stephanie answered.

Nicky pulled out from the hotel and headed to the Ristorante di Sorrento, a cozy Italian restaurant in downtown Southampton.

They had a wonderful dinner, talking about school, family, how Aaron and Michelle met, and Nicky's sports. It turned out Nicky was quite an athlete in college; a softball player who got a scholarship to play for West Virginia. Though Stephanie didn't play in college, she and Nicky had softball in common and talked about sports for quite awhile.

"How are the littleneck clams?" Stephanie asked. "I've never tried clams."

Nicky glanced at Stephanie and teased. "You sure you want to try them? You know they're an aphrodisiac?"

"There go the inhibitions," Aaron joked.

"I thought that was oysters." Stephanie frowned.

"Those, too," Aaron laughed.

"Aaron, don't tease her," Michelle scolded. "They're really very good, Stephanie. You should try them."

Stephanie joked about the effect of an aphrodisiac being wasted on her.

Their conversation turned to Long Island, and they gossiped about the Hamptons, the rich, the famous, the scandals, and the history. Stephanie enjoyed the laughter and casual atmosphere. Nobody discussed the case at all. It was refreshing to enjoy a glass of wine, great food, and conversation with no business mucking it up.

They finished dinner, and Aaron picked up the check.

Aaron and Michelle had to get home to their two kids, even though it was Saturday night. "We don't get many Saturday nights out," Michelle told them. "This has been a real treat."

"I'm so glad we got to meet you," Stephanie said, giving her a hug.

"You, too, Stephanie," she smiled. "Good luck on your case."

"Nicky's taking you out to a fun place," Aaron said, shaking Dave's hand. "Sorry we can't join you, but the kids do cut down on our social lives."

"We understand," Dave said.

"Nick's a lot of fun. She'll show you a good time," he added, looking over at Stephanie. "Enjoy yourselves."

"We will, Aaron, thanks," Stephanie smiled. "We'll see you in the morning."

"Ready to go?" Nicky asked, raising her arms and throwing a sexy dance move.

"Oh yeah," Stephanie said.

* * * *

Nicky took them to the Pelican's Perch down near the beach. The club was a little wild. A far cry from The Beat, Dave thought.

"This club's the mildest of the three I picked," she yelled to Dave over the loud music.

"This is the mild one?" Dave said, raising his voice.

"What?"

"This one's the mildest?" he repeated louder.

"Yeah, but it's still a great dance place."

Dave had not been out dancing in a long—a very long time. As it turned out, neither had Stephanie.

"All right, Dave, you're going to have to dance with both of us," Stephanie said, already moving to the music as she and Nicky pushed through the crowd searching for a table.

Nicky had her hands up, clapping to the beat, moving seductively through the mass of people. Dave noticed how her athletic body seemed to glide through the tight spaces between the bodies and tables in the crowded club.

"Follow me," she yelled over the noise, spotting a table at the edge of the dance floor.

Dave ordered a Manhattan, and the girls ordered Cosmopolitans. Stephanie explained to Dave that it was a Martini with vodka, cranberry juice, triple sec, and lemon or lime juice.

"A *sissy* martini?" he teased.

Nicky answered, "We prefer to call it a flavored martini. Very popular."

"Still," he smirked, "a sissy martini."

By the time the drinks arrived, both women were already up and dancing. Dave wasn't a bad dancer, but he didn't do much of it anymore. Ex-number-one had dragged him to dance classes years ago. He hated it at first, but enjoyed it once he learned some of the dances. He was a little rusty, so he decided to only dance if the women asked him.

Dave was polished at the waltz and the cha-cha, but they weren't playing many of those at this club—they were dancing something altogether different. As if on cue, Stephanie came over and asked him to dance. He was a little reluctant at first, but she wouldn't take no for an answer. Although a little raw, he loosened up as Stephanie and Nicky encouraged him.

Dave saw that Nicky was a good dancer, and he danced with her several times. She was playful and knew quite a few people at the club. Most of her friends were dancing, sometimes all together—at times as many as eight or nine of them.

He danced sometimes with none of them, and sometimes with all of them. He relaxed and allowed himself to have a great time. Of course, the Manhattans probably had something to do with that. He was not sure that 48-year-olds were supposed to have this much fun.

Dave danced, laughed, drank more than he should have, but he believed the dancing kept him fairly sober. It was nearly 1:00 a.m. when they decided to call it quits.

Nicky took them back to the hotel, chatting about how energized the evening had been, and Dave suggested they have breakfast together in the morning.

"As long as it's not before 10:00 o'clock," Stephanie said.

"No problem," Nicky said. "We're eating here, right?"

"Sounds good to me," Dave added.

"Okay, 10:00 it is," Nicky said, hugging Stephanie and then Dave.

"See you in the morning."

Dave headed for his room, a little smile on his face. Even though he was tired, he'd had a great evening. It was more activity than he'd had in a long time, and he was surely going to pay for it the next morning, he thought.

He stopped outside Stephanie's room to say good night.

Stephanie smiled. "I had a great time, Dave…and you're quite a dancer." She stepped forward to give him a hug.

It caught Dave by surprise. It was a firm embrace, warm—lasting longer than their previous hug. Her taut body pressed against him. Desire welled up inside. She felt good in his strong arms—secure—but he knew she was vulnerable. It made Dave feel a little awkward, but her body felt wonderful and he wasn't about to let go of this moment.

Stephanie looked up, and their eyes locked. Her misty blue eyes were soft, inviting, enticing him to go further, but at the same time causing him to feel slightly embarrassed. Tension mounted, and he had difficulty sorting out his feelings. Dave forced himself to gently push Stephanie away.

"Good night," he said, awkward, shaky.

As he approached his door, the jingle of her key resonated

through his body, touching every nerve. Inserting his key, he wondered if he had just missed an incredible opportunity?

Dave glanced over at Stephanie, breathed a deep sigh, and opened his door. He stepped inside, closed it, and leaned against the hard surface waiting for the smell of her perfume to fade.

Tomorrow they would return to their professional relationship, and she'd forget all about the little embrace.

He'd done the right thing. His imagination raced, replaying the scene in his mind. *How could that young, intelligent woman desire him?*

45

Sunday was a crisp and exhilarating fall morning.

Dave groaned as he tried to roll out of bed, sore in places he didn't know he had muscles. An experience everyone has had at one time or another, but Dave had not been in this situation for years. Not since he had to dig up four flower beds and plant a few trees about twelve years ago, at the request of ex-number-two.

Stephanie was already down-stairs having coffee.

"Good morning, Stephanie," Nicky said entering the restaurant, vivacious, bouncy, and ready to go.

"Morning, Nicky," Stephanie smiled. "Thanks for last night. We had a great time. I sure needed that," she added. "And I think Dave enjoyed it, too."

Dave walked in on their pleasantries. "You talking about me?" he asked, hearing part of the conversation.

"Yes, we were," Nicky said, cheerfully, a big grin on her face.

"Surprised this old guy could even get up, I'll bet?" Dave laughed, trying to hide how difficult it was to roll out of bed this morning.

"We were just saying that it looked like you were having a good time," Nicky said.

"I did," he said. "You two are great dancers."

"You did pretty well yourself, specially for an old guy," she teased.

Dave chuckled and turned to Stephanie. "Well, I told you I had lessons years ago. I guess they paid off last night. I got to dance with the two hottest women in the club."

He was surprised to see them both blush.

Dave ordered coffee, and their conversation turned to the reason Dave and Stephanie were there. Stephanie wanted to know more about the injuries to Wimkowski. Nicky repeated what the medical examiner told to her, but said that he could explain it in more detail.

They talked with Nicky about the possible connection with their case against Phillip Hobart.

"Aaron and I were wondering about the connections ourselves," Nicky said. "You said there have been five deaths now…in nine months?"

Dave nodded between sips of coffee. "Five…four of them supposedly accidents."

"It *is* difficult to believe that these are just coincidental. I see why you two are suspicious," Nicky agreed.

They finished breakfast and headed to the Southampton police station before heading out to the crime scene. Aaron had agreed to meet them at 11:30.

The station was quiet when they arrived. Aaron was already there waiting for them. Stephanie pulled out the paperwork she brought to discuss some of the reports with Aaron and Nicky before going out to the Wimkowski mansion. Aaron clarified Wimkowski's charges and his part in the misappropriation of corporation funds. He broke down the SEC's and attorney general's investigations for them. After about 30 minutes, Nicky suggested that they head out to the crime scene.

"There might still be some lab techs at the scene," Aaron told them, "but we'll be able to examine what we want."

"There isn't a whole lot to see," Nicky said, "without the body there, and the water extracted and filtered by now."

"That's okay," Stephanie said. "We just want to get a feel for the crime scene and the crime. Maybe we'll see something that no one else noticed, just because we have a different perspective."

The trip to Wimkowski's estate didn't take long. As they drove up the long drive, Dave shook his head. Like the others they had investigated during this case, it was a huge mansion. Another opulent abode, luxurious in its own way, oceanfront elegance, and with it came a high price tag. The only problem—it was purchased with investors' money, wrongfully taken and used by Wimkowski.

"The Mansion TriCorp investors built," Stephanie whispered, her voice cold and distant.

Aaron explained the timing of the accident as they walked through the house. They went to the kitchen, and Aaron showed them the garage entrance next to the laundry room. There were two doors from the garage to the house. The one nearest the kitchen was the one Wimkowski used to enter the house on Thursday night. The other entered the house off the front entry-way.

"The alarm was set from this security pad at 8:30 in the morning on Thursday," Aaron said.

"And you know that was Wimkowski leaving?"

Aaron nodded. "Pretty sure. It was then deactivated by the housekeeper at the pad in the entry-way at 9:15 that morning, based on the statement the housekeeper gave us, and confirmed by the alarm company."

"So she has the code?" Dave asked.

"Yes, she has it. She reactivated it at 5:30 on Thursday evening when she left," he continued.

"Do we know which door?" Dave asked.

"Yeah," Aaron said. "The front door, which is the same door the housekeeper always uses."

"At 11:09 p.m. this rear entrance alarm was deactivated. It was reactivated at 11:51 p.m. that night. The medical examiner determined the time of death as approximately midnight, or a little before."

"So he reactivated the alarm before taking a shower?" Dave asked.

"That's what we think," Aaron said.

"And this is where he reset the alarm, the same door he came in earlier?" Dave asked.

"He was downstairs," Aaron said. "You can reset the alarm from three downstairs stations and one upstairs, but this was the alarm that was reset."

Stephanie glanced at Aaron. "Anything disturbed?"

"Just his opened mail at the end of the kitchen counter. He had a glass of wine and left the glass in the sink, and left the bottle here on the counter," Aaron said, pointing to the partial ring on the counter where the bottle had been. "It was a $250 '93 Opus One. His prints were the only ones on the glass or the bottle."

"So it *appears* that he was downstairs from the time he got home until he reset the alarm?" Dave inquired, while sifting through the mail.

"That's the way we saw it," Nicky confirmed.

Dave looked up. "Could he have let someone in between the time he came home and the time of death?"

"If he did, there is no evidence of it," Nicky answered.

"After he set the alarm we think he headed upstairs to take a shower," Aaron offered.

They walked through the kitchen and into the living room, then turned up the stairway heading toward the master suite. The master suite was to the right of the landing at the top of the stairs.

"Could someone have entered undetected during that 40 plus minutes?" Dave asked.

"It's possible," Nicky conceded, "but there was no sign or evidence of *any* intruder."

"And," Aaron added, "no indication of exit from any door or window after the alarm was reactivated."

"Could someone have reset the alarm as they were leaving?" Stephanie asked.

"That person would have to know the code, but I guess it *is* possible," Aaron said, nodding. "But not likely. Our understanding is only five people knew the code."

"Who are they?" Dave asked.

Aaron raised his eyes as if compiling a mental list. "Let's see...Wimkowski, his wife, son, daughter, and his long-time housekeeper." He went on to explain, "the son is in Boston and the daughter is in Chicago."

"Then they're not even here?"

"No, the daughter was on a flight to Tokyo at the time of the accident," he said. "She's a flight attendant."

"You confirmed that and ruled her out, I take it?"

Aaron nodded. "She was definitely on the flight. We met her at the airport."

"And we do know the housekeeper returned at 9:00 a.m. and was pretty shook up about finding Wimkowski in the shower," Nicky added.

"That just leaves the wife," Dave smiled. "Where was she?"

"She's at her sisters in Arizona. She's on her way back from Phoenix today."

"Today?" Stephanie remarked. "She didn't rush home after she heard about his death?"

"They haven't been close in recent years. Separate bedrooms," Nicky whispered. "Even more separated since the indictment."

They entered the master suite. It was a big room with the master bath across the room to the right. As they entered the bathroom, the shower was on the right, just beyond the door, long counter on the left, with two sinks and a vanity area. A raised Jacuzzi tub was situated in the rear. The room was easily ten feet wide by eighteen feet long. Expensive mirror ran the entire fifteen-foot length of the counter.

The shower had two sides of glass on top of a fourteen-inch raised Italian marble wall which would account for the time it took the water to overflow onto the bathroom floor. It would also account for the amount of water exposure of the body, as listed in the medical examiner's report. The blood stains were still present on the edge of the marble tiled seat in the back of the shower, though some of it had been washed away by the water.

Dave noticed that the shower floor had tile designed to help prevent slipping in the shower. "What about the nonslip tile?" Dave asked. "Shouldn't that have helped prevent the fall?"

"The M.E. said that there is still some degree of surface slickness, and the fall would be exaggerated if the victim stepped on a bar of soap, or had soapy feet," Aaron answered.

"Was that the case?"

"The bar of soap was still in the soap tray when we arrived at the crime scene," Nicky interjected. "So that doesn't appear to be a factor."

The water had been extracted from the bathroom floor already, but the carpet was still soggy for several feet into the bedroom near the bathroom entrance. Aaron and Nicky were right. There was little evidence.

"Look at this bathroom," Stephanie remarked. "*Everything* here is perfect...almost untouched. If we didn't know better, you couldn't tell that anyone died in here."

"The entire house is immaculate," Aaron agreed. "The housekeeper makes sure everything is spotless. Our victim was very anal. As you can see, there are no signs of an intruder."

"There's no towel missing from a towel rack," Dave exclaimed. "Was there one over the shower railing?" He was examining the towels neatly hanging on the closest rack.

The towels were still hanging in their designated places, and nothing was disturbed on the bathroom counters. In fact, the only evidence of the accident was the blood stains on the edge of the tile on the shower seat. This was the cleanest crime scene Dave had ever seen.

"Everything is the same as it was, Dave. We didn't remove anything but the body and the water," Aaron assured him. "What are you thinking?"

Dave moved to the rack near the first sink, then turned and looked at the group. "These look like display towels. I don't think he used these to dry off."

"And your point is?" Stephanie asked.

"I can't afford display towels," Dave stated, "but if I could, I would have another one to dry off with. Where is it?"

Aaron's eyes widened. "Interesting point. Maybe he just forgot, but there was no towel over the rail when we arrived."

"What about the housekeeper? Would she have taken it?"

"She claims she never went into the bathroom," Aaron offered, "and she was visibly upset when we interviewed her."

"You think we should talk to her?" Stephanie asked Dave, then turned to Aaron and Nicky. "What do you think?"

"Her story checked out," Nicky spoke up. "I don't think she could add anything else."

Dave rubbed his forehead. "Did anyone from the lab check the laundry room...or a laundry basket? We should get them back out here to have a go at it," Dave said.

"We'll do that," Aaron said, opening his cell.

On the way downstairs, Dave asked about other evidence.

"We don't have anything to speak of," Nicky answered. "No blood or foot-prints...no tire marks, hairs, or fibers, that we could find."

"No witnesses?" Stephanie questioned Aaron.

He shook his head. "We did door-to-door, and no one in the neighborhood saw or heard anything out of the ordinary."

Dave knew what his partner was thinking. So similar to the other cases. "Alone. No witnesses," he said, quietly to himself.

46

The courier waited while Detective Doug Morris signed for the package. Doug had been adamant with his captain and firm with the president of Williams's bank. It had taken longer to get the files than he had anticipated, but his persistence paid off.

"Getting the bank records means we have to reopen the case," the lieutenant growled. "We've already closed it."

"Not necessarily," Doug had replied. "My load is light right now, and if you want, I can go over them on my own time."

The chief of detectives stared at him with a slight look of disgust. "Without reopening the case, we can't get a subpoena."

Doug smiled, "I'll just make it clear to the banks that it's in their best interests not to force me to get one."

"I don't like it," he mumbled. "Since your load's light, go ahead...but if the banks balk, you're out of business."

Doug had agreed to the lieutenant's terms. It took him a week to convince the new bank prez that this would be a good career move. That behind him, he was anxious to sift through Williams's and Porter's monthly statements as he'd promised Dave he would. He hadn't mentioned a word to Stephanie.

The fact that the lab had newly discovered evidence of tampering with the scaffolding increased Doug's resolve as he dug into the records.

An hour or so passed with nothing of any consequence from Porter's accounts popping out. He tired of the simple, mundane accounts of the retired oil man and requested help from his partner who had recently returned to duty.

"Gary," Doug whispered, not wanting the request to be heard by the wrong ears. "You mind checking these bank statements for me?"

"No prob, partner," he said enthusiastically, but quietly. "But I don't want the lieutenant to catch me."

"It's not like you have anything else to do."

"True," he said, then tilted his head to the side. "Does this have anything to do with the detective in Houston?"

"No," Doug lied, his face reddening, "I'm just helping out because our case may be involved."

He handed the remaining pages to his junior partner and dragged the bigger, more complicated stack from the contractor's bank to the center of the desk.

It was obvious to Doug that Williams had made a lot of money from the Galivan job. There were hundreds of entries in his business account, and large payments to his subs and his suppliers. It would be difficult to find any indiscretions in this mess.

Just as his helpful partner arrived at his desk, Doug's eyes caught something in Williams's personal account.

"I didn't see any—"

"Take a look at this, Gary," Doug interrupted. "What do you make of this entry?"

"That's a big deposit to have in an account without a name on the 'pay to' line, and the date fits."

"Yes, it does!" Doug raised his voice. "Ten thousand is a nice round number…a payment for services perhaps?"

47

The next stop would be the medical examiner's office. Stephanie wanted to see the body and ask the M.E. about the excessive damage to the skull, indicated in his preliminary report.

"The trip to the Suffolk County Corner's Office is about an hour from Southampton to Smithtown this time of year," Nicky explained. "It would be much longer just a month or so earlier. Sometimes it takes us two hours to get to the North County Complex in Hauppauge."

Stephanie frowned. "Where?"

"Hop-Pog," Nicky repeated. "It's in Smithtown, and it's spelled h-a-u-p-p-a-u-g-e."

"Hop-Pog?" Stephanie repeated inquisitively.

"You got it, Stephanie!" Nicky exclaimed.

"We'll be taking the L, I, E," Aaron told them. "But we know a couple of shortcuts so just sit back and enjoy the ride."

Light banter made the trip seem shorter than an hour. As they pulled into the complex, Stephanie glanced at Dave's watch. It was almost right on an hour.

Aaron introduced them to the medical examiner, who already had Wimkowski's body out on the examination table.

The body, stretched out on the cold stainless steeltable, was chalky and grossly wrinkled—considerably more than just being in the bathtub too long. Stephanie thought the body had a ghostly, ethereal look. The M.E. explained the reasons time of death was difficult to determine. The amount of time in the water, the ambient temperature of the air and water, the amount and temperature of the water from the water heater, and the rate of delivery were all part of the complicated formula. After taking everything into consideration, combined with the lividity of the body, he was able to determine that it was some time in the hour before midnight. The body had been in the water between nine and ten hours when it was found.

"What about the damage to the skull?" Stephanie asked the M.E. "I understand you felt it was excessive?"

He turned the head, exposing the right side, and pulled the examination lamp closer to the table. He pointed to the area of the skull behind the ear. "See the bruising here?"

Dave and Stephanie drew closer. "Yes," Stephanie answered.

"Here is the point of impact," he specified. "The damage starts here in the area where the parietal and temporal bones articulate. This is where these two overlap, and—"

Stephanie shook her head. "I'm a little rusty on my anatomy," she explained. "Had a class in college, but haven't used it much since graduation. So bear with me while I write this stuff down."

He paused for her, and then went on. "The damage in this area is excessive, but more importantly, is how these fractures generate outward from this point.

Stephanie noticed that Dave was getting impatient. "So what does that tell us?"

The M.E. took them over to the x-ray display and showed them the fractures of the parietal bone and the damage to the temporal bone, and how they generated away from the original injury. He took them back to the table and pointed to the areas he had shown them.

"In a normal fall of a man this size, there would be about half this much bruising and the fractures would not have been as long."

"So you don't think it was the fall that caused it?"

"Oh, yes, it was the fall," he was emphatic. "The injuries are consistent with a fall, but I can't explain the amount of damage."

"So it's the amount of damage that disturbs you?"

He pulled the lamp over placing it closer to the jaw. "One more thing…there is excessive damage to the mandible—the jawbone—that isn't consistent with a normal fall either." He ran his finger down the jawbone. "It appears that the head struck the seat twice."

"Twice…you mean like someone smashed his head against the seat?" Stephanie asked.

"More like bounced off the seat," he clarified.

"But you signed the death certificate," Dave questioned.

"Didn't really want to, but it's only the preliminary finding and there was no evidence to indicate it was anything other than an accident," he told them. "So I signed."

Stephanie stared at the M.E. "And you're sure no one hit him?"

"The damage was not caused by blunt force trauma. He was not struck by any blunt object prior to the fall," he assured her. "And no weapon was found at the crime scene."

He paused and looked up at Stephanie. "So…" He stopped again and just shrugged his shoulders, indicating his frustration. The shrug was not very professional, Stephanie thought, but was indicative of everything about these cases.

Stephanie asked, "If I were to tell you that we feel there is a conspiracy connecting all these deaths, would that change your finding?"

"I'm not sure it would change it, but it might explain the excessive damage and give me reason to look into it further," he told Stephanie. "We're so underbudgeted I can't waste time if there's no supporting evidence for further investigation."

"This case is just like the others," Stephanie said to the M.E., shaking her head. "I believe that it's more than coincidence. Even more amazing—*all* the victims were alone at the time of their accident and there were *no* witnesses. There is something more sinister going on here. We just have to prove it."

"Good luck," he said. "I sure would like to get the answer."

"I'll let you know if we come up with anything," Stephanie promised and shook his hand. "Thanks for your time, and the clarification."

"Yeah, thanks for coming in on Sunday, Doc," Aaron said.

They said good-bye and headed back to the station—another hour back to Southampton. They discussed the scene and the evidence the M.E. had shared with them. It was just as Aaron and Nicky said: there wasn't a lot of evidence, and though the medical examiner had his doubts about one aspect of the injury, on the surface, it appeared to be an accident.

Aaron told Stephanie he would continue to look through the reports to see if something they missed suddenly popped out at them. Like Stephanie and Dave, he thought that five dead executives from bankrupt corporations was too much of a coincidence to let go. She said good-bye to Aaron and promised to keep him informed.

* * * *

Nicky took them back to the hotel. On the way, Dave and Stephanie talked about getting a little rest before dinner. Dave thought a quiet evening would be welcome after the excitement of last night. He joked about needing at least a week before he could hit the dance floor again.

After a short rest and a hot shower, Dave met Stephanie in the lobby and grabbed a cab to a nearby restaurant Aaron had suggested. It was rare that they could actually sit down to have a peaceful meal together. Their meal at South Beach was far from quiet.

"Yep...I was married twice. Both were failures." Dave winced, as he recalled his past.

"Both were failures?"

Dave paused while the waitress set down the two glasses of wine they'd ordered. "I guess you could say the biggest problem was the job," he declared. "It's difficult to be married and be a cop."

"It was the same with my uncle." Stephanie frowned. "So, it's not just you, Dave."

"I'm aware of that, Steph, but I took the job home with me. That's not a good thing to do."

Stephanie nodded. "Difficult not to take it home, isn't it?"

"Damned hard," he grimaced. "This work affects your life, Stephanie. Don't let anyone tell you different."

Dave saw that Stephanie was listening intently as he described the downside of the job.

"You carry the job with you everywhere, every time you strap on your weapon," Dave explained. "It's there when you go out to dinner and when you go to the bathroom." He paused, his gaze fixed somewhere in the distance. "It's even there on a date." He sighed, took a long drink of his Merlot, then said, "I'm looking forward to retirement."

"What will you do when you retire?"

"Fish," he smiled. "I used to enjoy fishing, but I haven't taken the time to go. It's been more than six years."

"So you like fishing?" Stephanie prompted. "I'll bet you have some *good* fish stories." She laughed.

"I do," he said, laughing with her. "Used to go out with Captain Martin occasionally, but not in a long time. Now *he* can tell some whoppers."

"What else would you do?"

"I would probably go out to the range a lot more. I have a small collection of guns and enjoy the firing range," he confided. "A by-product of my ordnance training."

"Just four more years?"

"Yep, four more. Actually, less than four," he sighed. "That'll be the big 3-0h which will give me a damn decent retirement."

After a brief pause he looked at Stephanie. "I'm glad I got you as a partner, Steph." His gaze met hers. "Was a little skeptical at first," he confessed, "but I really enjoy working with you."

"Thanks, Dave," she said. "I was a little concerned myself when they told me I would be working with Dave Duncan. I had heard things, but I didn't really know you. I think the fact you had been a detective for so long intimidated me. But now I think we make a good team."

"Me, too," Dave said, smiling back at her.

Dave had not been able to talk to his partner like this in the first four months. She didn't seem to be interested in his life, and he didn't ask her much about hers. But, his feelings about her as a cop, as a person, and as a partner had changed.

Dave had wondered about her dating but had not felt comfortable talking about it before. As he asked her about it he noticed she was daydreaming.

She heard only part of his question, but enough to respond. "In answer to your question...I don't really date all that much."

Dave didn't hide the surprise in his voice. "I thought you were dating all the time. So I didn't ask. I know you've been busy since we caught this case, but what about all those nights since we've been together?"

Stephanie stopped as their second glass of wine arrived along with their salads. "I've been very selective the past couple of years," she intimated, after the waitress left. "Not many good dates."

She explained that looks were not nearly as important to her now as they were a few years ago. "Of course, I want to meet someone who is attractive, but I've discovered that personality is as important as looks. Maybe even more so," she told Dave, as she sipped her fresh glass of Chardonnay.

"What are you looking for?"

"I would just like to meet someone I enjoy being with...who wasn't overly vain, selfish, or macho. Macho is way overrated."

This surprised Dave, but she stated that she knew from experience, having met some real macho jerks in the past. Her model looks seemed to attract that kind of guy. Dinner arrived, and the conversation changed.

Dinner was exceptional. Good food, ambiance, enlightening conversation, and wonderful company. It was still fairly early, but they were tired, so they caught a cab back to the hotel, expecting to get a good night's sleep.

There was no mention of the moment they shared last night in front of their rooms. Neither of them brought it up.

Dave again wondered if he had imagined Steph's feelings for him. *Maybe he was just an old fool.*

48

Dave stared at the glass case in the entry lobby. Fourth Floor—Division 6; State of Texas v. Hobart—the sign in the lobby of the courthouse read.

Deputy District Attorney Eric Manly walked up to Dave, saying, "Well, our big trial starts today."

"You mean *your* big trial, don't you?" Dave replied, refraining from looking at Manly.

Manly ignored Dave's acerbic statement. "You ready to testify on Tuesday or Wednesday?"

"If I have to," Dave said, half-heartedly.

"What do you mean, *if you have to*?"

"Really don't think this one should go to jail," Dave said.

"But *you* arrested him!" Manly's eyes widened, then he said, "This is the best evidence we've had in a long time. What's the problem, Duncan?" His obnoxious voice taunted Dave. "What happened to the tough Dave Duncan?"

"I feel bad for Hobart, and what's happened to him," Dave said. "Day deserved it."

"Maybe, but we're not allowed to make that decision. It's up to a jury to decide his fate," Manly said sanctimoniously.

Dave and Stephanie had discussed their feelings many times about convicting Hobart for killing Benjamin Day. Though Dave knew it wasn't right to exonerate Hobart, his plight—his sheer desperation—touched Dave. He and Stephanie had different points of view about the value of prosecuting this case. The trial hadn't started, and they were in opposition on the subject.

"How about your lovely partner, Detective Fox?" he heard Manly say.

"I'm sure she's ready. She's been ready all week."

"Well, at least *someone* wants to help me convict Hobart."

"Nobody said he shouldn't be convicted. She's excited because it's her first big case," Dave replied. "I still disagree with your decision to go for the death penalty."

"I've got to get to court," Manly said, dismissing Dave. "We'll call you on Monday."

Their preparation for the trial began on Tuesday after their meeting with Captain Martin, when it became evident they weren't going to connect the other deaths to Hobart, or to a conspiracy involving Hobart.

"Drop the conspiracy," the captain had bellowed, after discovering they couldn't prove it. "We've got to get prepared for this trial."

Dave knew the captain was right, and with no more to go on they had to close the case. Somewhere deep in his gut, though, he felt Stephanie was right. There was a conspiracy—they just couldn't find it. Exposing a conspiracy would have been great for her career, but he knew they had to move on.

They met with Manly Wednesday to go over the material and questions for the trial. Stephanie had put her efforts into Hobart's case since returning from Southampton. Dave knew that she had prepared well, and that she was positive of a conviction in this case.

At Wednesday's meeting, it took Manly a whopping three minutes, thirty-four seconds to hit on Stephanie. He seemed to be slipping. Maybe he was preoccupied with the case. Dave showed her the watch on the way back to the station. It really was no longer a laughing matter, and Dave would be glad when this was over, for Stephanie's sake.

Manly really played this one to the media. As he left Dáve, he was stopped by a television news team and paused to answer a few of the reporter's questions.

"The evidence is overwhelming and we expect to prove capital murder and easily convict Phillip Hobart for the murder of Benjamin Day," Manly gloated. "Yes, we will start *voir dire* today and will be ready to start the trial either Monday or Tuesday."

"Are you still going for the death penalty?" the reporter asked.

"Yes, the death penalty is still on the table."

Dave grimaced as he heard the words. He wondered when Manly told the media he was seeking the death penalty. The sleazy bastard. That's even low by his standards. Did he also tell them that Hobart only had two or three months to live?

Manly knew about Hobart's terminal illness and knew that the death penalty would be for naught. Dave wondered how the public would feel about the trial if the press found out about Hobart's cancer?

Hobart's health had become more of an issue, with his strength weakening over the two weeks of his confinement. The cancer was beginning to take its toll. He still refused to post bail. Dave was now positive that Hobart was trying to speed up the trial process; he wanted to get the story of his frustrations, his desperation, his angst told in court before he died.

His treatment, which had been negligible until now, was increasing and being picked up by the state. He was trying to protect what little he had left of his assets so that he could leave something for his children.

Dave went to the clerk's office to pick up some paperwork they needed for another case that he and his old partner had been lead detectives on three years ago.

When Dave got back to the station, Stephanie was going over the scribbles in her notebook. He knew she didn't want to make any mistakes. This would be her first time testifying in a capital case.

"We need another case," Dave said, boredom and frustration in his voice.

"We have a couple," she replied.

"I mean something big enough to take our mind off *this* case. By the way, I saw your buddy," he sneered.

"My buddy?"

"Yep, Manly."

"Where?"

"At the courthouse." Dave paused. "I can't believe his grandstanding. He's still talking about asking for the death penalty! *The guy is dying.* Why ask for the death penalty?"

"Seriously?" Stephanie shook her head. "I never *really* thought he would pursue it."

"Well, he did. I've always thought he was sleazy, but not that sleazy. The guy only has two or three months to live," Dave reminded her. "What value would convicting him serve?"

"But he *killed* Benjamin Day, Dave!"

"Looks more like justifiable homicide to me," Dave said.

"Not really, it's a clear case of first degree murder," Stephanie stated. "He planned the whole thing."

"You have to admit, Stephanie, he had just cause. You may have done the same thing if you had lost everything."

"Maybe," she said. "But, it's still murder, and we've got to do our job."

"What happened to all that compassion they taught you in the academy?" Dave asked.

"What happened to your old school 'bust em and bag em' philosophy," she countered. "Dave, you're way too involved in this case."

"Admittedly, I have developed a level of sensitivity toward Hobart's plight."

"Sensitivity? *Dave, you're obsessed!*"

"Touché," he replied.

"No, I mean it, Dave," she said. "I know I haven't been a detective long, but I know you shouldn't get this involved with the suspect."

Dave knew Stephanie was right and thought about how the two of them had turned 180 degrees since they started investigating the Day murder. Of course, this was her first bust, a high-profile one at that, and she wanted to start with a good record.

Stephanie was still getting reports from the other police departments regarding their cases. Dave could see she had motivated each of them to find out more, to continue their search, officially or unofficially, for the clues that might tie them together into a neat little conspiracy.

"What's this?" Dave said, picking up a message from Detective Morris on Stephanie's desk. "Another call from Doug?" he teased.

"Yep," she said. "He just can't live without me, I guess."

"What's he want this time?"

"We need to talk about that, partner," she scowled. "We are partners, aren't we?"

"Of course, why do you ask?"

"I wonder," she said. "Doug asked me to relay a message to you."

Dave's eyes widened. An uneasy feeling swept through him. "A message from Doug...for me?"

"Yes. He said to tell you that the money trail didn't pan out," she relayed, shaking her head. "You two were following a money trail?"

Dave shifted his weight uneasily. "I won't lie to you, Steph. I asked Doug to dig through Williams's and Porter's bank accounts. I should have told you."

"It's okay. Doug explained it all to me. He told me you were trying to protect me."

"That was my intention...really," he said, softly.

"I know. He told me to tell you it was winnings from Vegas that Williams didn't report to the IRS."

"That's why I didn't tell you," he smiled. "In case it didn't work out."

Stephanie turned up a big grin. "That's sweet."

Dave smiled again and changed subjects. "Doug's calling almost every day, isn't he?"

"Yeah, he is."

"So what do you think about him?" Dave asked.

"He's all right," she replied. "Intelligent, interesting, and we share a common interest in police work."

"Any interest?" Dave was looking for some sign of emotion.

Despite their trip to New York, he was still reluctant to pry into her life. Since their dinner in Southampton, he felt closer, but, conversations with a female partner were quite different. This wasn't serious. It was teasing, so he took a little liberty.

"Maybe, but he is GU," she said.

"You think so?" he said. "I think he dresses pretty well."

"Not GQ, Dave," she laughed. "GU. Geographically Undesirable."

"I knew that," Dave said.

There was a brief silence, and Dave continued, "But he still dresses nice."

"Yes, he did," Stephanie grinned. "But he'll never make the cover of GQ with that tie he wore on Monday."

"And he wore it especially for you," Dave reminded her.

"Anyway," she said. "I've had long-distance relationships before, and they didn't really work. Don't need another one."

"It's not like you need to travel 1,500 miles for a date," Dave said.

"Maybe I do," she said, laughing.

"I didn't mean that," Dave apologized, realizing the mistake he'd made.

"Don't apologize. I can laugh about it. I think things are going to change real soon for me," she smiled.

"I still can't believe it, even though you told me. I thought guys would be hitting on you all the time—actually standing in line to take you out."

"*Guys like Manly*," she said, trying to make a point. "I have a friend who told me I intimidate men. I don't think I do it consciously, but maybe my girlfriend is right."

Dave wished he was fifteen years younger. If he was, he would definitely ask her out. It wasn't her personality that was intimidating. It was her looks.

"Maybe it's just that guys think you're unapproachable," Dave suggested.

Stephanie told Dave that she really hadn't had much fun dating when she did have a date. She told him it had been that way for the last couple of years. "It is more difficult than it should be," she said. "Dating is supposed to be *fun*, not *work*."

The phone rang on Stephanie's desk. It was Manly, calling to let them know the jury process may take longer than he had hoped. Five panels of jurors were originally brought into the courtroom and they had already dismissed more than half of them. They were waiting for three more panels from the jury room.

"It looks like we won't be called until late Tuesday, or Wednesday morning," Stephanie relayed to Dave.

"We already planned for that. He just wanted to talk to you," he said, smiling.

"See that?" she said, raising her voice. "These are the kind of guys I attract!"

"If I were fifteen years younger," Dave heard himself say.

"If you were fifteen years younger," she repeated, smiling at Dave. "You'd what?"

Dave just laughed—an embarrassed laugh—not sure why he blurted that out. He just stared at Stephanie and said nothing.

"You're not really my type, Dave, but you're starting to grow on me," she said, before he could say anything.

Dave laughed again. He knew they came from two different worlds, but he was really beginning to like Stephanie.

Unlike Stephanie's life, Dave had had it rough growing up in Chicago. He seemed to always be on the edge, flirting with trouble. Stephanie, on the other hand, came from a stable, nurturing home, an upper middle-class neighborhood, far removed from Chicago's South Side.

She was a good student and a good athlete, two things Dave never was, although he could have been, if he had applied himself. He was a good athlete when he was younger, but he needed the grades to play sports in school. It wasn't important enough to Dave. Stephanie applied herself in everything she did, and it fueled her success.

Their worlds were degrees apart, the homecoming queen and the rebel—but fate is fascinating. Their lives intertwined, pushed together, with no visible purpose—two unlikely partners.

"Wanna stop by The Beat tonight?" Dave asked.

"Not tonight. Maybe if we weren't on call. You remember what happened last time?" she reminded Dave. "Raincheck?"

"Sure, we'll do it again after we testify."

"Great," she said. "I did promise Rafe and Paul that I would come back."

When Dave left the squad, he headed toward The Beat, thinking about Stephanie going home to her cat. He wondered if she considered them two souls, different, but lost in the same night, searching, but stumbling into the same darkness, living the same boring existences.

49

The courtroom was noisy and packed when Stephanie arrived on Tuesday morning. Dave was already there. Manly and his two co-counsels were seated at the prosecution table, piles of paperwork and notebooks in front of them.

Camera crews from the big three, as well as CNN, MSNBC, the BBC, and a few other foreign crews crowded the courthouse steps when she arrived. Reporters crammed the hallway, and those who were fortunate enough to get in the courtroom were pressed against the wood-paneled walls in the back and along the sides.

Stephanie wanted to witness Manly's opening statement. She joined Dave in the first row, behind the prosecution table.

"Hey, Steph." Dave smiled as she slid in next to him.

"Mornin', Dave. Lotta people here," she said, looking around the courtroom.

"Yep. It's a big trial."

Stephanie leaned over and whispered, "I heard that Manly is pretty animated in court."

"You heard right," Dave whispered back. "I'm sure we're in for some good theater today."

"Is that why you wanted to see it?"

"That...and to get a feeling for the proceedings," Dave explained. "*And* Baker's demeanor and delivery."

"This case is important to Manly. It would be good for me, too, if Hobart gets convicted," she added in a soft voice.

"I know Steph, and you did a great job." Dave turned up a proud-of-you smile. "I don't see any way he won't be convicted."

"I know you don't want a conviction, Dave."

"Don't worry about that, Steph. He *is* guilty, and for that reason, he should go to jail," Dave said, patting Stephanie on the knee. "I just understand Hobart's—."

"All rise and come to order. The Honorable Stanton Neufeld presiding," the bailiff called.

The judge walked through the door, black robe flowing, spartan, confident, and took his place on the bench. The bailiff read the docket and commanded everyone to be seated.

"Are we ready to proceed, counsel?" the judge asked, looking first at Manly and then at Tony Baker.

"We are, Your Honor," they said, almost exactly in unison.

Baker rose. "Your Honor, I would—."

"Yes, Mr. Baker, what is your first motion?" Judge Neufeld interrupted, anticipating Baker's request.

"Defense requests a continuance, Your Honor."

"You were the one that wanted this speedy trial, Mr. Baker. And *now* you ask for a continuance?" the judge admonished. "On what grounds?"

"Sidebar, Your Honor?" Manly hastily requested.

"There is no jury, Mr. Manly, so please…I'm as curious as you are." Judge Neufeld looked sternly at defense counsel. "Mr. Baker?"

"We have had some new developments, Your Honor, that I haven't had sufficient time to weigh."

"His client has cancer, Your Honor, and now he wants to delay the trial," Manly blurted out, before Baker could speak.

"*Is this true*? Your client has *cancer*?" Neufeld asked, the shock clearly evident in his expression.

All over the courtroom journalists and reporters, pens scratching frantically in notebooks. Two or three ran out, surely hoping to scoop everyone. This was *big news* in this high-profile trial.

"The prosecution admits this is egregious to the defense, Your Honor, but *they* asked for the fast track on this trial. The prosecution *is* ready to go forward," Manly declared.

"Your Honor," Baker broke in. "I need time to evaluate what effect this has on our case."

"When did you discover this?" Neufeld asked, clearly annoyed.

"It doesn't matter, Your Honor, it's extrinsic," Manly interrupted.

"*I'll* decide that, Mr. Manly. Last time I checked, this was still *my* courtroom."

"Just last Wednesday, Your Honor," Baker answered.

"Mr. Baker, this court may have been more lenient had you brought this to my attention *before* we selected a jury," Neufeld said, irritated with the public defender. "Motion denied. Bailiff, bring in—"

"Your Honor."

"Mr. Baker?"

"I have another motion."

"I'm sure you do, Mr. Baker." The judge frowned. "Please, don't keep us in suspense."

"A motion to exclude all evidence collected illegally from my client's residence, Your Honor."

Judge Neufeld immediately denied the motion. "Bring it up in your appeal," Neufeld said. "The evidence is in. Anything else, Mr. Baker?"

"Not at this time, Your Honor. Thank you for asking." Baker smiled, looked down at the table, and then sat.

Judge Neufeld turned to the bailiff. "Bring in the jury."

The twelve jurors and two alternates shuffled in, split into two rows, and were seated. The judge welcomed and thanked them.

"Mr. Manly, are you ready with your opening statement?"

"I am, Your Honor."

Manly walked sprightly toward the jury. His suit seemed to fit better today, shirt tucked in neatly, tie more conservative and straight, and jacket tailored a little sharper. He stood erect—self-assured.

"Your Honor… ladies and gentlemen of the jury," he began.

"Your time is valuable as is the time of the court, so I will only ask you for a small portion of your time to present compelling evidence of a calculating, cold-blooded killer, who, after careful planning and almost flawless execution, took the life of Benjamin Day, a highly regarded citizen of the community—your community. I intend to further prove that the suspect shows no remorse for having committed this act of violence."

He paused, walked to the other end of the jury box and continued. "Now, the defense will try to play on your sympathy. They will show you evidence of undeniable losses in the stock market and will tell you that the victim—Mr. Day—was responsible for the defendant's—Mr. Hobart's—losses. They will tell you of his terminal illness, known by only a few individuals until today, and try to imply that this illness makes him somehow less responsible for this heinous crime." He took a deep breath.

"You will be instructed by the judge in the laws in this case, the laws related to murder—a capital offense. I will not only prove to you that Mr. Hobart was the individual who pulled the trigger, not once, not twice—but three times, ending the life of Benjamin Day, but I will also show you indisputable evidence that Mr. Hobart spent weeks planning this cold-blooded, calculated, iniquitous murder. The definition of murder will be clearly defined for you at the end of this trial, and you will see, beyond a reasonable doubt, that Mr. Hobart is, indeed, guilty of murder."

He paused and walked to the middle of the box. "You are here at great personal sacrifice of your time, your family, and your job, to assist the State of Texas. You have been asked by the state to represent the interests of the people of Texas. It is a difficult task, but I am confident that once you have heard and seen the evidence you will make the right decision—the only decision that can be reached in this case. Murder in the First Degree. Thank you."

"Wow! Where did that come from?" Stephanie said, leaning over to whisper in Dave's ear. "Where was the theater?"

Dave was as stunned as Stephanie. He had never heard Manly deliver such a powerful, cogent opening. "I still wish we hadn't told Manly about the cancer."

"We had to tell him. It was our duty," Stephanie said.

"I know that," Dave said. "If only you hadn't found out, Manly wouldn't be able to use it."

Baker got up, reached over, and squeezed Hobart gently on the shoulder. He buttoned his jacket and stepped from behind the table.

"Your Honor...ladies and gentlemen. As the assistant district attorney so aptly stated, your time is extremely valuable, and the service you are doing for the people of this great state, is invaluable.

"I will show you that the defendant—Phillip Hobart," he said, pointing to his client, "a man of unique integrity; a good family man; and honest, hardworkingman; a man of impeccable character—was himself the victim in this case."

Baker paused, looked at Hobart, a caring, almost tearful look, then turned and gazed soulfully at each of the jurors, making a couple of them squirm uneasily. It was a poignant moment—perfectly executed, preparing them for his explanation of the pain and emotional duress that Hobart was under, which he was about to place squarely on their collective shoulders.

"My client, was a victim of the uncaring, unscrupulous, and unethical activities of individuals given the responsibility of running the corporation for investors. Mr. Day's self-serving activities placed this man," pointing to Hobart, "under unbelievable duress, taking everything he had.

"I will show you that my client was decimated—despondent—and desperate. A man clearly of diminished capacity. He was no longer able to provide for his children, unable to pay for their education, was in jeopardy of losing his home and his dignity."

Hobart's advocate moved slowly to the other end of the jury box, allowing each juror to absorb, feel, and contemplate what he had just presented.

"What would any reasonable man or woman have done?" he said feebly, barely audible, forcing jurors to strain to hear what he was saying.

"How much could I have endured?" he boomed, angst evident in his sudden outburst, causing a few jurors to jump.

"What would any of you have done?" he said, compassionately, dolefully, playing again on the jurors' emotions.

Baker had taken the jury on an emotional ride, surely shaking some of their moral foundations. He paused, looked passionately at each juror. "I ask you again...can a man—violated as my client was—placed under such extreme duress—be held responsible for his actions...by any of us?"

Deafening silence.

Air conditioning hummed softly somewhere in the reticence, increasing in intensity, and finally a collective sigh pervaded the courtroom. An amplified sigh emanated through the microphone as Judge Neufeld gathered himself, banged his gavel, and called a recess for lunch.

"One-thirty, ladies and gentlemen. Be prompt. We start on time in this courtroom."

Stephanie carefully surveyed the jury. She wondered what they were thinking and what effect Baker's opening had on them.

50

*T*hey went down to lunch together, and Stephanie excused herself to answer a page from the office. She was gone for a little over 30 minutes. Dave had almost finished his lunch when she finally returned to the table. She sat down and began nibbling at the tuna salad Dave had ordered for her.

"What took you so long?" Dave asked, after she took a couple of bites of her tuna.

"I was just on the phone with the M.E. in Hauppauge," she said. She loved saying "hop pog" since she learned the proper pronunciation. "Hop Pog," she repeated, slowly. "You know, not too many people can pronounce that," she declared.

"And what did he want?" Dave asked.

"He wanted to give me some new information," she said, her excitement increasing.

"Oh, yeah. Anything of interest?"

"Lots. Want to hear about it?" she teased.

"Sure, but it doesn't matter. Our case is closed, and we're testifying *today*," he reminded her.

"I know, but this is pretty interesting stuff," she taunted.

"So...tell me!"

"Well, first of all." Stephanie went on to explain the new evidence the M.E. had uncovered. Information that—had they received it earlier—might have delayed the trial.

"The M.E. and a lab tech went back, checked the shower

doors, and found that one had no blood spatters on it, which would indicate that it was open at the time of the fall," Stephanie said. "Ordinarily that wouldn't be a concern, except the photos taken at the scene showed the doors were closed. The maid insisted that she never entered the bathroom, and she was positive the door was closed when she saw Mr. Wimkowski lying on the shower floor."

She explained that the M.E. also checked the floor outside the shower with Luminol and discovered blood spatters that had been wiped up. "He told me they were consistent with the spatters they found on the inside of the dam, below the door, that were barely obtainable because of the water." Stephanie looked up at Dave. "This is interesting. They were streaked, so it appeared someone had wiped up the blood before the water spilled out from the shower."

Dave stared blankly, deep in thought. "Hmmm, that is interesting," he mumbled.

Stephanie looked up from her notes. "You were right about the towel. They went through the water they collected from the bathroom floor and found some tiny white and light blue fibers—cotton towel fibers." She smiled. "The light blue fibers matched the towel they found in the washing machine, which also contained the victim's blood."

"In the washer?"

"The housekeeper had started a load of laundry before she discovered Wimkowski."

Dave shook his head. "And she didn't see the blood?"

"The M.E. told me there was only a small amount so she wouldn't have necessarily noticed it." She paused and raised her eyebrows. "There were no white towels in the bathroom, in the laundry, or linen closet that matched, so they don't know where the white fibers came from."

"*Wow!*" Dave said. "Sure raises some questions."

"And they should be answered, don't you think?"

"They probably should," Dave said. "If we weren't ready to testify against Hobart, they might reopen our case."

"*That's not all!*" she exclaimed, getting more excited. "I saved the best for last."

"There's more?"

"Yep. The M.E. tried a new forensic technique and found something intriguing. He covered the face with a new phosphorescent gel—let it dry for twenty minutes—and using the fluoroscope, looked at it with the help of a special high-intensity ultraviolet lamp." Stephanie beamed. "It's a brand new procedure."

"So what did he find?"

"He found some sub-dermal bruising on the wimkowski's face. Five distinct spots that would indicate someone had put their hand on his face and exerted some pressure."

"So what was the M.E.'s conclusion?"

"He felt that it indicated Wimkowski had been pushed, which would explain the excessive damage to the skull."

"Absent some other explanation, this is beginning to look like homicide," Dave said, shaking his head.

"It sure is," Stephanie said. "He said the Southampton police were considering reopening their case based on his new findings."

As a result of this new information, their conversation turned again to the other cases, as it had most of the week. The same unanswered questions, the same mantra. Was it a conspiracy? Who was killing these unscrupulous executives? Were all of them homicides? Did they miss some key element that would help connect all of them?

Manly came over before returning to the courtroom, and caught the tail end of Stephanie's statement. "Are you talking about the other cases?" he asked. "Anything new? Can we connect them to Hobart?"

"No," Stephanie answered. "Nothing new that we can pin on our suspect."

"So you think they were accidents after all?"

"I didn't say that," she said. "I just said that we had nothing new to connect with Hobart."

"Okay," he said, dropping it. "See you in the courtroom."

Stephanie watched him scurry off, his shouldered bag flying recklessly behind him. Stephanie could see that his suit had already begun a transformation. His shirt was pulled out slightly on one side, tie cocked to the left, his jacket already crumpled.

They finished lunch and headed up to Division 6. Manly was outside the courtroom talking with Jerry who was scheduled to testify later in the afternoon—following Dave and Stephanie.

"Hey Jerry," Stephanie smiled as they approached.

Jerry hadn't seen them for over a week, even though they were all preparing for this trial. "This one should be a slam dunk," he said to the two of them. "We've got *iron clad* evidence," he grinned.

"We sure do," Stephanie agreed, moderately excited about testifying. "It was teamwork."

"You two did a great job," Dave said, complimenting Stephanie and Jerry on their work.

"You all did a great job on this one," Manly interrupted. "Dave, you'll go first, then Stephanie, and then I'll call Jerry to finish it up." He paused, looked over at the clock and said, "Got to get into court. I'll see you when you're called."

Manly disappeared through the big mahogany doors, and the three of them continued their discussion in the hallway. Dave was called to testify first.

Jerry asked Stephanie if they had found anything new in the other cases, and she began to explain the new things each of the investigative teams had discovered.

Stephanie sat down on one of the benches. "Yep, they found some microscopic marks on the nuts from the scaffolding."

Jerry sat down beside her as he spoke. "And they couldn't match a tool to the marks?" Jerry asked. "Do you think they'd send them to us to examine?"

"They thought it might be homemade," she explained. "I don't know, Jerry, we could ask."

"Fascinating. It would be interesting if they would let us take a look at them."

They talked about the disappearance in Hawaii, and she explained the efforts of the search and rescue team. Jerry was also curious about the tracking device and grilled Stephanie about where, and how they found it. She explained the M.E.'s discoveries in Southampton. "They found the bruises with a special phosphorescent gel and ultraviolet lamp," she stated, knowing that Jerry would appreciate this new forensic technique.

"Bruises on the face?"

"Yep, the M.E. said it was clearly the impression of a hand in the face. He said he could even measure the size of the hand," Stephanie explained further.

"Wow!" Jerry exalted. "I have to get in touch with the Suffolk M.E."

Stephanie had enjoyed working with Jerry on this case. He was professional and extremely thorough. He did a great job gathering evidence when initially there didn't seem to be any. Stephanie knew there was no doubt in Jerry's mind that Hobart was the one who killed Benjamin Day, and she was sure he would prove it in the courtroom.

"So, what do you think, Jerry? Looks like more than coincidence now, doesn't it?"

Jerry nodded. "Sure does. You were right, Stephanie. Every one is looking more like a homicide."

51

In the courtroom, Manly was putting Dave through his organized series of questions. Dave had testified many times, so today's testimony would be fairly routine.

Manly: "And the scuff on the tire is what caught your attention."

Dave: "Yes."

Manly: "Upon closer investigation did you discover that the tires on the defendant's car matched the model of the impressions found at the crime scene?"

Dave: "Yes, they did."

Manly: "After making contact with the defendant, was there anything else that led you to believe Mr. Hobart might be a suspect?"

Dave: "Yes, there was."

Manly: "And could you tell the court what that was?"

Dave: "The defendant was wearing the same brand of running shoes as the impressions found at the crime scene."

Manly: "Adidas, adiStar Cushion Ms?" Manly read from the report.

Dave: "Yes."

Dave continued to answer Manly's questions, as well as Baker's when he began his cross examination. Baker had gone through the standard questions rapidly.

Baker: "Did anything contaminate any portion of the crime scene to the best of your knowledge, Detective Duncan?"

Dave: "No, not to the best of my knowledge."

Baker: "And nothing was disturbed in the residence prior to the arrival of the warrant?"

Dave: "No, nothing was touched."

Baker: "And you and your partner would never tamper with evidence at a crime scene, would you, Detective Duncan?"

Manly: "Objection!"

Baker: "Your partner didn't—."

Manly: "Objection, Your Honor. He's arguing with the—."

Baker: "Withdrawn."

Dave knew Baker wasn't going to waste many questions on him. His strategy was to save the damaging ones for the rookie—Stephanie Fox. He finished with Dave, and Manly called Stephanie to the stand.

Dave watched as Stephanie took the oath for the first time as a detective. She took a deep breath and waited for Manly's first question.

Manly: "Could you state your full name, and spell your last name for the court?"

Stephanie: "Stephanie Fox—F-O-X."

Manly: "And what is your position?"

Stephanie: "I'm a detective first grade with the Houston Police Department."

Manly: "How long have you been with the Houston Police Department, Detective Fox?"

Smart, Dave thought. Manly used her full tenure with the department, not just the short time she'd been a detective.

Stephanie: "For almost five years."

Manly: "Prior to that you were in the police academy?"

Stephanie: "Yes, the the Houston police academy."

Manly: "Could you tell the court about any additional education you've had in criminology?"

Stephanie: "I completed the criminology course at Plano Valley College before attending the academy." She looked over at the jury for the first time.

Dave could tell Stephanie was beginning to feel more comfortable as Manly asked his series of questions. *Good for you. Now just take it easy and stay alert.*

Manly: "You attended Plano for two years?"
Stephanie: "Yes."
Manly: "And you graduated from the criminology course?"
Stephanie: "Yes, I completed the course before enrolling in the academy."
Manly: "And I see you finished third in your class?"
Stephanie: "Yes, I did."
Manly: "Could you tell us how you did on the detective exam?"
Stephanie: "I finished second in the exam."

Stephanie answered all the questions Manly asked her and described the discovery of the evidence and the arrest of Hobart, pretty much matching Dave's testimony. He concluded his questioning and turned Stephanie over to Baker.

Baker's motion to exclude the evidence Dave and Stephanie had collected at Hobart's had already been denied. No doubt he would try to persuade the jury that the collection was unlawful and demonstrate that the prosecution was hiding that fact.

Baker: "And you claim Mr. Hobart invited you in the house?"
Stephanie: "Yes."
Baker: "Didn't you ask if you could use the phone?"
Stephanie: "Yes."
Baker: "So he didn't exactly *invite* you in?" Baker asked emphatically.
Stephanie: "Yes, he did ask us to come in," she said calmly.
Baker: "You mean *you* asked to come in, don't you?"
Manly: "Your Honor, asked and answered." Manly objected.
Neufeld: "Sustained."

Baker: "I'm sorry Your Honor, I'll rephrase. Detective Fox, did he actually ask you to come in and use the phone?"

Manly: "Your Honor."

Stephanie: "No. But he said it was all right to come in and use the phone when I asked him." Stephanie answered, before the judge could rule.

Baker: "*So you tricked him?*" He turned toward the jury and away from Stephanie.

Stephanie: "No, I didn't trick him—I did use the phone."

Manly: "Your Honor?"

Baker: "I'll move on, Your Honor. She told me what I needed to know."

He walked over and looked at Hobart, opened the cover of another file, and turned back to face Stephanie.

Baker: "You've been a detective how long…four months?"

Stephanie: "I was promoted in June."

Baker: "And you made detective in a short time, didn't you?"

Stephanie: "Yes, hard work and training can do that."

Baker: "Well…let me be one of the first to congratulate you, Ms. Fox."

Manly: "Objection—."

Stephanie stared mutely, not sure that his statement required her answer.

Baker: "So you've obviously testified before?"

Stephanie: "Yes."

Baker: "And as a detective, you've testified in capital cases such as this?"

Stephanie: "No, this is my first capital case…but all testimony must meet—."

Baker: "*First?*" Tony turned, a surprised expression on his face.

Stephanie: "Yes."

Baker: "First?" he said again, a little calmer, and shaking his head slowly.

Manly: "Objection!"

Neufeld: "Sustained."

Baker smiled at the jury as he completed his statement.

Baker: "Was this then, the first big case you've investigated?"

Stephanie: "Well…I guess so."

Baker: "So…I'll take that as a yes. You must have had a lot of questions?"

Stephanie: "Well…some."

Baker: "I'm sure," he said, sympathetically. "I don't know about you." He paused, looking at the jury. "But, I avoid buying a new car in the first year of a new model. They always have things go wrong. I know that we've all bought a new model and have had that happen." He smiled at the jury.

Manly: "Objection…counsel is testifying."

Most of the jury smiled, and about half nodded their heads.

Baker: "Could you have made a mistake or two on this—*your first big case*, Ms. Fox?"

Manly: "Your Honor, he's arguing with Detective Fox."

Neufeld: "Mr. Baker, do you have a point that is relevant?"

Baker: "Yes, Your Honor. It's regarding the collection of evidence."

Neufeld: "Then, please, get to the point."

Baker turned, walked back to the table, and picked up another folder. He opened it, acted like he was reading something.

Baker: "And how did you discover the evidence you gathered from Mr. Hobart's home? Evidence you found after you tricked Mr. Hobart and are now presenting in an effort to convict him."

Stephanie: "It was in plain sight. We didn't gather any evidence from inside the house until after arresting Mr. Hobart and obtaining a search warrant," Stephanie added, a little more flustered.

Baker: "So on what basis did you arrest Mr. Hobart?"

Stephanie: "On the basis of the matching tires, the smudge

from the curb on the right front tire, the running shoes he was wearing when he came outside, and learning from the phone call that he owned a .38 caliber, Smith and Wesson Model Ten."

Good. Dave thought she sounded more confident again.

Baker: "Is that so, Ms. Fox? How long were you in the house before the warrant arrived?"

Stephanie: "I don't know…maybe fifteen minutes."

Baker: "And your partner, Detective Duncan, was there with you?"

Stephanie: "Yes, he was."

Baker: "Was he invited in by my client?"

Stephanie: "Yes."

Baker: "Isn't it true that my client said *you* could come in?"

Stephanie: "Yes…but—"

Baker: "Did you hear him invite Detective Duncan in?"

Stephanie: "Well…no…I—"

Baker: "And though uninvited, he was there the whole time? The whole fifteen minutes or more?"

Stephanie: "Yes, he was—"

Baker: "Could it have been twenty minutes, or maybe twenty-five?"

Stephanie: "I don't think it was twenty-five, but—"

Baker: "But it could have been?"

Stephanie: "No, I don't think—"

Dave became concerned for Stephanie. Baker had opened the folder as if he had some evidence he was going to throw at her. *What does he have up his sleeve?*

Baker: "What would you say if I told you it was twenty-five?"

Stephanie: "It didn't seem that long."

Baker: "Yes…it is a long time. Long enough to mess with or plant some evidence?"

Manly: "*Objection*, argumentative," Manly shrieked.

Stephanie: "We didn't touch anything that was not in plain sight." Her voice elevated.

Neufeld: "Sustained."

Baker: "Withdrawn, Your Honor," the defense attorney said coolly. "What would you say, *Ms. Fox*, if I were to tell you that we have a fingerprint of your partner's from the inside of the defendant's residence?"

Stephanie: "We didn't—."

Manly: "*Objection*, sidebar, Your Honor?"

Neufeld: "You don't have to answer that, Detective Fox. Come," he motioned the two attorneys to the left side of the bench—his right.

Manly: "Your Honor, you didn't allow his question about planting evidence. He's trying to go down the same path."

Baker: "She said they didn't touch anything, Your Honor, and so did her partner, Detective Duncan."

Neufeld: "Do you *actually* have evidence that they did, Mr. Baker?"

Baker: "Yes…I do, Your Honor."

Neufeld: "*What*, Mr. Baker."

Baker: "We have Detective Duncan's fingerprint on the trophy case."

Manly: "But Your Hon—"

Neufeld: "I'll allow it, *but you had better not stray, Mr. Baker.*"

Baker: "Thank you, your Honor."

They returned to their tables and Phillip's attorney changed folders.

Baker: "We have Detective Duncan's fingerprint on the trophy case. Was that before or after the warrant, *Ms. Fox*?"

Manly: "*It's detective*, Your Honor."

Neufeld: "Mr. Baker, *you will address the detective properly.*"

Baker: "Sorry, Your Honor. Detective Fox…was it *before* or after?"

Stephanie: "It was before…Detective Duncan was—"

Baker: "Thank you, Detective Fox." He paused.

Manly: "Your Honor, the detective should be allowed to answer the question before counsel cuts—"

Baker: "I'll rephrase."

Baker paused and walked back to the table appearing to be thinking about his next question. He ran his finger along the table's edge, then turned back to Stephanie.

Baker: "So, you weren't being truthful about not touching anything before the warrant arrived?"

Stephanie: "I didn't know he had touched the trophy case. He was only pointing out—"

Baker: "So we can't expect the jury to believe the evidence gathered at my client's residence was collected legally, *can we*?"

Manly: "*Objection!*" Manly shouted.

Neufeld: "Sustained...Mr. Bake—"

Baker: Nothing further, Your Honor."

Baker closed the folder and dropped it confidently on top of the pile making sure the jury was aware of his confidence. He patted Hobart on the shoulder as he sat down.

Neufeld: "Redirect, Mr. Manly."

Manly: "Nothing at this time."

Stephanie finished her testimony and stepped back into the hallway. Dave joined her, and they wished Jerry good luck.

"How you feeling?" Dave asked, as they headed toward the exit to return to the station.

"Not good," she answered. "I'm glad it's over."

"You were up there a long time," he said.

"I thought I was doing okay until Baker asked about the evidence, and how we obtained it," she said. "Then he brought up your fingerprint on the trophy case."

Dave felt horrible about that. "I'm sorry, Steph, I really didn't think about accidently touching the door. We had so much evidence." He shrugged. "I didn't think anybody would get that fingerprint."

"Well, Baker did, and he sure caught me by surprise with it."

Dave smiled. "Tony Baker is turning out to be sharper than

anyone gave him credit for," he continued. "But, I am surprised Manly didn't clean it up in redirect."

"Well, it rattled me pretty good."

"Don't let it bother you, Steph. You did a great job on this case." He beamed, proud of her effort. "You did your job to help Manly convict him."

The light rain that had begun that morning increased in intensity as Dave held the door open for his partner and they stepped outside. They huddled for a minute under the portico of the courthouse waiting for a break in the inclement weather. Neither had brought an umbrella. They stood and stared at the rain in silence. One minute turned into five, and there was no sign of it letting up.

Finally Dave put his arm around Stephanie, and they walked through the heavy raindrops, down the steps, and away from the courthouse. He gave her a little squeeze, firm, reassuring, letting her know he believed she did a good job.

A broad smile, warm and inviting, turned up on Stephanie's rain-soaked face.

"Thank you, Dave," she said. "You never know…you might get your wish. He may get to spend his last months at home. Do you think he was part of a conspiracy, or was it just me?"

The skies opened up—a sudden downpour—as they reached the cover of the parking structure. Dave turned to face Stephanie. A flash of lightning ripped through the sky followed by a deafening boom of thunder. As the thunder subsided, Dave spoke up. "If there was a conspiracy, I'm afraid Hobart's prepared to take it with him to his grave." Dave paused. "It's a puzzle we'll never be able to put together."

52

The electric blue flash of light and thunderous cacophony, in stark contrast to the rain's tranquil symphony, ripped at the fabric of the dark San Francisco sky. The TransAmerica pyramid, just blocks away, stood defiant against the raging storm.

A well-dressed man in his late sixties stood perfectly still, mesmerized by the drops playing on the panes of glass in front of him. From his eighth floor office, he stared at the skyline and the gray clouds blanketing the city. The calming rythmn returned.

Lightning streaks across the sky, and the crash of thunder jogged him from his deep thoughts. He turned and walked to the side of his enormous antique mahogany desk.

A Friday edition of the *Houston Chronicle* was sitting on top of the neat desk. Slowly he ran his fingers over the headline as if he were reading it in braille, and read aloud, "Trial Begins in Day Murder." He paused, picked up the paper and added, "It's a shame this happened."

Byron Thursby: businessman, entrepreneur, multimillionaire, a man of integrity and wealth had been following the Hobart trial very closely. He was a well-respected member of San Francisco's upper class and the business community.

He handed the newspaper to the gentleman sitting in one of the overstuffed chairs in front of the desk.

"It is—*unfortunate*," the gentleman said in a calm and caring voice as he took the newspaper from his friend.

Ethan Penfel had been Byron Thursby's trusted friend and assistant for more than 30 years. He was a highly intelligent individual, a resourceful and astute businessman, and, like Thursby, a man of unquestionable integrity. That is probably why he had been with Thursby for so long, and why Thursby had time-tested and unwavering respect for Penfel.

From the credenza behind him, Thursby grabbed a couple of folders. Turning back, he looked at Penfel.

"They're calling him a cold-blooded killer," Thursby said.

"I don't think he cares," Penfel shrugged. "His terminal illness will take him before they can sentence him."

"It probably will. That will be better for him than spending the rest of his life in prison or waiting on death row for who knows how many years," Thursby said, returning to his task.

Thursby's eyes were drawn to the folder sitting in the upper left corner of his desk. He stared at it for a long moment, then pulled it in front of him. Hands trembling, he slowly opened it and lifted the weathered, yellowed newspaper article.

Skipping the first two paragraphs, which he now knew by heart, he focused on the third one. It angered him each time he read the accusatory voice of the journalist, who cited the victim's greed as the real cause of death.

Though Thursby acknowledged that greed was part of the story, nowhere in the article was the blame laid at the feet of the corrupt corporate executives who caused the desperation his friend, his teacher, his mentor had felt before killing himself. He repressed his anger, quietly tucked the article back into the folder, and moved it back to its permanent resting place.

Penfel had returned to the paper. It was difficult to read in the dimly lit room, a room, not dark merely from lack of lighting, but from the rich woods, the polished mahoganies, and the deep walnuts of the furniture and paneled walls of this lavish office in San Francisco's Market District.

A single window took up nearly a third of the west wall, the thick rich drapes, reminiscent of the late thirties, hung full length on either side of the window Thursby had stared out earlier. Thunder and lightning were still discernible outside.

The desk filled one corner of the large room. An expensive Renóir hung over the credenza behind Thursby. It was the first painting that Catherine, Thursby's wife and lifetime love, had purchased after he moved into the top floor of this historic building.

Cabinets and shelves were filled with books and numerous awards and plaques for philanthropy and business. The south wall of the office had an original Monét, Thursby's favorite artist, hanging above a bust of Andrew Carnegie, his mentor.

Penfel reached over and turned the desk lamp up one more level so that he could finish reading the cover story. He would pick up the Saturday, Monday, and Tuesday editions of the Houston paper from a newsstand in the Market District tomorrow, so they could keep up with the developments in the case.

As Penfel read, Thursby opened the top folder. It contained clippings from various newspapers. The middle tab had "Carston" written in black marking pen—bold capital letters. Newspaper articles from Maui, Houston, and the *Wall Street Journal* filled the folder. There were four other folders below that one. Each one had a hand-written name on the tab, and each was filled with similar newspaper articles.

Meanwhile, Penfel quietly read the story, seated comfortably in one of the soft, plush, overstuffed chairs across from Thursby. He turned the page. "It looks like the evidence is solid, and there's a lot of it," he said to Thursby. "If we can believe what the district attorney is telling the media."

Thursby looked up. "Yes, it looks like the investigators did a good job."

"Unfortunately for Hobart, *too good a job*," Penfel agreed. "*And very quick!*"

"Incredibly, in just two days," Thursby said. "Hobart needed a three-month investigation."

Penfel just nodded, and they both returned to what they were doing.

Thursby had shuffled through all the newspaper clippings in the folders. He turned and put the folders back neatly, in the same location from where he retrieved them. He took two more folders off the credenza and turned back to his desk.

The first folder contained a list of names, about eleven pages, some with black checkmarks. He read through the list. Each contained a short paragraph or two, to the right of the name.

Penfel came to the part in the article, a side-bar, chronicling Day's involvement, and his denial of involvement, in the Energy-Dyn scandal. Day had insisted that he had no knowledge of two-way trades, or shell trading companies or any other malfeasance. He claimed his selling of stocks during the fourteen-month period prior to the bankruptcy was fortuitous, but not illegal.

"Day claimed he knew *nothing* of the malfeasance at Energy-Dyn," Penfel said, breaking the silence in the room. "He didn't know subordinates were inflating the bottom line."

"That's why he was placed high on the list," Thursby said, looking across at Penfel.

"I know, and I agree, *totally*," Penfel answered. "He was either a crooked chairman, or incredibly incompetent."

"I would have to vote for crooked given a choice," Thursby said. "Call me cynical, but I just can't believe that selling more than $100 million worth of stock, months before the collapse of his corporation, was merely fortuitous."

Byron Thursby had a reputation of extreme integrity in his business and personal life. He was a millionaire many times over, a businessman whose word was his bond.

He was honest, fair, and ethical—qualities that were lacking in many of today's corporate executives. This really bothered Thursby. He demanded integrity from everyone around him, whether it was in business or in his personal relationships. He took care of his employees, many of whom were millionaires now, and, in turn, his employees rewarded him with success and wealth.

Some of the executives in charge today had forgotten the basic principle of running a public corporation. That principle was responsibility to the employees, creditors, and investors.

He also felt that bankruptcy today was far too easy and became the coward's way out. Thursby felt that bankruptcy laws were far too forgiving, and that the leniency of the laws was exacerbating the problem.

Each individual on the list had forgotten those principles—or never had them. Or maybe it was sheer greed. Whatever the reason, they *were* on the list.

He wondered where the colleges and universities were in this equation. What on earth were they teaching? Surely *they* should share in the responsibility for this mess. He looked up at Penfel who had just finished reading the article.

"We are sending a message regarding corporate governance, aren't we, Ethan?" Thursby asked, looking for affirmation.

"I think so, Byron," he stated, emphatically.

Penfel's conviction was reassuring. "The Day murder didn't change that, did it?"

"I don't think so," Penfel answered. "I think the message is still evident to those for whom it is intended."

"It would have been much better if Hobart hadn't been caught," Thursby said.

"Probably," Penfel confirmed. "It would have looked more like the others. Unsolved, it would have left everyone a little more uncomfortable,"

"Do you think the business world is getting the point?"

"I'm sure they are," Penfel said. "Five executives dead in such a short time-span. And all from failed or bankrupt corporations under investigation by the government. I think they get it."

"That was our intention, but do you think it has been too subtle?"

"It *is* our intention, Byron, and I think smart executives are paying attention and getting the message. It is covered extensively in all the business publications and the business news telecasts. So I think executives are becoming aware that this is more than a coincidence."

Every executive strives to move up in the corporation, and one reward is the key to the executive restroom. Receiving that key put an executive on an elite list and was a corporate cliché for having arrived. Losing that key could be devastating. Thursby was not asking for the key back: he was taking it.

With Penfel's help, they had compiled a list of more than 75 corporate executives who were wholly or in part responsible for the failures of their corporations. It was an elite list, but not one any of the executives would aspire to be on. Responsible for losses in the billions, affecting hundreds of millions of people—each had varying degrees of culpability.

Each individual was put on the list after careful investigation, evaluation, and research. Each sold millions of dollars worth of stock before their corporations filed bankruptcy, obviously, evidence of knowledge of their imminent failure.

The message was to become more apparent with each death—all accidents. A series of coincidences that would eventually lead to an undeniable truth. That truth was simple: corporate executives of bankrupt corporations, who were involved in the improprieties and wrongdoing were dying. It was hoped that other executives would pick up on the inscrutable message as the number of dead executives—all of them greedy, selfish, arrogant, and ambivalent to their charges' rights—increased.

The business sections reported all of the accidents and continued to report them. *The Wall Street Journal* even brought up the coincidence theory in its article about Wimkowski. For the first time, it broached the possibility that these deaths were connected, but had no evidence, no reliable sources, to substantiate that theory. So the story faded, and Wimkowski's death, like the others, was listed as accidental.

53

*T*hursby's plan was to send a message to only those for whom it was intended. He could justify the elimination of those who were guilty, but could not live with any collateral damage from what he was doing.

Benjamin Day was on that list, so neither Thursby nor Penfel believed the misfortune of Hobart's murdering Day, or being caught for his murder, would alter the message. Maybe it would take a little focus off the others for a short time, but the Wimkowski death brought them right back to the point.

Wimkowski's death could not be stopped even if they had wanted to. Once the selection was made, the request sent, and the plan put in motion, it could not be reversed. There was no way to contact the individual whose services had been contracted once they had received *the package*.

Carston was the first on the list. He had been selected because of his part in the collapse of EnergyDyn. At the time, it was the largest bankruptcy in history. The stocks' immediate and permanent decline affected millions of investors and ran into the billions of dollars. In its corporate annual report for the year 2000, Energy-Dyn listed nearly $50 billion in assets. Where was it? In the world of magic, it would have surely been touted as the quintessential misdirection. So where did it go? Stephen Carston had the answer.

Carston's disappearance was a work of art.

"Mr. Smith orchestrated a perfect first accident," Thursby said to Penfel. "Carston was on vacation and just seemed to disappear—*poof.*"

"He did. And you're right, it was brilliant," Penfel said.

"*It did raise some suspicions though*," Thursby said, expressing a concern.

"Yes, it did. At one point, the police thought he had faked his own death," Penfel countered, "but they didn't suspect that he had been murdered."

"The message would have been in jeopardy right from the start, if the Maui Police Department had determined he faked his own death."

"But they didn't, *because* of the job Mr. Smith did," Penfel reiterated.

The selected individual's name and details were sent to one of three operatives. All were military trained in areas of stealth, deception, communications, firearms, combat, electronics, as well as explosives.

Their task, once they received this special package, was to plan and execute an extermination. The death had to appear to be accidental, and unpremeditated. For his part, the operative received $5,000 in cash, with the package, as immediate operating capital, and a deposit of $95,000 wired to a numbered account in a Swiss bank, for the operation.

Upon successful completion, the operatives would place newspaper clippings of the accident and death of the selected individual in a pre-addressed envelope, and mail it to an address in San Francisco. Penfel would retrieve them, and an additional $150,000 was transferred to another numbered account in the Caymans as final payment.

The Carston drowning was planned in less than a month. Each of the others took two to four months to plan and execute.

Mr. Smith was chosen for the first task. He caught Carston out snorkeling. Though Thursby and Penfel were not given specific details, they knew of the type of accident chosen, and the outcome, from the newspaper accounts of the death or disappearance.

Expert in covert operations, Smith developed the plan for Carston's demise. He knew that Carston would be vacationing in

Hawaii and followed him to Maui where he would meet with an accident.

While in Kahanapali, Smith discovered that Carston planned to snorkel every day. He devised a plan for Carston to disappear at one of his favorite spots. His preparation required finding out Carston's schedule and snorkeling locations, without actually being connected to him in any way.

He was able to do this with a casual meeting and conversation in the bar with Carston himself at the hotel. During the conversation, they discussed diving and snorkeling. Carston extolled his trip to Molokini that day. His glowing description of the aquarium-like atmosphere was so enticing, it momentarily distracted Smith from his task. Discovering Carston's snorkeling location for that Thursday, Smith was able to put the final touches on his plan.

That day Smith anchored his rented boat near Ulua Beach and scanned the beach through highpowered binoculars searching for Carston. He rented the boat in Lahaina. It was the same one he rented the previous three days to eliminate suspicion.

Carston was there—at Ulua Beach. He had described it to Smith and explained that it was his favorite place to snorkel on the island. This section of beach, with its rugged point, was a favorite of many who came to the west side of the island. He looked relaxed as he stood waist-deep and moved his hand through the water. But that would soon change.

The rocky point, a random structure of weathered rocks and bright coral, stretched out from the beach for over a quarter mile, providing a wonderful playground for the fish and sea creatures that lived there—a snorkeler's dream.

As Carston readied his snorkeling gear, Smith donned the final pieces of his diving gear, slipped quietly into the water, and headed toward the point. Carston was a good swimmer, but would be no match for Smith, an ex-Navy Seal.

Luring Carston out to a more secluded area of the point with the promise of seeing something spectacular was Smith's idea. It was easier than he expected. Carston had been easily drawn to a shiny object beyond the end of the point. Once Carston turned the corner, Smith drew his weapon and took aim. A well-placed shot from his Trident Underwater pneumatic pistol, equipped with a custom-made tranquilizer tip, would be all he needed to execute his plan.

He set the pistol on the low power setting, and from six feet away he fired. The 16 inch dart coursed through the water, with a high pitched whine, and struck Carston in the shoulder. The tranquilizer drug began to take affect on impact, and in just under a minute, Smith was able to drag Carston's limp body out to his boat, anchored about 100 yards beyond the end of the point.

He lashed him to the side of the boat, just under the waterline, to avoid detection, and headed further out to sea—a normal, enjoyable day of diving.

When he reached his destination he tied heavy weights, two 25 pound discs, to chains wrapped around Carston's lifeless body and watched as he disappeared in the deep blue depths of the Pacific Ocean.

Newspapers reported Carston's disappearance as a drowning. That was enough for Thursby and Penfel. The first assignment was executed. Their plan was in motion.

"Mr. Jones did an equally fine job with Galivan," Thursby stated.

"He did," Penfel conceded. "The fall from the scaffolding was almost poetic—Galivan's fall from grace."

"I would be curious to find out how he lured him out on the scaffold," Thursby said.

"We'll never know exactly, but it had the desired effect." Penfel smiled at his long-time friend. "The newspaper clippings gave us some information."

Thursby nodded. "That it did."

The newspaper accounts did not fully reveal the ultimate brilliance of Jones's nearly perfect deception.

Jones spent several weeks in the Boca Raton area formulating Galivan's demise. Several days at the construction site, posing as one of the workers, was all he needed to get the lay of the land, schedules, and pictures, in order to form his strategy.

As an ex-Army Ranger he was good at observation and had purchased the right tool belt and boots to blend in perfectly with the others. His training allowed him to pass as a journeyman electrician. After a few days at the site, Jones decided that a fall from the third-story scaffolding would do the trick.

A well-conceived phone call from a pay phone would be all he required to get Galivan out to the property on Friday evening after the crews had gone home.

Posing as a building inspector, he informed Galivan that he had uncovered some code violations and corruption within the building department that he needed to discuss with him privately before breaking it open. He played on Galivan's greed, explaining that he might be able to retrieve more than a million bucks on his project. A million that Galivan could put back in his own greedy pocket—a million reasons to meet out at the construction site. The sheer mention of that kind of money piqued Galivan's interest sufficiently to get him to meet at any time Jones suggested.

So, Jones, pretending to be Mr. Johnston, of the Boca Raton Building Department, requested a meeting at six o'clock on Friday evening. He promised to show Galivan several areas of infraction and expose the fraud that was costing him a lot of money.

Jones knew no one would be on the scaffolding on Friday, so under the cover of darkness on Thursday night, he removed fifteen nuts, including the two in a strategic location.

Galivan arrived on time, promptly at 6:00 p.m. The crews were gone, and an unsuspecting Galivan obediently followed Mr. Johnston to the third-floor balcony. Directing Galivan to step out on the scaffolding to see the first violation was all Jones needed. Galivan's weight caused the altered plank to immediately give way, and the three story fall proved to be fatal.

A stoic Mr. Jones drove away in his borrowed work truck, emblazoned with Boca Raton decals on the side, returned it to the Public Works yard, and walked calmly to his waiting rental car. He returned to the hotel and got a good night's sleep.

Jones enjoyed the South Florida beaches on Saturday. He drove down to Miami on Sunday and decided to have lunch at a popular South Beach restaurant—the News Cafe. On Monday, he gathered up the five newspapers he had purchased and headed home to Pensacola, never to be seen in Boca Raton again.

The last two accidents were equally efficient. The results were what Thursby and Penfel were looking for. Digást's mishap went as planned.

It was simple actually, but effective. Mr. Gray was confronted with obstacles not inherent in the other operations. The closely knit mountain town of Coudersport presented a unique problem.

Mr. Gray had to devise a plan that would not raise the suspicions of local residents. He could pose as a tourist, maybe two times, but more than that and he would run the risk of being noticed.

After his two visits he decided that Digást's accident would have to occur outside the cozy Alleghany mountain town to avoid detection. The curvy, mountainous terrain of Highway 6 would provide the perfect opportunity to create the young executive's unfortunate accident. He picked the location for the accident and worked on the timing and execution.

Digást's frequent trips to, and late night returns from, Pittsburgh and Philadelphia would make Gray's task much easier.

He attached a state-of-the-art transmitter to the frame of Digást's Porsche and tracked him several times before he put his plan into motion. He ran Digást off the road and into the Alleghany River about eight miles outside of Coudersport.

It worked to Gray's satisfaction, as he stuffed the newspaper clippings into the envelope to send to Penfel. Local newspapers did an excellent job describing this tragic and unfortunate traffic fatality of one of Coudersport's most prominent citizens.

The forth accident had already been set in motion before Hobart killed Day. But Thursby and Penfel couldn't have stopped Wimkowski's accident even if they had wanted to. It worked out exceedingly well though, and may have had an even greater impact coming on the heels of Day's murder.

The Wimkowski operation was a study in patience. Mr. Smith put his years of training to the test and the outcome was testimony to the excellent training he received in the military.

He snuck into the Wimkowski home while the housekeeper was there and the alarm was off. He waited patiently all afternoon, undetected, while the housekeeper performed her daily duties. It was easy for him to hide in the huge house.

She left, resetting the alarm, and Smith cased the entire house, finalizing last-minute details. He waited patiently until Wimkowski returned home and took care of business downstairs. Smith watched silently as Wimkowski got something to eat and drink, listened to the stock report, shuffled through his mail, and listened to his phone messages. It was late, and after resetting the alarm, Wimkowski headed upstairs to take a shower and retire for the evening.

Smith sprung into action, donned his surgical booties, exited his hiding place and ascended the stairs to confront his victim. When Wimkowski entered the shower, Smith pounced, swiftly, surreptitiously, and, in a matter of seconds, completed the assignment.

It had gone smoother than he had anticipated, and with half the expected effort. There was no struggle and little clean-up required. He wiped up the blood from the bathroom floor with a towel, closed the shower door, and headed downstairs to patiently wait for the housekeeper to return at 9:00 a.m.

The housekeeper arrived at her usual time on Friday morning, turned off the alarm, and went about her daily routine. At the appropriate time, Smith exited the house, slipped out the gate, and, dressed in a jogging suit with a towel around his neck, jogged down the beach and back to his room at the Southampton Inn.

A perfectly executed plan and an unfortunate turn of events for Wimkowski. It is said that 50 percent of all accidents occurred within one mile of the home.

Benjamin Day was high on the list and may have been the next victim if Phillip Hobart had not stepped in. Since Day was on their list of victims, Thursby gave serious thought to helping Hobart by paying for his defense. Penfel made the offer—anonymously.

Thursby would have covered all the costs of Hobart's legal defense if he hadn't declined, and if Penfel hadn't found out about Hobart's terminal cancer. The illness was obviously paramount in his decision to reject Thursby's generosity.

The media was accommodating in delivering the sad news of Hobart's illness. They were always quick to jump on a story—any story that would boost their ratings. Baker's motion for a continuance, citing his client's cancer, was a revelation on the first day of the trial and provided the media with hundreds of journalistic inches. Thursby was sure that Hobart was anxious to tell his story, and that it would be well covered by all the big newspapers and cable and network news.

Thursby turned back to his list and, again, ran his finger slowly over the names. He went past Carston and the checkmarks next to Galivan, Digást, and Wimkowski.

Benjamin Day also had a checkmark, a new one, next to his name. It was like a lottery. But this selection was particularly important. Thursby wanted this "accident" to drive home the message: corporate malfeasance will not be tolerated, and there would be a price to pay.

He would give this decision a lot of thought before choosing the final victim.

54

His finger stopped next to a name on the second page of the list. He thought for a moment then looked up at Penfel sitting across the desk from him. "Stan Bonsell," he said quietly to himself, but loud enough for Penfel to hear.

"No, Byron, I don't think so. Someone a little more involved and more obvious."

"You're right, as usual," he said, looking down at the list. He glanced at Penfel again. "I was trying to pick executives from different sectors."

"Not a bad idea, but Bonsell has already pleaded guilty, trying to protect his family members. It sounds like he will be getting a pretty stiff sentence." After a brief pause, he added, "I think we'll have to choose another, Byron—someone stronger."

"How about Barry Sinteck?" Thursby asked, placing his finger on the name and reading the short paragraph.

Thunder rumbled outside, rolling through the city and dissipating somewhere in the north.

"CEO of Trans Ocean Communications; feigned any knowledge or responsibility for the failure of the company; sold $135 million in corporate stock in the months prior to filing bankruptcy; offered a settlement to the pension fund of the employees who lost their pensions, as a gesture of goodwill; and is still denying any responsibility."

Penfel nodded, a sign of immediate approval. This was the

one that would make the message clear to all corporate executives. They had agreed that if all went according to plan it would take five or six "accidents" for most executives to realize these deaths were more than coincidental. Thursby wanted to be sure they would make the connection.

The government was trying to send its own message, by passing a bill requiring CEOs and CFOs to sign the quarterly reports certifying the authenticity and validity of the numbers on the financial report. As is typical of Congress, politicians overreacted to correct a situation they helped create.

The CEOs had always been required to certify the financial reports, and the SEC had the authority to monitor and take action when it found infractions, but Congress had tied the hands of the SEC in wielding that authority.

Thursby had long felt that the government managed to screw up most everything it became involved in, and what happened was in part the government's responsibility, but the public would never see any of their elected officials stepping forward to take responsibility. Members of Congress had always been good at covering up their ineptitude by finger pointing, or convening a subcommittee hearing.

Thursby always thought that members of Congress should be put in jail, right along with these corporate executives. "Real" jail with real convicts whose mothers or aunts or fathers had lost money in the collapses of these corporations.

"They should have put Millkin and Keating away in a real prison years ago. If they had, these scandals probably wouldn't have occurred," Thursby stated. "Executives would have gotten the message that white collar crime doesn't pay—years ago."

Thursby's thoughts returned to the task at hand. Penfel, as usual, waited patiently while his friend and boss went off on his tangent.

"So you think Sinteck is the right choice?"

"I think so." Penfel smiled, confirming Thursby's choice. "He's well known, as culpable as any of them, and only the second CEO."

"You're right," Thursby said. "Day was chairman, Wimkowski

a CEO. The others were CFOs and COOs. We'll go with Sinteck," he confirmed, tapping his finger on Sinteck's name.

Thursby reached for his marker, opened the lid, and placed a neat checkmark to the left of Barry Sinteck. On a new folder he wrote, "Sinteck," neatly on the tab—in bold capital letters.

Sinteck's name was on the second page of the list. He was one of the top fifteen, which also included Day and Carston, from EnergyDyn. Further down the list, on page three, in the twenty-fifth position was a well-known figure who destroyed her company and the trust of her investors by selling her position in Bonsell's corporation after receiving insider information. She was the first, of only four women, on the list.

The list of 75 was neatly typed and tucked inside a green file folder with third cut tabs. Thursby was always well organized, and this was no exception.

Once the decision was made, Penfel reached for a brown leather briefcase in the other overstuffed chair. Grasping both latches he snapped the locks open and pulled out his own file folder. He got out a pair of gloves and put them on before opening it.

Thursby put on a pair he had taken from his desk drawer. They were standard poly-surgical gloves—the kind you can get at any medical supply store. He pulled a file folder out of his locked file cabinet and two large padded envelopes out of the bottom drawer of his desk.

"Who do you think we should use for this one?" Thursby asked.

"I think we should use Mr. Smith again," Penfel said. "He did an excellent job in Hawaii…and in Southampton."

"He did," Thursby agreed. "But Mr. Jones did an equally fine job in Florida also. And we just gave Mr. Smith Southampton, so he's done two jobs for us."

Penfel agreed. "Mr. Jones would be a good choice.

"Let's spread the wealth around!"

Penfel nodded his head in agreement and extracted a manila envelope from his briefcase. This one contained mailing labels. He got up and stood in front of the desk. Thursby handed him the two padded envelopes.

He peeled a label from the backing and placed it squarely in the middle of the smaller envelope. He then pulled a label off another page and repeated the procedure with the large envelope.

Penfel picked up the folder he had taken out, selected a letter and handed it to Thursby. He handed the envelopes back to him. Thursby added the letter to the items he had gathered from several other files and slid them inside a new manila folder.

Those items included: pictures of Sinteck; a list of addresses, including homes, offices, clubs, and professional organizations; a time-line of places he frequented; and a list of sports, leisure activities, and hobbies. The letter was addressed to Mr. Jones.

All letters had been typed on a standard Compaq computer, printed on a standard computer paper on a popular Canon inkjet printer. All very difficult to trace should something go wrong and the envelopes intercepted or inadvertently opened.

Thursby placed the folder in the smaller of the two envelopes. Penfel extracted three stacks of 100, 50, and 20 dollar bills from the case. He counted out $5,000 and handed it to Thursby, who placed the bills, evenly distributed, in a thin box that would accommodate the stacks of cash neatly, and then slid it in the envelope along with the manila folder.

Penfel took the small envelope from Thursby after he carefully sealed it. He pulled a flat of stamps from his briefcase and placed the required amount to mail it from Denver to Pensacola. He then slid it in the larger envelope and secured it just as carefully. He placed the postage required to send the larger envelope from Seattle to Denver. An old colleague in Denver would open it, and mail the smaller envelope on to Pensacola, to Mr. Jones.

They had used this method of mail, combined with courier, to deliver some of their most important documents, deals, products, and ideas, for many years. The envelope was ready to send to Mr. Jones in Pensacola by way of Denver, after Penfel mailed it from Seattle. This final victim would complete the plan Thursby had devised and initiated almost a year ago.

"Have you thought anymore about the morality of what we're doing Ethan?" Thursby asked his old friend. "This would be called vigilantism."

"A couple of times," Penfel answered. "I see it more as taking from the rich and unscrupulous, and helping out the poor—almost like Robin Hood," he added, a philosophical tone in his voice.

"You've been a loyal and trusted friend for many years, Ethan, but you didn't have to involve yourself in this."

"I don't have a problem with it," Penfel assured him. "You know I would tell you if it did. I only hope it accomplishes what we wanted it to."

Thursby had discussed his plan thoroughly with his friend after having decided that he would go through with it. He had become so frustrated with the breadth of the corporate scandals and the number of people it destroyed, he believed someone should do something.

It seemed like a new scandal hit Wall Street every week. Though he hadn't personally lost much money in any of the scandals, he felt an urge to act—felt some responsibility as a member of this elite community.

This wasn't easy for him. Thursby spent many sleepless nights pondering, debating, and agonizing, over the morality of his decision. Was he playing God? Did he have the right to?

He pondered those questions, but he was frustrated with Congress and its failures, and the justice system and its method of administering justice to white collar criminals.

Finally, after numerous nights of labored sleep and burdensome dreams, he made the decision to wield his own justice. He hoped to send the appropriate message to his contemporaries, corporate executives. What emerged was the best of four possible plans that he had devised.

He looked up at Ethan holding the envelope in his hands. "What did I do to deserve a friend as loyal as you?" Thursby said, a tear forming in the corner of his eye.

"I've been wondering that same thing for quite awhile," Penfel said, laughing. "What did you do to deserve me?"

Thursby laughed.

"I'm serious, Ethan, friendship like this is extremely rare these days. I may not tell you this as often as I should." Thursby paused, sighed deeply, an emotional sigh, and continued. "I have always been thankful that you came into my life 30 years ago. So was Catherine."

"I feel the same way, Byron," Penfel said, looking at Thursby with a caring smile.

The dim room was dead silent, the emotion heavy, momentarily gripping the two men.

"Did you take your medication?" Penfel asked, breaking the silence.

"Don't worry about me," Thursby said. "*I will take it*—now go, and give a dying man his last wish."

Ethan looked at Byron, his best friend, tears forming in the corners of both eyes. His flight to Seattle would depart in an hour and a half. He wiped his eyes with his sleeve and looked at Byron again, a look of absolute admiration.

Thursby had told no one about his illness. Ethan was the only one who knew. They were so close Thursby wouldn't have been able to keep it from him anyway. He had lived a good and fruitful life, but that would soon come to an end, and his friend Ethan would be alone, surviving his wife Margaret, Catherine, and now himself. Thursby felt worse about leaving Ethan alone and lonely, than he did about his own death.

Ethan turned without a word and walked through the double doors at the end of the darkened room. The doors closed behind him.

Byron watched Ethan leave and stared at the doors as they closed. His office was dark and quiet, and suddenly cold, causing him to shiver. His life had been evaluated, and he had evaluated other's lives.

This was the last victim and, hopefully, the final message. It was...

The Final Audit.

Acknowledgements

I gratefully acknowledge the support and contribution of the individuals who helped, motivated, and encouraged me through this long, exciting, and rewarding process. Writing this novel was a labor of love and persistence, and each of the people listed here had an important roll in the completion of this first of hopefully a long list of novels.

I am eternally grateful to my family members who endured more than three years of my endless updates, excuses, and, exuberance and never seemed to lose interest.

A book would never be what it is without the patient and expert help from those who edit the writer's work. For that I relied on the expertise of Robyn Conley O'Brien to do my editing, Denise Vitola who did the copy editing, and Sherry Roberts who did a final proofreading and copy editing. Some of the things that may counter usual writing conventions were solely my doing.

I am especially grateful to some incredible people whose advice was very important to the success of this first novel, who read way more than anyone should be required to read, and did it graciously, and unselfishly: David Hirstein, Jerry O'Brien, Judy Wallace, John Goodnight, Christina Peterson, Ken Bell, and Dana Watson.

To the Managers, Assistant Managers, and Baristas at Starbucks, Brea II, and Seattle's Best in Brea, for putting up with my endless hours of writing, and rewriting, and for being such great listeners.

Many readers read the manuscript more than once. Their time and input were invaluable to the success of "Final Audit": Claire Hardman, Sam Pazzo, Elisabeth Sammons, Gay Taylor, Darla Brown, Rosie Nicol, Rey Agustin, and David Stillion.

...and also to those who provided wonderful insights and

suggestions: Sally Bagheri, Karen Bakotich, Leslie Brown, Debra Brunner, Vince Campolongo, Ana Ceja, Craig Coy, Joe Dobashi, Scott Fowler, Judy Fox, Larry Fox, Carol Frank, Joni Garabedian, Connie Gayhart, Jean Giorgi, Jane Goodnight, Jana Hamilton, Linda Hollenbeck, Ron Kelly, Warren LaRose, Renee Larum, Tracy Lee, Kathy McKinnell, Allen Meyers, Jim Miller, Nancy Mirande, KaCee Moore, Nick Mosouris, Ken Palmer, Debbie Pasquali, Nicole Powers, Natalie Randazzo, Tanya Reilly, Kathleen Robb, Sandra Rojo, John Saunders, Bernice Sellitto, Joan Stepp, Elizabeth Strahan, Marc Taylor, Rhonda Taylor, Carol This, Bob Trout, Melanie Wagner, David Watson, Janice Webster, Scott Wegenke, Sandy Willis, Sharon Willmer, Patrice Wilson, Mary Wories.

Research is an important part of any novel and "Final Audit" was no exception. Some very generous individuals gave of their time and expertise to help me enhance this novel. As a new author, I dreaded having to bother people to gather information, but my first contact changed all that. I picked up the phone, dialed a small town in Pennsylvania and spoke with two warm and gracious ladies at the Coudersport Chamber of Commerce. I would like to thank Nila and Dolores for their selfless assistance, setting the stage for my continued research. I would also like to thank the following individuals for their help: Mike Dreyfus at Trident Underwater; Tony Magaldi of the News Cafe; Matt at Adidas USA; Neil Lasater at Turner's Gun Shop; David Ryan in Legislator Lynne Nowick's office; Pascal at Scandal's; and Dimitri at Versace in Beverly Hills.

My sincere thanks to Jaimarie and Cindy Sutherland for taking the time to photograph the author at my favorite Starbucks—the photo which is shown on the back cover of the book.

Special Note: There are two special individuals who, during my research in South Beach, made such a wonderful impression that I included them in my book. They are John Rice, the outgoing host at Scandal's and Vadim, who plays a soulful, sultry Sax.

Epilogue

"Final Audit" is about corruption and greed. It's about executive's whose avarice went unchecked, whose ethics were questionable, and whose audacity was abhorrent. The number of Boards who failed their investors was appalling. It teetered on the edge of criminal negligence. Accounting firms failed miserably in complying with the law, in fear of losing their big clients, and are also complicit.

It is also about the weakness and incompetence of Congress. As Arthur Levitt, at the Securities and Exchange Commission, fought to control the rampant creative accounting, in an effort to prevent a collapse, Congress tried to find ways to limit his authority. It's about the business schools at universities and colleges in this country, and their complicity in the collapse of the many corporations over the last three years.

The collapse of these huge corporations may have been prevented had any of the factions above upheld their charge. In the aftermath they have all expressed outrage and surprise, but continue to point the finger at others to divert attention from themselves. None seem willing to stand up and admit responsibility.

Until we restore 'real' accountability, until the Security and Exchange Commission adopts and enforces tougher policies, until Congress gets off their dead asses and enacts legislation that no longer favors big business at the expense of hard working Americans, until universities and colleges stress ethics, and until investors put aside their greed and apathy, the problem will not go away but only be in a period of remission.

Investors need to become educated. If you fail to learn from the past, don't expect sympathy or support in the future. If you choose to remain in the dark and go blindly into your investments I will gladly chronicle your pain and losses—and laugh—all the way to the 'bank'.